SHADOW COUNTRY

A NOVEL

CRAIG HIGGINSON

CATALYST PRESS
El Paso, Texas

Published by Catalyst Press.
www.catalystpress.org

In North America, this book is distributed by Consortium Book Sales & Distribution, a division of Ingram. Phone: 612/746-2600
cbsdinfo@ingramcontent.com
www.cbsd.com

First published in South Africa as *The Ghost of Sam Webster* by Picador Africa in 2023.

This edition, first printing
9 8 7 6 5 4 3 2 1

Cover design by publicide
ISBN 978-1-960803-43-6
Library of Congress Control Number 2025944325

Praise for *Shadow Country*

"A beautiful page-turner … with characters so rich and deep that by the end of the story you feel as though you know them personally, and the final few pages make you dread the imminent absence of them in your life … cleaves the messiness of a South African colonial landscape, littered with bloody history and damaged people, as it is, highlighted with a dangerous beauty and a mystery, replete with an unbreakable thread of a red herring. You won't be able to stop until you finish."
—Robyn Sassen

"Craig Higginson is an extraordinary talent."
—Margaret von Klemperer

"I'm tempted to make this the shortest review you'll ever read! Buy this book and relish it. It is a rare gem."
—*The Star*

"An extraordinary book … Higginson writes so beautifully, with so much care, so much integrity and beauty … it feels spiritually uplifting having finished it … and that is quite a rare and remarkable achievement, to leave a reader with a feeling of hope."
—Vanessa Levenstein

Novels by Craig Higginson

Embodied Laughter, 1998

The Hill, 2005

Last Summer, 2010

The Landscape Painter, 2011

The Dream House, 2015

The White Room, 2018

The Book of Gifts, 2020

PROLOGUE

THE RIVER

All night, she is rolled around in the Buffalo River

The river turns her this way and that, worrying at her like an unwanted thought. Try as it might, it can't unravel her. She is rippled and revolved, sucked in and spat out, perfectly paced with the mood of the water. She is half fish and half girl, and both halves are equally dead.

The girl belongs to no one. She has no home, no parents, no name. Her tongue fills her mouth, swollen and dark, like a sod of earth. Her hair is one long weed trailing her. Her head is a thoughtless rock. Her hands move rhythmically, and her arms drift at her sides, opening to accommodate the willow trees, the breathing herds of cattle, the weeping, starless heavens. But these gestures are without meaning. She is nothing but the body of a girl being moved swiftly along, her story long gone with her. She is equal to the broken branches and the rolling stones that accompany her. She has no more history, and no less history, than they do.

A storm hangs over the Drakensberg

It is like the smoke above a great fire, pumping water into unseen flames, until every hill is filled with it and every bird on every branch drips with it. A whole embankment dissolves and consumes a village, filling every room of every house with sticky muck, digesting grandmothers, television sets, chickens and children. The whole landscape is on the move. The air is filled with a distant roaring. The old world lies numb, no longer recognising itself. Mountain streams bounce beyond their bounds to join rivers that have never been there before. Where there was once an elegant waterfall hemmed in by bracken and ferns, there is now a mound of rubble. Where the river circumvented a pasture filled with grazing, honey-colored ponies, there is now an abandoned lake. Where the river curved left, it now veers right.

Her body is found on a Sunday morning

Zwelibanzi Zimba is grazing his grandmother's goats in the rain when he sees the dark-blue anorak washed up against the rocks. He has been rained on for a week now and he no longer notices the rain. But he likes the look of that anorak. It is the only thing of color in a world of diminishing grays. It floats near the edge of the river. Something forbidden but tempting. He suspects it has been washed down from the campsite where the people from England come to dwell with their stories of the dead.

Zwelibanzi walks into the water until it reaches his hips, his feet finding their way amongst the stones. Usually, there is no water here. He is walking across a piece of land where before he has sat and roasted a mealie cob. He has never experienced the uMzinyathi River like this. So angry and restless. A bad mood looking for a place to settle. But even under these conditions he knows the river.

He has been crossing and re-crossing it since he first learned how to walk. The nearest bridge is a mile away. In weather like this, it will be deep underwater.

He stops when he sees her face. It is so pale that it seems to have no eyes, no mouth. The face is a blank space waiting to be filled in. It is no longer human. It no longer needs eyes from which to see or a mouth from which to speak. The girl's hair lies against the rock like a rope that has just been used to strangle her. Her hand is a small, folded star. Her body is a larger, folded star. All around her, the water boils its blood-colored froth.

Zwelibanzi only stops running when he reaches the priest's house

There he learns that the priest is away, preaching at Msinga Top. He tells the wife instead.

"A dead body? Uqinisekile?"

"Yebo, Mesis. Ngisibone silele emadwaleni."

"Uthintile anything?"

"Cha, Mesis."

"Ungasondeli kuso. Ngizoshayela amapolice."

He returns to the river and waits with his goats in the rain for the police. The rain carries on falling on the dead girl with as much indifference as it falls on him. The goats continue to graze at the edge of the river as if nothing has changed. A heron stands on the opposite bank like a folded umbrella, its hunger a wet pebble sitting inside it. But now that Zwelibanzi knows that the girl is there, he can think of nothing else, look at nothing else. She is lying pressed into the rocks while the river urges her this way and that, trying to draw her away to the sea.

He chooses a rock from which to watch her. He is known to have the patience of a kingfisher. He also understands that somewhere in the world there is a family that is waiting for her to come home. They will be pleased with him for finding the girl. But not so pleased when they understand what has happened to her. Although the lower half of her body is submerged in the water, she is wearing nothing except the dark-blue anorak. Zwelibanzi tries not to think too much about this. Or about how she might have come to be there. It will be the police's job to worry about that.

When the police arrive, it is three hours later. Zwelibanzi suspects they have come from Greytown. He watches the splattered white bakkie dodging the dark-red termite mounds, the engine laboring over the sodden earth. The vehicle stops where the earth flattens out and after three heartbeats the policemen emerge. A small, round one and then a taller, more attenuated one. They look up at the sky as if cursing their fate, but they do nothing to protect themselves. They come like cats over the wet grass. Their boots are soon heavy with the orange mud. The priest's wife stays inside the vehicle for a moment and then she too emerges, balancing under a black umbrella, jumping from rock to rock. She is one of the few white people to whom Zwelibanzi has ever spoken. The memory of her isiZulu makes him smile.

Zwelibanzi finds he is relieved that he will no longer have to carry the dead girl alone inside his head. The men arrive and nod at him. They look at the girl and murmur between themselves. The priest's wife—a pale-limbed, wet-eyed woman—stands as if for protection amongst the scattering of goats.

"Akufanele sithinte umzimba," the thinner man says.

"Kepha ungathathwa ngumfula," the other man says.

The current is getting stronger. The policemen are worried the girl will be washed away. They link arms and wade into the water, the two men becoming the beginning of a bridge between the girl and the place where Zwelibanzi stands waiting. The river, sensing this new invasion, grows deeper and stronger, working against the two men from surprising angles. The river has never been more confident. It will carry on growing until it has swallowed the world.

The policemen, who looked sturdy enough in their blue-gray uniforms and muddy boots when standing on the shore, are now two big babies, floundering. The smaller man is leading the way. He is clearly the one in charge. He is leading by example. The other man keeps looking upriver as if expecting a huge wave to come hurtling around the corner to consume them. But the smaller man isn't letting his gaze stray away from the body of the girl. There is something doomed and heroic about this smaller man. The way he is prepared to take on a whole river in order to reach something that is already dead.

A bloated cow, its legs stuck out like sticks, floats past them, but neither of the men pays it any attention. The first man has already reached the girl. He is holding onto a rock that is only one rock away from her head. He shouts something to the other man, his words lost in the wildness of the water. Now that they have reached the girl, they are unsure of what to do. Neither of them has looked at her face. The smaller man maneuvers himself around the crop of rocks that holds her so that there is a man on either side of the body. The water is building up against them, thumping up against their shoulders, cascading now and again over the smaller man's head.

Time has slowed right down, as if Zwelibanzi's whole life was nothing but a preparation for this moment. The two men pull at the girl for a while, trying to wrestle her away from the rocks. She wobbles, a large doll filled with water, her head flopping from side to side. While the smaller man pushes his hands under her shoulders, the other man wraps an arm around her ankles, both of their faces averted. The girl has become little more than a problem they have to deliver to the shore.

As the smaller man hauls her toward himself, the anorak is lifted briefly—and then, before anyone can grasp the horror of what is happening, her body flops forward into the water, and the taller man's free arm waves briefly, and the three of them spin away together with the current. Zwelibanzi follows them downriver, just as the taller man, who was always the less committed of the two, releases the girl—but the smaller man is still holding onto her for dear life, shouting something to the other man, perhaps calling for help, perhaps reprimanding him for letting go—and then, at the moment when it looks as if he may be able to find a rock and get a foothold against the river, he too lets go of the girl and grabs onto a half-submerged sapling instead. The dark-blue anorak bobs like a balloon for a moment. The water revolves around the girl and gives her the once-over and swallows her whole.

The girl has vanished.

The river becomes a river again.

Zwelibanzi stops running. There is nowhere left to go.

The dead girl is later identified as Sam Webster

She is the seventeen-year-old daughter of Bruce Webster, the famous historian. The Zulus in the area call him "Isicabu," which is an abbreviation of "isicabucabu," the isiZulu word for "spider." Bruce Webster runs a luxury lodge on a mountain overlooking iSandlwana. The tales he has spun about the Anglo-Zulu wars are so famous that they even reached the ears of the British Queen. The two young princes have stayed at Mr. Webster's lodge. When Sam was a young girl, she was once seen on the shoulders of the Prince of Wales, walking across the battlefield where the whitewashed cairns still mark the piled-up bodies of the British dead.

PART ONE

THE WRITER

Last summer, Daniel learned the names of all the butterflies

He was planning to write about his disgraced ancestor, the soldier and lepidopterist, Lieutenant Charles Hawthorne, who fought—although perhaps not as hard as he ought to have—at the Battle of iSandlwana in 1879. For this, Daniel traveled to Zululand and stayed at Bruce Webster's lodge. There he became friendly with the family and he met Sam, Bruce's daughter, who had recently turned sixteen. Sam was the kind of girl Daniel would most likely have fallen in love with when he was a boy. She was also the kind of girl who would not have noticed him as he entered her atmosphere, all awkward angles, to approach her sun.

He stares at the ceiling of his old bedroom

He has been living in his mother's house since the day she died.

There are florescent stars above his bed that he stuck there when he was about nine. They have not been painted over since. He remembers that he did his best to recreate the constellations. The Southern Cross, the Pointers, the Seven Sisters—and his sister's ill-fated star sign, Scorpio. He remembers looking up at the stars on the ceiling as if he was lying under the night sky, staring into infinite space. These days, all he sees are the stickers. The crooked dimensions. The failed representations. Everywhere he looks in his mother's house, all he finds is failure, all he finds is loss. Not only has he lost his sister and his father and his mother—he has also lost the boy who stuck those stickers across the ceiling, believing he could map an inner landscape and an outer landscape, so that there would no longer be any division between himself and the stars.

As a boy, Daniel knew every part of what was always referred to by his parents as "the plot." The house, which is situated between Johannesburg and Pretoria, has always been long and low and unattractive. Although it might have appeared modern in the sixties, it now resembles a poor person's home, with its missing rooftiles, rusted gutters and khakibos growing tall in the pond where the rinkhals used to emerge from the rockery to drink. Below the house is his father's collection of decayed army trucks. On the other side of the driveway, which is still no more than a dirt track lined with aloes, is the round concrete reservoir and the broken windmill where some red and golden bishops still nest in the reeds. Below the reservoir, in what was the peach orchard—now a few black skeletons overgrown with black-eyed Susans—his father used to feed the guineafowl, carrying chickenfeed inside the Second World War helmet that had belonged to his father. After his mother's death, Daniel found the helmet inside his grandfather's army trunk and restarted the tradition. The guineafowl are long gone, but he has been feeding the doves, sparrows and weaverbirds instead.

It is interesting, what having a cowardly ancestor has done to the men in his family. Lieutenant Charles Hawthorne is notorious for three times abandoning his fellow soldiers at the height of battle. Once at a rocky outcrop as the army was withdrawing back to the camp at iSandlwana, again on the retreat between iSandlwana and Fugitives' Drift, where Charles was accused of abandoning a higher-ranking officer, and finally after he had crossed the Buffalo River, when he was said to have made off with another man's horse. Charles is inevitably depicted in the history books as a disappointment in the otherwise heroic narrative of iSandlwana and Fugitives' Drift.

Yet it has always seemed to Daniel that each of the accounts that condemns his ancestor is little more than speculation. The rest of his actions on that dark day—it became dark literally, since, at the height of the battle, the moon eclipsed the sun—are left unmentioned. That Charles was part of an army of a few thousand men that faced a Zulu force of over twenty thousand soldiers, and that the British army spent most of the day retreating as fast as possible—these circumstances, in the story of Daniel's butterfly-collecting ancestor, are passed without comment.

Charles Hawthorne's own father had died honorably in the Second Anglo-Ashanti War in present-day Ghana. Charles himself left behind a son who died in Verdun, who in turn left behind a son who was torpedoed by a German U-boat off the coast of East London, South Africa. Daniel's own father fought in the Zimbabwean War of Independence, which he preferred to call the Rhodesian Bush War. He was said to have behaved as heroically as his father and grandfather before him, flying supplies over the border from South Africa at night over bush occupied by hostile forces and once landing a plane with a blasted tail in the middle of a game reserve, where he was soon surrounded by a pride of hungry lions. The shame associated with Daniel's disgraced ancestor gave birth to a line of men who might have come straight out of the pages of a Ryder Haggard or Wilbur Smith novel.

But what if Charles was merely like the rest of us? What if he was merely human, sometimes mastering his fear and sometimes allowing his fear to master him? What if he found during those hours of mass slaughter that he did not believe in the whole endeavor? What if it wasn't the Zulus he was trying to get away from, but something he had discovered inside his fellow British soldiers? Or even inside himself?

These are questions that had always interested Daniel. After the publication of his most recent novel, he decided to do some reading about the Anglo-Zulu War. In the formal historical accounts, he soon came across the version of Charles Hawthorne that he had come to expect. The famous coward. The man who had thrice betrayed his fellow man, like Peter betraying Christ. It was only when Daniel started to look further, into the journal entries and correspondence of the soldiers who had reputedly fought alongside Charles, that he found the traces of an altogether different version of events.

By this point, Daniel had already read about the famous historian, Bruce Webster. He had even listened to recordings of Webster's stirring narrations of the events surrounding iSandlwana and Rorke's Drift. During a break from work that winter, he decided to pay Webster Lodge a visit and conduct some further investigations. He drove down from Johannesburg, leaving the national road after crossing the Vaal River and heading off across the open country, along tarmac roads with potholes that were filled with cow dung and dirt roads criss-crossed by low cement bridges and the dongas left from long-forgotten floods. At first, he was disappointed in the landscape. Everything was dry and dead-looking and covered in a fine patina of red dust. It was difficult to imagine that any of the events described so stirringly in the history books could ever have taken place in somewhere so mundane, so commonplace. When he entered the iSandlwana valley, with its randomly arranged homesteads and its lodges—some of them grandly arranged down a mountain—he came upon the modest, lion-shaped mountain of iSandlwana. Was this what everyone had been fighting over? Seen from the road, the mountain looked meagre and the village flanking it was a mess. Although the veranda and the yard of each homestead had been swept clean, the boundaries of the properties and the sides of the dirt roads were piled with rubbish. Scraggy chickens and wizened goats wandered around in the ruined road. Something synthetic and toxic-smelling was being burned in a nearby bonfire.

Daniel tried to summon up some feeling for the men who had fought and died in this valley, both British and Zulu. But he did not find much to work with. Whatever had happened here, it had nothing to do with him. He had felt a similarly defeated, dead feeling whenever he had tried to read the history books—to find out more about what the Zulus called "the day of the dead moon." He only ever got as far as the Zulu army being discovered by Charlie Raw and his troops. He found that he had no stomach for what happened next, which seemed to him little more than a scene of mass slaughter. He also found the representation of the participants generally inadequate. The way the Zulu soldiers were mythologized like figures out of Rousseau, and the British portrayed as jolly good fellows who spent the day cracking jokes while everyone around them was being slaughtered en masse.

Zululand—or perhaps it was only this small part of it—seemed to be a giant graveyard. Everywhere the dead lay buried. The violently slaughtered. Thousands of British soldiers lay buried inside the cairns scattered around the lion-mountain of iSandlwana and thousands of Zulu soldiers lay in the ditches from the aftermath at Rorke's Drift. But there were also the dead from the early 1990s. When whole families and homesteads were massacred during the build-up to the first democratic elections. And the air was thick with more recent acts of violence. Random stabbings, assassinations of local community leaders and politicians, farm murders—and the murder and rape of women and children.

When Daniel went to visit the local chapel, St. Vincent's Church, he came across an old white woman fixing the stained-glass windows. She told Daniel that her brother had been a tour guide at one of the lodges and that he had recently been murdered. Shot by an unknown group of men who had also beaten and gang-raped his wife. The woman was using the money raised after his death to fix these historic windows.

Daniel was so surrounded by such stories that he wondered whether any progress had been made in the area since the Anglo-Zulu War a hundred and fifty years previously. Zululand seemed entirely overrun by the dead. Even the lives of the living seemed determined by the dead and the needs of the dead. He decided that there was no reason to write his ancestor book. He would leave the dead to their own devices and have no further involvement in any of it.

Then he met Bruce Webster. At first, Bruce struck Daniel as a man from a particular mold. A man of considerable wealth who loved the bush, spoke fluent isiZulu, liked a large Scotch and a good story—and was thoroughly satisfied with himself. He was the usual colonial type who was passing himself off as a benefactor and a liberal. And yes—he was also a typical product of the prestigious boarding school he had attended. Their first conversation took place at the lodge's bar, during which Daniel was more interested in having his suspicions about Webster confirmed than in finding out anything else about the man. After their second drink, Daniel told Bruce something about his book, describing it as an idea on which he had already given up.

"He was very remarkable for his time, your great-grandfather," Bruce responded.

Except from Daniel's grandmother, this was the first positive thing anyone had ever said to Daniel about Charles.

"He was?"

"You've probably heard about the hearing in Pietermaritzburg he attended after the Battle of iSandlwana?"

"It was an inquiry into a friend's death. Another distant relative of mine, as it turns out."

"The hearing was about a great deal more than that. Lieutenant Hawthorne spoke with unusual honesty about what had taken place."

Bruce waved for another drink from the elderly Zulu barman.

"The transcript is still buried somewhere in the military archives in Pietermaritzburg, if you're interested. I've sent one or two men in that general direction over the years, but Hawthorne's story is not the kind of thing people want to read about. Or write about. It's a story about shame, you see. Shame is one thing that people do everything they can to forget."

"Are you saying it's a story about Charles's shame?"

"It's about a great deal more than his shame. It is a story about shame generally. All Charles was guilty of in the end was a determination to save a friend."

Daniel was invited across for dinner at the Websters' house the following evening. There Bruce gave Daniel a copy of an old photograph taken of Lieutenant Charles Hawthorne with his Native Contingent at the camp of Sandspruit a couple of weeks before the Battle of iSandlwana. In the photograph, Charles is sitting surrounded by soldiers carrying assegais, wrapped in blankets and wearing their Native Contingent headbands. Charles turned out to be an innocuous-looking man with the usual moustache and a melancholic, abstracted gaze that had—at least according to Bruce—survived all the way down the family line to Daniel himself.

On that same evening, Daniel also met Caroline and her two children, Sam and Matthew. It transpired that Sam was studying one of Daniel's novels at school and the girl believed that they had a bona fide celebrity in the house. By the end of dinner, Daniel had agreed to visit Sam's school to talk with her class about his book. His new novel, which he had already started to call his "ancestor book," had also sprung back to life.

The shape of Daniel's narrative quickly formed over the weeks that followed. He had the main idea, with some fragments arranged around it, rather like the scattered cairns around the mountain of iSandlwana. It turned out that the transcript of Hawthorne's testimony was no longer to be found in the archive where Bruce had last seen it. But Bruce had made detailed notes and he dug these up and handed them over to Daniel. Charles Hawthorne's account of the events contained several clear omissions and it also seemed that he was being careful not to incriminate certain people—but there was enough there to provide a small window into the internal world of Daniel's protagonist.

By the time Daniel left the area and returned to Johannesburg, he had the shape of his ancestor book secure inside him. He also believed that he and Bruce Webster had become firm friends. As with most performers, Daniel had found that there was a more tentative and subtler man to be found sitting not too far behind the construct of Bruce Webster. Bruce had listened to Daniel's stories—both real and imaginary—with a degree of attention that Daniel had never experienced from any older man—or woman—before.

Later that winter, Daniel's mother died. The book that he had planned, with its stone lion lying at the heart of it, began to fade, like some legend he had once heard. As with several other writing ideas that he had started to develop over previous years, the ancestor book would be lost in the realm of the unconscious, making its appearance only in fragments, in daydreams and nightmares—never again resolving into a meaningful or coherent whole.

Every story has the same ending

Every story ends with the same abandoned room, filled with the same accumulation of meaningless junk. Every night, when Daniel turns out his mother's bedside lamp, he watches the stars fade until he is lying once again in the dark. He realizes that his preoccupation with Sam's disappearance is unfathomable and pointless. Yet her story keeps flowing through him. It flows with the authority of the Buffalo River itself.

Christmas passes and the new year begins. Each night as he lies in his old bed, he imagines driving down to KwaZulu-Natal and standing at the river's edge on those black rocks as he had two years ago. He imagines following the Buffalo River all the way to the Tugela River and the Indian Ocean. He has heard that there are tiger sharks patrolling the river's mouth, roving the muddy water, waiting for whatever the river has to offer. He thinks of Ophelia. He thinks of Lucy Gray and Lorelei. But these young women could not be further from Sam Webster, who existed in what people like to call the real world and whose bright spirit had been experienced by all who encountered her.

A few days later, he finds himself driving down to KwaZulu-Natal

On the way to Webster Lodge, he stops at Sam's old school. The fountain skitters as it did before in the quad. Water splashes the stone boy's face. It embraces an emerald-green thigh. Where the statue of the boy David stands in the water, speckled koi hang suspended, their pectorals slowly stirring. The world of the school could not be further from the world of those fish. Their rippled heaven contains a tower, a clock and a haggard, looming god who bends down to look at them, eclipsing their light.

Daniel has already booked a room at the lodge. He made his

reservation over the phone with old Moses, who did not recognize his name or his voice. Daniel would like to arrive incognito. Perhaps under another name. It is far too early to intrude on the Websters' grief. It is only around six weeks since Sam disappeared, reappeared and disappeared again.

He booked one of the least-expensive rooms, named after a so-called "drummer boy." Each of the rooms at the lodge has been designed by Caroline Webster, Bruce's wife, and named after a serviceman who fought in the Anglo-Zulu War. The bridal suite is the Lord Chelmsford Room, occupying prime position near the top of the mountain, just beneath the dining area and swimming pool. As the lodge winds down the mountain, the rooms reflect the hierarchy of a British battalion. Daniel's room is right at the bottom, named after Damiel McEwan, a twenty-three-year-old Welshman who was said to have been slain at iSandlwana and slung up on a wagon with a meat hook, his severed genitals stuffed into his mouth. This is not information included in the lodge's publicity material. It is information Daniel found on doing some further research. The degree to which the account is Victorian propaganda was difficult to assess. But Daniel knows that the best propaganda gives itself grit by carrying a grain of truth.

Daniel reads on a noticeboard outside the school chapel that the first service of the school year will take place in half an hour, so he drifts off amongst the poplars, passing through cool bars of light, circumventing a scuffed hockey field and stopping at the swimming pool, where a dead frog floats pearl-belly upwards.

When the bell tower starts its funereal gong, Daniel follows the sound back up to the main school buildings, which are Victorian Gothic. He enters the wood-panelled chapel and finds a place at the back with some parents. Above them is a wooden cross with a carved Christ hanging there—a man made of little more than kindling. The girls, freshly returned from the Christmas holidays, have entered ahead of them, their bottle-green blazers glowing in the blue-bottle light. All the shades of blonde, black and brunette hair are there, with every conceivable texture and arrangement of braid, plait and ponytail. Then the organ blasts through the packed room. An army descending into battle, swords bristling, pennants rippling. Everyone stands to attention. As the first hymn begins—"Onward Christian Soldiers"—Daniel has to wipe the wetness from his face, feeling a sense of loss he has not begun to comprehend.

The chaplain steps up to the lectern to explain the difference between demons and daemons. He is a slender man, all elbows and knees, with ears too large for his attentive head. A simian saint, he is modeling what it is to be a good man. Sunlight streams into the room from a high widow above his head, illuminating his ears to animate the act of listening, as if to suggest that God gets wind of everything through this man, through this particular pair of ears.

The chaplain invites each of them to locate their spirit animal, their shadow-self, their "Patronus." Which makes the girls laugh appreciatively. He asks them to breathe in as leopards, owls or koala bears and then to breathe out as leopards, owls or koala bears. He asks them to feel the weight of their animals inside their bodies. To feel the gaze of their animals running through them. Daniel tries to locate inside himself a spirit animal, but he finds nothing there. Only the alien ghost of Sam Webster—her pulse skipping one step ahead of him.

"This is what it is to have the Holy Spirit inside of you," the chaplain says. "Can you feel how powerful you have become? Can you see how straight is the path to Righteousness?"

Daniel understands what the sermon is about. The chaplain is trying to start the new year from a place of purpose in the absence of Sam. He is providing them with metaphors through which to make the incoherent coherent again. Daniel looks around the congregation for anyone he might know and sees only Dr. Lopez,

Sam's unobtrusively beautiful English teacher, whom he met on his previous visit to the school.

After the service, Daniel searches for Sam's name along the corridors. He finds that she is still in the previous year's debating and equestrian teams, but that her name has been erased from the previous year's tennis team, with a single red line by a teacher's pen.

The land deepens and steepens as he approaches Zululand

The mountain road is shining with rainwater. As the sunlight strengthens, a violet haze rises up from the earth, turning gold as it reaches the light. He sees bony cattle standing idly amongst the pond-sized puddles. Unattended goats are trotting fussily along the grassy verge. A dead owl lies flattened in the road, two pied crows picking away at the lattice of feathers and bones. There are weaver-bird nests woven into the barbed wire fences and the same crops of potholes filled in with cattle dung. A man carries a headless brown-and-white rabbit he most probably snared. Under a grove of gum trees, farm laborers stand in a group, waiting to be fetched for work. The trees around them are more like the memories of trees. The car passes a homestead where a running child scatters chickens and an old woman wrapped in a tartan blanket lifts a hand toward the swirling gray void of the sky as if to feel the texture of heaven. A black dog, enormous and narrow and with a tunnel-vision gaze, appears suddenly and trots across the road, right in front of Daniel's car. Daniel brakes and hoots, missing the dog by inches. But the dog does not flinch. Its mouth is smiling obscenely and the tongue is long and red and sloppy. The dog seems to have been running like this for days, for weeks, for all eternity.

The car crosses rivers and vleis named after animals that have since been hunted down and slaughtered. Blesbok, crocodiles, elephants and hippos—"sea-cows" in Afrikaans. Sometimes, it passes a field containing nothing but a broken windmill and a thousand dark-red anthills. Most of the rivers are no more than oxidized orange runnels, intricate dongas composed of ancient stalagmites, where aloes cling to the bleached earth and a strip of olive-green wanders along the dredges, carrying the memory of the last storm.

Despite the grandeur of the landscape, Daniel is once again struck by the air of neglect. Plastic packets have been blown up against the fences. Junctions glitter with smashed glass. Several shops and one stone church have been completely burned out. He passes an old farmhouse that is surrounded by heaps of broken machinery. The house has been re-assembled out of rubbish—the roof made from sheets of found tin and plastic sheeting, pinned down by bricks and tractor tires, the windows boarded up with Masonite, the entrance steps assembled out of beer crates.

Soon the sky starts to accommodate patches of light—and then a whole vista of blue. Daniel knows that it is still too early to encounter iSandlwana, the mountain that Sam used to call "her mountain"—the sleeping sphinx that, in a weird coincidence, exactly replicated the insignia of the 24th Regiment who died in its shadow. But Daniel keeps thinking that he can see Sam's mountain anyway, approaching in the distance. Yet every mountain turns out to be too flat or too long, or too backed like a weasel or a camel. Daniel has arrived in a land of shadows, and he could carry on driving forever, like someone lost at sea, the same wave rising and falling, repeated interminably.

It is raining hard when he arrives at the lodge

His mother's car—a battered Toyota Corolla—wades through a stream of water as he turns into the entrance and rattles over the cattle grid. He has been driving for an hour over a rutted road and the back end of the car is splattered with black mud. A toothless old man emerges from a stone hut at the boom, holding a plastic-covered clipboard. They are both pleased to find Daniel's name on the list of expected guests and Daniel is given a slip of wet paper welcoming him to the lodge and giving him directions to his room. The wiper on his side of the car leaves a smear in its wake and the rain keeps up a ticking dance on the roof. This is what it is to feel alive, Daniel remembers, as he passes into the grounds of the lodge.

One of the changes Bruce Webster made to the lodge after he inherited it from his father was to have the land established as a game reserve and a natural heritage site. The entrance road of the lodge consists of two strips of cement weaving through five kilometers of bush, washed away in places and patched up in others with darker cement. Daniel sees a gathering of rain-streaked impala, frozen in time, staring at him with their eternal gaze. There is also a single giraffe nosing its way toward the fresh foliage of an acacia tree. Daniel is surprised to encounter Nguni cattle mixed in amongst the zebras and blesbok at a waterhole. He once heard that Nguni cattle are well known for attacking snakes on sight, which is one of the reasons snakes stay away from Zulu homesteads. But whose cattle these are is a mystery. Is Bruce trying his hand at beef farming on the side?

Daniel stops to get out and urinate at a turning. He is surrounded by birdsong. The sonic pulse of some bird whose name he doesn't know—and, further off, near the banks of the Buffalo River, the clear note of a shrike—and the plaintive mourning of an emerald-spotted wood-dove. For much of the year, this is a place without water. When Daniel came to the lodge previously, it was midwinter and everything was a shade of brown. The nights were cold and clear and the days were warm and clear, and every part of the landscape was in deep need of rain. Now he has arrived in an altogether different land. A land with more water than it could ever contain. Everywhere around him, there is evidence of new growth—the fresh grass, which would have been burned down the previous winter, and the thick thornbush sprigging bright-green all around him. In the days of the Anglo-Zulu War, this landscape was wholly different and the soldiers often struggled to find firewood. They had to burn the dead leaves of aloes and dried-out cattle and horse dung. Back then, the grass was taller than a man and able to conceal an army of over twenty thousand Zulu soldiers. When the Zulu soldiers advanced, they would sometimes place their shields ahead of them, so that the whole land was on the move, like Birnam Wood advancing toward Dunsinane.

He climbs back into the car and continues along the track toward the lodge buildings, passing through a black metal gate where another guard is evidently expecting him. Daniel parks outside the shop and reception building, under a large and dripping ficus tree. He remembers the shop from before. It sells CDs of Bruce Webster's narrations, and beaded and woven artefacts produced by local women. There are display cases containing various finds on the grounds of the lodge: Martini-Henri rifle cartridges, both live and spent, as well as musket balls, brass tent-clips, service buttons, buckles and regimental numbers and badges. At Reception, he finds Moses standing behind the oversized wooden desk, as a priest might stand behind an altar. Now that he sees Daniel's face, the old man immediately remembers him as the man who writes for television.

"How long will you be staying?" Moses asks with warmth, as if recalling Daniel as a more good-humored man than Daniel imagines himself to be.

"Could you check me in for the next week?"

Daniel still has a week left of summer holiday before he has to start work again. As he only goes into the studios for story meetings, he is generally able to work from home. He is the script editor for a show that is reputed to be the most authentically Zulu program on television. This is in spite of the fact that—apart from the Head Writer, Zee—it is written by a team of middle-aged white men who live in the Johannesburg suburb of Parkview.

"We have many rooms," Moses says. "Business is quiet these last days."

Daniel is not sure whether this is an allusion to Sam's disappearance or to some broader issue and he does not ask. He remembers Moses as a man who does each thing in its allotted time and place. To bring up Sam at such a moment would be beneath both of their dignities. Daniel also remembers that Moses is a respected induna in his community. His people are the Ngobese family of Chief Sihayo's clan. They were living in the area, on both sides of the river, long before Bruce Webster's father bought the land. Moses's ancestors had fought bravely against the British in the Anglo-Zulu War and it was said that the Websters' actual home—a glass-and-steel structure near the summit of the hill—was built on top of an important Ngobese burial site. Over the last years, there have been several land claims in the area, but most remain unresolved.

A man whom Daniel does not recognize loads his luggage into a golf cart and drives him up to his room. Guest cars are not usually permitted beyond the parking area and guests either need to walk up the series of wooden walkways that have been built between the ascending rooms or they must take a cart up the trail that leads to the top of the hill, where the swimming pool, bar and dining area are to be found. The Websters' glass house is off to one side, with a wider view of the Buffalo River and the neighboring hills of Zululand. Below it are the stables and then the library—where, on his former visit, Daniel spent several happy hours of writing and research.

Daniel also stayed in the Damiel McEwan Room on his previous visit and he remembers it well. There are framed pictures on the walls depicting battle scenes as well as photographs of the men who fought and died there. There is a coffee station, a bar fridge and a sitting area with sliding doors that lead onto two wrought-iron chairs on a wooden deck. The double bed is enclosed in mosquito netting and the bathroom consists of a standing bath and an outside shower, which is screened off by stripped wattle poles. From the outside shower and the deck there is a decent view of iSandlwana—the stone head of the lion only just managing to peer above the ascending hills of Zululand. From here the river can be heard but it can't be seen. The Damiel McEwan room is the most remote, stuck off to the side and at the bottom of the hill. It has the longest walk toward the restaurant and the longest walk back from the bar—and is usually reserved for younger, fitter guests who are less likely to misjudge the wooden walkway steps.

Daniel showers and brushes his teeth and makes himself some coffee, the thick white towel marked with the golden lion-mountain insignia of Webster Lodge wrapped around his hips. He glances at himself in the mirror and is pleased with what he finds there. For a man of thirty-two, he still has a slender body and some visible sign of stomach muscles. He has a thick mop of dark hair that is showing no signs of thinning—and the kind of good looks that make people turn to look at him when he enters a room, although there is something withdrawn about him and almost apologetic that usually discourages people from looking again.

He arranges his clothes in the cupboard and puts away his suitcase. Then he angles the desk toward the sliding glass doors, so that he will be able to see the head of the lion-mountain when he is working—even though right now the scene outside is engulfed in wisps of white cloud. He sees that there is a large wasp bumping into the glass from outside and in the eaves he notices a wasp nest, where a few wasps are circling dangerously. This is not and never has been a benevolent landscape. The wooden walkways were built by Bruce after a guest came face to face with a black mamba one afternoon on his journey back from lunch.

Daniel plugs in his computer, but he does not open it. He hasn't written a word of his ancestor novel since the day his mother died.

He is hoping this week to make a fresh start. The only hard evidence he has that his novel ever existed is a series of notes, bits of scenes, fragments of dialog and images jotted down in no particular order. He climbs into the enormous bed—noting that the linen is still good, the pillows still soft and thick—and falls into the absolute and determined sleep of a very tired man, or a sick child.

When it is time for dinner, he buttons his coat
and steps into the night

It is raining more thinly now and the rain wets his face but makes no sound. All around him, there is a great hush, the rain moving through the land with a single breath that will probably outlast the night. He has barely eaten today, he realizes, and is very hungry. He takes the walkway uphill in the direction of the dining area, hearing the call of nightjars and of zebras yipping from the banks of the river. Whenever the thunder rumbles, it feels like something subsiding deep inside the earth rather than something skyward, and there is no visible light in the sky afterwards to dispute this. All he has to guide himself by are the lamps arranged at intervals along the walkway—but the lamps are too widely spaced for such conditions, and between each smudge of light he has to walk for a moment in the dark.

He passes only one figure as he ascends—a tall, big-boned woman in khaki slacks and a white shirt who is making no attempt to keep herself dry. At her side walks a long-limbed wolf. At first, Daniel thinks it is only the woman's shadow, created by that weird lamplight, until he realizes that the shadow is a living thing, a daemon in the flesh. Only when they have passed him and continued down the walkway does Daniel realize that the wolf is only the Websters' dog—Jane—and that the woman is Caroline Webster, rendered almost unrecongnizable by grief.

The next morning, in the blue hour, he slides open the door

A long bank of mist is hanging above the river and a slither of moon is visible in an apricot-pink sky. The head of iSandlwana lours above the mountains, exactly as he remembers it. He makes himself some coffee and sits outside on a wrought-iron chair. The previous night, when he had not been able to see the lion-mountain, he had almost forgotten to think about it—but now that it is here, once again in front of him, he realizes that he felt it even during his hours of sleep, as you might experience something denser than the darkness, pushing back at you through the night.

As he watches the light of a new day grow, the mist rises and fills the whole valley—and when he next remembers to look for the mist, he finds it gone and the landscape restored. A paradise flycatcher is sitting on a nearby dead branch, ascending now and again with a flurry of its long tail to catch an insect before alighting again. Two brown-hooded kingfishers call to each other from different trees—and are gone again in a sizzle of electric-blue. Now that Daniel is here, exactly where he planned to be, he feels slightly foolish. An impostor. He stares at the mountain as you might stare at some edifice from an ancient culture that you can never hope to comprehend.

It took him a long time to fall asleep the previous night. He lay in his strangely shrouded bed, keeping very still, waiting for the ghost of Sam Webster to appear. Sam had once described to him how the dead would gather around her bed when she was a small girl. She never said whether these were the dead who had been buried directly under her house—the restless ancestors of Moses Ngobese—or whether they were the British and Zulu soldiers who had been buried in the hills around them.

When Daniel did finally fall asleep, he had a pedestrian dream involving himself and some boys he had barely known at boarding school. In the dream, they were dressed in bee suits, hats and veils, and a sick-looking boy was smoking a beehive as he cut away the sheet of wax that concealed the honey. There had never been any beehives at Daniel's school and he has never before worn a bee suit, let alone extracted honey from a hive. Yet in the dream he knew exactly what he was doing. Even now, he can remember the moment he lifted the wax sheet away from the hive to reveal the rich and glaucous honey, which smelled of ginger and eucalyptus.

There are waffles for breakfast

Moses watches as a waitress places a slippery fried egg and some charred bits of bacon next to Daniel's waffle on the plate. Moses has a disinterested stoicism about him that Daniel associates with warriors, with men who know that the next battle will come to them whether they go out to look for it or not.

"Honey?" Moses asks.

"Thanks."

On Moses's wrist is a strip of goatskin and a copper bangle. Around his neck is a string of white beads, with the occasional red bead interspersed. Daniel now remembers that Moses—despite being a man whose job it is to oversee the serving of eggs—is also a traditional healer of some kind. When Moses hands Daniel the little pot of honey, he looks at him probingly.

"How is the writing for television?" he asks.

"Fine, thanks."

As Daniel likes to relate, the poet WH Auden once tried to write for television. He gave up, however, because he said he found it impossible to imitate other people's bad writing. Daniel sometimes jokes that his job is to make twelve bad script writers sound like one bad script writer. But instead of saying any of this, he asks:

"And how is Mr. Webster doing?"

"He is very bad."

"And Mrs. Webster?"

"She is very bad."

"I'm sorry. It's a terrible thing."

"Yes, a terrible thing."

Not knowing what else to say, Daniel smiles his thanks at Moses and moves outside to the wooden deck. There is a row of lemon-yellow umbrellas looking down on the swimming pool, where a young man made out of various shades of gold is standing in the shallow end. As Daniel grinds pepper over his eggs, the man steps out of the water and saunters over to the lounger below Daniel. There he starts to dry himself appreciatively with a Webster Lodge towel.

"You must have checked in last night," the man says, sounding English and surprisingly familiar.

"Yesterday afternoon."

"I'm Tim Greene."

He says this as if his name is widely known—and he extends a wet hand. Daniel can already guess that he is the new intern from England. He looks pretty much like the previous intern, only his hair is shorter and a steelier shade of gold.

"Are you coming on my tour this morning?" Tim Greene asks him pleasantly.

"Actually, I hadn't thought about it."

"You'd be very welcome. It's been unusually quiet over the new year, but I have a very knowledgeable couple from England. And a few South Africans. Have you been on the tour before?"

"I was last here just over a year ago."

"Before my time," Tim Greene says, smiling strangely.

"I hear Bruce is in a bad way," Daniel says.

"Bruce? He's doing okay."

"He must be pretty devastated."

"You mean about Sam?" Tim says this as if Sam has merely moved countries, not been seen dead in the middle of a flooded river. "The trouble with Bruce," he adds, "is that he doesn't actually believe that Sam is dead."

This is the last thing Daniel expects to hear. Tim looks amused by whatever expression has found its way to his face.

"But—she was seen."

"You mean the woman on the river? Bruce believes that was someone else."

"But Sam was identified—wasn't she?"

"Bruce went and talked to the kid who first saw her. He believes the woman he described was older. She'd also been in the water for a few days, so—you know, hard to identify. At least with any certainty. '

"Right."

Daniel glances across at Tim Greene and finds him looking right back into him. There's something about the younger man's gaze that unnerves him. Perhaps it's simply that Tim's eyes are too close together. He has been designed to be more predator than prey.

"What's your name anyway?" Tim asks.

"Daniel. Daniel Hawthorne."

"Ah yes. The writer. Caroline has talked about you."

"She has?"

"She said you were writing a book about Charles Hawthorne. The notorious coward."

"That's the one."

"What's your book called?"

"I'm not sure. "The Butterfly Collector" is my working title, but I'll need something catchier than that."

Tim gives him a sample of his smile. For an English person, he has remarkably good teeth.

"Tell me something," Daniel says. "If Bruce doesn't think Sam is dead, what does he believe? Does he think she was abducted, or that she just—ran away?"

"You'll have to ask him about that," Tim says, continuing to wipe the lustre of wet gold away from his skin. "Every day, he has a new theory. You know what Bruce is like. After a while, it gets hard to keep up. It's pure denial, if you want my opinion. It's merely his way of trying to survive—all this."

"And Caroline?"

"What about her?"

"I saw her last night. She walked straight past me without recognising me. She looked—pretty awful."

"That's because Caroline knows the truth."

Daniel listens to Bruce Webster's narration all the way to iSandlwana

He is seated in the back seat of the lodge's minivan, the window slid open to the smell of wood-smoke and wet earth. Tim Greene is in the front with Moses, who is driving rather dolefully. There are five other guests sitting between them. The minivan passes through the gates of the lodge, rumbles past the fabled buildings of Rorke's Drift and crosses the cement bridge over the Buffalo River and into Zululand. This—they are told—is where the central column of the British army crossed into Zululand in 1879 under the command of Lord Chelmsford.

They are listening over the minibus CD player to Bruce's account of the historic events as they unfolded—and the river crossing in the mist in the morning, during which two men drowned. The journey across the plain toward the camp of iSandlwana. Now only a twenty-minute drive away. Which took nine days due to the muddy trader's track that had to be cleared of rocks for the passage of around five thousand men, five thousand oxen, five hundred mules and horses, as well as goats, sheep, the pet dogs of officers—and a domesticated monkey.

Soon they are surrounded by Zulu homesteads, with the round, thatched ancestral hut at the center—where family disputes are resolved, weddings planned and the ancestors communed with—and the huts of the wives and other family members arranged in a circle around them. There are fruit trees and mealie fields and the occasional crop of cannabis. Cows, goats and dogs wander around the road, their ownership known by all who live here. The locals they pass wave with deference toward the figure of Moses.

Moses slows to show them the wagon tracks the British army left across a sandstone riverbed and they stop for a refreshment break at St. Vincent's Church, where there is a museum that the other guests climb out to visit. Daniel investigates the grounds of the church, taking photographs with his phone and trying to find a way into the church building but finding it locked. Afterwards, they drive through the gates and into the heritage site of iSandlwana itself, the mountain still facing away from them. Its summit is teeming with tourists from another lodge, their voices audible even from where Moses parks. All around them are the whitewashed cairns concealing more British dead—the smaller ones containing six to ten bodies, the larger ones containing the bodies of up to ninety men.

"Can I show you something?" Tim says quietly to Daniel while the other guests are helping themselves to rusks and coffee. Daniel follows him to a nearby cairn, where Tim lifts a whitewashed rock. "See that?" he says. "Human teeth."

Daniel can see a few loose teeth lying there in the dirt and he touches one of them. It still has its pearly sheen. He thinks of *Hamlet*. Here hung the lips I kissed I know not how oft.

"These are the teeth of the soldiers?"

"Some of the skeletons are beginning to emerge," Tim says. "See here." He points out where several broken-off ribs have become visible amongst the stones. "In the old days, Bruce used to come here and cover them up—especially after it had rained. But no one bothers anymore. In fact, the bones attract more visitors."

Daniel bends down and takes a photo of the bones and the teeth. He wonders whether these are the bones of any of the men he intends to write about. This might be Private Mowbray or Captain Sprite. Daniel already has all of his characters lined up like chess pieces, ready to advance, but so far he has lacked the inclination and energy to move them. He looks away from the bones when Tim's phone gives off a beep.

"Tell me," Daniel says, "do you think someone could do the walk with me—from iSandlwana to Fugitives' Drift? In my novel, some of my characters manage to escape the battle on horseback and they journey to the river and back into Natal. I'd like to walk it, if possible, just to experience it?"

"Sure," says Tim, "I'd be happy to take you. When would you like to go?"

"How about now?"

"I have to finish the tour. But I could take you tomorrow?"

"That would be perfect—thanks."

Moses and Tim carry camp chairs to a gathering of wattles—and there Tim narrates the familiar story. The arrival of the army at the base of the mountain, the reports of Zulu soldier movement to the south-east of the camp, and Lord Chelmsford and others taking most of the fighting men deeper into Zululand, leaving the camp under-resourced and more or less undefended. The surprise of Lieutenant Raw coming across the Zulu army only eight miles away, to the north-east of the camp—twenty-five thousand soldiers and around fifteen thousand women and children, who were there to cook and care for them. The army standing and crying out "Usutu!" and hitting their spears against their shields and the women behind them ululating—and the whole army moving forward with a single intention toward the few dozen men who had appeared at the ridge like little clay figures on clay horses.

Daniel is familiar with the narrative that evolves from there, which is Bruce's narrative even as it is recited by Tim Greene. The account of the one-day battle that took place in that devil's triangle between iSandlwana, Fugitives' Drift and Rorke's Drift, leaving thousands of men lying dead at the end of it, each side having endured extraordinary victory and extraordinary defeat. Despite his better qualities, Bruce's public mode of storytelling is one of sentimental self-aggrandizement. Even when he is praising the pluckiness of a humble British messenger or the nobility of an anonymous Zulu soldier, he manages to turn the anecdote into an opportunity for what Thomas Hobbes, speaking of human laughter, called self-applause.

When Tim arrives at a natural interval in his narrative—the death of Lieutenant-Colonel Durnford, only a hundred yards from where they are sitting—they have another coffee break and wander toward the shoulder of the lion-mountain. From this point, you can see even further into the haze of hills from which the Zulu army attacked. The white cairns lying across the plain ahead of them look freshly painted, as if they were placed there only recently and only in order to provide evidence that the battle took place. Interspersed between the cairns are more Nguni cattle and some zebras and wildebeest that have crossed the river from Webster Lodge. There are also several goats—two of them standing inside a small tree as they crop the new growth.

Now that Tim's narrative has been placed on pause, the lodge guests return with some relief to the everyday comforts of coffee and cheese-and-pickle sandwiches. Daniel finds a rock next to a British couple he greeted briefly at breakfast. They are sitting in the shade of a buffalo-thorn bush, wearing their matching khaki-green anoraks. The man is talking at the top of his voice, sounding like an out-of-work actor—the kind of fellow who might have been cast as one of the less memorable lords in a history play at the Royal Shakespeare Company.

"Someone ought to write a musical," the man is saying to his wife.

"A what, dear?"

"A musical."

"About what, dear?"

"iSandlwana, of course."

"It wouldn't have a very happy ending."

"Does *Les Misérables* have a happy ending?"

"To be honest, I can't remember."

"To be honest, neither can I."

Tim has also found a rock nearby, but he is absorbed in tapping messages into his phone. Daniel has not yet decided what he thinks of Tim Greene. He has a surface dazzle beyond which it is difficult to see without a good pair of sunglasses—and yet there is also some kind of fissure running through him, like the cracked glass across the face of a watch under which the time keeps ticking.

"Caroline says you must come for a drink tonight," Tim says, looking up toward Daniel with his vacant, friendly face.

"Sorry—what?"

"Caroline and Bruce. They want you to come for a drink at their house."

Daniel combs his hair in the dark

He has always preferred interiors that are cavernous and uninhabited—except by him. Although he has been in several relationships since leaving school, and although each time he has chosen a different type of girl, each time the relationship has ended in the same place—with him having done everything he could think of to make the girl happy, and the girl saying in the end that she had never been happy, and him realising that, in truth, he had never been happy either.

He is not apprehensive about this meeting with the Websters. Perhaps because he has never been intimidated by the presence of death. Since the slow death of his younger sister, which lasted two years and finally happened when he was ten, the idea of loss has been a familiar companion. His most recent girlfriend said to him when they were breaking up that it was life he was afraid of, not death. He replied that he did not understand what she meant by this. Was he not living as full a life as anyone else? She said she hoped that one day he would find whatever it was he was looking for, because it clearly wasn't anywhere inside her—nor in any other person she had met.

The sun is sinking into a purplish hunk of cloud when Daniel emerges from his drummer-boy room, his hair combed back wetly, his face still smarting from a blunt razorblade. The winding walkway takes him through thickening indigenous bush before he follows a path that veers away from the rest of the lodge buildings and toward the library, the stables and the glass house.

The Websters' house has been featured in several architectural and interior-design magazines and the architect is said to be someone famous—although Daniel never managed to catch the person's name. Where every other building at the lodge has been designed to blend into the landscape—they are each made from local sandstone and the roofs are covered in montane grass—the Websters' house has been constructed so as to draw the utmost attention to itself. From this angle, the glass rooms have caught the declining sun so that the whole structure is like a large ember gradually losing its light.

He finds Bruce sitting in the glass veranda. At his right hand is a tumbler of Monkey Shoulder and at his left is the family wolfhound, Jane. Bruce appears more or less as he was when Daniel last saw him, facing his mountain like a baby eagle. Featherless, short-sighted, without any immediate prospect of flight. Of Caroline, there is no evidence.

"Hello, Bruce," Daniel says. "It's good to see you."

Bruce eyes him, perhaps weighing up the sincerity of this statement. "Get yourself a drink," he says.

At the drinks table, Daniel takes a moment to take in the view. The mountain is a hunched shadow across the graying sky. Although the land between them is dark, some of the homesteads of Zululand twinkle in the space before the lion's feet like gold coins. A sprinkled peace offering. Daniel tastes his drink and realizes that he has overdone the gin, but since this is the Websters' house he does not add more tonic.

"Where's Caroline?" he asks.

"I'm sure she'll be through in a moment."

Only now does Daniel realize that Bruce is already drunk. Daniel had seen him drunk on his previous visit, but back then he was full of ideas and the drink only fuelled him. Now he is like a man from a Graham Greene novel, waiting to be taken out to a courtyard to be shot.

This is not the first time Daniel has seen Bruce in the weeks since Sam's disappearance. The Websters appeared on television on the same day that the girl's body was seen. It was the usual appeal to the public to inform the police of anything they might know about the case. There had been something unusual about Sam's case even then. It emerged that it had taken the Websters a week even to report that Sam was missing—and her body was seen on the river three days later. There had been some speculation about this in the press, but the Websters claimed that Sam had had a fight with her mother and had threatened to run away from home—so initially the family didn't think anything bad had happened. They thought she was hiding out with her boyfriend or one of her friends. When she left the house, she had taken with her a small red suitcase, her phone and her passport. She had officially left school on that same day and they thought she was trying to demonstrate her new independence. But after a week of no word from her—either to the Websters or to any of her friends—the family had started to panic.

Daniel remembers that in the television interview Bruce had said something about how their love would outlast the killer's hate. Bruce had looked dreadful onscreen—his gray tonsure in more than usual disarray, his face swollen and crazed—while Caroline looked like a neatly folded napkin that concealed something distasteful—a piece of gristle. After Bruce's statement, the two detectives produced examples of the digital watch the girl was wearing, the phone she was using and the colorful charity beads she had around her left wrist. None of these items was seen on the dead girl in the river, however. Only the unfamiliar, dark-blue anorak. As for the red suitcase and the passport, they had never been seen again.

"How's your book coming along?" Bruce asks.

"I recently made a new start," Daniel lies.

"I'd be interested to read it. Right now I could do with the distraction."

"Of course. I'll send you what I've done in the morning."

Daniel decides he can always cobble something together before Bruce wakes up. He has arranged to meet Tim at Reception at ten the next morning—so he will have a few hours before in which to work. His earliest notes for his novel are the most detailed, but they dwindle into almost nothing as his characters approach iSandlwana.

"How have you been holding up?" Daniel asks, finding a wicker chair alongside Bruce.

"Well—you know."

"I'm really sorry about—all of it."

"Thanks."

They say nothing more, but Daniel can feel that the other man likes to have him here. He likes to have him here as a man likes a dog at his side. Or a lion-mountain before him. Yet Daniel is not used to being silent with Bruce. A silent Bruce is an unknown entity. With a silent Bruce, there was no telling what might happen next.

"Christmas must have been awful without her."

"Every day is awful without her."

"Sorry—that came out wrong," Daniel says. "I suppose Matthew's back at school?"

"Matthew started this week—yes. He hated it last year. I'm hoping that this year something will shift. But with everything that's happened with Sam. Well, none of that is going to help."

"Have you heard—anything new?"

"Nothing new."

"And the police? They have nothing new—to go on?"

"The police have absolutely nothing new to go on."

By the time Caroline comes through, the moon hasn't yet ascended and the valley has been reduced to a shadowy void. Caroline is wearing a plain silk dressing gown and her hair hasn't been washed or brushed. She seems to have applied her lipstick a moment too late, as if her face had already moved off. Previously, Caroline was one of those people who wore her body as you might ride a horse. With an air of easy command. Now she looks earthbound and lost.

"Hello, Caroline," Daniel says, half standing.

"Hello," she says briefly. "Would you like something to eat?"

"Not especially, thanks."

"I can ask Moses to bring up something from the restaurant. I can't remember the last time I cooked. It is so utterly pointless to cook, don't you think? People are generally better off eating toast."

"I'm honestly fine, thanks."

But Caroline has already forgotten her question and walked across to the drinks table, the cord of her dressing gown swaying behind her like something designed to attract the attention of a cat—although these days there is no cat in this house.

"Another drink?" Caroline asks.

"I'm good, thanks," Daniel says.

She pours herself a large whisky and drops in a few afterthoughts of ice.

"What have you come here to do?" she asks.

"I thought I'd—well, I thought I might carry on with my book."

She laughs. "Is Bruce helping you with that? There's nothing Bruce likes more than the prospect of another book."

Daniel realizes only now that Caroline has barely looked at him since her arrival—and that everything she has said and done has been directed, in some way, toward her husband.

"Perhaps I should go," Daniel says, turning to Bruce.

"Don't be silly," Caroline says. "You've only just arrived."

She finds a chair that is angled toward them and fishes out a dead fly from her drink—flicking it toward the dog, which duly snaps at it. Daniel can see some broken veins running up one of Caroline's calves. Little worms nosing about in vain for an entrance to the dark. He remembers that Caroline made some sort of pass at him when he was last at the lodge. It had come out as a joke and he had taken it as such. But it had been far from a joke. Since that moment, Caroline had cooled toward him. From her frank look in his direction, however, there's no telling whether she remembers any of this or not.

"You're looking suntanned," she says with a note of accusation. "Have you been away somewhere nice for the holidays?"

"Me? No, but I do go walking. I suppose it must be that."

"It suits you," she says. "And are you still doing lots of writing in your spare time?"

"To be honest, not much since my mother died."

"Your mother died? I'm sorry to hear that."

Caroline does not sound especially sorry, but then what is a dead mother alongside a murdered child? Although Bruce has not stirred since Caroline's arrival, there appears to be a private war going on between them. Bruce and Caroline have always seemed to hate one another—but this new, dead thing between them, is this what happens after hate, when all the blood has been drained away from it?

"Are you still writing for your television show?"

"Right now, we're on holiday."

"I watched a few episodes after you left that last time. It really is complete schlock, isn't it?"

"I'm afraid it probably is."

"I thought at the time of how you sit in judgment of Bruce—don't deny it—and his style of storytelling. 'Essentially colonial' is how you think of it, not so?"

"Mrs. Webster, I really—"

"Colonial and full of self-importance. And yes, I have to say I agree. It's a particular kind of liberal romanticism. But are you and your friends who write for television any better? Have you ever considered what you might be romanticising? What you might be trying to colonize?"

"I'm not sure I understand."

"You know what I thought when I watched your show?" she continues. "I thought how you writers—you people actually writing the show—were doing terrible harm. I thought you were inviting terrible harm. Most of the men, for example, were criminals. They were psychopathic killers. Yet we were also being asked to believe that they were honorable Zulu men and good fathers. I mean—is that not a bit disgusting? And yet you carry on doing it. I suppose you'll say you're doing it for the money. I suppose you'll tell me that you have no choice. That if you were to leave the job, you would immediately be replaced by some other sop. But that's all a lie, isn't it? You don't care what you're doing. You don't care about the consequences of your actions. You don't actually care that you're helping to fuel this great beast that's devouring our children—children like Sam—every single day. The whole world is imploding in on everyone anyway, so you may as well make yourselves a quick buck."

"I'm very sorry," Daniel says—almost inaudibly.

"Why don't you give him a job, Bruce?" Caroline asks, turning on her husband.

"What's that?"

"Tim will be going back to England as soon as the police allow it. I'm pretty sure you'll be wanting a replacement."

"No, Caroline," Bruce says. "I think you mean that you will be wanting a replacement."

Daniel excuses himself an hour later

He mutters something about needing the bathroom, but in truth he is preparing his escape. Except for that one occasion when Caroline showed him her bedroom—and her bed—he has never been deeper into the Websters' glass house than the open-plan kitchen area. The only possible route to the guest bathroom is the passage that leads off from the kitchen, where he finds dimly lit abstract paintings in dusty oranges, salmon-pinks and slashes of lime green. The first door on the right is ajar and there he discovers a boy's bedroom, all in blue, with framed pictures of a malachite kingfisher and a rainbow trout, and a large model of a Lancaster bomber suspended with fishing line over the bed. The room has the same designed quality as the rest of the house—as if, even in here, an actual living family member is yet to move in.

He tries the door opposite and enters a room that smells of old oranges. He switches on the light and the first thing he notices is an unmade bed. On the pillow is a well-worn rabbit with ears as long as its body and a smile drawn across its velvety muzzle with a marker pen. There are used coffee mugs all around the room and a crumpled tissue that has missed the half-filled metal bin. At the desk, which is made from smoky emerald glass, a spectrum of colored pencils lies spilled across a drawing pad. There are also a few hair ties on the desk and a hairbrush still holding some copper-colored hair. Sam's hair. The wardrobe door is standing open, revealing a rack of dark-green school clothes and a dark-blue coat. Daniel realizes that the citrus smell is coming from a tub of body cream that has been left open beside the bed. On the walls are posters of Thom Yorke from Radiohead and Claire Danes wearing angel's wings in Baz Luhrmann's *Romeo and Juliet.* There is also a basket full of mottled black-and-white springer spaniel puppies. It's the room of a teenage girl who hasn't yet managed to relinquish her childhood ideas about herself. On the floor, Daniel sees a boy's sock, and on the pad he finds a surprisingly lively drawing of what appears to be a pygmy kingfisher.

He walks over to the bedside table and picks up a framed recent photograph of Sam holding a Siamese cat—more of a kitten, really. He looks long and hard at Sam's eyes, at the color of her eyes, which are green at first glance, but are actually made up of blue-grays and chestnut-grays that are flecked with a dusty gold. It is difficult to imagine that these eyes, this gaze, have gone forever from the world.

"What are you doing?"

He turns to find Caroline filling the doorway. She is holding her drink and her other hand is rested on the wolfhound's head. In the unforgiving brightness of the room, she looks ten years older than she did when Daniel last saw her properly. Twenty years. More like the mother of the woman she was until recently.

"I'm sorry. I was looking—for the bathroom."

Caroline waves away an invisible fly.

"Don't lie to me, you little shit."

Daniel blinks and tries to smile.

"You know what?" Caroline says, standing aside for him and

slopping her drink. “Just get out. Get the fuck out of my fucking house.”

THE BUTTERFLY COLLECTOR

"You must be Hawthorne?"

Charles turns to find a young officer standing directly in front of him, taking up less space than his voice suggested. There is something about the officer's manner that Charles immediately recognizes, even as he knows that he has never encountered this man before. In the fading light of Dartmouth harbor, all Charles can see of his face is that he has a moustache in the English style and that there is something slender and fine-boned about him, something more of the poet than of the soldier.

"I am indeed Hawthorne," Charles says, taking the other man's hand. "And you are?"

"Grace. Lieutenant William Grace. I'm to be your cabin companion for the trip. I must say—I was getting concerned that you'd missed the boat."

"There was a muddle with my luggage. It was sent to Victoria instead of Paddington. But everything was resolved in the end."

"I'm glad to hear it."

Grace glances across at the pile of bags belonging to those who boarded late. Amongst Charles's luggage is a new pair of leather boots that he bought that afternoon at Dean's, as well as his old leather knapsack, which contains his butterfly-collecting equipment.

"Can I help to bring anything down?" Grace asks.

"Thank you. I would appreciate that."

Charles finds their cabin in a state of chaos. Grace has already had a fire lit and all of his belongings are arranged as if he stood at the cabin door and merely threw them inside, leaving them to settle where they landed. There is a sheathed sword and a woman's touring hat decked with peacock and ostrich feathers on one of the bunks, a blue patrol coat on another, three pipes attached to an uneven rack at the fireplace, an open tin of tobacco and a decanter of brandy on the mantelpiece, as well as two leather boots at opposite ends of the room with a shoe tree emerging from only one of them. Most surprising of all, however, is the Fox Terrier puppy lying fast asleep on a folded greatcoat by the fire.

"That's Pip," Grace says. "A gift for my sister. Along with the hat."

"Your sister?"

"I have a sister who lives in Kalk Bay. A fishing village not far from Cape Town."

"But are dogs allowed?"

"What are they going to do? Throw him overboard?"

When Grace goes over to pick up the sleeping dog, it comes to life in his hands and eagerly licks his face. Will Grace has regular, carefully drawn features that manage not to draw undue attention to themselves, but he has eyes that are both surprisingly dark and surprisingly blue. Charles, who is usually slow to make up his mind about anything, feels drawn to the other man at once.

Grace is still holding onto the weighty leather knapsack. "And what are you carrying in this?" he asks pleasantly.

Charles takes the knapsack and lays out his killing jars, pill boxes, cork-lined pocket boxes, zinc relaxing boxes, entomological pins and other bits of equipment on the less-cluttered bunk. This includes three small bottles of cyanide, each still marked with the hand-drawn skull and crossbones Charles's father drew on the label when Charles was a child—and, of course, his butterfly net, which he recently adjusted while still posted in Templemore. He had taken his old collapsible cane-framed umbrella net and converted it into one of those new-fangled kite nets, which have a longer Y-shaped brass ferrule that Charles had brazed together. He had also replaced the old netting with a finer mercerized cotton, which had a higher tensile strength than ordinary muslin.

"I collect butterflies in my spare time," Charles says unnecessarily.

"Do you think that any of this will help to defend you against a Zulu attack?" Grace laughs.

"I suppose we shall have to find out," smiles Charles.

"Come," says Grace, handing Pip across to Charles. "I have a good bottle of claret we could share before we go up for dinner. Fancy a glass?"

"Why not."

Charles learns that William Grace, who had been previously posted in India, had spent most of his youth in Natal, where he had acquired a fair knowledge of the Zulu language. This was why he had applied for a new posting in South Africa, which he had received only three days before, directly from the hand of Sir Martin Dillon. Grace had asked to be attached to one of the Native Contingents so that he could practice his language skills on the Native soldiers. Apart from his sister in Cape Town and an aunt in Durban, he had no other living family of whom he was aware. He seems to Charles to carry a curious blend of candor and internal bewilderment—and

Charles, who remains a private man in most public circumstances, is relieved that he is required to disclose little about himself in return.

They find the saloon almost empty by the time they head up for dinner. Most of the men have already moved through to an adjoining room, where they are arranged around the standing piano, singing "It Ain't All Honey and It Ain't All Jam." Charles helps himself to some sponge pudding and looks across to find that, instead of joining him for dinner, William Grace has joined the other singers with his confident baritone.

Charles is asleep by the time Grace returns to the cabin

He is woken by the sound of a man sobbing. He sits up to find Grace holding onto the dog by the fire. Charles has never witnessed another man weeping before—and, at first, he thinks he is laughing silently, until he sees Grace wiping his hand across his face.

"Grace? Is everything all right?"

"Quite all right," Grace says, laughing through his tears in embarrassment. "I'm afraid I might have had too much to drink. It can make one rather emotional."

"I see."

Charles does not intend to sound judgmental, but this is the tone that comes out of him—a tone that has absorbed the air of the world in which he was raised. But Grace is too drunk to notice this—or perhaps he simply does not care.

"Would you like to talk about it?"

"Talking is of no help," Grace says. "I have tried talking before. But the truth is, you can't trust anyone, can you? It is those closest to you who betray you, I find. It is better not to think about it."

"To think about what?"

"Anything of any importance."

This last utterance is made with a note of bitterness and reproach—reproach against phantoms that seem to have entered the cabin, even though they are surrounded by nothing but the darkness and the sea.

"The dreadful thing is that I have no faith. I have no faith in God. I sometimes feel it would be better to die. It would be easier to die. That is what I am hoping for, if you would like to know. I am hoping to find my death at the hands of the Zulu army. I want to feel the divine justice of a blade in my heart."

"That is the drink talking," Charles says mildly, beginning to sound more like himself.

"Do you believe in God, the Creator, as they speak about in church?" Grace asks, turning to look at him.

"If there is evidence of a creator anywhere," says Charles, "it is surely in the life cycle of a butterfly."

"A butterfly? What on earth are you talking about?"

"Did you know," Charles continues, "that when the caterpillar dies inside the chrysalis, it uses its own digestive juices to consume itself, to dissolve itself into a soup? It spares only those body parts that it will require for its next manifestation of life. No one yet understands what takes place inside the chrysalis, but usually within about a fortnight, or perhaps a few months, the soup reforms itself into a perfected butterfly. Depending on such factors as the weather, or the flowering of a particular plant, the butterfly then breaks free. It pumps blood into its new wings and often it has to assemble its own proboscis so that it will be able to feed. A few moments later, it flies off, already knowing everything it will need to know in order to survive and procreate."

Grace is staring at him as one might toward a rising sun.

"What magic is passing through the earth," Charles continues, "to enable such a simple and yet infinitely complicated event to take place? What magic tells every migrating butterfly to emerge at the same moment as hundreds of other butterflies and travel across cities, mountain ranges and seas—each one sharing the same notion of home?"

"I have no idea," says Grace. "I have never had any notion of home."

"Neither have I," says Charles. "But is that not a reason to be happy? Everywhere we go, the same miracle is passing through the earth. All we need to do is allow ourselves to become a part of it."

"You are a good man," Grace says after a moment.

"Me? I am not a good man. I am merely a man."

"Do you mind if I ask you something—terrible?"

"Not at all."

"Would you mind if I came and lay down next to you?"

Charles says nothing to this. For the first time since their departure, he becomes fully aware of the sea, moving beneath them and around them like some huge, breathing animal.

"I think it would be a better idea if you went to sleep," he says.

A few days later, they are visited by a thousand blue butterflies

Charles is standing at the stern when the first batch arrives, hovering around the foam of the propellers. Charles looks for any sign of land, but he finds none. There is only the aquamarine calm of the sea and the paler cobalt dome of the sky and the glimmers of blue iridescence coming off these small, blue butterflies.

"They've probably come in from Cape Verde," someone says.

Charles turns to find a large man in a cream-colored linen suit standing next to him, cutting a cigar. He has fleshy, wet lips and the melancholy expression of some old hunting dog. Charles has noticed the man before, watching him and William Grace from across the saloon, full of some unsmiling insinuation that, at the time, entirely unsettled Charles.

"But where are they headed?" Charles asks. "There is nothing out there but the sea."

"They are headed where each of us is headed, my friend," the man says, lighting his cigar with melancholy satisfaction.

The butterflies, steadily growing in number, are hovering merrily over the white water, showing no intention of landing anywhere on the ship. They seem to have emerged not from the land but from the phosphorescence of the ocean itself.

Charles catches several specimens with his net, along with a few wasps. The other officers smile at the sight of a soldier with a butterfly net, but Charles pays them no attention. The *Lycaena* have a deep-blue velvety patch in the discal area of the forewing, with gray-centerd marginal spots on the underside. He releases each specimen into a glass-bottomed pill box to be examined before transferring the best three into the killing jar, which has a base of plaster of Paris suffused with sodium cyanide. When the butterflies are dead, he pins them into the first of his cork-lined pocket boxes, which he slips into the drawer next to his bunk.

Throughout all this, Grace is lying half dressed in his bed, watching him, Pip's head just visible from under the blanket. The two men have not alluded to Grace's drunkenness on that first night, nor to his strange request. The morning afterwards, Charles had woken to find Grace breathing evenly from the safety of his own bunk—and, in the days that followed, Grace had behaved as if nothing unusual had taken place.

It was not the first time Charles had received this kind of proposal from a fellow officer—and Charles, as he had with Grace, had found himself kindly declining the offer. There had been a man in his former regiment called Captain Rowlston who was rumored to be preying on younger privates—and, after an official complaint was made, it was suggested by Rowlston's superiors that, for the sake of the regiment, he should find a suitable means of ending his own life. Rowlston had ridden off to a picturesque spot by a nearby river, placed the muzzle of his rifle into his mouth, passed a riding crop across the trigger and fired the rifle using his feet.

The idea of spending months in the exclusive company of other men did indeed attract some queer fish—as it did to the priesthood. Even today, soldiers were encouraged not to marry and not to have children—and, although contemporary novels were full of tales of young soldiers seducing a range of women, both married and unmarried, there were other events that were never written about and were spoken about only rarely. Charles, who had grown up in the all-male austerity of boarding school and then military life, had always found himself listening with interest and some shame to these tales. In some way, he felt that they implicated him.

With William Grace, however, Charles feels something altogether new. Since the first few minutes of meeting one another, they have slipped into a companionship that is found only between old friends. Yet it is also more than friendship. There is a feeling of mutual empathy and consideration that Charles has never experienced with another man before. Sometimes, the air inside their cabin feels too thick to breathe, too suffused with an unknown new drug, as if the two of them have entered a killing jar of their own devising.

"Do you feel nothing when they die?" Grace asks.

"Sorry—what?"

"The butterflies. Do you not mind killing them?"

"If I do not preserve them," says Charles, "how will there be any evidence that they were ever here?"

Charles soon forgets what it is to have the earth beneath his feet

They have been at sea for so long that the earth is difficult to imagine. Often, it seems that the ship is making no progress at all, so flat and constant are the horizons. But Charles knows that the rest of the soldiers feel differently. Already he has registered a gradual change in the air around them—as you might feel the change in the air before a thunderstorm—or, indeed, before an impending war. Where Charles continues to stand alone, a man adrift between two continents, the rest of the men draw together, their bodies taller, their voices louder and more difficult to distinguish. In the evenings when they gather around the piano, infected with cheap sherry, they even manage to sing in harmony.

William Grace has by now established himself—at least in Charles's mind—as two people. He is Lieutenant Will Grace, or Gracie, a regular Tom Jones with a ready laugh and a buoyant spirit who is inevitably liked by all who encounter him—and he is the shadow-man Charles finds alone in the cabin, brooding by the fire and holding onto his dog as a child might cling to a stuffed rabbit while an ocean revolves unevenly around him, one porthole away. Sometimes, this other man has a half-empty bottle of wine in his hand, and at other times he is sucking distractedly on his pipe, his gaze lingering over lost horizons. Yet he always appears relieved to see Charles, since any company at such moments is perhaps better than his own. But if Charles comes too close to him, either through an unexpected turn in the conversation or through some unconscious physical gesture, the other man withdraws inside himself like an exotic sea creature returning to its shell.

On their last night at sea, as if the world has finally caught up with the brooding moods of William Grace, their ship encounters a famous southeaster—the sort of weather through which the Cape of Storms has acquired its reputation and its name. The saloon is soon emptied of men—and the saloon table of crockery and cutlery—and Charles comes downstairs to look for his friend. He finds him sitting on Charles's bunk, one of the small bottles with the skull and crossbones label in one hand.

"Grace, what are you doing?"

"What would it take?" Grace asks, making no attempt to hide the bottle. "One sip?"

"I have no idea," Charles lies, taking the bottle away from him and putting it back inside its special pouch in the leather knapsack. "What were you doing with it anyway? You can't possibly be considering taking your life."

"I only wanted to look at it," says Grace, giving Charles one of his best smiles. "I wanted to look death clean in the face. We shall soon be looking death in the face. I suppose I wanted to get used to the sensation. Tell me something, Charles—are you afraid?"

"Of dying?"

"Of behaving badly. Of being named a coward."

"I haven't really thought about it," says Charles. "I suppose when the time comes, all one needs to do is one's duty. I think the training carries one through the whole endeavor. At least, that has been my experience. Did you see much action in India?"

"None at all, to be honest."

"Well perhaps we shall see none at all in Africa too."

Grace has moved across to the fire now, where he picks up his dog.

"You're a good friend, Charles," he says. "I sometimes feel that I might tell you anything."

"You may tell me whatever is in your heart."

"May I?" Grace laughs at this idea—as if Charles might not be able to take it.

"Of course you may. I know your heart, anyway. I know there is much goodness inside it."

"And much that is bad?"

"I do not believe that."

"That is because you are good. You expect to find only the same goodness in others."

"Believe me, I have learned to expect nothing at all."

Grace looks across at him now, his large indigo eyes inscrutable. "You care for me, Charles, do you not?"

"I do care for you."

"I mean—in a way that is not entirely—natural."

"I have no idea of what you're talking about," Charles laughs. "Yet Nature is, after all, a very curious and complicated thing—is it not?"

The city of Cape Town lies flat against the mountain

All Charles can see of the fabled mountain, however, is a brilliant green hill shaped like a pyramid and a shadow of blue-gray rock ascending into cloud. The buildings of the city are roofed in terracotta-colored tiles and they gleam white in the late-afternoon light. There is a forest of masts along the harbor wall and numerous smaller vessels rolling about in the swells like corks. As soon as the ship is lying at anchor, they are surrounded by surfboats offering to ferry them to the shore. A moody, splattering rain has started up and the lead-colored sea feels malicious. But Grace—who carries his own sunlight along with him whenever he appears in public—seems oblivious to the mood of the place. With the ostrich-feather hat balanced on his head and Pip tucked under his arm, and a white cloud of screeching gulls surrounding him, he summons a surfboat and starts his descent.

Although the sea is reputed to be filled with man-eating white sharks, the only sign of sea life are a few seals, floating fatly in the swells and flapping their weighty flippers from side to side. Mr. Silver—the man with the cream-colored suit Charles met when the blue butterflies appeared—accompanies Charles and Grace to the shore, anxious to get back to his shop. Charles has already arranged to visit him the next morning to acquire an extra pair of boots.

"Is there a train to Kalk Bay?" Grace asks Mr. Silver.

"The tracks are still under construction," says Silver. "I should get myself a Cape cart. There are always several lined up outside the harbor entrance."

"Thanks," says Grace. "You take good care of yourself."

"And you take good care of each other," says Silver, that insinuating smile running all the way through his large form.

With a change of clothes, Charles's butterfly-collecting equipment, the shivering dog and what is left of the hat, they drive off in the rain and are soon ascending a track that takes them away from the city and into a wider valley filled with farmland. At the end of a great plain is the glitter of what appears to be a fishing village—and beyond it, coming from a direction Charles had not anticipated, another wrinkled expanse of shining sea. Now and again, the declining light breaks through the low, swirling of cloud and ignites patches of emerald light.

"It is a scene straight out of Turner," Charles says to Grace.

"Out of where?"

"It is unlike anything I had imagined for Africa."

"Well Cape Town has never really been Africa," Grace says with a short laugh.

Except for two wagonloads of military men from Simonstown, there is little traffic on the road to Kalk Bay. By the time they pass through the seaside settlement of Muizenberg, it is so dark that Charles can barely see the straw beneath his boots. But the driver continues as confidently as before, the wheels of his cart jolting their bones with every bump and ditch. Soon they can hear the roar and thump of the sea and their cart comes to a halt outside a modest stone cottage covered in thick thatch.

"I believe," says Grace, "that we have arrived at my sister's house."

Grace's sister immediately offers them onion soup

She is a smaller, neater version of her brother. Accepting the gifts of the hat and the dog with much hilarity, she sits the two men down at a butter-stained wooden table by the fire and pours them each a large glass of the local red wine. It soon emerges that she has become engaged to an ostrich farmer called Grobbelaar out at Oudtshoorn who is twice her age, dyspeptic and incredibly rich. Grace's sister tells them that white ostrich feathers, per pound, are almost as valuable as diamonds and have come to be known locally as "white gold."

"And this Grobbelaar has never been married?" asks Grace.

"His former wife died in childbirth. But she left behind three sons."

"So you are prepared to play the evil stepmother?"

"Oh, they're all grown up. They're about my age, in fact."

"You might have been better off marrying one of the sons."

"I think poor Tertius is hoping for a second batch."

"At least you will be able to repair the hat," Charles jokes.

Lydia Grace—for this is her name—meets Charles's gaze as any man might. "What about you, Mr. Hawthorne? What do you do?"

"He's a lieutenant," corrects Grace, "and he spends all his spare time butterfly collecting."

"Butterfly collecting? What on earth for?"

"It's something I have always done," says Charles. "I grew up collecting butterflies with my father in Somerset—and I suppose the habit stuck."

"Then you shall have to meet Mr. Trimen. He is renting one of the neighboring cottages. He is the current Curator of the South African Museum in Cape Town. He even stayed in my cottage once—and he left me the prettiest tray of butterflies you ever saw in your life."

"That sounds wonderful."

Charles wakes to the sound of the sea

Yet his bed is ominously still.

"Have we run aground?" he asks, sitting up.

He finds himself in a room filled with light, a large tray of blue butterflies hanging on the wall across from him. He turns to find Grace asleep next to him, and gradually he recalls the events of the previous night—the two men agreeing to sleep in the same bed since there were no other beds, and Grace cleaning his teeth at the open window and climbing in next to Charles and falling instantly asleep. Charles lay there for a long time, feeling strangely elated and inspired, but he did nothing to interfere with the sleep of his friend. Later, Lydia arrived with a lamp at the door and looked down at them—until Pip hopped onto the bed and settled himself between them, and the young woman, who was in every way as attractive as her brother, smiled and retired.

Charles gets dressed and steps outside to encounter a glorious and blustery day, the southeaster having almost spent itself. The cloud is beginning to thin around the mountain above Kalk Bay, and the sea, which is turquoise-green at the shore break and a deeper royal blue toward the horizon, is flecked throughout with white. A solitary fisherman stands amongst the rocks, surrounded by a tattered flotilla of gulls, and nearer the cottage is the raw furrow that has been dug out of the earth to prepare for the new railway track.

"How are you feeling this morning?"

He turns to find Lydia standing close to him, her nut-colored hair tied back. She is wearing a simple yellow dress and is even more beautiful than she was the night before. She seems to Charles to carry in her bright spirit something of the mountain and the sea. She is a wild flower, entirely at home in this landscape, even though she might have been supplanted from an altogether different place.

"Very well, thank you."

"And my brother? Is he still asleep?"

"When I last saw him—yes."

Lydia glances up at Charles again. It is the first time Charles has looked properly into her eyes, and there he finds the same shade of indigo-blue.

"How has William been?" she asks.

"He has been well," says Charles.

"Well?"

"Very well—I believe."

"And is that all?"

"Well, he is—he does seem quite complicated."

"Yes, he most certainly is," smiles Lydia. "He has always been complicated, Lieutenant Hawthorne. But he is also the very best of us. The very best of any of us."

"I do see that. I do know that."

"And what about you, Lieutenant?"

"Me?"

"Are you also complicated?"

"Terribly complicated," laughs Charles.

He is surprised to find her laughing back. "Poor William," she says. "He has finally met his match."

Lydia picks up the dog and tucks him under her arm—as was Grace's habit at sea. "There is only one thing that I would like to ask of you," she says with sudden earnestness.

"Please—anything."

"Please ensure that whatever takes place over the next months, you will bring my brother back alive. Promise that you will not leave him on the battlefield to die alone."

"I promise," says Charles, "that I shall do everything in my power to look after him."

"Thank you," says Lydia, switching back to her sunny disposition as rapidly as she clouded over. "Oh yes," she adds, "I almost forgot to tell you that I have spoken with Mr. Trimen. He will be setting off directly after breakfast in search of specimens, if you would care to join him?"

"I should be delighted."

"Then perhaps I had better get you something to eat."

A lepidopterist is never quite at peace in the natural world

He is constantly scouring his surroundings, searching for that flash of movement and color that might lead to a fresh discovery. He knows that such an event is both a chance happening, a happy coincidence, as well as something mapped out and intricately intended. A particular south-east-facing slope, for example, might catch a moisture-laden breeze coming in from the sea, and there a shrub that favors sandy soil might be flourishing that shields a particular leguminous flowering plant from the afternoon sun. On this site, a species of antelope, combined with a seasonal fire pattern, might create a mosaic of open patches. Each of these conditions may be required in order for a specific butterfly species to establish itself and flourish. The slightest change in such an environment might lead an entire butterfly subspecies into extinction.

But the lepidopterist in foreign lands knows nothing about this. He is left to stumble through the unknown world, surrounded by an enormous puzzle, the pieces too subtle and numerous to be fitted together. He must rely on his own experience of the world, as well as his instincts, to find a specimen of interest—and he must also rely on such local experts as Mr. Roland Trimen, whom Charles meets directly after breakfast, standing at the entrance to Lydia's cottage, armed with a leather satchel and a butterfly net. Trimen is a dark-bearded man of about Charles's height, with a pleasant, interested face that reminds Charles of his own father when he was still agile and middle-aged.

"I hear you have an interest in butterflies," Trimen says, stepping inside at Lydia's invitation.

"Indeed, I do."

"You found anything of interest?"

"We only landed last night, but I did encounter some interesting *Lycaena* on the trip. I believe they might have flown across from Cape Verde. Hundreds of them. They appeared to have been drawn to the white foam churned up by the propellers."

"Interesting," says Trimen. "Did you manage to catch anything?"

"I have some here," says Charles, taking out and opening the pocket box containing his three specimens.

"Ah yes," says Trimen. "*Azanus albus*, I believe. First identified by Stoll in the early 1780s. I first saw these in some numbers swarming around some thorn trees in Griqualand. Like many species, they were attracted to the puddles of urine left by our horses. Perhaps these ones were drawn to the waste outlet at the ship's heads?"

"I suppose it is possible," says Charles, impressed.

"Today I am on the lookout for the *Zeritis protumnus*. There are some good examples up in these hills—and what appear to be some interesting variants that I should like to investigate." He slings his satchel across his shoulder and sends a wink across to Lydia. "Are you prepared for a quick gander?"

"Absolutely."

As soon as they have left the cottage, circumventing Miss Grace's neat apiary and vegetable patch, Trimen launches into a dissertation on the fauna and flora of the area, assuring Charles that there are more plant species to be found on a single slope of this mountain than there are in the whole of England.

Trimen points out a languorous *Acraea horta*, hovering near its host plant, the Cape peach, as well as the spectacular *Zeritis thysbe*, named by Trimen himself some years previously, which is a small orange butterfly with opalescent blue bases to the wings that light up in all the colors of the rainbow when the sunlight plays upon them. Charles also catches a good example of the *Danais chrysippus*, also recently renamed by Trimen, which is, according to Charles's companion, the first butterfly ever to be represented in a work of art—on a fresco of Nebamun's tomb.

"To find our *protumnus*," Trimen says, "we shall have to climb all the way to the summit. Are you out of breath?"

"Not at all," pants Charles.

Charles has already learned from Lydia Grace that Trimen first came to the country on account of his weak lungs, yet there is little evidence of this as Trimen leaps across mountain streams and plunges further into the fynbos, which is not unlike the heather of the Scottish Highlands. The fynbos comes in all shapes and colors and is punctuated by a thousand different flowering plants, as well as silver trees and protea shrubs. Trimen points out a vivid blue butterfly circling some prominent rocks, which he calls the *Lycaena asteris*, as well as the famous *Meneris tulbaghia*, which has nut-brown wings and blue eyespots and skips away as soon as it registers their movement.

Far below them, the Atlantic Ocean stretches out like a great sheet of metal. Two military vessels are lying at anchor outside the harbor of Simonstown, but otherwise there are no other ships at sea. As they ascend along the mountain path, thin cloud swirls around them and gradually consumes them, so that only occasionally do they catch sight of a glint of ocean or a line of shore. Everything around them is a shade of olive-gray and lilac-gray and it feels more like the close of day than the height of morning. Mottled rock formations, splashed with vivid orange and green lichen, rise up all around them like ancient burial mounds, and an iridescent honey-eater—officially called a "sunbird"—twitters for a moment around Charles's head before ascending into cloud.

Now that Charles has arrived here, on African soil, the prospect of the impending war closes in on him. He remembers Grace's question: are you afraid of being named a coward? Charles's own father, Brigadier General Arthur Hawthorne, had died in the Second Ashanti

War when Charles was a boy of about nine. Charles's father was always represented in their family tales as an honorable man who had died "trying to rescue the Natives from one another, if not themselves." A large watercolor of his father, wearing his red serge coat ornamented with regimental badges, hung prominently above the fireplace, overseeing every meal Charles ever ate as a child—at least, those he ate when he was not at boarding school.

As a boy, Charles had inherited two things from his father. A love of lepidoptery and an unquestioning allegiance to the British Empire, which was best expressed through serving abroad in the military. After completing a degree in the Sciences in Edinburgh, Charles had surprised his mother by putting in an application to join the Duke of Edinburgh's Regiment in Templemore, Ireland. He had been promoted to the position of adjutant when the first disturbances broke out in Zululand. His mother was surprised by his decision to join the army because it was always assumed that Charles would not be suited to following in his father's exemplaryfootsteps. He was too solitary and delicate. He had suffered too frequently from a weak chest as a child. As for Charles, by then he had lost his childhood faith in the British Empire. His primary reason for joining the army—even if he never came anywhere near to admitting this to himself—was because he hoped to meet other men like himself, "complicated" men like William Grace, who was currently sleeping off his hangover in Charles's bed.

PART TWO

THE GHOST OF SAM WEBSTER

Sam

Sam is sitting in the enclosed glass veranda of her family's house

She is watching her mountain and waiting for the first bat to appear. Her feet are pressed at odd angles against the metal railing, bare and splayed, lucent in the amber-colored light. Her hair is gilded around the edges with gold. She is wearing a faded blue dress and swaying back and forth on a wicker chair, her long arms along the armrests—leisurely, but not quite at ease.

She never tires of watching her mountain. In the fading light of dusk, it resembles the jawbone of a cow. When she was younger, she imagined that her mountain was a headstone above an enormous grave. In certain lights, she could make out the beginning of her name across the stone. Later, wherever she was in the outside world, all she had to do was close her eyes in order to find the mountain's shape inside her. The mountain had become part of her body. It provided her with a touchstone in the form of a monument.

When Sam first started to draw the things of the world, the object she liked to draw most was her mountain. The whitewashed cairns arranged around its feet were the abandoned hats of mountain elves. She used the same blue for the sky that she used for her brother's eyes. She used the same green for the grass that she used for apples and mambas. But the mountain itself was always as dark as thunder. It stood high above their house, brooding and grumbling, looking for the best place to strike.

The name of the mountain is iSandlwana. It means "the second stomach of the cow" in isiZulu. She learned in Biology that the second stomach of the cow, like the first stomach, is used to carry unchewed food. This food has to be regurgitated and masticated before it is ready to go to the third and fourth stomachs for digestion. When she first learned the true meaning of its name, it gave the mountain a new reality. It was no longer a solid thing, a headstone made only of rock, but something with a rich and mysterious interior life. It became a great, shaggy cathedral, overgrown with grass and bush, but without any light inside it. Later, she learned its older Zulu name, "Buyavangama," which meant a kind of mumbling. She was told by Brian, one of the lodge's guides who had grown up in the area, that this name was given because the mountain gave off echoes whenever people passed close to it. The people believed the mountain was a sacred place. A portal into another world from which the ancestors talked back at them.

Sam is not alone on the glass balcony. Her father is sitting there too, drinking his whisky and shuffling through some printed sheets of paper. Her father hates to read anything off a screen. When he writes, which is rare these days, he only ever uses a fountain pen. Her father is angled toward the mountain, his crystal tumbler filled to the brim with ice and golden light. Her father slugs down at least half a bottle of Monkey Shoulder every evening between five and six o'clock. Yet he never gets drunk. At his feet lies Jane, who is ragged like an old rug and as narrow as an anteater. Her tongue is hanging out, almost translucent in the light—a thing too long for swallowing.

Usually, Sam avoids her father at this hour. His sentimentality can be more unsettling than his temper, which is rare and terrible to witness. Her father is not so different from her mountain. Solid and familiar enough when viewed from a distance. Full of dangerous rumblings when approached too closely.

"Sam, I need your help," her father says.

"Okay—"

"I have to choose an intern. Which one of these fellows would you pick?"

He hands across the sheaf of papers and Sam pages through the biographies, the photographs, the printed letters. Every year, her father takes on at least one posh young man from England who is hoping to spend his gap year in South Africa. Bruce finds that the guests like to have such a man around. It helps them to imagine the kind of young officer who might have fought and died in this place a hundred and fifty years ago.

"I also need someone who can write," her father says.

The subtext is that the British intern also needs to be good-looking, since everything at Webster Lodge has to be aesthetically pleasing. With the obvious exception of her mother, who looks like a retired carthorse. And her father, who is balding and red-faced and always a bit out of breath.

"Why write?"

"I'd like to dictate my memoirs. I need someone who can turn my random musings into elegant prose."

By now, the mountain has grown as dark as a funeral and the

first bats have been released amongst the stars. A nightjar can be heard, asking the "good Lord to deliver us." At the edge of the river, a campfire flares as more wood is added to its flames. Soon the sky will be full of stars. A dense white rainbow across the sky. Sam read somewhere that the San believed that the stars in the sky were the campfires of the departed. The night sky was an endless grave. On such nights as this, when the sky is clear and there is no wind, the guests are invited for sundowners on a wooden deck at the river's edge. Here they are told stories about the heroic men who fought and died here. These stories are as familiar to Sam as *Hansel and Gretel*, *Cinderella* and *Rumpelstiltskin*. They too contain abandoned children, witches and ancestors who come down to intervene in the lives of the living—and the making of promises that are impossible to keep.

"This one here," Sam says with some irony.

She holds out a sheet of paper with a picture of a young man who is as handsome as any young prince from any picture book.

"This one here is perfect."

Sam has an official boyfriend called Tom

"Shouldn't all official boyfriends be called Tom?" she once asked her best friend, Jess. Tom is a round, reliable name, the color of a tomato. It is the very opposite of the name Bruce, which is a mountain-brown name you soon stub your toe on.

Her boyfriend Tom has a sheen that runs all the way through him. From his glossy dark eyes and raven-colored hair to the daily shine of his polished shoes. Tom always expects his optimism to be reflected back at him from everyone he meets. Sam loves him with the same impatient tenderness with which she loves her horse. As soon as she thinks she has settled on her idea of him, and is beginning to look for ways to extricate herself from their relationship, he surprises her with a handful of porcupine quills. Or the scarlet feather of a turaco's wing. Or a bracelet woven, in the Zulu fashion, out of the long savannah grass.

Sam likes to go riding with Tom in the hills around the lodge. He is not as good a rider as she is, but then who is? Tom rides like someone trying to angle a large thread through a large needle. The reins and stirrups are always too long for him and he is always one pace behind his horse. But in the end he manages to keep up. She remembers the first time she took him across the river and up to her mountain. He was riding Sam's brother's horse—a fluffy ex-school pony called Pedlar, with the myopic gaze of a wildebeest—and she was riding Meg, her new horse, who is part-Arab but also a phantom horse, silvery and solemn, like a unicorn. Sam hadn't liked the name Meg at first. It was a peckish, russet, meddlesome name. But after she had ridden Meg for a few days, she realized that the horse's name was like her own name. Samantha. A name full of doom, speculation and fairy dust.

Tom seemed unnerved to be riding through such an enormous graveyard. The whitewashed cairns struck him as gruesome and unnecessary. They marked the place where something very bad had happened and then they said nothing more about it. This was what most people experienced when they first came here. The sense of both violence and silence. Of something violent having been silenced. This was why the place needed someone like her father, who could stand on any anthill or rock and wave his knobkerrie in the air until the scattered cairns became sites of heroic resistance, of fights to the death, of opportunities for noble phrases to be spoken. With his magic stick, her father could mobilize whole armies, slow down flying spears and bullets, and find the individual faces amongst the piles of nameless dead.

But Sam had simply cantered ahead, leaving Tom to absorb the weirdness of the place in which she grew up. She was not about to tell him that she belonged to this place in a way that she had never expected any boy to understand—and that if he ever wanted to call her his own, as crazy as that would sound, he would have to pass through this valley of death in order to reach her. She often felt as she rode through here that she was little more than one of the ghosts roaming about. She used to see them at night when she was a child. They would leave their dry cocoons on the mountain and gather around her bed like wingless moths. They smelled of rotting wood, disintegrating bandages and formaldehyde. There was no point in turning on the light. She had tried that the first time she saw them, gathered all around her. They had vanished immediately. But she had known they were still standing there. They had simply become invisible. Like a drawing made with a magic pen that can only be seen in the dark.

That first time, she and Tom rode to a place at the paws of the lion-mountain from which there was a good view of the battlefield. Her father often brought guests to this spot to give them what he called "a clearer perspective." He told her once that he would like his ashes to be sprinkled in this place, with this view. This was just like her father. To want to spend the rest of eternity with these phantoms.

"This place is pretty creepy," Tom said.

"Tell me about it," said Sam.

"But I like it."

"You do?"

They had dismounted and he was sitting next to her. She could feel his hotness through his shirt. She could feel the strangeness of her mountain passing through him. A dark wind coming off a hidden fire. She looked down at his hands, which were reddish from the reins and wholly unfamiliar, and she was about to touch the nearest hand, with its smell of boy and leather and horse, when he turned and they kissed.

By the time they had re-crossed the river and returned to the lodge, Tom was her official boyfriend. All they did that afternoon was kiss, and afterwards they did not speak about it. But Tom had passed an important test. He had ridden through the wasteland of her childhood and come out still wanting her.

Caroline

Caroline has been swatting the same fly for a hundred years

Always, it comes back at her, and back at her, with the same singularity. If it was there when she was a girl, she had never noticed it. But these days the fly is at the very center of her life. They are engaged in a battle that Caroline knows she will never win. She knows from living inside a battlefield that the flies always win. They arrive with their picnic bundle of eggs and feed them into the dead before the blood inside them has even dried.

Perhaps this is her fate. To spend her days alone in this beautiful glass house above the hills with only flies for company. Her husband left years ago, even though he turns up at the end of each day, leaving his boots at the door and greeting her like some half-remembered guest.

She has just swatted the latest fly when Moses
calls up from Reception

The fly has left a smear across a new cookbook—across Nigella Lawson's cheek. Moses tells her that the young man from England has arrived and she remembers only now that before Bruce left for

Johannesburg he asked her to welcome the new intern and give him dinner. As usual, she had only been half listening.

"Could you give him one of the drummer-boy rooms?" she asks.

"Yebo, Ma."

"And then could you drive him up to the house?"

She has some leek and potato soup that she could defrost and she decides that she could do with the distraction. She hates the house at night without Matthew inside it. Her son only recently started at his new school, as a weekly boarder—which was also Bruce's old school, as it happened. As for Sam, these days she and Caroline got on far better when Sam was out of sight.

Jane follows her as she moves out to the balcony, her claws clicking on the polished cement. Caroline doesn't look toward the mountain. In general, she tries not to notice it. She has never liked the mountain—the way it dominates the landscape like a fortress protecting nothing but rock. Soon she can see the lights of the golf cart threading up the long track toward the house. A little duiker is surprised by the headlamps at a turning, looking as pale as the ghost of a duiker before it bolts back into a bush.

Back inside, she has time to light the candles. Abstract oil paintings the colors of apricot and salmon-pink and lime-green quiver between the bookshelves and Bruce's collection of African artefacts. Sometimes, she has to remind herself that this is her home. These are her choices. There was some idea about herself that was enduring still when she chose these paintings, these artefacts. It was a world in which such things mattered. When it mattered how much mauve there was in a particular shade of blue. Or how one image was placed against another. As if a conversation could be initiated. And connection was possible.

She moves through to the kitchen to greet the new intern. She sees that he is about as beautiful as it is possible for a young man to be. Although perhaps too squared off at the corners for her liking.

"Hello," she says. "You must be Tom."

"Tim. Timothy Greene."

"Sorry, yes—Tom is the name of—someone else."

A look of confusion settles into Tim Greene's face. She wonders if this is his natural expression or something that is only passing through him. He runs a hand through his golden hair and flicks rainwater onto her Nguni mat. Then he offers her his large, wet hand. They hold onto each other for a moment, like two doctors trying to find out which one of them has the fever. Caroline is the first to let go.

"How was your trip?" she asks.

"Fine, thanks."

He turns away from her then and unzips his dark-blue anorak. The garment still has the "special offer" tag inside the collar. He holds the anorak for a moment before dropping it, with some deliberation, onto the new leather armchair. When Jane approaches him, he rests a hand on her head, like someone giving benediction. The wolfhound sways her ropey tail.

"Where is everyone?" he asks.

Under his easy English air, he has a predatory, lupine watchfulness that Caroline likes. All the previous interns had been fresh-faced, earnest boys straight out of some English public school. This one is very much a man. A young sailor who has already managed to circumnavigate the globe.

"I'm afraid that Bruce is still in Johannesburg. He'll be back in a day or two."

"Okay."

He waits for her to say more.

"We also have two children, Sam and Matthew. They're at school. They'll only be home on Saturday."

"And how old are they?"

"Matthew is fourteen and Sam just turned seventeen."

"Two boys?"

"Sam is—very much a girl."

He nods—amused from some private place he clearly has no intention of sharing. He has a large, mobile mouth and violet-blue eyes that his smile doesn't access, as if his thoughts are somewhere below the scene, running along the foundations of her life, her world, looking for some faultline of which she is unaware.

"Are you hungry?" she asks.

"Always."

Bruce

Bruce is an autumn man

He likes to have the long months of winter well within his sights. He knows that winter is where we're all headed and that it can come at any moment. His father grew up in Stoke-on-Trent after the war and he taught his son that the man who survives is the man who garners supplies for the days of austerity. Perhaps this is why Bruce has always been drawn to spiders. Those self-sufficient planners for the future who produce all the weaponry they will ever need from inside themselves. His Zulu nickname is "Isicabu," an allusion to the "isicabucabu." In the eyes of the locals, he is both an incidental creature and a thing with predatory intent.

But spiders are also spinners of yarn that disorientate their victims with a will-o'-the-wisp. A gossamer of light. Hasn't all of his success come from this precise talent? Of course, he inherited some land from his father. A rocky hill in the middle of a graveyard fit only to graze a few tick-ridden cattle. But Bruce Webster, the web-spinner, was the one to come up with the design that could knit each of these rocks together. Without this grand web of words, there would be no reason to stay at Webster Lodge. There were several other lodges in the area, some far better situated than Bruce's, yet none of them was nearly as successful.

But today Bruce is surrounded
by the overwhelming evidence of spring

The season arrived like an itch coming from a place he could no longer reach. It made him wonder how many springs he might have left in him. Was this the last one? Or would he have another one, another two? Concealed safely inside his fawn-colored Land Cruiser, with its recently replaced leather upholstery and reconditioned engine, he watches the blossom floating toward him from a nearby crab-apple tree. He looks through the windscreen—and at the pawmarks of Sam's Siamese cat, which are printed in dust across the glass. Ahead of him stands the school chapel where, on a morning not unlike this one, he and Caroline were unhappily married. Already, there are schoolgirls pouring through the archway and into the parking lot, chattering like starlings. Bruce has never felt more desolate.

A year ago, he was diagnosed with prostate cancer. He was told that the cancer was not advanced and that it could be dealt with now or in a year's time. He decided to do nothing more about it. Yesterday, he was told that his PS-marker had increased significantly and he was advised to consider immediate treatment. In the meantime, he has been given some strong prescription painkillers. He has been told they might make him sleepy and he has also been told that under no circumstances is he to mix them with alcohol. He decided to store the painkillers for a rainier day and chose the alcohol instead.

Caroline knows nothing about any of this and probably thinks he has another woman in Johannesburg. And, in a way, the cancer does feel like a forbidden relationship. A feeling of toxicity has filtered into every aspect of his life, blighting every opportunity for happiness before it can get established. Bruce has been notorious for his affairs, but the truth is that they have been fewer and further between than anyone might have imagined. Perhaps the only woman he has ever really loved is his daughter. Yes—and maybe his mother when he was a boy and hadn't yet learned how to look at her directly.

"Planet Dad!"

He turns to see Sam's laughing face at the car window.

"I've been calling you for like—the last half hour! Have you finally gone deaf?"

Their first encounter on the Saturday morning pick-up always makes Bruce's heart leap. For a moment, he is once again the man whose daughter liked to climb into his arms as you might climb into a tree. At her side stands her friend Jess, who is paler than Sam in every way, but still bright and pretty. A moon alongside Sam's sun.

"Hello, Sam. Hello, Jess."

The girls throw their bags into the boot alongside a sack of birdseed and climb onto the back seat. Since she was a small girl, Sam has always sat in the back when she is with a friend. The birdseed gives the car the smell of haylofts. Of farms experienced during childhood. Bruce kissed a girl in a hayloft once. Later, she became a doctor. Or was it a vet? He has always been far too charged with sex. Even into middle age, he was like a boy still trying to experience the glory of sex for the first time. Until a year ago, he had wanted to experience every variety of woman the world might have to offer before he was dead.

He had fallen in love with far more women than he had ever managed to make love to. Even during his school days, women struck him as another world, as another way of being in the world. He admired everything about them. Their verbiage and their laughter, but most of all their strength. Their instinct for the truth and their ability to name it. The truth was something that had always eluded him. He only knew what it was when it was already too late to do anything about it. He had tried to find it in women, in loving women. He knew that it was in their bodies, somehow. Women were more embodied than men, in his opinion. From their bodies, they had made all the people who had ever lived in the world. They knew that the body was the center of everything. That a disembodied life was not a life worth living. It was not a life that was living. If he could get closer to women's bodies—the mystery of them, the smell of them, the fluidity of them, the elastic endurance of them—then he would get closer to the mystery of life.

"Dad—is that okay?" Sam is asking.

"Is what okay?"

"Jess. Is it okay if she spends the weekend?"

"As long as her parents know."

The girls laugh. They are both wearing their straw boaters—Sam's perched at the back of her head in a way that manages to be both engaging and ironic.

"Gee, Dad, do you really think we'd abduct the girl without telling anyone?"

"Just checking."

Bruce reverses into the row of expensive cars headed toward the exit. A green haze of leaves is passing through the peach trees and a crop of crocuses lies across a bank of grass. The sunbirds in their early summer plumage are busy amongst the crimson blossoms of the coral trees. The sky is a saturated blue. Bruce is beginning to like the idea of the world without him. It will become clearer and cleaner. No longer clouded by his own interests.

The previous morning, when his doctor did the upside-down drawing of his private parts, the doctor showed him where he had "spots" on one side of his prostate and cancer developing on the other. The doctor suggested a recently developed course of treatment that involved shooting radioactive pellets into the affected area. He gave Bruce the number of an oncologist in Pretoria whom he was told to phone urgently. Bruce left the doctor's card behind at the airport inside the hired car and only realized his error when he was sitting uncomfortably on the plane. Since then, he has done nothing to get the number, let alone use it.

"We have a new intern," he says to Sam.

"Oh yeah?"

"The young man you chose from England."

"Who I chose?"

"You picked out his CV."

"Oh—him."

Bruce looks in the mirror to learn Sam's expression, but he finds nothing there. Perhaps she is thinking how risible her father is for wanting to write his memoirs. Not knowing that he'd gone off the idea before he'd even recruited the chap.

"What's he like?" Sam asks.

"Timothy? Haven't met him yet. I've been in Joburg and only got home late last night. But your mother has been entertaining him."

"I'm sure she has," Sam laughs.

"You must promise to be polite to him."

"Why wouldn't I be?"

"He mentioned in his CV that he could ride a horse. I thought maybe you could take him for a ride?"

The girls exchange an amused look.

"I was actually hoping to be with Tom today," Sam says, only now appearing to remember. "He has a tennis match in like half an hour. I was hoping we could watch it and then Tom could come home with us?"

"Your brother will be anxious to get home."

"Matty loves Tom. He won't mind watching."

"And I have a lot to get on with at the lodge."

"Oh come on, Dad. For once, why can't you let yourself off the hook?"

Bruce slows at an old railway crossing and a minibus taxi honks and veers past him, almost hitting an old man walking his goat, which he has tethered to his hand with a piece of orange bale string.

"We could hang out," Sam continues. "You could tell me about your Joburg trip."

"As long as you take Tim out after lunch."

"We will. We promise."

Bruce finds that he doesn't mind the smile of undisguised triumph his daughter sends across to her friend. She will remember such moments as this when he is gone and she will know that she was happy. And that, for a moment, even as the little black spiders were weaving their webs through his body, her father was too.

Sam

It isn't even time for lunch

Yet she arrives to find her mother sitting in the glass veranda with the new English boy, drinking large, pink goblets of gin and tonic. The new intern is the only thing that is completely visible inside that glass box. He is sitting in the sunlight as though it has been arranged there just for him. Sam can see at once that her mother is already completely transfixed by the boy. Her mother is one of those women who only comes alive when there are men about. As if other women, when left to their devices, are as dull as she is.

"Mr. Webster," the new intern says, standing, "it's such a pleasure to meet you."

"You too," her father says, taking his hand. "Sorry I never saw you last night."

"I thought you'd want to spend some time alone with your wife."

This comes out wrong—and in several directions at once—and Sam is the only one left smiling.

"This is my son Matthew and my daughter Sam," her father says. "These are her friends. Jessica and Tom."

"I'm Tim Greene," the intern says, as if he might actually be the next James Bond.

He steps forward to shake everyone's hand and it soon becomes apparent that there are too many hands to shake and that he should never have started the whole thing in the first place. Everyone laughs except for Sam—and Sam knows, with an animal instinct, that Tim Greene is truly only aware of her. At the moment he takes her hand, she feels a jolt running through her, a neural realignment that almost hurts.

"How was the match?" Caroline is asking Tom.

Tom is wearing his number ones and his cheeks are still flushed from the tennis match. He smells of his schoolboy deodorant and everything about him is neat and trim. Even placed alongside Tim Greene, Tom is the handsomest boy Sam has ever seen. And yet right now she no longer recognizes him. He is the boyfriend of someone else.

"It was okay thanks, Mrs. Webster."

"Tom won in three straight sets," Sam says, directing this statement, for some reason, toward Tim.

"You're always far too modest," Caroline says to Tom.

Meanwhile, Matty has slipped away and is helping himself to a handful of fresh figs. Sam's father is looking around with a detached smile of what appears to be regret. Where the yellow light gives everyone else a holiday look, an air of wealth and leisure, her father's face is mottled like a fish. Only now, with a creeping of familiar guilt, does Sam remember that she was supposed to talk to him about his Joburg trip. Instead, she spent the whole match sitting with Jess and some other boys at the other side of the court, eating wine gums and tanning her legs in the sun.

Tim Greene has agreed to ride her horse

He is the first to leave the stable yard and he is sitting up there on her horse as if he's just won a battle. Sam, who is following closely behind on her mother's large chestnut, regrets her show of generosity. She can see that Meg doesn't like the feel of her new rider either. A horse like Meg has a sense of decency, of decorum, that most humans lack—and already she suspects that her new rider is not to be trusted.

Sam read somewhere that a horse's brain, like the human brain, is divided into two hemispheres, but that the two parts of a horse's brain are barely connected, so that a horse has two brains, working almost independently. This is why you have to help a horse to integrate the two worlds it experiences. Just because it sees a suspicious bush approaching on the left does not mean that it will be prepared to see it appear again on the right. Sam can feel that Meg is yet to fit her new rider into a coherent whole—or decide whether he will be treating her as an obstacle or a horse.

They take the path along the back of the library and up into the densely wooded hills. The purple-crested turacos can be heard calling from deep within the bush. They are entering the wildest, highest part of the lodge, the area that the tourists seldom visit. It is here that a twelve-foot python was seen last summer and it is here where most of the wild animals live. Soon Sam falls behind with Tom, who is riding Matty's horse with his usual misdirected earnestness, not thinking ill of anything. Where everything around them seems to carry two brains, Tom steadily retains his only one.

"Hey," she says.

"Hey," he replies.

Tim breaks into a slow canter ahead of them and they follow him up the path that leads to the boundary fence of the lodge, Jess doing her best to keep up with him. If Sam is honest, Jess has been annoying her all afternoon. The way she made sure she sat right next to Tim at lunch and pretended to listen to everything he had to say. When actually Jess never listens to anything. Jess also knew that Sam wouldn't approve of this, but she did it anyway. It was her revenge over Tom. Because Jess had liked Tom first.

They meet the contour path along the ridge and slow to a steady trot. The ten-foot electric fence to the left of them ticks thickly. There is a loose bundle of porcupine quills where the grass has been cropped. There is also a headless snake that Sam identifies as a rinkhals. They are riding in the direction of the long grass plain and the waterfall—and soon they leave the fence behind as it veers back through the bush. To their right, the hills of Zululand unfold in a ripple of earth and thornbush and rock. The clouds coming in from the Drakensberg are almost too bright to look at. Sam knows from experience that it will rain hard tonight.

When the path reaches the grassy plateau that runs along the summit of the hill, they come upon a herd of wildebeest, which gallop alongside the horses for a while, their heads down, a rising line of orange dust in their wake. The horses have merged for a moment with a collective flow that stretches back to the beginning of remembered time—even though these wildebeest are her father's property and about as tame as cattle.

There's also a troop of baboons squatting on the rocks at the far end of the plain. It takes them longer to react to the shape of a horse than they would to the shape of a man—or a girl. The dominant male sits on the highest rock, dipping his head as the riders approach. The females pull their young deeper into the shadows cast by their bodies in the afternoon sun. The baboon troop is one of the few things at the lodge that refuses to bend itself to her father's will. Sam has always felt a strange kinship with them as a result.

Soon she is riding alongside Tim Greene. It's apparent that he and Meg have fallen into a more natural rhythm by now, Tim leaving the horse to find her footing between the tufts of grass, anthills, columns of aloes and perpetual rocks. Tim turns to her and laughs with his crazy blue eyes—and she decides that maybe he can't be all bad after all.

They hear the waterfall before they see it. It is surrounded by tall reeds and drops from a dark-blue, kidney-shaped pool at the far end of the plain into an indigenous forest where three-hundred-year-old yellowwoods grow, venerable and still.

When Sam was about ten, she and her friend Simon—Moses's son—came across two male black mambas fighting for territory at the edge of this pool, no more than ten meters away from where their horses had stopped. The two snakes were oblivious at first to their presence. They were looping and dipping and striking at each other, appearing to float in the air, their tails forever restless and rippling. They seemed like one snake doing battle with itself, like two sides to the same thought. Simon told her with his eyes to go back along the track on which they had come. Sam nodded and was about to turn her horse away when she realized that the snakes had disappeared. There was a wind blowing and the reeds were hissing all around them. As if the landscape itself was speaking. Speaking for those two snakes. The horses were stamping and snorting, a tremor running through them. They had seen the snakes—with both sides of their brains—and the truth of the snakes, the knowledge of them, had taken over their bodies. Sam's horse swung around and bolted—and she left the horse to flee, knowing that she was powerless to stop it anyway.

It would be years before Sam would agree to visit the waterfall again. In that time, she encountered many other snakes at the lodge—cobras, adders, boomslangs, pythons and even a few smaller black mambas. But there was something about those two male mambas, and the idea of a single snake doing battle with itself, that always haunted her.

"Careful," she says to the others, "there's a sheer drop just ahead of us."

Tim, however, takes her horse right to the edge of the precipice.

"Can't we get down?" he asks, standing in his stirrups and peering.

"There's a path around the side," Sam says. "Follow me."

The pool at the bottom of the waterfall is smoky-green in the afternoon light. The pebbles on the bottom of the pool are white and round as the eggs of ducks. Sam leads them down the steep zig-zagging path and into the hush of the forest. Then she slips off her horse, tethers her to a tree stump and immediately starts to undress.

Soon everyone is undressed and standing around the glowing water. The reflected light illuminates their bodies, like wood fairies out of a children's book. Sam and Jess are wearing their dark-green swimming costumes from school and Tom is in his pale-blue boxer shorts, which are patterned with lemons and limes. Sam is careful not to look across at Tim—not even once.

"Watch out for snakes," she laughs.

Simon told her once about a pool in the Transkei where he was swimming with some friends when they came face to face with a black mamba. The snake was swimming in the same pool with them and making no attempt to attack or escape. They had carefully climbed out of the pool and run away, the snake still circling the pool like some vile thought breeding off its own malevolence.

"As in—water snakes?" asks Tim.

"As in swimming snakes," says Sam, still not looking directly back at him.

She steps onto her usual rock and dives toward the deepest part of the pool. At this time in the afternoon, half of the pool lies in shadow and half of it lies in light. When she emerges, she flicks her hair and glances back at them and laughs. The cold is painful and pleasant at the same time. Like when she whacked her ankle bone against Tom's stirrup earlier on the ride.

"Is it cold?" Tom shouts.

Instead of answering, she ducks back underwater and swims hard to where the waterfall lands in the pool. The bubbles are dense around her, making it impossible to see anything. She has to feel her way up along the rocks before resurfacing behind the wall of water. Here there is a green rock where you can sit quite comfortably, but you have to move carefully. Matty once slipped and cut his thigh so badly that they had to walk their horses back home in the dark.

A wet head emerges next to her, sleek as an otter's—and, before she can identify who it is, she is being kissed, a kiss that lasts for the longest minute in her life. When she feels the face of the boy to find out who it is, she is relieved and a bit disappointed to find the face of Tom.

Caroline

Matthew is alone in his room

He is lying with his back to the door, the silver bomber revolving slowly above his bed, looking for a place to settle. His hair is thick and wheat-colored. A crop that comes from no member of Bruce's family. The hair is entirely from Caroline. Yet she wonders where he has gone. Her long-limbed boy who was, until recently, so full of immediately available mischief. He still has his oversized feet, which he has been falling over since he was a toddler. He has always been like Caroline in this too. She also grew up in a body that was forever intent on misrepresenting her. Looking down at him, she knows from the way that he is curled around Bluebell, Sam's Siamese cat, that he has been crying and that he is crying still. All through lunch, she now realizes, he barely lifted his eyes from his plate.

"You didn't go to the waterfall," she says.

"Tom is riding Pedlar."

"You could have taken Spare Pony."

"I wasn't asked."

Caroline feels a rush of impatience. It is triggered more by a helpless grief than by any form of anger. The Matthew her son used to be was never so hungry, in some insistent way, for disappointment.

"Why don't the two of us do something else?"

"Like what?"

There's a sunbeam at the foot of Matthew's bed, filled with motes, sending a shadow off the boy's foot that renders it into a sundial. Caroline steps into this light and the motes flurry around them like ants disturbed from their nest. The cat, which is barely more than a kitten, stretches her four chocolate-colored limbs and yawns ecstatically.

"We could take Jane for a walk."

It was Matthew who had named the wolfhound. The name still makes her smile.

"It's okay, thanks."

Matthew has been at his new school for almost year, but still it feels wrong and difficult. Caroline recently spoke to Matthew's housemaster about her son's unhappiness, but the housemaster, a traditional and impatient man, proved to be of little help. "The boy needs to find his feet," the housemaster said, as if Matthew's oversized feet could simply be exchanged for someone else's.

"Have you had a good week at school?" she asks.

"Not too bad, thanks."

By which he means about as bad as all the weeks that have come before.

"Have you made any new friends?"

"Not really."

"I thought you liked the Gatsheni boy?"

"I do like him."

By which he means the Gatsheni boy does not like him back. Or not sufficiently.

"You know Dad says he comes from royal lineage?"

"Sorry?"

"Gatsheni is an important Zulu family. I mean, historically."

"I didn't know that."

There is a flat disappointment in the boy's voice that he generally reserves, these days, for his father. Caroline knows her son has always wished for another kind of father. A father whose world contained a more prominent, more interesting, more loveable version of his son. The truth is that the only person Bruce has ever loved properly is Sam. Matthew has always been Caroline's boy—and, if she is honest, she is partly responsible for this. She never shared Matthew with Bruce the way she shared Sam. It was Caroline who decided Bruce was not good enough for Matthew. Long before Matthew felt that he was not good enough for Bruce.

"How about a driving lesson?"

At this, the boy wipes his face and sits up.

"Do you think we could take Dad's car?"

"I don't see why not."

Matthew starts the engine at his first attempt

Bruce's fawn-colored Land Cruiser is too large for him in every sense. His hands are wrapped around the steering wheel as if he is steering an old ship and the bonnet stretches ahead of them like a coffin—large enough to contain the whole family.

"Do you want me to release the handbrake?" she asks.

"Thanks."

This is the third time Caroline has given Matthew a driving lesson in Bruce's car. His first lessons had been in Caroline's old silver Audi. On none of these three occasions, however, has Caroline asked Bruce if she could use his car. The former Bruce did not like his things to be tampered with. The mess in his study down at Reception was his mess, not anyone else's. The selection of books that were to be displayed in the library were his choice, no one else's. He had even flown into a rage when Caroline had edited, without consulting him, a passage he had written for the lodge's website—this was because he never knew where to place a comma and so generally left them out. Yet none of the driving lessons had provoked his usual response. This current Bruce had only nodded and smiled, as if the car, until recently his pride and joy, had already been given away to someone else. Caroline suspects this is all because of his new woman in Johannesburg. The woman he is always so sad to come away from. Well, Bruce was welcome to his secrets. These days Caroline has more than enough secrets of her own.

Matthew's flaxen head is alert and angled forward as the car creaks into motion. This suddenly feels dangerous and precarious—and she knows that what she is doing is wrong, and that it would make her husband angry, and that she is risking the life of her son—but she decides she can always pull the handbrake or, if necessary, take over the steering. At the sight of the driveway dropping down ahead of them, Matthew presses too hard on the brake pedal and the car lets out a strangled sound and stops.

"It's okay," Caroline says, "just start again—and let the weight of the car carry you down the hill."

Looking at the sky beyond Matthew's head, she can see that another storm is approaching—and the children are still not back from the waterfall. How like strangers to one another they have all become. Of course, Sam moved across to the enemy's camp years ago. But even Matthew, whose heartbeat is usually so companionably skipping alongside her own—even Matthew is like some other boy, sitting there so delightedly in his father's oversized car. Yet Caroline knows that if anyone has become unrecongnizable it is her. Even if the rest of the family hasn't yet noticed it.

"There's no need to accelerate," she says.

The boy—for boy he was—had arrived in the rain in his dark-blue anorak and eaten her soup and laughed at her jokes and lit the fire and opened another bottle of wine without even asking her—and then, without any preamble, they were rutting on her leather couch like two teenagers at a party, the zip of his anorak cutting into her face.

"Am I going too fast?"

And him fresh off the plane from England.

"Mom?"

"No, Matthew, you're doing just fine."

What kind of a man did that? Arrived in some foreign field and immediately planted his seed in the nearest woman—a woman old enough to be his mother? Caroline has never been conventionally attractive, even when she was younger. God knew—she was already half dead. Was it this that had drawn the boy to her in the first place? Not the life in her, but the death in her?

"Are you sure this isn't going too fast?"

"The brake is there whenever you need it."

Afterwards, the boy had buttoned his jeans and made some joke. He said he had a headache, suddenly. His brain was trying to split itself in two. Then he swallowed the rest of his wine, slipped into his anorak and went out into the rain—already knowing his way to his room in the dark as if he'd been living there for years.

"Careful of that bump."

It's unlikely that it will ever happen again. It's not advisable that it should. But the dreadful infraction thumps on inside her like another glowing heart. Even now, she can summon up every detail about him. The fluidity and confidence of his body. The gritty tangle of his hair. The slow rasp of his cheek. The salty bitterness of his long, fine tongue. It was his hunger that surprised her the most. His desire to sniff out every part of her and fill it with himself, himself, himself.

"How does it feel?" she asks Matthew.

"It feels okay, thanks."

Afterwards, he went all soft inside her arms, like a little cat.

"Are you still feeling scared?" she asks her son.

"No."

"Be honest," she laughs—the young woman she once was ringing falsely in her ears.

"Well—maybe just a bit."

PART THREE

THE WRITER

Daniel's mother died on his birthday

He was in the story room at the television studio when he received the call from Victoria, his mother's domestic worker. Victoria had been with their family since he was four months old. She had been there for the death of his sister and she had been there for his father's departure, but in all this time she had never before called Daniel on his phone.

At the center of the story room on a large wooden table was the chocolate-fudge cake Daniel had brought that morning for his fellow writers. He wasn't particularly fond of his fellow writers. The head writer was a woman called Zee, who dressed like Minnie Mouse—or was it Lolita?—and spent all her money on designer handbags. The producers loved her because she was an indefatigable source of cliché. Zee never had anything nice to say about anyone unless a compliment would cast her in a better light. In the eighteen months Daniel had been working there, he had tried hard to find something to like about her and recently he had started to admit defeat. When he told Zee that his mother was dead and that he would have to leave the meeting, she tried, in her defense, to arrange her face into an expression approaching concern.

"I'll get Anthony to edit your scripts this week," she said generously.

Daniel drove more deliberately than usual toward his mother's house. The plot where she lived was not far from the Kyalami Racetrack. His weekends as a boy were often accompanied by the angry swarming of motorbikes and cars. His mother had an electric fence around the property, but it had not worked for years, and often she would forget to lock the kitchen door at night. So Daniel had been waiting for a call like this. Victoria had not told him how his mother had died, but he assumed it was murder. Apart from having type-two diabetes, his mother was in relatively good health.

It was winter in Johannesburg and the aloes along the driveway were all in bloom. The peaches from the previous summer were stuck to the branches of the surviving peach trees. Desiccated black hearts. The ficus tree stood huge and immoveable at the top of the driveway and the drab, shallow bungalow lay, as ever, in its shadow. Victoria was waiting in the shade of the tree with her husband, Legion, who had married Victoria a few years ago and now worked as a groundsman. Legion had been given his name because his father had worked for the French Foreign Legion. An ambulance was visible under the tree, its back doors closed, and Daniel's mother's cream-colored Toyota Corolla was parked in its usual place next to it. When Daniel climbed out of his car, Victoria and Legion came forward as if he might need propping up. But Daniel did not need propping up.

"She is in the house," Legion said.

Legion was a minister at his church and he told Daniel that he had prayed for his mother when he and Victoria had found her.

"Thanks," Daniel said.

His mother was lying on the kitchen floor. One of the old dog blankets had been carefully placed over her so that her feet were sticking out the one end and her hair was sticking out the other. Her feet were too yellow and thin, almost like a child's feet, and her hair was the same winter brown it had been throughout her life. People always commented on his mother's hair. How, at sixty-five, she barely had a gray hair on her head.

There were two paramedics sitting at the avocado-green kitchen table. There were printed forms and a ballpoint pen waiting for Daniel. He had a sense that these people had gone through this procedure many times before. Sitting next to the dead and waiting for their lives to be signed away, their deaths recorded.

"What happened?" Daniel asked the nearest man, who was perhaps in his mid-fifties and seemed to have been chain-smoking for the whole of his adult life.

"It looks like a major cardiovascular event."

"Right."

"Your maid says she was diabetic."

"Yes."

"Late onset?"

"Yes."

"That's the most likely cause of death."

Daniel heard a sobbing sound and turned to see Victoria standing by the sink, her feet placed where her slippers had worn the linoleum down to the cement. Legion was at the door, his cloth hat in his hands. Legion and Victoria were both from Zimbabwe. Most of Legion's cattle had died in the previous year's drought.

"If you can please sign these papers," the younger paramedic said.

"Sure."

"Do you have a particular morgue you like to work with?" the older paramedic asked.

Daniel looked at him.

"I'll phone someone," the paramedic said.

When the paramedics were gone, Daniel stood in the garden under the dead willow tree. His mother's garden had been reduced to bald earth and a few stray acacia bushes when the drought restrictions were first introduced. What remained of the lawn had been eaten away, first by the ants and then by the termites.

Daniel stared at the khakibos growing in the pond and the rockery where he imagined the rinkhals still lived—even though it had not been seen for fifteen years. He could still recall the fluid, insinuating movement of the snake. It moved like something made of myth rather than flesh. It was his worst fear, his deepest terror, made manifest. He remembered how it paused and considered him before it drank, its large, black eyes observing him without expression, without judgment. They were creatures from two entirely distinct worlds. For a moment, all they did was watch each other, waiting to see which of them would be the first to attack. But when the pale, forked animal standing there made no move, the snake dipped its head and drank. Then it was gone, its after-image burned into Daniel like some internal lighting strike that would shift his world-view forever.

His mother's dog had died a few weeks previously, but its old white turds were still lying about in the dust. The vet had said it was probably rat poison and warned that it might have been intentional. Criminals sometimes killed off the family dog a day or two before an attack—or before a heart attack, Daniel now thought.

He went to see his mother the following morning

He wanted to look at her once more before she was gone from the world forever. The previous day, he had not wanted to look at her with everyone else watching him and assessing his level of care.

There was a wall of red dust moving through the pale-gray buildings of central Johannesburg. He had to close his eyes against the oncoming storm as he moved from his car to the yellow-brick building of the morgue. He had chosen this morgue because it was in sight of the university. His mother had found a job there as the secretary of the Fine Art Department so that Daniel could get a remission in fees.

One of the undertakers who had come to the house to collect the body led him down steep cement stairs and through a vacant, dank room. He left Daniel alone in another, brighter room that contained little more than the trolley on which his mother's body lay. Daniel had been uncertain about coming here, and a few times he had almost phoned to cancel the visit. Now that he was here, however, he wondered how he would ever be able to leave.

He took a plastic chair and sat at some distance from the body. He sat there like someone sitting in attendance at someone else's mourning. He looked first at the trolley, at the wheels of the trolley, which had been wheeling the dead for decades, and then he looked at the dark-blue blanket that covered her body, with its woven insignia of an ascending dove. He wondered when the blanket had last been washed. At the far end of the room, there was a dusty white coffin with gold handles. The windows were high and frosted and one of them was broken and boarded up. Then he heard the thunder outside, coming to test the immensity of the heavens, coming to measure the scale of the emptiness.

Only then did Daniel look at his mother's face. She was lying on a plastic sheet, her head without a pillow, her hair wet and recently combed by a hand that had only ever known her dead. Her hair was neater and flatter than it had been in life and it was still that famous winter brown. He knew that her body lay under the blanket, but he did not want to think about that. All he had access to, like a doorway back into the mystery of her, was her face. Yet the face was not her face. The undertaker had blushed her cheeks, but the color had not entered into the lines that time had written there. The bottom half of her face had collapsed back into itself, making the nose prouder, the cheekbones more prominent, the mouth more reticent. It was the face of someone with opinions he had never given his mother credit for during her life.

Daniel had to sit with her for a long time before she started to look like herself. He saw that the ears were still her ears, as was the forehead and the two tufts of her eyebrows. She was so deeply dead, so stubborn and solemn about it—and yes, he could recognize something of her characteristic resolution in that.

At first, it had been impossible to look at her, but now he could look at nothing else. It was years since he had touched her. It was years since she had been touched. He fingered her brown hair briefly and then he stood and walked away.

Breakfast is served inside a tinkling vacancy

He helps himself to coffee and honey and toast and chooses a table at the far end of the deck in the bright-green shade of a fever tree. In the crown of the tree, out of the reach of snakes, is a chattering crown of weaverbird nests. The little yellow birds sway in the branches like tufts of pollen. Daniel angles his chair toward the view of iSandlwana and away from the British couple who are still wearing their matching anoraks. There is no evidence of Moses, Tim Greene or the Websters. He eats his toast alone and without appetite. The scene in Sam's bedroom the previous night is sitting inside him like a bad conscience, festering. He watches a crested barbet nipping at a pawpaw skin that has been left on one of the tables. The company of this bird—and the single zebra blue butterfly that flies brokenly across his line of sight—are perhaps as close as he has ever come to feeling at home. Without these everyday constellations, he would very soon be lost.

The taste of the honey reminds him of an account written

by a war artist a few months after the battle of iSandlwana. The British army had retreated from Zululand after the battle since there had been no opportunity to bury the dead. The war artist was with the first British troops to return to the site—and there they found bodies that were severely mutilated and decayed. Some of the soldiers, however, were still recongnizable from the beards and moustaches on their leathery faces. Others could be identified from letters and old photographs still in their pockets. Anything of monetary or potential trade value had long ago been stolen. The war artist followed the trail of retreating bodies in the direction of the Buffalo River and Fugitives' Drift—and there, high above a ravine, he found a hive of bees inside the ribcage of a dead soldier. The artist stooped down to taste the honey, located just where the man's heart had been, and not one of the bees made any move to attack him.

"What the hell are you doing here?"

Daniel looks up to find an acquaintance of his, the Africa correspondent of a large English broadsheet, munching on a yellow apple. He is long-faced and sandy-haired and a famous drinker.

"David," Daniel says, "good to see you."

David had written a couple of fantasy novels that always had something to do with orcs in their titles. They had been published internationally but had not sold well. He and Daniel had spoken together at literary events and Daniel had once had dinner with him and his boyfriend at their house in Johannesburg.

"So what are you doing here?" David asks again.

"Oh," Daniel says, "researching a historical novel."

"I see."

"I suppose you're here for the Webster case?"

Daniel has already noticed a few people who appear to be journalists wandering around the lodge. The Websters have made no new public statements since appearing on television and so far they have refused to answer any questions from the press.

"Do you have any leads?" Daniel asks.

"Nothing yet. I'm investigating the land angle," David says. "Vengeance killing. That's the most likely explanation. Do you know the family at all?"

"Slightly," Daniel says.

"You couldn't get me in there, could you?"

Daniel recalls the expression on Caroline's face when he last saw her. "It's unlikely," he says.

"Well let's have lunch, or something," David says. "Maybe tomorrow? I could tell you about my new novel. *Orc Uprising*."

"That sounds wonderful," Daniel says with his best smile.

Daniel meets Tim Greene, as arranged, outside Reception at ten

Tim is wearing a red-and-white striped rugby jersey and he observes Daniel's approach with an ironic air. Standing at the minivan in the shade of the ficus tree is a pale-haired, pale-eyed family Daniel has not seen before. They are speaking quietly and complacently while the mother rubs sunblock onto the youngest boy's face and neck. Daniel sits where he sat before, at the back of the minivan, while Tim takes the front seat with Moses and the other guide, who is called Brian. Soon they are following the same journey as they did the day before, past the sliding gate to Rorke's Drift, across the cement bridge into Zululand, and stopping off at the museum and St. Vincent's Church before arriving at iSandlwana.

Daniel and Tim set off straight away across the battlefield—crossing over the "nek" in front of the mountain where the few survivors of the battle fled—only to be met by the four thousand soldiers from the Zulu army's right horn, who had barely engaged in any fighting and would later break off, against the explicit orders of their king, to enter enemy territory and attack the field hospital at Rorke's Drift.

All along the route into the next valley, Daniel and Tim encounter more stone cairns marking the bodies of the dead. Sometimes, these occur in long lines of stones, like the burial mounds at the summit of Spion Kop—which Daniel visited several years before in order to research another book. From this angle, as they face the stone lion, the mountain is tall and thin and top-heavy. A child's sandcastle. The rocks at its upper reaches are overhanging precariously in places and look as if at any moment they might collapse.

Earlier that morning, in the hours between breakfast and meeting Tim, Daniel had made good progress on his ancestor book. Charles was currently in Cape Town, surrounded by the fynbos and butterflies. As Daniel and Tim continue to walk, Daniel notes several swallowtails, grass yellows and commodores—and makes a mental note to put them into the war sections of his book.

"I saw Caroline earlier this morning," Tim says, sounding almost glum, almost sardonic.

"Oh yes?"

"Looking for you, as it happens. She thought you might have bolted."

Daniel says nothing to this.

"Apparently, you caused quite a stir last night. Either that, or Caroline did."

"Yes—"

"Anyway, she said she was feeling bad about the way she spoke to you and she wanted to apologize. I was surprised. Not by the verbal abuse. Caroline often gets abusive when she's drunk. I was just surprised by the fact that she even remembered the abuse the next day—and cared enough to come and apologize. She must actually like you."

"Well—"

"So what happened there?"

"I was looking for the bathroom and I walked into Sam's bedroom instead."

"I see. Matthew sleeps there now."

"Right."

"Have you met Matthew?"

"The last time I was here. But I'm sure he's very different now."

Tim gives off an obscure laugh. He's rather too pleased with his private knowledge of the Websters. There's something overtly proprietorial about it.

By now, they are descending the stone path in the direction of the Buffalo River. The river is still at least five kilometers off, however, and there is no sign of it from here. At the time of the battle, the grass was six to eight feet high and there were few trees, but the ground was littered with the same rocks that are here still. Daniel remembers reading accounts of horses and oxen falling and breaking their legs.

Soon they come across the precipitous dongas Daniel has also read about—steep cracks in the earth that appear almost out of nowhere and that sealed the fate of several other men and their animals. This area is followed by a further series of dongas—the passage so narrow in places that two men would have struggled to pass one another without touching. But Tim seems far away from their immediate surroundings—and disinclined to give the usual history tour.

"Where are you from, exactly?" Daniel asks.

"England. Surely you've realized that?"

"I mean—where in England. Where did you grow up?"

Tim tells Daniel that his parents own a pub in the countryside near the town of Amesbury. The River Avon runs along the bottom of their garden, where there are wooden tables and benches for the patrons and the usual ducks and swans. When Tim's father died of a heart attack, a wealthy uncle paid for him to go to Marlborough. There he was Captain of the First XV and the head of his house. All of this information is delivered with a certain subtle bitterness. Tim might have been describing the accomplishments of a twin brother who forever outshone him.

"Does your mother live there still?" Daniel asks.

"With my younger sister. Yeah. They don't exactly understand what I'm doing here."

"And do you understand what you're doing here?"

"I did," he says, "until a month ago."

They reach the foot of another mountain. The white cairns have faded away from the path—not, according to Tim, because the fleeing soldiers were no longer being killed, but because they were no longer being buried. When they reach the top of the hill, they are both breathing heavily and stop in the shade of a straight-arm thornbush to look back at the mountain and drink.

"Let me show you something," Tim says.

He leaves the path and heads off along an animal track through some tall and ancient aloes. They soon come across a clearing and an overhanging rock, which forms a shallow cave. From here, there is a good view of iSandlwana, which is no longer quite facing them—as well as a view of the Buffalo River curving toward them on the right.

"I came here once with Sam," Tim says. "With Sam and Matthew. We were on horses and we spent the night." He walks across to where some charred logs are huddled inside a circle of stones. "This was the fire I built. Weird, isn't it? That our fire should still be here—as if we visited only a few days ago."

"Were you very close with Sam?" Daniel asks.

"Sam? Everyone loves Sam."

"You're speaking about her in the present tense."

Tim wipes the sweat from his face—a gesture that makes it seem he might be crying. Daniel has the tact to keep his eyes averted.

"You can carry on loving people even after they're gone," Tim says, moving away and back to the path.

As Daniel remains standing there, he can once again feel the ghost of Sam Webster hovering around him, casting itself about, restless and blind, like a fishnet plunged inside the sea.

Daniel is woken by the thump of thunder

It echoes like great drums bouncing back and forth across the heavens. He sits up and waits for the rain to arrive—and he is beginning to think that it won't arrive and is sighing back into his pillows when the storm reaches him—with a force behind it so ancient and inevitable that it feels intended. This is not a place God has abandoned, he thinks. This is a place that has ignited his attention. And, by the sound of things, his disapproval.

All night, the rain hammers against the mountain. All night, Daniel lies awake in his stone house and feels the rain descending, spattering every available surface and running through every available crack. In the morning, he expects the mountain to be nothing but rock, emerging from the earth like a gravestone, with the lion of iSandlwana sullen and smoldering. But he can feel that the houses the Websters built will stand firm, like barnacles that have withstood a hundred years of thunderous seas. Only further down the valley will it be a different story. For those who built their dwellings out of tin sheets and mud, plastic bags and wattle sticks.

In the morning, the trees are dripping under a bright, blank sky

The storm has moved on. Sunbirds chitter in the wild dagga, nabbing midges in the golden haze. A chameleon, blotched green and gold, edges along the wooden railing of the walkway. Daniel leaves the wooden path and takes the gravel track instead, which is more direct. He passes through a tall crop of silvery-blue cabbage trees and startles a duiker at a turning. They stare at each other in mutual fright before the antelope leaps over a bush and disappears without a sound.

Today there is a white police van with a blue-and-yellow stripe along the side of it standing alone amongst the coffee-colored puddles outside the dining area. It's a Sunday morning, so Daniel is surprised to see this. The breakfast area is already busy with weekend guests, but he sees no evidence of the police. Nor is there any evidence of David and his journalist companions—who have, most probably, moved on to another story, a story with more immediate blood inside it.

Daniel smiles at the pale-eyed family with whom he drove to iSandlwana two days earlier and he notices that the British couple with the matching anoraks has been replaced by an older, trimmer German couple whose anoraks are made from the same cloth, but in different shades of blue.

Tim Greene is sitting at his usual table under the fever tree. Today, Tim has a girl with him—and Daniel is wondering where he might have seen her before when Tim stands and introduces her as Sam's schoolfriend, Jess. There's something steely and watchful running through Jess. Daniel imagines that were he to touch her hand he might get an electric shock.

"We've met before," the girl says.

"At your school, it must have been. How are you these days?"

She gives Daniel a sad look, perhaps denoting mourning for Sam.

"I'm sorry. I'm sure it's been a very bad time—for everyone."

"Yes."

Jess leans back in her chair and gazes across the valley, past the mountain and toward the fading blue hills beyond it. There's something self-dramatising about her grief, Daniel decides. Under the table, he notices that her thigh is rested against Tim's.

"You should go and visit Dr. Lopez," Jess says, turning back to Daniel.

"I should?"

"She spent like the whole of last year talking about your book. At every opportunity. I know she'd love to see you again."

There's a shadow of implication in this that Jess wants Daniel to register and feel flattered by. As he remembers it, however, Dr. Lopez is married and has a son.

"I was there the other day," he says. "At the school. Passing through."

"Oh yes?"

"I sat in on a chapel service. The priest talked about spirit animals."

"Did he? I never used to listen in chapel. It was always the same thing being said in a slightly different way. We were supposed to feel bad about ourselves. Bad about feeling more alive than the priest and the rest of them. You know what I mean?"

"I do," Daniel says, trying to sound diplomatic. "And what are you doing this year?"

"I'm going to Cape Town to study Law. I leave in a couple of weeks."

"That sounds interesting."

"To be honest, I can't wait. I need to get the hell away from this place."

Daniel nods in a way that is intended to be meaningless and finds a place at a neighboring table. He places his coffee next to some redwing starling excrement. Since his last visit, Daniel has found a change in the lodge that he suspects has much to do with Sam's disappearance. Usually, every moment of a guest's experience was overseen by some well-trained member of staff. A bit of redwing starling excrement would not have been permitted for more than a moment on any table—and by now there would have been a waiter there to wipe it away.

The previous evening, Daniel had been invited to the Websters for an early dinner—at Caroline's request. Matthew was home for the weekend, but he stayed locked in his room—or Sam's room—and Caroline spent much of the evening trying too hard to make peace between them. She kept topping up his drink—and, as the evening progressed, she became less accurate in this and everything else. Daniel suspected that everything Caroline tried to do at the moment missed its mark. She was without a coherent center from which to operate. Then she went to bed, forgetting, after all her hospitality, to mention anything about dinner or even say good-night. Bruce spent the remainder of the evening quizzing Daniel about his butterfly-collector book, insisting he wanted to read each of the sections as they were written. They mentioned Sam only when Daniel was preparing to leave—the thought of dinner long-abandoned. Bruce really did seem to be in denial. The girl on the river wasn't Sam. Sam was elsewhere. Although Bruce admitted that he had no idea where.

"I can tell Dr. Lopez you're here, if you like?" Jess asks. "You could go and talk to the new Grade 12s. They'll be studying your book again this year."

"Why not," Daniel says politely.

"Nina zinja zabantu abamhlophe!"

They turn to see a young man dressed in a black Adidas tracksuit and expensive-looking fluorescent-yellow trainers. He is emerging from the bush around the staff houses to the left, where a single line of blue smoke is ascending while a cock crows. Following closely behind the young man are two policemen, the one small and round and the other tall and thin.

"And now?" Tim says.

"Who is that?" asks Jess.

"Simon."

"Nina zimpimpi bastards! Ngabe uyazi ukuthi unenkululeko yakho? Kungani ubopha umfowenu?"

The two policemen are looking suitably chastised. They do nothing to interrupt Simon's flow of verbiage—as if everything that is being said, whatever it might be, contains a level of substance, a level of justice. The three figures pass right below the deck, circumventing the swimming pool and the three children swimming there, paused in their game of Marco Polo by the sound of the man's tirade.

"Who is Simon?" asks Jess as the figures pass around the side of the building.

"Moses's son. He's forever getting himself into trouble."

"For what?" Jess asks.

"Politics, mainly."

"Politics?"

"Last year he also hit a girl. A fellow university student. The parents wanted to press charges, but Bruce, who has paid for Simon's entire education, managed to talk them out of it. You know Bruce—he hates to admit defeat."

"What's he studying?" Daniel asks.

"Engineering, can you believe? Although Caroline says he's far more likely to blow up bridges than to build any."

The police van soon emerges on the track leading back down the hill. They watch as it slithers through a gathering of mud, rights itself, turns a corner and is consumed again by the bush.

"Did he know Sam?" Jess asks.

"Simon? Sure he did. They practically grew up together."

"They were close?"

"For a while. But Simon was a year or two older and they grew apart."

"Funny that Sam never mentioned him."

The van appears again on the dirt road at the bottom of the hill, the engine still audible as the gears rise in confidence. Daniel hears a quiet sigh and turns to see Moses, who is standing not far from their table, watching the little white dot progressing into the green hills.

"Have they taken him in?" Tim asks.

"They have not taken him in," Moses says, sounding pained and disappointed. "The boy is sitting inside, eating his breakfast."

"What did they want with him?"

"Something about clothes. A blue anorak. Simon said he knows nothing about it."

Tim nods, mutters something about needing the bathroom and heads inside.

"Literature is concerned with fitting untested language into untested situations"

This is Daniel's opening remark to the class of twenty-odd schoolgirls. He can see, however, that they are more interested in him as a man than they are in him as a writer—or the book they will be tasked with reading this year. He can hear a weed-eater somewhere in the distance and the clatter of a fountain through the open door. The sunlight of midsummer is pouring in through an open sash window. On the walls are posters of famous writers. Shakespeare, Oscar Wilde, Sylvia Plath and Chimamanda Ngozi Adichie. There's also a poster of the cover of his own novel that Dr. Lopez would have acquired at a teachers' conference. The image of a wooden farm fence on a muddy track, fading off into the mist.

Dr. Lopez has taken a seat at the back of the class and is sitting inside a stretched square of light. She seems younger than Daniel remembers. More in her twenties than her early thirties, which is where he placed her the previous year. She's a woman with a large bush of ungovernable black hair. Her face is pale and dark-eyed, her gaze never quite settling anywhere. There is something straight and serious about her mouth that Daniel likes. She also has a small birthmark under her left eye that he has never had an opportunity to look at properly. It is like a tear, or the stain of a tear, splashed across her skin. A sign of suffering. Past suffering, perhaps. Suffering reduced to its proper scale.

"The worst thing your English teacher can tell you," he says with an amused glance in her direction, "is to tell you to write about what you know. Rather, you should write about what you don't yet know about, but would like to find out more about. The process of writing will track the process of learning, the process of discovery."

Some of the girls turn back and smile at Dr. Lopez, and Daniel imagines a new glow about her. She might have told her students exactly this. To write out of their own experience. Since that is the one clear thing that they have and that no one else could ever take away from them.

Daniel can feel that the girls in the room, who are all about seventeen, are not feeling inclined to take anything seriously today—least of all him. He is struck by how untested they seem by the horrors of the world. But he likes their confidence, even if it's no more than a front they're putting up while their real interior lives take place elsewhere. At their age, Daniel had no such confidence, no such protective shield.

Their table overlooks the parking lot

Dr. Lopez has taken him out for a compensatory lunch. They order a pint of Peroni and the puttanesca. Dr. Lopez tells him that this is her son's favorite restaurant. She shows him a photograph of the boy on her phone. A child sitting on a gray donkey. The misty, rust-colored hills of a KwaZulu-Natal Midlands winter in the background. The boy shares his mother's mop of black hair and her long, shy smile. He looks proud of himself under his mother's gaze and entirely oblivious to the donkey's bored expression.

"His name is Rafael," she says.

"He's your only child?"

"There is only me and him."

Daniel doesn't ask where her husband is and she doesn't tell him.

"I'm sorry about the class today," she says instead. "I think they're all still in holiday mode. And we only started reading the first few pages of your book this week. Last year, the girls found your novel quite slow to start—but once it had really taken off, they were rivetted."

"They were?"

"What did Sam say?" Dr. Lopez asks herself. "Yes—she said you are always looking for the light. For the light left in the world. I liked that."

The mention of Sam's name renders them silent for a moment. Dr. Lopez slips away her phone and the image on her phone as if to protect her son from some malign force in the world that has so far spared him.

"It's awful that no one knows what happened to her," Daniel says.

"Yes."

"The way she disappeared like that—and was then seen on the river before disappearing again. It's the not knowing that makes it even more difficult."

"Yes."

Dr. Lopez—she has asked Daniel to call her Natasha, but he has yet to use her name—lets out a long sigh. She looks more familiar now, although there still seem to be several women competing for attention inside her.

"The thing about Sam," she says, "is that she disappeared long before she disappeared. Something had happened to her. By the end of last year, she was no longer the same girl."

"You mean she seemed—unhappy?"

"Not unhappy. It was as if she had become careless. Careless with herself and everything around her. She no longer seemed to care about anything."

"When I met her, she was such a dedicated student."

"She was the kind of student every teacher wants in their class. She was the kind of girl who not only had a hunger to learn, but she infected her classmates with a hunger to learn. She could have been the Head Girl if she'd wanted to be. She was a natural leader. But by the end she only wanted to be left alone."

"She had a friend in Jessica, didn't she?"

"Not in those last months—no."

They drink their beer and stare down into the parking area, where cars are reversing out of spaces or finding their way into spaces, like a game being played by an unseen hand.

"So you never got to the bottom of what had happened to her?" Daniel asks.

"No."

"Did you ever speak with Bruce and Caroline about it?"

"I did. Caroline seemed angry with Sam. I think it had something to do with Sam's boyfriend. To be honest, when she disappeared we thought she'd run away. We thought she'd gone to England with her new boyfriend. We never imagined she could have been—murdered. And yet, when I learned the news, something about it made sense. There was such an air of violence around her toward the end. As if she was already living in the dark."

Bruce is sitting on a rock on the side of the road

He is wearing a yellowing shirt and gazing across at the stretch of river and the lion-mountain beyond it. The wolfhound is panting in empathy with her owner, who looks as if all the blood has been drained out of him. At first glance, Daniel barely recognizes Bruce. He seems like a far more apologetic, far less successful man. Perhaps this is what a great shock does. It turns a man at the height of his powers into some shadow version of himself. Into the man he might have been had his life been characterized by a series of failures. Bruce glances across at Daniel and almost smiles. As if divining Daniel's thoughts, he says:

"Cancer. I have cancer. It metastasized a few months ago."

"Sorry?"

"I think you heard me correctly."

The dog pants on as if she already knows this news. Daniel looks around for a companion rock on which to sit, but there isn't one. So he carries on standing there, at the edge of Bruce's shadow.

"Are you getting treatment?"

"There is no treatment. At least, not for me."

Not knowing what else to do, Daniel stares at the mountain. It sometimes seems that the mountain is listening and waiting—waiting for the world to wake up and worship it.

"I've been given opioids. But I prefer whisky. I'm told the two aren't designed to mix."

"I'm—sorry."

"I'm not."

"But what about Matthew?" Daniel asks.

"Matthew?"

"He needs you. I'm sure Caroline does too."

At this, Bruce doesn't even attempt to laugh. "Just before Sam went, I decided to get treatment. I decided that, for some reason, she needed me—she needed to be protected. But now that she's gone, there's no point. I was too late. Too late to do whatever I was supposed to do. I never saw the signs."

Through this speech, they hear the sound of a car engine approaching from somewhere below them. Now the police van appears around the bend and ascends the track toward them.

"And this?" says Bruce with irritation.

"You weren't expecting them?"

"Why would I be expecting them? It's probably to do with that bloody Simon again."

Bruce stands with difficulty and steps into the road. He has been sitting at the junction where the road divides, one half going up to his house and the other half cutting across toward the restaurant buildings. Jane follows him into the road with her solemn, all-knowing tread. When the policemen see him, they stop at the entrance to Bruce's driveway and emerge from the vehicle. Both of them are wearing the same grave, rehearsed expression. Daniel recognizes them as the two men who were here to question Simon. Bruce introduces them as Superintendent Ndlovu and Detective Dlamini.

"Mr. Webster, we're sorry to disturb you."

"Don't worry," says Bruce. "I'm already disturbed."

The two men nod without comment. Neither of them has glanced at Daniel since being introduced, and he withdraws to a discreet distance, near Bruce's rock.

"I'm afraid there has been—a new development," Dlamini says.

"Oh yes?"

"Earlier this afternoon, a body was found."

Bruce looks at him.

"It was the body of a young woman. She was found in the river."

The wolfhound steps forward and sniffs Dlamini's hand.

"Mr. Webster," Ndlovu says, "we wonder if you could come with us? The body—it needs to be formally identified."

THE BUTTERFLY COLLECTOR

They do not find the *Zeritis protumnus*

But Charles leaves Trimen far from disappointed, armed, as he is, with bound copies of his two-volume *Rhopalocera africae australis*—the first comprehensive book to have been written on the butterfly species of South Africa—as well as some other locally produced publications Trimen thought might be of interest. When Charles and William climb into their Cape cart, it feels to Charles as if a whole week has passed, even if William spent much of it asleep. Lydia hands Charles two jars of honey from the apiary behind her house, as well as a warm loaf of bread wrapped in muslin cloth.

"When all of this is over, will you come back to visit me?" she says to Charles.

"I shall."

"Remember your promise. Whatever happens, you will keep William safe."

"That's hardly likely," laughs William, overhearing them. "We shall be facing the entire might of the Zulu army."

"We will come back to find you," says Charles. "We promise."

As their cart heads off, Pip trots after them for several yards until Lydia calls him back. Their last view of the scene is of the little dog being lifted into the air and held against Lydia's yellow dress, in the position of her heart.

"Charles—I do believe you are in love with my sister," observes William with a laugh.

"I think I might be," laughs Charles.

"Then you had better marry her. I'd rather have you as a brother-in-law than that ostrich-farmer chap. He sounds perfectly hideous."

The cart drops them off on Adderley Street, within sight of the curved glass roof of the train station. At the sound of a large bronze bell, several young women hurry past them toward their train, holding their hats against the wind. The streets of the city are wide and generous and filled with carts, pedestrians and the occasional omnibus. Their first port of call is Mr. Silver's shop, where Charles buys a second pair of leather boots designed by Silver himself—with the knee-cap lengthened in order to protect the horseman while riding through thorny bushes. The rest of the soldiers are to be given two pairs of identical boots for the campaign, with no distinction between the left and the right foot. The boots will need to be softened and stretched through a combination of the men's urine and the long march from Durban to Pietermaritzburg—and then into the "thousand hills" of Zululand.

Charles and William have an excellent lunch of Karoo lamb and more Cape wine, where they are joined by two high-spirited officers from the *Edinburgh Castle*—who afterwards hail a phaeton to take "young Gracie" to a nearby bordello called The White Room, leaving Charles to find his own way back to the ship.

Charles spends that evening paging through his new butterfly books

In one obscure article, Charles reads that some species of butterflies are born with insufficiently developed mouths and gradually starve themselves to death, spending their brief lives using up whatever energy they have to copulate. Charles learns that the writer kept a *Zeritis protumnus*—one of the species that lacks the ability to feed—in captivity for two weeks before it finally died. Because they do not need to frequent flowers, these butterflies are found near ant colonies, often in the hundreds, where they lay their eggs. The writer observes that when the larvae hatch, they appear to find shelter in the ant nests, where they live as parasites, the ants feeding them mouth-to-mouth, as cuckoos do. The writer wonders whether the ants and the grubs in their care know anything about the greater process in which they are involved—and that their labors will one day result in the dun-colored *Zeritis protumnus*, a creature incapable of feeding itself yet immediately capable of flight.

William returns to their cabin only in the small hours, climbing into his bunk without bothering to get undressed.

"William?" says Charles.

"What is it?"

"Are you well?"

"I am very tired."

"I shall see you in the morning, then?"

"As you do every other morning, Charles."

Charles lies in his bunk without moving for a moment, listening to the other man's breathing. The sea is rolling them through its dark landscape and somewhere out across the water a large bell tolls—and Charles can't remember when he last felt this alone, or this afraid.

Leaving the bulk of their luggage onboard to be offloaded later, they catch a boat to shore and all the soldiers scatter, the privates moving on to the canvas-tented camp, which is said to be infested with cockroaches the size of mice. Most of the officers head for the train station, and the train that leads toward but does not quite reach Pietermaritzburg because the track is still under construction.

Charles has had almost no contact with the privates onboard the ship, although he has seen William in conversation with a few of them on more than one occasion. Many had been drawn to the war by the prospect of decent clothing and three meals a day. The only requirement is that they be in good health and are no less than five feet and six inches in height. As for the officers, many are second or third sons who have little prospect of inheriting their ancestral lands. Several of these officers set off to check into The Emperor Hotel—William's two friends from The White Room, Bayley and Sprite, are amongst them—while others go straight to see General Bellairs, the General Officer Commanding, to receive their orders. At the dock, they encounter a local war photographer, a bearded man with an instantly forgettable face, who insists on taking their photograph.

Soon William and Charles are met by his aunt's gleaming yellow-and-black brougham, which takes them up a macadam road to the Berea, where they arrive at a gracious double-story house that overlooks the harbor and the bluff. Charles has with him his overnight bag, butterfly books and leather knapsack. The *Azanus albus* from Cape Verde he has left behind for the South African Museum. Trimen has also given him a list of moths and butterflies for which he is to look out during his journey into Natal and Zululand—in the hope that he will be able to add to the collection of the Durban Museum.

"I do worry about you, Charles," smiles William as Charles hoists his bags over his shoulder. "Do you not think you should be leaving all of that paraphernalia behind?"

Charles knows that there is something protective about this suggestion. There has been a haze of talk around Charles. It started before their arrival in Cape Town, but in the last few days during the final journey to Durban it has grown into an almost audible hum. Charles knows that Lieutenant Bayley and Captain Sprite, for example, have turned decisively against him. It is not simply his butterfly net. It is Charles's habit of keeping to himself, of missing the countless opportunities to demonstrate a kinship that he has never felt. This has made him an object of quiet suspicion—and the only thing that has protected him thus far has been the friendship of William, who manages to be loved and embraced by all who encounter him.

Mrs. Highwood, William's handsome and corpulent aunt, is waiting to meet them on the veranda with her dark-haired daughter, Isabella. As they pour drinks, the child, who is wearing a jade-green dress, descends the steps to the front lawn, where she is soon engaged in teaching her yellow Labrador puppy how to sit. A large black butterfly with pale-yellow spots and blue tail-spots appears over some red flowers—before breaking off again in an agile, swooping flight to settle nearer the child. Charles has already observed some of these butterflies—called *Papilio demoleus* in Trimen's book—drinking, in some numbers, from the urine-soaked puddles in the stable yard behind the house. There he also saw an example of the spectacular *Papilio nireuslyaeus*, first named by Doubleday in 1845, another large black *papilionid* with conspicuous blue-green upperside bands. Without comment, Charles takes up his net and stalks across the soft lawn—and, with a practiced flick of his wrist, he captures the *demoleus* the moment it senses his presence and floats upward. The child comes over to watch him as he takes the butterfly between his forefinger and thumb and pins it directly into one of his cork-lined pocket boxes.

"Why did you do that?" the child asks.

Her eyes, which Charles now observes are the identical color of the *nireuslyaeus*'s markings, are magnified with tears.

"It's for the new museum," Charles says.

"Which new museum?"

"Here in Durban. I'm collecting butterflies so that people like you can go there to admire them."

"But—you killed it."

"I'm sure that it did not feel any pain."

But this last statement is delivered into a place that the child has already vacated—and Charles watches her running away from him, her puppy yapping after her as if this were all a game.

They spend the evening drinking whisky on the veranda

Bats the size of pigeons flit in and out of the lamplight. Far beneath them, at the other end of the overgrown city, the harbor lights embrace the darkness of the sea. The air is alive with crickets and strange sounds of mourning and lamentation—an owl, a stray dog searching for a place to settle, the screech of some creature in distress whose name remains unknown to Charles. Where Cape Town was like something out of the Scottish Highlands, all gray rock and heather and unusual angles of rich golden light, Durban is like some wet corner in the tropics, the air thick with mosquitoes. At least five translucent, sand-colored geckos lurk on each wall, moving only to make a kill, their large black eyes wet and glistening.

Charles can feel a great darkness moving toward them. It is not only the war advancing—man by man, from every homestead across the length of Zululand—but something that seemed to enter all the men on board the *Edinburgh Castle*. A force like hate that disguised itself as patriotism. It was as old as the world. It was what made one race wipe another race from the face of the earth with indifference, as you might wipe the moisture from a window on a winter morning to get a better view. No one cared about anything except this ancient impulse in each man to have the world repeated back at himself, in his own image, in a hall of mirrors. Charles knew that William was going to sacrifice himself to this force, this darkness—not because he wanted to, but because it was what their civilization expected.

"I'm not sure what we are to do," Charles says when William's aunt has retired, at last, to bed.

"About what?" asks William—the words slurred and petulant with drink and no longer masked as they were in the presence of his aunt.

"About anything."

"Charles, you're not making any sense."

"I'm afraid for us," says Charles. "I'm afraid of where we're headed. I'm afraid of what we might have to do. Of what we might become. Whatever lies in store for us, I know that it can't end well."

"It will end—and that's all that matters," William says.

The horse-drawn omnibus fetches them
the following morning at Berea

It stops at several picturesque locations along the way—Rooi Koppies, Cowies Hill, Pinetown, Fields Hill, Botha's Hill, Padley and Camperdown—each place triggering some unclouded childhood memory in William of walking and hunting with his long-departed father. They are deposited in Pietermaritzburg, outside the Plow Hotel, which was once an officer's mess. Having confirmed that their luggage will be arriving later that morning, they set off to report to General Clifford at Headquarters. Charlies and William see Clifford separately. Charles is given a position in a regiment under the command of Captain Sprite and William is placed in a regiment under Commandant Hamilton-Browne. When Charles hears the name "Sprite," it is with some misgiving, but he is grateful to be in the same contingent as his friend, even if not the same regiment. They are offered ten shillings a day staff pay—as well as a carbine and a horse, both of which are to be fetched from Government Supplies the next morning and returned after the war. Charles is encouraged to buy an extra pony to carry his supplies as well as extra saddlery.

To celebrate, they take a cart to the Maritzburg Club, where mention of William's father's name—once a well-known and respected trader in the area—immediately leads to both William and Charles being made honorary members for life. At the bar, they come upon the imposing, ginger-haired figure of Captain Sprite, who manages to greet Charles like an old friend when he sees the gleaming numbers of his regiment on Charles's shoulder straps.

"Ah, Hawthorne, old fellow!" he says. "You're welcome to the regiment, I'm sure!"

"I'm pleased to be in it," Charles says, dropping the "sir" because of the informal nature of their meeting—and immediately regretting it.

"And we will be pleased to have you," says Sprite, moving forward to greet William, a more genuine smile finding its way onto his face. "Gracie, old boy!"

"Hello, Sprite. I hear you'll be having my friend Hawthorne under your command. You will have to keep a good eye on him."

"I plan to do that, my dear fellow," laughs Sprite. "And I trust that he'll be leaving behind that butterfly net!"

One of the butterflies Charles is to look out for
is the *Papilio ophidicephalus*

This butterfly is reputed to be the largest known butterfly in southern Africa and was described only a year previously by Oberthür—a man best known for having named dozens of new genera of moths. As with many butterflies, the *ophidicephalus* defends itself by means of color—the black and yellow markings signaling to birds and other predators that it may be unpalatable. Mimicry was a phenomenon that had only recently been described by HW Bates, following his experiences with Alfred Russel Wallace in the Amazon. He had presented a paper to the Linnean Society in 1861 and published it as "Contributions to an Insect Fauna of the Amazon Valley" in the Society's *Transactions* in 1862. This paper, which was amongst those Trimen had given Charles, presented the theory that unpalatable species often evolved bright colors and patterns to demonstrate to insectivores that they were indeed unpalatable. Palatable species had then evolved to look like them, deriving protection from sight predators, such as birds, through the resemblance.

This idea is something on which Charles reflects as he stands in the bar of the Maritzburg Club in a room full of scarlet serge coats. Since the Indian Mutiny of 1857, all the units based in India have come to wear a dust-colored "khaki" uniform in order to conceal themselves from the enemy. The red coats being worn at present date back to those conflicts in which it was difficult to distinguish between friend and foe through the gunpowder fog of war. But here in Zululand the enemy would be all too easy to distinguish—and the red coats of the British would be no more than a red flag to the Zulu army, who always attacked in the horn formation of the bull.

Charles and William, being of the Cavalry of the Natal Native Contingent, are wearing the blue patrol jackets that they brought with them from London. But these will be of no more protection than the red coats against the bright-green hills of Zululand. Charles finds himself hoping that their flagrant display of color will be like the famous eyespots on the wings of butterflies. When the wings of these butterflies are abruptly opened, the eyespots, which resemble the eyes of owls, are displayed, disorientating the predator and giving the butterfly enough time to escape. It seems that predators, like all bullies, do not like to be looked at by eyes more penetrating than their own.

That evening, Charles also meets Commandant Hamilton-Browne—or "Maori Browne," as he is referred to by his friends—who by his own account blew up his father with a squib cigar, fought against the Sioux in America, hunted down bushrangers in Australia and was reduced to eating a child to survive while fighting the Maoris in New Zealand. Charles instantly dislikes the man—and all the men being so happily regaled by him. Yet William immediately disappears into them, reminding Charles of other butterflies in Trimen's book, camouflaged to resemble dead leaves or bird droppings – or, in the case of the *D'Urbania limbata*, another newly discovered species Charles is to look out for, the lichen on the rocks that the butterfly likes to frequent.

It takes four days of laboring through the rain and mud
to reach the camp

Charles's company is separated from William's on the first day while on the road to Greytown, as many of the spruits and rivers have been rendered impassable by the recent floods. Charles arrives at a camp named Sandspruit only to learn that William's regiment has moved further on, to the camp at Helpmekaar. Charles is yet to meet the men who are to be under his command, but he arrives to find his tent already pitched. His ponies are unsaddled and divested of their traps and taken away by a groom called Sunshine to be cleaned and fed.

Charles has been feeling quietly and inexplicably miserable since their departure from Pietermaritzburg, but the difficulty of the journey has been such that no one appears to have noticed. Due to the quality of his horsemanship, he has won the temporary respect of Captain Sprite, and he has been careful to keep his butterfly net out of sight. The government-supplied bay is a studious mountain pony named Robin Hood and the extra pony he acquired in Pietermaritzburg is a sturdy gray he named Clifton Lass.

Charles's deep-sleeping tent companion is a Lieutenant Tyrell, a fellow who still manages to smell of onions even when there are no onions about. Tyrell is some associate of Sprite and the two of them often play cards and drink together in the evenings. Charles suspects Tyrell to be an informant to Sprite. He once encountered Tyrell rifling through his belongings when Charles was out—and Tyrell had muttered something about wanting to borrow his knife. But Tyrell has a natural, easy disposition and Charles senses that the man likes him, in spite of himself. As with William, there is probably an altogether different man locked inside Tyrell that their life in the service does not permit. In civilian life, Tyrell would probably have married and had dozens of chubby blond children like himself—and it would not have occurred to him to act duplicitously.

Over the weeks that follow, the inclement weather endures and several of the tents are washed away, the pegs not being sufficient to lodge them into the rocky earth. When it is not raining, the sun is hot and high and the air is full of flies—the creatures managing to find their way into every mug of coffee and every mouthful of food. At night, large mosquitoes fill the air with their insistent song, their proboscides able to penetrate the cotton of Charles's nightshirt. The men survive mainly off Australian and Chicago beef in tins, as well as grainy coffee and increasingly musty biscuits. There is also a ration of sugar and salt—and preserved carrots and lime juice in the absence of vegetables. Whenever an ox breaks its leg or becomes sick, it is slaughtered and fed to the men—boiled, roasted or stewed, yet tasting much the same however it is cooked. Whenever a patch of pumpkins is discovered, the winnings are soon made into a mash, fritters or pies. Most of the officers have with them some rum and there is talk of the more senior officers having whisky and even champagne.

Charles spends his days drilling and training the new recruits and he hears nothing further from William. The Natives continue to arrive from all over the country to be conscripted. They are each overseen by leaders from their own villages and each man is supplied with a blanket and a red cloth, which is to be worn as a headband in order to distinguish them from the Zulu army. In each battalion, only a hundred Natives are armed and the rest are supplied with the pangas used for cutting sugarcane. Yet they are more at home with their assegais and shields. The war photographer Charles remembers from the dock at Durban takes a photograph of Charles with his men, promising to give him a print in the unlikely event that their paths should cross again.

On Christmas Day, the men are given a day of rest and Charles takes Clifton Lass across to Helpmekaar in search of William. The camp is situated along the summit of a long, flat mountain which looks down onto the Buffalo River and the hills of Zululand that lie beyond. This seems to be a clear provocation to Charles. The British are declaring that they are preparing their advance into enemy territory, even though the date of the final ultimatum is yet to be reached. Charles is directed to William's tent at the far end of the camp, where he finds William asleep—his tent in the condition of disarray Charles has come to expect from his friend.

"William? God man—are you still asleep? It's nearly twelve o'clock."

"Charles?" says William, barely moving his head. "Could that be you? I thought I'd never see you again."

The tent smells of something rotten—as if there is a dead rat nearby. William's unshaven face appears jaundiced in the yellowish light.

"What is wrong?" Charles asks, sitting on the ground next you him. "Too much rum last night?"

"I have a fever of some kind," says William, "but I'm sure it will pass."

William manages to sit up on one elbow to get a better look at him.

"When did you last wash?" Charles asks.

"Oh, some days ago. There's no point in this heat. One is sweating again before one has even dried oneself."

"You must make more of an effort," says Charles with a gradual smile. "You look dreadful—and you smell even worse."

From outside, they can hear the voices of men—the laughter of Maori Browne clearly audible. William does not appear to notice, however. He is merely watching Charles from across a great, shimmering plain.

"I wish we were in the same regiment," Charles says.

"I do too. I have been missing you more than I can say. How have you been holding up?"

"I have been keeping myself busy with the new recruits."

"Any new butterflies that you've managed to collect?"

"I have not taken out my butterfly net."

"And Sprite? Has he been difficult?"

"He's been away this last week to consult with some Natives in the Umsinga district. We've barely crossed paths since our arrival."

"You must keep it that way, Charles. He has taken a strong disliking to you. He thinks you're like that Rowlston chap you once told me about. The man who was disgraced and shot himself in the head."

"But I am nothing at all like him."

"Of course you aren't. But Sprite doesn't know that. I think he believes you have developed unnatural feelings toward me, can you believe? He once said as much. He thinks you're a threat to the integrity of the regiment. He's looking for any reason to destroy you. You can't afford to slip up—not for a minute."

"Not even for one minute?" asks Charles with a smile.

William smiles back at him. "We have wasted so much time," he says.

"What do you mean?"

"On the ship. At my sister's house. Oh, Charles, what is to become of us?"

"We have to live through this war. We will be able to make more sense of things afterwards."

William reaches for Charles's hand and presses it.

"You ought not to have come," he says, his eyes shining with emotion in the strange light of the tent. "You ought to have remained with your men."

"My place is here," says Charles. "With you."

On the morning they cross into Zululand, they are engulfed in a thick mist

At the smell of the river, Clifton Lass snorts and strains against the lead rope, but Charles clicks her onwards. They have been warned about crocodiles, but these are less of a threat when compared to the prospect of the Zulu army. Charles knows that the mist will soon clear and that the long procession of the British will be exposed—while the Zulus in the area will remain entirely invisible, their numbers wholly unknown.

Charles hears the river before he sees it—and, before he has decided to step into the current, he finds that the muddy, moiling water is already all around him, reaching as far as his saddle flaps. Clifton Lass tosses her head and buries her nose in the water, and Charles has to pull her head up and kick her forward before she is tempted to roll.

From further downstream, from Jim Rorke's old crossing place, he can hear the men singing "The Warwickshire Lad" and he can feel the blood of all their ancestors stretching back in time. This incursion into hostile territory before dawn feels like something ageless, forbidden and abiding. Everything about their advance has been ordered and planned, verified by map and compass, sunlight and starlight. But Charles knows that this is all an illusion. They are crossing into a place without maps, where there be only dragons.

A few days after visiting William, Charles's regiment had proceeded on to Helpmekaar in preparation for the probable invasion into Zululand. He had only seen William in the distance—and, being under the permanent gaze of Captain Sprite, he had made no attempt to approach him. His friend looked much improved as he walked up and down the columns, speaking and laughing easily with his men in what sounded to Charles like perfect Zulu. On one occasion not long after dinner, Charles had not been able to help himself and he had wandered into the section of the camp where William shared a tent with Bayley—but he had found the two men sitting outside with some other officers, playing a card game—Twenty-five or All Fours.

The next morning, Charles had taken advantage of the change in weather to saddle up Clifton Lass and go in search of some of the butterflies on Trimen's list. This included the *Papilio euphranor*, a large black butterfly with yellow spots, which Charles had seen sitting on the shoulder of one of the officers, perhaps attracted to the shining scarlet of his serge coat—as well as South Africa's largest known pierid, the rapidly flying white-and-yellow *Eronia varia*, which favors moist, forested areas and has splashes of dusty orange-red on the upperside forewings and conspicuous olive-green eyes. Charles caught one *euphranor* and two *varias* and pinned them into his collection tins.

He was riding back into camp, deciding that he would leave his collection and most of his equipment behind at Helpmekaar, when he encountered Captain Sprite emerging from a tent, holding a pet monkey on a leash. Sprite had acquired the forlorn creature in Sandspruit and, when he wasn't on duty, it was condemned to accompany him everywhere.

"Hawthorne, where have you been?"

"Oh, I went off to look at the view, sir. On a good, clear day like this, you can see all the way into Zululand."

His disassembled butterfly net was in the leather bag Charles used on fieldtrips, which was less cumbersome than the knapsack—and thankfully it did not draw Sprite's attention.

"You see anything interesting?"

"Definite movement amongst the hills, sir. Something throwing up dust. A herd of cattle, I thought. And further off, a thin column of pale-blue smoke."

"Yes, there are definitely some Zulus in Zululand," observed Sprite, with a caustic tone that was characteristic. "We've been seeing their beacon fires at night. We believe they're exchanging messages all the way to Cetshwayo in Ulundi."

"Yes, sir."

"Are your men fit and ready?"

"As fit and ready as they will ever be, sir."

"Good man. I've been impressed with your general attitude. I have to say—your friend quite misled me concerning you."

"My friend, sir?"

"Lieutenant Grace."

"I am not sure I understand you, sir."

"Never had a good thing to say about you. Never had a bad thing either, mind you. But he never took any of the opportunities available to him to come to your defense."

With that, Sprite walked off, chatting to his mute monkey as if he had not left Charles with a knife twisting inside his breast.

They are ascending the first valley when they hear the singing

They can't see much through the mist, which still hangs like an ocean fog around them, and at first there is only the sound of their horses breathing, and the clatter of their hooves as they pick their way through the anthills and the stones—and then they hear it, the voice of a few hundred men, singing what sounds like a war chant from beyond the line of rocks above them.

"Do you think we ought to call up more men, sir?" Sprite asks another officer whose name Charles does not yet know.

"If they were planning to attack," the other man says, "they would have done so at dawn. No—they are only trying to unsettle us. I don't imagine that the bulk of the Zulu army is anywhere near these hills."

The troops below them are arranging themselves in the receive-cavalry formation, their red and blue coats emblazoned across the bright-green plateau. Behind them, the processions of wagons, horses, oxen and slaughter animals continue to cross the drifts along the river—a procedure that is anticipated to last all day. Charles can see only glimpses of the scene as they ascend, but the little painted soldiers, with their comical horses and oxen, and their white wagons placed at odd angles against the uneven earth, look like a game being played by children.

As the light around them grows, Charles observes several rust-brown butterflies feeding on the yellow flowers around them, their eyespots clearly visible as they rapidly open and close their wings—and the whole mountain seems to him to be alive and breathing, as if it was the land itself that was alive. They are the dream, he thinks. The child's game, the passing folly. Were Charles to die here—or if all of them were to die here—their presence would be forgotten with the blink of an eye.

That night, he lies awake in his tent, his head on a rock and his feet in a puddle

He listens beyond the sound of the rain, waiting for the first sign of a Zulu attack. He has been told that ever since the Battle of Blood River the Zulus prefer to attack in the open field and at sunrise. This is of no help, however, since it is the light of day that Charles fears the most. He also keeps returning to the insinuations of Captain Sprite, turning them this way and that, holding them against the light and then the dark. He knows William Grace better than any man present, perhaps better than any man alive, but that is not to say that his friend is incapable of betraying him—or of offering him up as a sacrifice.

When the bugle sounds the reveille, Charles emerges from his tent to find Sunshine standing outside with his horse and a tin mug filled with watery coffee. Sunshine is wearing a large black trench coat, Wellington boots and a round velvet hat that is placed at the back of his head, giving him a haphazard appearance. Sunshine speaks little English and he and Charles have learned to communicate through a range of gestures and smiles. Charles has never asked the groom to bring him coffee, but Sunshine continues to insist that it is necessary for Charles to drink a mug of coffee before mounting his horse. The previous evening, he and Charles had shared looks of commiseration when another of the grooms was flogged by a drummer boy for apparently stealing rum. The drummer boy was a large-armed Welshman in his early twenties called Damiel McEwan who had already flogged several other men for minor offenses in Helpmekaar. McEwan had tied the groom to a triangle of poles made from spontoons and given him three hundred lashes with a cat-o'-nine-tails—a number that was considered moderate for such a crime. Afterwards, Sunshine had splashed salt water across the man's mauled back, but he was already unconscious from the pain.

"I am sorry," Charles said later when he came to check up on the horses.

"Leya ndoda izobulawa, khona okugida kuyibheka," was all Sunshine said in his incomprehensible tongue.

Today Charles is to be part of a group of men that will join Colonel Glynn's contingent and head up Jim Rorke's old wagon track to investigate the line of hills at the edge of the next valley. There have been reports of Zulus hidden in the sandstone cliffs along that ridge and this contingent is to investigate their numbers while the bulk of the army continues toward the mountain shaped like a lion cut out of the rock—the mountain referred to as "Isandhlwana." The passage has been slow over this terrain and often it takes up to thirty-six oxen to haul a single wagon. The spectre of the stone lion resembles exactly the sphinx on the badge of the 24th Regiment, which strikes many of the men as an omen—whether for good or ill is yet to be determined.

Charles feeds Clifton Lass some extra cubes from his tea-stained helmet before mounting and riding across to the other horsemen who are gathering beyond the line of tents. He has slipped a cork-lined collecting tin and a few entomological pins into one of his ammunition pockets—a decision he trusts he will not come to regret. His heart sinks when he sees William exchanging words with Lieutenant Bayley, who is also serving under Colonel Glynn. Bayley is a dark-haired man with a wild, bushy beard that gives him the air of a Cossack. The previous evening, during the flogging, Bayley had been one of the men egging McEwan on—and, when Bayley had walked away, he had spat at the whipped man's supine form as if his punishment had been insufficient.

The sun is high and the grass is singing with cicadas by the time they leave the wagon track and enter the uninterrupted crop of eight-foot grass. As they approach the drift of a river, they encounter an assortment of mottled cattle, standing apparently unattended, as well as hundreds of bright-yellow butterflies, which are happily settled on the urine-soaked mud. Charles is wondering whether he might be able to leave the column to take a closer look at the butterflies when the first shots are fired. They are coming from the cliffs that rise at the far side of the riverbank, yet Charles can see no one there.

Lieutenant Bayley and the other men around him are unaffected by the shots. The Zulus are said to have an assortment of outmoded rifles and muskets that they have traded from Europeans, as well as ammunition that is often homemade. In the unlikely event that anyone were to be hit at such a range, the bullets would most probably fail to pierce their uniforms, let alone their flesh. None of the Zulu rifles would ever be as effective as the new Martini-Henrys of the British, which were sighted up to 1500 yards and could be reloaded in a few seconds. The Zulus were said to have no chance of killing anyone—since their rifles were more or less useless and it was doubtful that they would ever be able to get close enough to throw their spears.

Clifton Lass, who has been trained to endure such noises, merely tosses her head at the sound of the rifle fire and Charles nudges her forward. Charles sees that William has already reached the opposite bank and is trotting on his large, glistening bay toward some rocks to shelter from the enemy fire. Charles crosses the river and continues further uphill to where more mottled cattle are milling around a rocky track. There he joins some soldiers from his own regiment. He is about to offer words of encouragement to one of them when the man is hit in the thigh. The man drops to the earth, letting out a high cry, his leg lying at an unlikely angle, snapped off at the midpoint of the femur.

When the man has been attended to, Charles tethers Clifton Lass to a bush and continues on foot up the track. Here he encounters more of the yellow butterflies, and he bends down to examine the marginal black bands on the upperside of the forewings. The butterflies are most likely *Terias brigitta*—another taxon from Trimen's list.

"Hawthorne has been hit!" William shouts worriedly from the scattered rocks below.

Charles catches one of the yellow butterflies in his hand as it ascends. "No, he has not!" he shouts, standing up again as another bullet zips past his head.

The army arrives at the stone lion of Isandhlwana a few days later

They have been watching this mountain since their arrival in Zululand, aware that it is a destination of sorts. Charles has seen it as nothing more than the first of many such mountains that will mark their passage into Zululand. They approach from behind the mountain's haunches and head toward the camp assembled along the mountain's left flank. The sun is descending behind a mustard-yellow cloud that hangs across the sky like the distress signal left by a long-extinguished fire. Since flushing the warriors from Chief Sihayo's clan from their stronghold, and burning the village of another clan further into the hills, they have encountered almost no resistance from the enemy along the way—and since Charles's apparent brush with death amongst the yellow butterflies, he and William have spent as much time together as possible, their decision to avoid one another in public long discarded, like that smoke signal above the hills.

"I do believe the army is waiting for us at Ulundi," William says as they approach the shadow of Isandhlwana. "I believe they have gathered there to protect their king."

Charles says nothing to this, but he knows that the natural world is filled with prevaricators—turtles that lure their prey by making their tongues resemble a flailing worm and female dragonflies that play dead in order to avoid unwanted male attention. There is even a possum that can emit an odor from an anal gland that exactly replicates the smell of decaying flesh.

"I hope you're right," is all Charles says.

PART FOUR

THE WRITER

No one told Daniel that his sister was sick

Lucy had been alive for two years. It would take another two years for her to die. When she was born, Daniel held the bundle and was photographed. The boy of six holding the new baby. Back then, Lucy did not seem to Daniel to be alive to any of them yet. She was still firmly intent on some other world, some deeper shadow-world. Although she sucked in air and milk, she was acquiring them from another source, a place that everyone around her was too old or too preoccupied to reach.

Daniel was not one of those children who feels threatened by a new sibling. Perhaps he thought that Lucy would always be a baby, existing in that other realm. When she opened her eyes and started to make sounds and communicate, he continued to believe that nothing she could do would ever touch him. Not personally. She would learn how to walk and talk and tie her shoelaces as he had.

She would go to school and learn how to draw her own name as you might draw a picture of a house. As a place to inhabit. Lucy was simply growing up in her big brother's shadow, looking around for her own sources of light.

It was soon accepted that Lucy was much cleverer than Daniel. She was very much the second child, but she was also more interested in the workings of the world than Daniel had ever been. "Why?" was one of the first questions that came to her lips. As she grew older, she kept returning to it, as a bird might return to its favorite perch. After a few "whys," the conversation always ended up being about God and his intentions. That was where her questions and her family's answers inevitably came to a halt. "It's this way because God willed it," her father would say. "I have no idea why he willed it. He had to will something, didn't he? Otherwise nothing would exist."

Lucy had a round face and blue-gray eyes and mouse-colored hair that knotted easily. She also laughed easily. Daniel had never laughed so naturally or so well. Every bit of Lucy's body would be filled up with each new hilarity. She would literally roll around with laughter on the carpet or the lawn. Soon the rest of the family would be laughing too—even when they didn't know the reason.

Daniel didn't notice when Lucy first grew quieter. Or when that whisper started up around her. One day the whisper wasn't there and the next day it was. He could feel that something very bad was taking place. But no one talked to him about anything. People came and went without explanation. His sister would be gone for whole days. Then whole nights. All he was ever told was that she was feeling unwell or that she was going for more tests.

It was the same with Lucy's head of abundant, shining hair. The one day it was there and the next day there were patches where Daniel could see her scalp. Then she started to wear a pink-knitted hat. When Daniel next saw the hat being removed, she had no hair at all. Daniel supposed all of this must have taken weeks or even months to develop. But it happened in fits and starts. Like lightning flashes slowed down. So that the speed of light was experienced in slow, sickening blasts.

Then Lucy stopped coming home. Daniel started to visit her at weekends with his parents. She was in a hospital in Pretoria. In a room surrounded by trees. There were lots of colored numbers and letters on the walls. There were drawings of rainbows made with thick crayon. There were two rows of beds filled with children. Most of them had no hair. They had the same milky glow about them. The same voices gone meek. The same bruises along their little arms and legs. Daniel was very kind, apparently. They had to wear face masks. He would read to Lucy. Her favorite book was about a lizard that had lost his tail and spent all his time searching for it. Only to find that he had grown a new tail. A tail much stronger and more brightly colored than the one for which he had been grieving.

Daniel's father had some geese on the plot back then. They had chickens too—and a pond of orange fish. The geese would often chase Daniel up and down the driveway and he was scared of them. One day when he and his parents returned home from the hospital, one of the brown-and-white geese ran honking up to his father and he picked up a metal rake and beat the goose to death. Then he threw the rake at the sky and walked into the house. Daniel's mother put the goose in a black binbag and threw it away. The goose had made a strangled, gargling sound when his father was done with it.

Lucy came home only once more. There was nothing else they could do for her. She and Daniel's mother lived in the darkest room at the furthest end of the house, sleeping on a mattress on the floor. It was said that she was afraid of the light. Electric light hurt her eyes, so it was easier for her to be in the dark, with a single vanilla-scented candle burning in the glass jar—the jar usually used for cereal so that the horrible gray moths didn't lay their eggs inside it.

It took a long time for Lucy to die. One morning, Daniel's father took him out for breakfast. They had never done this before. Only the two of them. His father ordered the full English breakfast, but he only moved the eggs and sausages and fried tomatoes and hash browns around his plate. When the bill came, he wept. He did not know how to tell his son that Lucy was dead. Daniel understood only when they arrived home and passed the sleek, black car in the driveway. His father drove over one of the aloes to get away from it. The car snarled and stalled. They walked together up the driveway toward the battened-down house. It was the last thing Daniel would ever do with his father again.

Since then, Daniel has had an aversion to lightbulbs

When he gets up in the morning, he tries to remain for as long as possible in the dark. He has said in interviews that every person is born into each new day with a pocket of gold dust. In his case, this gold dust has to be used up immediately and constructively before the world arrives around him, nosing its way into his shadow-places, sniffing about inside him in the form of text messages, or cats that need feeding, or dustbins that have to be wheeled out to the street. It is in this underground state that he tries to write each morning—finding his way from the underworld and back into the light of day with that single thread of ore with which he has been provided. If he sits down later in the day to write, he runs the risk of sounding like everyone else.

Only now does he remember that he resigned from his job

He did this at some point during his second bottle of wine. He had been waiting to hear that Bruce had identified the body of his daughter. At one point, he had left his room and walked up to the house, wondering whether he might be needed. But the house seemed uninhabited. He returned to his room, poured another glass of wine and resigned from his job.

He is about to sit down to start his work for the day when he breaks his morning rule and looks at his phone. There are three missed calls, but none of them is from Bruce. They are all from the Head Writer, Zee. The phone starts to buzz again.

"Hello?"

"It's Zee."

"Hello, Zee."

"What the fuck?"

"Sorry?"

"What the fuck did you quit for?"

Daniel doesn't know the answer to this, but he says, "I think we both know why."

"We do?"

"I'm not very good at the job. And the truth is—I don't want to be."

"What the fuck is that supposed to mean?"

"I'm not sure that the cost is worth it. I mean for the salary."

"Jesus—are you drunk, or what?"

"I was when I quit, but I'm perfectly sober now."

"It's the very beginning of the year and you're supposed to give like—at least a month's notice!"

"Let's face it, Zee, our lives will be a whole lot better off without each other."

"Are you having some sort of nervous breakdown?"

"Probably."

"Where are you now?"

"iSandlwana."

"Where?"

"It's an important battle site."

"Don't tell me you're working on another show. Who poached you? What the fuck is it called?"

"There is no other show."

"Then what are you doing there?"

"To be honest, I don't know."

"iSandlwana—wait—isn't that where the Webster kid disappeared? Don't tell me you're writing a TV show about that?"

"Don't worry, I'm not writing a TV show about that."

"So what the fuck am I supposed to do now?"

"I'm sure you'll think of something, Zee. You always do."

He leaves his room and follows the walkway down to Reception

Some of the grass yellow butterflies—the butterflies Charles would have called *Terias brigitta*—have escaped from his ancestor book and entered the world. They are moving in a tattered cloud in the direction of iSandlwana and he follows them down the hill. This often happens to him—he loses himself between what is considered real and what has been invented. He floats somewhere between these two worlds, not quite inhabiting either, but present in both. He remembers Flaubert, who famously said "Madame Bovary, c'est moi"—and became ill when his protagonist became ill, spending days unable to move from the couch in his study.

"Are you going for a walk?"

Daniel has reached the large puddle of the carpark. Bruce's fawn-colored Land Cruiser is sloshing, tank-like, through the mud. His head is a pink balloon straining against its string at the open window.

"Come for a drive," Bruce says. "I'm headed for Greytown."

Daniel climbs into the car and finds a place amongst Bruce's papers. Bruce is surprisingly chipper today. A man who has had a good day at the races.

"The dead woman," he starts before Daniel has even closed the door, "it wasn't Sam—it was someone else, someone quite a lot older than Sam." Bruce glances across at Daniel's face. "Sorry—I suppose I should've put you out of your misery, but I wasn't supposed to talk about it. Not before the public statement."

"Who was it then?"

"The woman? Not sure. She'll be hard to identify."

"Well—that's a bit of a relief, isn't it?"

"Yes, and a bit of a coincidence," says Bruce. "Two young women disappearing at more or less the same time. The police implied that there may be some kind of serial killer on the loose. Which is premature, don't you think? Especially since only one body has been found."

"And the anorak? Did they find that?"

"Only the woman. There was no sign of the anorak. A pity—since it's the only piece of evidence. Apart from the body. Or what's left of it. Strange, but I always knew it wasn't Sam. The girl in the anorak. At first, the police tried to tell me this was a different girl from the one they'd seen on the river. They said they didn't see how the body could have traveled from where it was first seen by the goatherd to where it was found. It was an area they had only looked at superficially before, not long after the body was seen. But I reminded them that the river was in flood—and a body could have traveled twice that distance. I'm sure Sam is still out there. Alive somewhere. I can feel it, you know? There isn't an absence in the world where Sam is meant to be."

"Isn't it just as bad—not knowing where she is, or what's happening with her?"

"Perhaps she just needed some time away from us."

"But to leave you and Caroline to suffer like this? That doesn't sound like Sam."

"Maybe she just went to a place where she wouldn't be able to see the news—and where she could forget her old life completely."

"But where could she have gone?"

"Who knows? Namibia? Swaziland? Cape Town? Sam has always been different from Matthew. If Matthew goes off to sulk, you can always find him on the same rock, or sitting under the same tree. Sam never likes to do the same thing twice."

"So they're back to square one. About Sam, I mean."

"They never left square one. As you know, crimes are hardly ever solved in this country. Too many bodies. Not enough will to get to the truth."

Bruce is still wearing the same yellowish shirt he had on the previous day and Daniel can see that he didn't even attempt to sleep. Bruce is someone entirely lost. A man wandering around in a street in which a bomb has just gone off. The air around him is still ringing, and no one knows yet which is left or which is right, which is up or which is down—and no one has yet started to distinguish between the living and the dead.

Detective Dlamini's office smells of chicory and boiled eggs

His hands are pressed together, forming a rudimentary church. He is sitting back in his swivel chair and Daniel can see a stain of what might be mayonnaise below the pocket of his mint-green shirt. Dlamini is a disjointed, angular man who speaks in fits and starts, as if he has already said everything he is about to say and knows that it will be a disappointment.

"We have identified the girl," he says. "She was reported missing three years ago."

"Three years ago?" says Bruce, aghast.

The policeman looks across at Bruce and decides not to laugh. "Don't worry," he says, "we now know where she has been living. She was a high-class prostitute, working in Durban and sometimes Pietermaritzburg. When she was last seen, in early December, she was staying at your lodge."

"Are you being serious?"

"Very serious, I'm afraid. She came as the companion of a prominent businessman. He owns a logistics company. Randeria by name. When he saw her picture in the news this morning, he immediately came forward and confessed."

"To killing her?"

This time, Dlamini does laugh, but it is a sound entirely without humor. "He confessed to taking her to your lodge. He has a wife and children. He wants to keep the whole thing hush-hush, as you can imagine."

"I'm sure he does."

"We're still unclear about the cause of death. It seems the woman suffered a blow to the head and had a broken leg. But whether this happened before or after her death is unclear. The river could have done that after her death. It could have been the cause of death while she was in the water. Or she might have been killed and thrown in the river. It's impossible to tell. She'd been dead for several weeks."

"But was she definitely murdered? I mean—it can't have been suicide?"

"There was no sign of any water inside her lungs. Suicide is not impossible, but as this stage it looks unlikely."

Bruce looks at the detective squarely. "You have a body, but you have no clear idea about anything?"

"We have witnesses from when she was still alive. That is something we can begin to work with. Randeria says that he left the woman there at your lodge. He says she had found a new friend. The last time he saw her, she was sitting at Reception with your man, Moses. She was tapping messages into her phone."

Bruce sits back and glances across at Daniel. "And this new friend," he says. "Do you have any idea of who it was?"

"No idea. But Randeria argues quite convincingly that he was safely back home with the wife and kids by the time we believe the murder took place. Which means, I'm sorry to say, Mr. Webster, that we'll have to talk again to the staff at your lodge."

The river lies there like a great, wet snake

Bruce does not look at it as they drive home, but Daniel knows that they are both aware of it. They are close to the place where Sam's body was believed to have been seen—and then, as in some cruel conjurer's trick, replaced by the body of some other woman, a woman last seen at the Websters' lodge. As Bruce had said, it was quite a coincidence. Two young women both disappearing on what seems to have been the same night. But then this was a country in which thousands of children were trafficked every year. Of those who were officially trafficked, only one percent was ever found.

"Do you think Moses might be involved in any of this?" Daniel asks.

"Moses?"

"They say that the last person to see the victim alive must be the killer."

"He can't possibly have been the killer."

"Then what about Simon? I heard he has a history of violence."

Bruce gives a grunt of disapproval. "I suppose you've been talking to Caroline."

"No—not Caroline."

"Greene then?"

"Yes—Tim."

"Do you know that I fired that little bastard?" Bruce asks, suddenly violent.

"You fired Tim?"

"A couple of days before Sam disappeared. I said he had to pack his bags and go."

"Why did you do that?"

"Because I didn't trust him. He was after my family."

"You mean—he was after Caroline?"

"And Sam. Or Sam. Who knows?"

"You think he and Sam were—having a relationship?"

"Greene claimed to be in love with her. But the only person that bastard is capable of loving is himself."

"So why is he still here?"

"When I came home, Sam was gone, but he was still there. I didn't really think about it. He was just there—and since then I haven't done anything more to get rid of him. He even spent Christmas day with us, can you believe. And yes—I'm also still paying the bastard's salary. Even though he doesn't do much around the place. Just takes the occasional tour."

"What are you saying?" Daniel asks. "That Tim might be in some way responsible?"

"At the time, I told the police all about it, naturally. They questioned him and decided to let him go." Bruce slows as a crop of potholes comes into sight on the shining road ahead of them. "I don't believe Simon is capable of killing anyone. As for Greene—I have no idea. Maybe that woman just ran off and fell into the water. Or maybe she wanted to die. Maybe she wanted to drown herself but her head hit a rock before she could go under. Who knows? But she sounded a bit lost, don't you think? Maybe everyone is looking for a crime where no crime took place."

"And the dark-blue anorak?" Daniel asks. "It sounds like a man's anorak. It is strange that the woman was wearing only that."

"Perhaps," says Bruce, "but all that matters is that the woman wasn't Sam. Which means—we still have hope."

The next day, Daniel finds Tim sitting alone with his breakfast

Tim appears to eat only once a day, when he has the full English breakfast, his two fried eggs mashed into the toast and the hash browns criss-crossed with honey. He eats quickly and efficiently, getting every ingredient into every mouthful and leaving no uneaten food on his plate.

"I hear you're staying on," says Tim.

"News travels fast. Did Bruce tell you that?"

"No—Caroline."

Tim always says Caroline's name as if she belongs, in some way, to him. As if she is employed by him. Or indebted to him. Or has been rendered powerless before him. It is strange that Tim should mention this first—this awareness that Daniel has quit his job—rather than the fact that the dead woman was not Sam. The suggestion is that Daniel is being discussed by the two of them and that his staying on is, for some reason, significant. Is there something that they are afraid Daniel might discover? Some store of knowledge that the two of them are carrying that Bruce is not? Daniel can't begin to imagine what this might be. But he can feel it there, concealed somewhere in their vicinity, like a bag of snakes.

"I quit my job," Daniel says. "It was a bit dumb, I know."

"Sometimes life is too short."

"Exactly."

Daniel sits across from Tim and has a better look at him. Tim has the kind of face that is slightly different each time you encounter him. On some days, he is impossibly good-looking. On others, he is like a schoolboy who hasn't yet grown into his face. Today, his face is swollen with tiredness. Almost to the point of ugliness.

There is something about the way Tim moves that has drawn Daniel's attention before. It's not that he has an actual limp or any other identifiable disfigurement, but he carries inside his body what appears to be some internal injury, some Achilles heel. Yet he is also one of those people who treats himself with reverence. As if he has been set apart from the rest of humanity and belongs to some higher order of existence or intelligence. The air he breathes is rarer.

The food and drink he consumes are more considered and refined. Everything he does—the drying of his body, the combing of his hair, even the arrangement of a napkin across his lap—has a ritualistic, almost devotional quality. He seems moved by his own mortality. Moved by the transitory nature of his many wonderful attributes.

"Late night?" Daniel asks.

"Something like that."

"Were you with Jess?"

"Jessica?" Tim looks almost affronted. "No, I was with Caroline."

"Caroline?"

"Bruce went up to Joburg to see his girlfriend."

"Bruce has a girlfriend in Joburg?"

"It's actually cancer. But Caroline doesn't know that. She thinks the cancer is her husband's lover. And who knows—maybe it is."

Tim can see from Daniel's unchanged expression that he knows about the cancer.

"How did you know about Bruce's illness?" Daniel asks.

"He told me in a moment of weakness. Or a moment of drink. I was sworn to secrecy. Poor Caroline."

"Why poor Caroline?"

"She's always the person who never gets to know. About anything."

"Why do you think Bruce hasn't told her?"

"I suppose he thinks there's enough going on."

Since the woman's body was found, the police have been very present, interviewing the staff at the lodge, going through all the records and contacting previous guests. Several of the journalists have also returned. Along with Daniel's novelist friend, David. Daniel doesn't blame Bruce for wanting to disappear. Wherever it is he went.

"Do you still think that Sam is dead?" Daniel asks.

Tim doesn't look at him. "I have no idea of what to think," he says at last.

Daniel sees now that there are two love bites on Tim's throat. The kind of marks that might have been left by a teenage girl who doesn't yet know how to get her fill of the boy with whom she's making out. Tim notices the direction of his gaze, but he doesn't attempt to hide the marks and he doesn't say anything about them. Daniel understands then that Tim has never taken him seriously. Tim's kind never have. They only ever go by the brightness of the sword.

"Surely Caroline has a few secrets of her own?" Daniel asks.

At this, Tim laughs and finally looks at him. "Like what?" he says, a challenge in his gaze.

"Like—whatever's going on between you and her."

Tim's eyes are a blue that reflects nothing back at you. The color fades almost to white around the irises, as if the darkness burning through the pupils has scorched out the light. He laughs again—and returns to his neat arrangement of bacon and eggs.

"It isn't anything serious," he says.

"What isn't?"

"Whatever's going on between me and Caroline. The fact is—we're both as riddled with guilt and shame and all the rest of it as each other. Maybe we do what we do because we have nothing left to do. You know what I mean?"

"Not really."

"No—of course you don't."

"To be alive to a sunbird"

Daniel writes this phrase on the notepad supplied for his room, the gold outline of the lion-mountain stamped into the bottom of each page. Now that he has nothing left to do but write his butterfly-collector book, he finds inside himself a dead place where the urge to write is meant to be. He wonders where the impulse to write came from in the first place. "Impulse" isn't a bad word for it. The sense of an internal pulse beating back at life, defining a space for itself. Impulse, coming from "impulsis," "to strike against, to incite or to shock."

After his sister died, Daniel and his parents walked around like the ghosts of themselves, passing one another without touching. His father started to be away for work for longer periods. His mother never changed out of her pink toweling dressing gown, and only occasionally appeared in the kitchen to eat cheese and crackers or hang up the laundry, which she would leave outside for days, lost to the wind and the rain. Daniel wandered around the plot trying to shoot the mousebirds from the peach trees with his pellet gun. Once, he carved a bamboo flute that never quite worked. He would also sit in the shade of the willow tree and wait for the rinkhals to reappear. It never did. At the end of that year, his father said that he would have to go to boarding school. His mother didn't put up a fight. Her fight had been to keep Lucy alive. Daniel only realized later that he was sent to boarding school so that his father could leave the house without having to leave his son still inside it.

Daniel ought to be "alive" to the malachite sunbird chittering outside his window, swaying on the crest of an ouehout bush. When he was at boarding school, the sight of a sunbird could make him happy for the rest of the day. He realizes only now that it was not the sunbird itself that was important. Nor was it the little leap it produced inside him. It was something that happened between himself and the sunbird. A call and a response to life. A tentative constellation between two separate entities that, in some way, came from the same source. He thinks of Shelley's skylark, that twittering spark, that last fragment from the Great Fire, ascending into the blue air—and then dropping as if, at the very height of life, its life has left it. He looks around inside himself for some remnant, some spark with which he might be able to work. The only thing he finds there is a woman's face. The face of Natasha Lopez. A pale moon. A lantern in the dark.

The sound of banging wakes him from his reverie and he finds David standing at his door, a bottle of cheap red wine held like a blunt instrument in one hand.

"There you are," David says. "I've been looking for you since breakfast."

"Oh yes? Come in."

They fill two glasses and find a place on the wooden deck. The sunbird is still there, but David does not notice it. Daniel remembers only now that David went to the same school that he did, although they never knew one another then. David is probably ten years older. But David thinks this makes them allies of some kind.

"I see you're pretty tight with all the prime suspects," David says.

"I am? And who are they?"

"That's the question, isn't it?" David laughs. "But it must be someone close to her, wouldn't you say?"

"I thought you were pursuing the land issue."

"I am. I even had a chat with an old induna called Mpanza. And your friend Moses."

"My friend?"

"I've seen you two talking."

"Only to pass the time. I haven't spoken to him or anyone else very much about the case. To be honest, I've been more concerned with my ancestor book."

"Are you saying that you still have no idea of who killed Sam Webster?"

"I'm not even sure she's dead."

As Daniel says these words, however, he knows that he does not believe them. Something very bad must have happened to Sam. Otherwise she would still be here. Like that sunbird. Every bit of it bursting with life. Shining amongst them. The green eye of summer.

THE GHOST OF SAM WEBSTER

Sam

She counts fifteen vultures in the air

They are climbing the thermals above the Buffalo River, carving contradictory circles in the washed-out air, disheveled and dark, endlessly patient, observing everything. There have always been vultures in this sky, waiting to see who would be the next to fall. Most people who passed through here treated them as if the birds were on the lookout for something that existed in some other hemisphere. But Sam has always known that their gaze includes her.

"One of Bruce's wildebeests is dead," Tim explains.

That morning—a Saturday morning—Tim fetched Sam from school in her father's Land Cruiser. He was sitting framed in the window exactly where her father usually sat, his linen shirt the same color as the sky, the sleeves rolled up to reveal his strong brown arms, copper bangles and colorfully beaded charity bracelets. Tim hadn't cut his hair, it seemed, since his arrival at the lodge. Now he looked like a surfer. Yet his completely unapologetic way of approaching the world made it clear that he was far from being a native of this place.

"Struck by lightning. On the other side of river," he continues. "Would you like to go and take a look?"

They are sitting in the glass balcony, drinking beer. Apparently, her father was too unwell to pick her and Matty up—so he sent Tim instead. Her father has never been too sick to pick them up. He has always been the very picture of health. In spite of his drinking and the fact that he barely exercised, he bypassed all coughs and colds and stomach bugs. He liked to joke that he distracted all viruses with whisky. So Sam suspects that there is some other reason for his absence. There is some other drama playing out. Most likely between her parents. Since their return an hour ago, she has seen no sign of either of them.

"Why would I want to go and look at a dead wildebeest?"

"I thought it might be interesting."

They turn to Matty, who is drinking Caroline's homemade lemonade some distance away and trying to outstare Sam's mountain. Matty is still wearing his tennis kit. He never gets out of his school clothes the second he gets home, as Sam does. Sam always feels the need to shower and change—and start the day again.

"We could take the horses," Tim suggests.

Sam sends Tim what is intended to be a neutral expression.

"Didn't you say there was a cave up there?" he asks. "Maybe we could camp for the night."

This is something Sam and Matty used to do with their father several years ago. They would cross the river into Zululand and ride up to the summit of the mountain across from the lodge. There they would sleep at the edge of the cave—with its view of iSandlwana, the velvet-black hills and the long swarm of stars, migrating from one universe to another across the sky.

"These days there are leopards," says Matty. "Dad says he's even seen their tracks. Right outside that cave."

"Leopards?" says Tim, glancing across at her, waiting for her to deny the absurdity of the claim. But it was true. The leopards had never entirely left these hills. In recent years, they had started to return and grow in confidence. Recently, a heavily pregnant female had been caught in the ghostly green light of a night camera on the grounds of the lodge, sauntering along a track Sam had walked a hundred times before.

"I'm only going if Matty comes," Sam says, giving the space between the two boys her best smile.

They cross the river not far from the coffin-shaped rock

This is the rock to which Melvill, Coghill and Higginson famously clung while trying to save the Queen's Colors—the flag of the Staffordshire Regiment that had been carried out of the battle and was lost in the river, only to be found again several days later, surprisingly intact. It was a story on which the historians always liked to linger. This last attempt to save a shred of regimental dignity in the wake of such an ignominious defeat. These days, however, the coffin-shaped rock was almost covered over with river sand and it looked like any other rock.

In an acacia above the greenish water, a battered-looking fish eagle watches their passing. A pied kingfisher hovers and dips and disappears into the moving water with a splash—emerging again and hovering further downriver before dropping down with another splash. Sam takes them across a stretch of water that is deeper and less rocky—the site of the famous whirlpool where several men, horses and cattle were drowned as they fled iSandlwana. She has crossed this river many times before and she knows its every intention. When they studied *Hamlet* at school, she imagined this very place for Ophelia's death. It could not have been further from the flowery green bower where Ophelia could no longer find the will to live, but Sam was a girl who lived in South Africa, and her imagination was shaped by this place. The closest she has ever come to the green, wet light of England is Tim Greene himself—currently riding, like his precursors, with wholly misplaced confidence into Zululand.

They find thirteen of the birds standing in the grass. This area was once the marsh where the right horn of the Zulu army surrounded some of the few surviving British soldiers and their horses and butchered them. The necks and trousers of the vultures are sticky with gore and the flattened area around the dead wildebeest is like another, darker shadow. The birds seem oblivious to the riders as they approach. They hop and skip around the carcass, dipping their heads into a dripping hole there, tearing away a ribbon of flesh there, their collusion and eagerness giving the scene the atmosphere of a ghoulish prank. A pair of jackals, their muzzles and paws marked with the same muck, stand and watch the approaching riders from a distance, their tongues hanging from the sides of their mouths, scarlet and spent. When the vultures finally see the horses, they squawk and shuffle, undignified as chickens—and then, one by one, they skip away from the wreck, their wings extended wide, beating against the dead weight in their bellies, until they are unfolded into pale angels capable of transcendent flight.

There are several pied crows stalking amongst the ruins of the dead animal. One squats on a curved horn, another wipes its beak against a hipbone, surrounded by an iridescent haze of flies. When the last of the vultures is gone, the crows relinquish their posts, flapping not far above the shapes of the horses in order to arrange themselves on the bones of a dead willow—another victim of a lightning blast.

Sam looks across at Matty and sees that he's regarding her with a blanched, yearning expression. He's always been more fearful of the workings of the world than she has—and from places that, before Matty had looked into them, had never struck her as particularly frightening at all.

"They're huge," says Tim, standing in his stirrups in his usual way and watching the last of the vultures depart.

"Yeah," says Sam, "they're always bigger up close than you'd think."

The rest of the wildebeest herd is grazing nearby. They appear to have forgotten about their companion—an old male that once dominated this doleful herd. Sam and Matty have always known this wildebeest. They had even come up with a name for him.

"It's Woodstock," Sam says.

"Poor Woodstock," Matty says.

"At least he died before he knew what had hit him."

"Yeah, it can't have been too painful."

They stare down at the once proud and glossy body, now the picking place for thieves, and they share an ancient, knowing look—the look of two siblings who have grown up under the same skies and somehow endured.

They approach the lion-mountain in the shadow of its gaze

As they approach, the whitewashed cairns begin to accumulate. They ride into the series of dongas through which the remnants of the British army fled. In one section, they have to dismount because the passage is too narrow and overgrown for a mounted rider to pass. When they ascend the rocky path that leads to the base of the mountain, they see that the summit is teeming with visitors, their voices clearly audible as they shriek and laugh and take selfies—as if they are the first people to discover this place.

Sam shows Tim a cairn where the bones and the teeth of the dead are spilling out of the arrangement of earth and rocks. Sam says that her father usually comes here to cover the dead whenever they are exposed like this, but in recent months he hasn't been himself.

"Perhaps it's the drink," she says. "Perhaps his liver is finally giving up."

But she doesn't believe this. The light has simply gone out of him, that's all. He has run out of words. Or the energy required to mobilize the words. This place has claimed even her father, after all. It has drained the life out of him. Just as it drains the life out of everything.

They pass through the main gates to the iSandlwana battle site and ascend through the first homesteads and past the museum and the stone church. The people smile and wave at Sam and Matty. They know the children of old Isicabu well. For a while, a crocodile of children follows them, dancing and chattering, asking for sweets. An old woman who is digging up the earth in front of her homestead stops and watches them pass, arms akimbo, looking like every other old woman in that place whose name Sam will never know.

Leaving the valley behind them, they pass a whitewashed circle of Shembe stones and some recently constructed school buildings, and they continue along the Nyoni Ridge toward the Ngwebeni River. It was around here that Lieutenant Charlie Raw and his men were following a group of herders and their cattle up a gorge when they came across about forty thousand Zulus—twenty-five thousand fighting soldiers, and the women and children who were accompanying them. The Zulu army was so large that their passing flattened the grass—and it was still flattened six months later when the British re-entered Zululand to begin their second and final assault.

As Bruce liked to narrate it, the Zulus were crouched in neat lines behind a ridge when they were first discovered, humming like bees, waiting for "the day of the dead moon" to pass. For the Zulus, the movements of the planets and the stars were connected to the attitude of their ancestral spirits. An eclipse, like an earthquake, foretold great calamity. The army was delaying its advance for one more day. But the chance discovery of their position meant there was nothing left for them to do but to rise up and attack.

Sam has learned from her father how to read the lines of this landscape like a fortune teller, tracing the different pathways from their source and to their fate. This is the lifeline, this the deathline. Here there was the victory, here the defeat. As she and Tim descend into the trough where the Zulus were hidden—Matty riding a skeptical distance behind them—Sam points out the lines of retreat and attack, hoping to distract them from that other line that is growing up between them, that crooked love line that is finding its way across the earth like floodwater.

Sam doesn't understand what it is about Tim Greene that renders her so defenseless. She has always prided herself on being like her mountain. A fortress of rock, its internal echoing places little more than a source of speculation. Initially, when she had allowed her official boyfriend Tom some access to her inner life, he had moved from cave to cave like an explorer handed a lamp and given a special pass into some antique tomb. Here was a room filled with green summer light and birdsong. There was a cave of stars revolving like a mirrorball, while human shadows danced around a naked flame. But there were whole parts of her that Tom had never seen. Whole parts of her that had lain in the dark until Tim came along—like some explorer from an antique land.

As for Tim, what is surprising is that there's nothing about him that seems intent on seducing her. He carries this assumption that everything that needs to be understood between them has been understood already—and that nothing further needs to be said. She can tell from Matty's silence that he knows all of this and hates Tim for it. Matty is riding behind them so silently, and so potently, that sometimes Sam has to look back at him to make sure that it is really Matty sitting there, and not Tom.

"This is where the battle began," she says to Tim.

Tim looks around at the scene of the crime. There's no evidence of any army. Only a small bird standing on a nearby rock, shrieking at their arrival, glaring at them as it trills its orange-pink throat. Further off are more homesteads and some grazing cattle. And yes, above them are the vultures, still drawing their slow spirals inside the sky.

"That morning, Chelmsford had already left the camp with most of the army," she continues, "so the camp of iSandlwana lay more or less undefended. When the Zulus saw the British men on the hill, they all stood in unison and started their attack—and they didn't stop until every man left in the camp of iSandlwana was dead."

Sam has always despised that knack her father has of making himself appear heroic through narrating the heroic deeds of others, whether they were British or Zulu. But however ironic she tries to sound whenever she narrates this tale, she feels his presence running through her words like a current, a current so strong that it burns away what might remain of her own ideas about these events.

"Let's go down," Tim says, riding forward. "I want to stand where the Zulu army stood."

She lets him ride on and waits for Matty to catch up.

"I can see what's happening," Matty says. There are fresh tears in his eyes, making them look like blue marbles seen through ice.

"I don't know why you have to care so much," she says.

"I care because you're destroying everything."

"Oh, for God's sake."

"I'm being serious." He glances across at Tim. "Don't you see what he's doing? He's going to take everything from us. He's going to take everything—until there's nothing left."

Tim feeds more wood into the flames

All around them is the immense night. The horses snorting warmly from where they have been tethered. An eagle-owl sobbing from a nearby stinkwood tree. A thousand reed frogs squeaking from the river below. The low cloud moving fast, only sometimes separating to reveal that other realm, where the stars are revolving silently. Matty is sitting at the edge of the cave in his school trench coat. He has hardly said a word since they arrived and set up camp. In Sam's experience, he can go mute like this for days. Often, it doesn't mean anything. But tonight it means everything.

She has always taken special care of her brother. She also knows that he has always loved her the best—with that clear-eyed gaze of his, inquisitive and animated, always looking for the angle from which to laugh. They have laughed together as she has never laughed with anyone else. She has also told him each of her secrets. She has told him about every boy she has ever liked and what has happened with every boy she has ever liked. She has come to him with every important problem, knowing that his solution will always be cleaner and quicker than any adult perspective. Adults saw the world as if through one of those cataracts over an old eye, clouded with useless knowledge and disappointment. In the eyes of her friends, including Jess, Sam has always been the winner. Only Matty knows the true list of her gains and losses.

But she is powerless to stop this thing between herself and Tim. It is impossible to know what gives Tim his special quality. If you were to break down the parts of him, you would find each one entirely human. Yet there is some grand design in the arrangement of his parts that might have come from the sketchbook of some Renaissance artist.

"I'm going to bed," Matty says eventually.

He has been behaving badly all night and she and Tim have

pretended not to notice. Sam knows how unfair this is. It is she who is in the wrong, yet Matty is the one taking the blame. It is another one of the ways he has of showing her that he loves her. And that she is not deserving of such a love. At least—not as long as she continues on this slow suicide mission with Tim.

"Okay," she says. "Goodnight."

It is a final act of betrayal, this declaration that she will not withdraw, that she will remain here at the flames with this demon, this strange god who still walks around in the innocuous form of a boy.

"Goodnight," says Tim.

But Matty doesn't answer him. Out in the dark, one of the horses nickers and stamps. Tim throws more wood into the flames.

"What's the worst thing you've ever done?" she asks him when Matty is gone.

He looks across at her without smiling. "This."

"And the best?"

"This."

Caroline

She hates her husband

She especially hates the sound of his voice. That newly acquired Britishness that he cultivated in England while he was failing to complete his degree. She had been acquainted with him only passingly before he left for England. They had been at the same two schools that Sam and Matthew now attended. Caroline would see her future husband at socials, where he appeared with a lumpy tie and distracted hair, speaking with a loudness that people only adopt when they don't expect to be taken seriously. All she knew about him in those days was that he lived "deep in Zululand" and that he could speak isiZulu "like a native"—although no one seemed to have asked an actual "native" how true this was. She and Bruce also crossed paths on the polocrosse field and at the Royal Show, where they would exchange a disinterested nod from the relative perspectives of their horses. Bruce always looked better on a horse than he ever did on the ground—like Napoleon.

By the time Bruce returned from England, he had acquired that new accent—but he had also learned to speak in a way that made people take him seriously. He sounded like someone with something important to say. He was able to find his way into places through language in the very places where language usually failed. He wasn't a buffoon, after all. He was a poet, a web-weaver, an unlikely magician. She and Bruce met once again at the farm of a mutual friend and went for a walk around a muddy lake and within the year they were married. All their friends from school were at the wedding, which took place in Caroline's old school chapel. It seemed to everyone that it was all an elaborate joke—right up to the final "I do." Then the laughter subsided and she found herself alone with a man she barely knew. But in her experience there was nothing that a firm hand and a good riding crop could not fix.

From the start, they lived on the family "farm" at iSandlwana. By then, Bruce's father was dead from liver cancer and his mother was in a retirement home in Howick. Bruce was already establishing himself as a raconteur. A word that Caroline never managed to get to grips with. Which was perhaps the point of it. Bruce's new angle on the Anglo-Zulu War was that he would tell the tale from the Zulu perspective, which Caroline soon realized was simply another version of the Bruce Webster perspective. He was ridiculous, the way he stood on every available anthill and waved his knobkerrie about. But this was exactly what his clients expected. Especially the British ones—who had come all the way to this mound of rocks in the middle of nowhere to find a place that they could finally call indisputably British.

While Caroline was making these discoveries about her husband, she was also making some even worse discoveries about herself. Behind all her efficiency and drive, she found a little drubbing thump of what she came to recognize as fear. Whenever she sat still for too long, she could hear its insistent drum. Whatever she did, she could not get away from it. So she did her best to keep busy. She refurbished every interior space inside the lodge. She redesigned the gardens along the wooden walkways. She hired and fired long lines of kitchen and domestic staff. She distracted herself with a wide range of recipes and an even wider range of wines. And yes, she produced two children, to whom she tried to teach everything she knew. Which turned out to be surprisingly little. But that small heartbeat kept skipping along inside her, absorbing the poison in the world and feeding it back into her blood. It took her twenty years to realize that since the day she had been married to Bruce Webster she had been depressed.

"Moses knows"

"Sorry—what?"

Caroline can't explain how she has come to understand this, but she knows from the hardness in Moses's voice and the deflection of his gaze that—at least from where Moses is standing—she has become too degrading to look at.

Tim Greene merely laughs at this. "So what if he knows?"

"He could ruin everything."

"By doing what? By telling Bruce?"

Tim sits up on an elbow and leans over and kisses her neck. The morning light has stretched itself across her bed. As if arranged there just for him.

"You don't understand," she says.

"What don't I understand?"

"To a traditional man like Moses, a cheating wife is a piece of rubbish that deserves death. That's what started the Anglo-Zulu War in the first place. A Zulu chief sending his two sons to invade Natal in order to track down the two wives who had betrayed him."

"You aren't married to Moses. You're married to Bruce."

"Believe me—I'm married to more than Bruce."

Instead of answering, Tim pushes her over and climbs on top of her and slides himself back into her. She lets out an involuntary gasp and he laughs appreciatively. Is this his way of leaving her? Is this his way of saying goodbye? She wonders this every time this happens. Yet it continues to happen. Once or twice a week. Since the moment of his arrival at the lodge, they have been meeting in his drummer-boy room or in her room if Bruce is away for the night. They only ever make love in the middle of the week. Maybe because they are trying to get as far away from the weekends as possible. It isn't Sam that Caroline feels bad about, but Matthew—and for reasons that she has not even tried to understand.

"Why are we doing this?" she asks, perhaps for the tenth time.

"Because it's fun."

"Fun? That's ridiculous. You should get yourself an actual girlfriend."

"That's the last thing I want. All those text messages in the middle of the night you're expected to answer. All those promises you're expected to remember—and keep."

"You could have chosen a younger married woman."

"She'd only want to leave her husband and marry me. I'd spend the rest of my adult life being hated by her children. Now, for once, can't you stop talking so we can get on with this?"

She hears the click of claws on the screeded concrete at the open door. There she finds the face of Jane, watching her. Jane, who usually moves silently through the world, emits a low growl. Everything Jane does is specific and deliberate. The previous autumn, she had waited until all the apples were ripe in the apple tree outside the kitchen and then she had climbed right inside the tree and eaten every apple within reach.

"Hurry up," Caroline says.

"What?"

"I think there's someone outside."

"The dog just hates me—that's all."

Caroline looks again toward Jane and finds her gone. Her growl comes from the kitchen a moment later. It is the particular sound she only ever makes when there is someone unwanted outside the kitchen door.

"I have to go."

She withdraws from him and pulls on her dressing gown, which is patterned with scarlet poinsettias. A fitting garment for a scarlet woman.

"Caroline—bloody hell!"

Bluebell, Sam's cat, is sitting at the kitchen window, peering out as she might at a dove or an approaching car. Jane is still grumbling at the crack under the kitchen door.

Outside, Caroline can see some indunas standing amongst the olive trees. Mpanza, the oldest and most senior of them, is staring directly at her—as if he already knows that she is alone in the house with her young lover and the timing of his appearance is intended as a kind of statement.

"Ngiyaxolisa," she says through the window, "kodwa umyeni wami akekho okwamanje."

It is rude to speak to him like this—half dressed, through the window and without the usual formal exchange of greetings—but she feels she is being ambushed and shamed, and rudeness is her only available form of defense.

Mpanza is what Bruce calls "a troublemaker." He lives on the neighboring farm and is at least ninety years old. He is an uncle to Moses, apparently, and is said to be related to a chief who was especially honored at iSandlwana—just as every properly posh American sailed to the New World in the *Fortune* or the *Mayflower*.

"Singalinda," the old man says.

"I'm not sure when he'll be back. It may be tomorrow."

"Sizolinda," the old man says—this time for the benefit of his men.

The other indunas nod and start picking up the stones that line the edge of her flowerbed. For an awful moment, Caroline imagines they are about to throw the rocks through the window, so premeditated the collective movement seems. But then she sees that they are only arranging the rocks in a neat circle in the sun. One of the indunas finds an old tin bucket for Mpanza to sit on and Mpanza takes his seat as if he has done this demonstration of waiting a thousand times before. Usually, Moses would be part of a gathering like this, but today—out of some delicacy, or for the sake of his job—he has decided to stay away.

"What do they want?"

Tim has appeared wearing nothing but a white towel around his hips—and his rainbow-colored beads. As he enters, he throws two red-and-green painkillers into his mouth and swallows them like Smarties, without water. After sex, he often has a sudden and extreme headache. He also prefers to use the children's shower instead of Bruce's. An act of fastidiousness that strikes Caroline as rather too little, rather too late.

"They want our land."

"I beg your pardon?"

"They have made another appeal to the court and I suppose they're here to negotiate. Apparently, when Bruce's father first bought the land, one or two homesteads were moved to the neighboring farm—although the story at the time was that the people were moving out of their own volition to be closer to their place of work. Now they're saying that they were forcibly removed. Of course, Bruce's father is no longer around to dispute this. As old Mpanza very well knows."

"But Bruce's father bought the land, fair and square?"

"It's a lot more complicated than that."

Tim pours himself some lukewarm coffee. Outside, the men are sitting close together and one of them is rolling a cigarette out of newspaper and tobacco. Two citrus swallowtails circle their heads, providing a kind of halo, a kind of blessing. For some reason,

Caroline feels like an imposter inside her own house.

"What are they going to do?" asks Tim. "Sit there all day?"

"They have been waiting for a hundred and fifty years," Caroline says. "What's another afternoon?"

Bruce

Sam's school always brings back the indignity of his childhood

He remembers the boy he was and wishes he could go back in time and repair his actions, his relationships, his most important ideas about himself and others. While he was still at school, he thought it was better to be the class clown than it was to be invisible. He discovered that if you made enough jokes, people would eventually learn to laugh at them. But Bruce never felt particularly amusing. As soon as he was left alone, he would sink into a restless misery that could only be alleviated by more jokes, more clowning. And whenever he was faced with girls, his jokes fell flat. He found that he didn't have the confidence to pull off his usual persona—and so became a shambling fool instead, either too sentimental or too cynical for any girl's liking. For Bruce, growing up was a prolonged obstacle course set up in the wrong direction.

Only recently did he realize that his need to aggrandize his family home with sweeping historical narratives was no more than an extension of his clowning. He had returned from university in England one credit short of attaining his degree, but with a new acquisition: the gift of talking. He was still a shambling fool, but he knew what his listeners needed in order to feel better about themselves. That's because he needed the same thing. People wanted to experience the illusion of order, the illusion of significance. In the world Bruce learned to conjure up for his guests, there was such a thing as heroic action, as a moral universe. There was still room for patriotism.

For several years, he came to believe in his own stories. He needed to believe in them in order to be convincing. The height of his new-found celebrity came when the Prince of Wales stayed at the lodge. He occupied the Lord Chelmsford Room and was photographed walking across the iSandlwana battlefield with Sam perched on his broad, tweed shoulders. Only then did Bruce come to accept that perhaps he might actually have accomplished something. When the Prince returned to where he belonged, Sam, who was about four at the time, famously asked:

"Dada, why is the Prince only the Prince of Whales? Why isn't he also the Prince of dolphins and sharks and all the other fish?"

"Because whales are the biggest of all the fish," Bruce replied, "and therefore the most important."

After that, several other celebrities came to visit the lodge. There was the middle-aged American actor whose cookie-cutter face had appeared on every movie screen around the world. There was the owner of a multinational company whose branding had been emblazoned across record shops, gyms and every international airport. There was that religious leader who had won the Nobel Peace Prize and whose sayings were constantly being reiterated at political rallies and in schoolboy speeches. These men—for men they all were—wanted to test themselves against the songlines that storytellers such as Bruce had woven across this landscape. They wanted Bruce to cast them in the roles they imagined might have been assigned for them. Dashing soldiers. Charismatic leaders. Sources of enlightenment and wisdom. The bulk of these men arrived in the wake of the Prince of Wales like over-indulged children, staying in the Lord Chelmsford Room and expecting to be treated like princes. They left with little idea of how banal and commonplace the Battle of iSandlwana really was. It was merely another site of mass slaughter that had taken place, and was still taking place, around the world.

Bruce often wondered whether he might have found a happier ending to his story had he married differently. Had he wedded a companion who could think of him as highly as he tried to think of himself. But Caroline was never quite up to that task. Getting married here, in this school chapel, on the site of his childhood humiliation—that had been his second mistake. The first was choosing Caroline. He woke up one morning not long after his marriage only to realize that—to his wife at least—all his actions were ridiculous. He was ridiculous. The class clown had finally been exposed for the stuffed man that he really was.

He and Caroline have been summoned to Dr. Lopez's classroom

It is a large room tucked away at the back of the school with high sash windows and Japanese maples crowding to get in. On the walls are large images of "women writers who resisted convention" as well as other canonized writers and prescribed novels—including the cover of young Hawthorne's novel, which has been composed as an allegory of ghostly trees and suffocating mist.

"So what's the problem?" Caroline asks as soon as they are seated in front of the teacher.

Bruce is accustomed to Caroline's manner, which comes across as rudeness but is merely an old awkwardness—but he can see from the slight hardening of Dr. Lopez's smile that Dr. Lopez is not. He wonders briefly what it might be like to return to school as an adult, as Dr. Lopez has, and to feed all your remaining energy into the idealism of the next generation—as if your own life is not maimed and shamed and exhausted.

"Oh, there isn't a problem, as such," says the teacher, "but I was sitting down with each of the girls to talk through their university choices for next year, and—"

"And?"

"And I was surprised to hear that Sam has no intentions of going to university."

Bruce can feel Caroline looking across at him, but he does not return her gaze.

"Where is she planning to go instead?" asks Caroline with a stab at humor.

"She said she was going to live in England."

"England?"

Caroline attempts another glance in his direction.

"But she doesn't have a British passport," Bruce says, feeling the need to be obtuse.

Dr. Lopez is watching them, her eyes so glossy and dark that there is not much distinction between the pupil and the iris. "She told me that her boyfriend has a British passport."

"Tom?" says Caroline. "Believe me, Tom is very much a South African."

"I think she said his name was Tim—not Tom."

"Tim?" says Bruce.

"You must be mistaken," Caroline says, flushing. "Her boyfriend's name is most definitely Tom."

Usually, Caroline walks one step behind him

But now she wants to get away—and back to the car so that she can yell at him. Bruce has obviously known from day one that Caroline has developed one of her infatuations with Tim Greene. It's not the first time this has happened and it probably won't be the last. Her infatuations have been tolerated by everyone exactly as Caroline's drinking has. But to behave like that, in front of Sam's teacher, at Sam's school—that was two steps too far.

"Do you really think she intends to marry him?" Caroline asks as soon as they're inside the safety of the car.

"I have absolutely no idea."

"How else does she plan on living in England?"

"Again—I have no idea."

"Well thank you at last for your honesty, Bruce."

"Caroline, really—"

"Clearly that Lopez woman has made a mistake. Tim—Tom. The names are practically interchangeable."

"But the two boys are rather different."

"It's completely ridiculous. And this idea of not going to university—"

"When Sam comes home this weekend, we will ask her about all of it."

"Don't worry. I will most certainly be asking Sam about all of it. The bitch."

"For God's sake, Caroline. Can't you get a grip?"

By now, Bruce has reversed the car and is waving cheerily as they pass the uniformed guard at the raised wooden boom.

"Aren't you even the least bit concerned?" Caroline asks.

"Of course I'm concerned. It's clear that Sam has to go to university. Even if she takes a gap year to think about it."

"And what about Tim? What about that?"

"Don't worry about Tim," Bruce says. "I'll tell the little bastard that if he lays a hand on her, I'll get him arrested for statutory rape."

They arrive home to a wall of thorns

Branches from some of the acacia trees at the bottom of the driveway have been broken off and arranged thickly across the gravel road—

within clear sight of their house. Bruce retrieves the loaded pistol from under his seat and climbs out of the car. He can feel something watching him, but perhaps this is only his own fear reflected back at him.

A piece of paper has been struck through one of the thorns and it is flapping there like a wish, or a prayer. Bruce pulls it off and sees that it is a piece of Webster Lodge stationery. A sheet from one of the notepads, emblazoned with the golden lion-mountain. The paper has been left entirely blank, but the lion has been stuck through at its heart.

Bruce knows what this means. A year ago, a wall of thorns was built across the driveway of a neighboring farmer who had a long-standing land claim against him. Three days later, the farmer was shot in the back of the head, and the wife hacked to death with a panga—the implement traditionally used to cut down sugarcane.

"What is going on?" asks Caroline.

She has emerged from the car and is standing next to him.

"It's a message from Mpanza," says Bruce.

He hands her the blank page and she looks at it.

"But it doesn't say anything."

"Believe me, it says everything that needs to be said."

He gets back into the car and drives up the rocky bank and around the wall of thorns toward the house, leaving Caroline standing in the sunlight, the white note still shining in her hand.

Later that afternoon, he finds Moses standing
at the barrier of thorns

The older man seems hesitant to pass beyond that point—and he is looking uncomfortable, even resentful, as if he has been tasked with standing there against his will. If he passes that point, does he fear that it will be perceived as a show of allegiance toward the

Websters? Or is there some spell at work, some piece of witchcraft of which Bruce is not aware?

"What do you know about all this?" Bruce asks as soon as the other man is within hearing. The question has come out as an accusation, and immediately Moses seems affronted—whether out of the lack of ceremony or wounded innocence is unclear.

"Uzokwenzenjani?" Moses asks instead.

"I am going to do nothing," says Bruce.

"Laba bantu ngeke bahambe."

"And I am not going away either."

"Bazobuya! Lababantu banodlame."

"Well, I have a gun to defend myself."

Bruce is too annoyed to speak isiZulu. Moses will find this insulting, but that is Bruce's intention. He is suggesting that he will not enter into dialog with Moses on this or any related subject.

"I am happy to speak with Mpanza and his men," Bruce says, relenting slightly, "about giving them more land for their cattle to graze, but I'm not prepared to hand over the land for nothing, and I'm not prepared to rent it to them so they can overgraze it with their goats. I'm trying to protect the wildlife here."

"They say your wild animals are making all their cattle blind."

"Then they're welcome to move their cattle somewhere else," says Bruce. "I would have preferred not to have had them here in the first place."

"They say this is their land and their home. This is where their cattle belong."

"Well that there is my home," says Bruce, pointing up at the glass box on the hill. "That is where I live. And that is where me and my family belong. I will not be intimidated by these underhand threats. If your friends have something to say, they must come and say it directly to my face."

Moses shakes his head, looking very tired. "I'm not here as a messenger," he says.

"Then what are you here for?"

Moses appears to think about this—more generally than Bruce intended.

"I'm here to tell you that you need to make peace with these men," he says. "Because this here—it is only the start."

"Listen to me," says Bruce, deciding to treat Moses as a messenger whether he likes it or not. "They know the procedure. If they want to follow up their claims, they must do it through the courts. The government makes the policies, not me. If their claims are valid, they will receive whatever compensation the government deems fit."

"They do not respect you enough for that," Moses says—or half mutters bitterly as he turns away.

"What are you—?"

There is something in Moses's gaze that silences him.

"They are talking," Moses says.

"Who is talking?"

"Isicabu, they are talking about you. And they are talking about your wife."

Bruce feels a rage rising up inside him. He does not yet know where it comes from or what it might be directed against, but it comes so readily and so thickly that for a moment he can't speak. "What are they saying about me and my wife?"

"They are saying that she is no longer your wife."

"I beg your pardon?"

"They are saying that these days she belongs to someone else."

Sam

Matty finds the dead kitten inside the circle of stones

Her throat has been cut and she is lying in a pool that looks too large and dark to have come from her. There are already dozens of spidery-gray ants crawling in and out of her velvety black ears, pausing at the pink tip of her tongue, climbing over the scar where, a few months earlier, she was spayed.

"Sam!" Matty shouts.

When Sam first got Bluebell, she knew the little creature had been here before. She seemed so happy to be back in the world, exactly as she had left it. She arrived so self-sufficient and discreet, already knowing how to feed herself, clean herself and bury her own waste. She was especially proud of her long black legs and her long black tail, which waved about like a sensor tracking the movement of the planets. She had a round, fluffy mask of a face that put Sam in mind of a racoon. Even though she didn't know what an actual racoon looked like.

Bluebell loved having her rabbit-fur tummy scratched. As soon as Sam was up in the morning, she would be there, weaving and purring between her legs, her bottlebrush tail flared. She would alight on the kitchen table without a sound and watch Sam make her morning tea. The kitten's appetite was limitless—not only for food, but for every electric stirring of the world, which she would immediately have to seek out and investigate.

At eight months, Caroline had Bluebell spayed. Her pale-pink stomach became the site of a gash fed on by a dozen green nylon spiders. Apparently, her ovaries had been so far back inside her body that the vet had to cut and dig deeper than usual to find them. Sam knew her kitten's body was not ready to relinquish her eggs, even though the kitten herself knew nothing about them.

"Sam!"

Sam emerges from the kitchen, still wearing her clothes from school. Already she knows something terrible has happened, but she is not prepared for this. Bluebell is lying there, entirely still, her monkey-spirit long-lost to her. Her paws are soft and untested, powdered with dust from when she last walked, and her whiskers are slightly crinkled as if in memory of the confines of the womb. Her throat has been cut by a hand accustomed to slaughtering chickens without a moment of thought.

"I'm sorry," Matty says, as if this is something he has done.

Sam bends down and brushes away an ant that has paused at the firmly closed eye. "What should we do?" she asks.

"Bury her," is all Matty says.

"The bastards!"

Her father says this a few minutes later. The family of four is standing inside the circle of stones, the dead kitten lying where a sacrificial fire ought to be.

"What kind of a monster would do a thing like this?"

"Calm down," her mother says. "There's no point in yelling about it."

The scene feels more like a reflection on them, for some reason, than it is on the person or people who did this. Recently, there has been an air of crisis in their family that Sam can't understand. A week ago, her parents cross-examined her about her relations with Tim and—obviously—she denied everything. She told them that she already had a perfectly good boyfriend in Tom. Obviously she was planning on going to university next year. She merely said all that about going to England with her new boyfriend to get Dr. Lopez off her back. But there is more than only this going on. They feel like strangers, the four of them standing there. As though each of them is carrying their own private source of shame.

"We need to bury her," Matty says again, as if by burying the cat the rest of the family's secrets might be concealed forever.

Sam has an old silk dressing gown, patterned with lemon-yellow spots, that has been torn where the cord is attached. While Matty digs a hole in the shade of an olive tree, she places Bluebell on the robe and brushes off the ants and flicks them away from the dried gash at her throat. There are a few shiny green flies circling the body too, their senses quickened by the smell of death. Sam folds the dressing gown over and around the cat before any more insects can get at her. She wonders how long it will take for the silk to rot.

She has seen death many times before. Once, she saw a woman who had just been stabbed by another woman because the first woman had slept with the second woman's husband. She still remembers the familiar red-handled knife that was last seen cutting carrots and was now sticking out of the woman's chest. Sam also remembers the look of surprise on the dead woman's face—and was surprised herself that such an expression could outlast the body that had contained it. On another occasion, Sam saw a man on a motorbike being hit by an oncoming truck. When he landed on the grass just ahead of where her father's car had stopped, half his head was missing and she saw the pale bulge of the man's brain. It had the color and wetness of chewing gum.

Sam has also been present at the death of animals. She held her old sheepdog, Tess, when the vet injected her—and she felt the body release and lighten as the spirit went out of her. On one occasion, she saw a horse with a broken leg being shot. She has also seen several animals killed at the hand of her father, both wild and domestic. But this death feels totally different. A targeted act of hate. Administered efficiently. "We know where your heart lies," the killer is saying, and saying it directly to Sam. "And we will stamp on it and stamp on it and grind it into the dust."

By the time the hole has been dug, her father has gone back inside the house and her mother has drifted away toward the stables like a sleepwalker, a large goblet of frosted white wine aloft in one hand. Matty glances across at Sam. He looks like he is about to be sick.

"I don't know why you're blaming Dad," he says, still panting from the effort of digging.

"Who says I'm blaming Dad?"

"I saw the way you looked at him."

"I don't know why he can't treat people with more respect."

"Do you call this respect?"

"No," says Sam, "but he's the one who started it."

Tim is there by the time they bury the dead cat

He heard the news from Sam's mother—who, it would seem, never misses a chance to message him. They consider the bundle of dressing gown in its hole. It is round and speckled like an Easter egg. Sam remembers that she bought the dressing gown on a trip to London a long time ago. When her mother was another mother and she was another girl.

"Have you called the police?" Tim asks.

This is something no one—including Sam—has thought about.

"What would be the point of that?"

"They can go and confront the people who did this."

"The people who did this would only deny it."

"They should know there are consequences to their actions."

"They want there to be consequences to their actions. That's exactly why they did it."

Sam looks up at the sky and sees that another storm is coming in across the hills. The wind is warm and smells of horse. The first clouds are already filtering across the sun. "Will you take me away?" she says, turning to Tim.

"What's that?"

"Tonight. Can you take me away somewhere?"

"Where would you like to go?"

"Anywhere I've never been before."

"All right."

She knows that there is some weird pact between her mother and Tim. This idea was confirmed for Sam when her mother kept trying to question her after the meeting with Dr. Lopez. No doubt, her mother has done some dreadful thing to embarrass herself, and Sam can see that Tim has been doing his best to appear tactful, even if he can't help speaking to her mother with a rough kindness that sounds completely fake.

Now Matty walks across the shadow of the two of them and kneels before the pile of damper earth. Without consulting anyone, he starts to push the earth back into the hole.

"Goodbye, Bluebell," he says.

A pink earthworm becomes visible and instantly starts squirming away from the light. Then it too is consumed by the landslide. When Matty is finished, he pats the mound as you might a dog, to comfort it.

Sam is wearing Tim's dark-blue anorak

It still has its "special offer" tag attached to the collar from when he bought it at Heathrow. When she puts her hand in one of the pockets, she finds a boarding pass and a pair of cheap earphones. "Did you steal these from the airplane?" she asks with a dry laugh.

"What?"

"These earphones."

He looks at them as if he has never seen them before.

"I suppose I must have. You can have them, if you like."

She throws the earphones into her father's cubbyhole and folds the boarding pass into a tube so that it resembles a joint. "Do we have anything to smoke?"

"We can easily organize something."

Tim is driving her father's fawn-colored Land Cruiser and holding a bright-green lighter, which he now uses to light a cigarette. He is driving the car as if he has killed off her father and taken possession of his car—and the rest of his possessions—his daughter included.

"What are you really doing here?" she asks.

"What do you mean?"

"Of all the places you could have come, why did you choose this place?"

"Actually, I chose it because of you," he says, exhaling his first cloud of smoke.

"Seriously."

"I am being serious."

He slows at the exit of the lodge and the Land Cruiser clunks over the cattle grid. A guard holding an umbrella and a clipboard sends them a salute, perhaps thinking it is Bruce inside the car. The lion-mountain to their right is facing away from them and they continue in a wide circle around its haunches, only slowing for a stray yellow dog and some mottled Nguni cattle—and the eroded runnels that cross the badly rutted road.

"I was trolling through a whole lot of Facebook pages," Tim says, "and I saw your photograph. You were riding a horse."

"What are you even talking about?"

"There was a picture of you on the Webster Lodge Facebook page. I thought—wow, that's the most beautiful girl I've seen in my life."

"Oh come on—"

"The comments below said that you were Bruce Webster's daughter—Sam. I searched Sam Webster's Facebook page and there I found a picture of you sitting on the grass with a yellow hockey stick across your lap. 'That's the girl I'm going to marry,' I said to myself."

She looks at him and laughs. He's joking, of course. But he's doing it with unusual earnestness.

"And I came here," he continues, "and found you."

"You're silly," she says, taking the cigarette from his mouth, the butt still wet from his lips.

He takes her to a shebeen called Rosie's Place

It is a low, mud-brick building with a tin roof and dusty metal-framed windows covered by burglar bars and wire mesh. The name of the shebeen has been painted above the whitewashed entrance in uneven black letters, the paint of the "i" dripping all the way down to the lintel. There is an old eucalyptus tree standing over the building like a worn-down wishing bone. There are also a few old cars and taxis parked outside. The kinds of vehicles that have been patched up and repainted so many times that their origin, like their ownership, has become indeterminate, like Theseus's ship.

"Is this where we're going?" asks Sam, trying not to sound too nervous.

"This is where we're getting our dope," says Tim.

Exposed in the headlights is an assorted huddle of young men dressed in an urban Jozi style that looks out of place in this rural location. They stare blankly back at Bruce Webster's car until Tim extinguishes the lights—and then they return to their quarts and cigarettes.

"Fancy coming in for a drink?" Tim asks.

"Why not?"

There is only standing room inside the shebeen. The room smells of beer and working bodies and cannabis smoke. The bar has a zinc counter and the shelves where the drinks are displayed are made of pine boards unevenly mounted—as if by someone already drunk. At a long table, some men are playing Morabaraba. Most of the patrons are farmworkers or builders, blear-eyed and strangely fatalistic. When Tim and Sam enter the place, there is a change of temperature, a cooling off, as if they are from the police. But Tim looks around and smiles at everyone—and Sam smiles and looks at no one—and they are soon subsumed by the crowd. It is clear from the way Tim greets a few of the regulars and heads straight to the bar that he has been here before. Sam has no idea how many of these men know she is Bruce's daughter. Quite possibly, it is all of them.

There's no sign of Rosie at Rosie's Place and Sam has to look hard to see any women there. The room feels entirely male to her. It's like walking into a men's bathroom by mistake and encountering a row of urinals. But she finds that she feels safer with Tim, who orders their beers and finds the corner of a table for them as if his arrival was announced ahead of them.

"How many times have you been here before?" she asks after they have clinked the bases of their beer bottles. They are drinking quarts of Black Label, like most of the people in the room.

"I come here at least once a week."

"No!"

"Why not? The people are friendly and the beer is cheap."

Everything Tim says sounds like a joke, yet there is something about him that is deadly serious. He is so much more level than the boys she knows through school. There was a similar quality in Tom that had drawn her to him, but Tom was still very much a boy. For example, Tom had said to her a few weeks ago that he had never experienced prejudice before. Sam knew that this was untrue. Tom had been surrounded by prejudice, just like everyone else. He had simply lacked the insight to notice it. This suggested about him a stoppage of the imagination. Some limit to his empathy. Tom was the sweetest boy she had ever known, but sometimes she wondered whether he would one day become a very dull man. With Tim, you felt that he saw everything, understood everything, and that, whatever came his way, he would feel himself equal to it. Even if his life was at risk, he would be able to place himself in the right perspective, giving his life no more and no less importance than it deserved. It was why he was able to sit in a place like this and appear completely at home. Were anyone to come and challenge them, he would meet them with a confidence and a danger to match their own.

She removes the dark-blue anorak and hangs it on the back of her plastic chair. There's nothing in the pockets except for the bright-green cigarette lighter. As for the anorak, it's the property of Tim, so it gives off the air of something untouchable.

"My father would kill me if he saw me here."

"Would he?"

"Then he would kill you."

Tim laughs. "It's all good," he says generally, his meaning perhaps deliberately obtuse.

"Is it?" she says. "I sometimes wonder if there's any good in the world. I mean—even Bluebell could play with a half-dead lizard for a whole afternoon. It didn't seem to occur to her that the lizard might have been suffering."

"Maybe the cat and the lizard are just two sides to the same thing," Tim says.

Sam looks at him. "What is that supposed to mean?"

"Like those two black mambas you told me about. You know—maybe the cat and the lizard are just the same life form playing with itself. I sometimes think that God's like that. He's in everything, you know? Mirroring himself back at himself, or herself, so that everything's just the same thing. Good and evil are just—a matter of perspective."

"I didn't take you for a believer," Sam says.

"Believe me, I'm not. At least—not in the traditional sense. It's just that I'm not so sure we're even alive. Not in the way we think we are. Which is why we can't be dead. Not in the way we imagine it. We're just part of this other big thing with its own laws that govern us. And we can't even begin to access it."

One of the young men who was standing outside comes over and hands Tim a bank bag of cannabis. Nothing audible is said between them, and Sam is expecting the man to go away again when he greets her by name.

"Sam?"

Simon is wearing jeans and a sky-blue hoodie with rainbow colors wrapped around the right sleeve. Sam realizes then that he has been standing at the door, watching her since they first entered the place. She has been aware of his presence all along, but had decided not to look at his face.

"What are you doing here?" he asks.

"Having a drink," says Sam.

"Why don't you join us?" asks Tim.

Simon tried to kiss Sam once. At the stables when she was about twelve. Maybe thirteen. There were a lot of things at the time that made this feel too complicated—and she had rejected him. Since then, they have barely spoken. But she has always remained aware of his growing hostility. Like the news of a storm in a neighboring valley when above you the sky is still bright blue.

"I don't want to disturb you," Simon says, looking across at her with his usual woundedness.

"Please," says Sam, a bit over-enthusiastic, "we'd love for you to join us."

As Tim stuffs the bag of cannabis into the anorak pocket, which is still hanging from Sam's chair, Simon finds a place across from them. He too is drinking beer. Although his bottle is almost full.

"Aren't you supposed to be at university?" Sam asks.

"I'm done with exams," says Simon. "I'm just waiting for my results."

"Oh—right."

She knows that Simon has always hated the fact that her father pays all his expenses. She wonders whether he has ever shared this fact with his political friends back at varsity.

"Did you know what Simon is studying?" she asks Tim.

"Actually, I do," says Tim. "But he's the man who is more likely to blow up bridges than ever to build any."

There is a moment of stunned silence—and then Simon explodes with laughter. "That's exactly who I am," he says.

Caroline

She blames herself for the dead cat

She knows that the gash across its throat is intended, in some way, for her. The indunas are telling the old spider that he has a witch in his house. But does Bruce know that he has a witch in his house? And would he even care? Why else would he leave her here, alone and undefended? He is no doubt down at the lodge's bar, drinking himself into a stupor under the gaze of Moses, as he does whenever he finds Caroline too much to look at.

Perhaps the men who did this are trying to reduce her powers. Perhaps they want to tell her that she, who acts so freely, like one possessed of such power, has no freedom and no such power. They want her to know that she has been seen. Her shame has been witnessed. She only continues to exist because those with the power of life and death have decided, at least for a while, to permit it.

She can see that Sam blames Bruce for the dead cat. Both Sam and Bruce think this is about the land. The land that was stolen and has never been comfortably occupied by the thieves who live in their glass house like people with nothing left to hide. What neither Sam nor Bruce are asking, however, is why this message has come now. What have the Websters done recently that they have never done before? Caroline is the only person in this house who has been behaving differently. She is the only one who could have drawn the attention of the indunas. She with her white neck, soft as the neck of a small cat.

She pours herself another drink, barely bothering to splash in the tonic. She is sitting in the glass veranda, waiting for Sam and Tim to return. She understands exactly what Sam is up to. Sam who was given all the gifts that somehow bypassed Caroline. Confidence, grace, intelligence, beauty. A father's love. Sam has always taken exactly what she wanted and now she wants Tim.

Caroline hadn't been fooled when Sam denied her feelings for the boy. When she later spoke with Tim about it, he denied everything and she decided to believe him. It was more likely, she told herself, that Sam was only trying to torment Caroline. She wanted Caroline to think that she could take Tim with the same disregard with which she took everything else. As if nothing else was good enough for her and she was only passing through. How Caroline hated her right now. How she wanted her dead.

"Shit."

It is Tim's voice, coming from inside the house. In the blindness of her rage, Caroline hadn't noticed the headlights. But Tim won't have seen her either—sitting inside her wicker armchair in the dark.

"What is it?" Sam asks, sounding drunk and irreverent.

"We left the damned anorak behind."

"It doesn't matter, does it?"

"That's an Eden Park jacket."

"Maybe someone handed it in. You can go there and check tomorrow. Do you want a last drink of something?"

"I'm okay, thanks. I'd better be heading off."

"Why not stay a bit longer?"

"Not with your parents in the house. I'll see you tomorrow, all right?"

A moment later, the door clicks closed. Caroline can half hear, half imagine, the gravel-crunch of Tim's footsteps leaving them alone in the house. Caroline stands, the blood thumping hot inside her head.

"Where the hell have you been?" she says, re-entering the house.

She finds Sam already drifting through to her room.

"I went out."

"I'm aware of that. Where did you go?"

"Some pub. For a drink. Dad said we could take his car."

"Do you know how late it is?"

"It's only around one o'clock."

"Your Finals start next week. Right now, you should be revising for your exams."

"At one o'clock in the morning?"

"You know what I mean."

"Actually, I don't. I have no idea what you mean. I went out for a drink, like any normal teenager. Now I'm going to bed."

"Don't you walk out on me, young lady!"

"Why not, Mom? You walked out on me years ago."

PART FIVE

THE WRITER

When Daniel was ten years old, he learned
that he had two mothers

He had returned home from his first half-term at boarding to find his father gone from the house. His mother told him that she didn't know when he'd be back—and that he'd never really been present when he was present, so it wouldn't make much difference anyway.

"He's found a flat nearer his office," his mother continued. "But he's gone fishing, or something, for the weekend, so you wouldn't have been able to see him—even if you'd wanted to."

"It's okay," Daniel said.

It would have been a shameful thing to admit, but he wasn't sad to see his father go. His father was an angry, watchful god whenever he was in the house. He lived in a world in which every single thing was angled against him. Every piece of furniture. Every expired lightbulb. Every fried egg that broke. Every word that was offered to find a way back to him. He was a god who wielded a thunderbolt in the form of a common garden rake.

"You should also know," his mother said, "that he has found another woman."

At first, Daniel didn't understand what this meant. Another woman? Who was the first woman? Had he found a first woman before this other woman? Then he realized that the first woman was his mother. Or the woman his mother had been before she had been a mother. A mother with one barely visible son and one wholly invisible daughter.

"Sorry?"

"Her name is Jane, in case you're wondering."

"Jane?"

"Or Mary. I can't exactly remember which."

"But—does that mean you're getting a divorce?"

"The papers went through last week. He actually asked for a divorce weeks before he moved out. I'm sorry, Daniel."

"It's okay," Daniel said once more, not feeling very much at all.

To change the subject, his mother told him that she had decided to use her horse, Tessa, for breeding. At the end of half-term, they were to drive her down to a stud farm not far from Daniel's school. Only later would Daniel realize that his mother was trying to clear the house of every living thing so that she could be alone with her grief.

By then, the geese had been given away to a neighbor and the chickens had wandered off to be stolen, run over or eaten. The only domestic animal that remained on the plot was the golden cocker spaniel that had been Lucy's second birthday present—given to her a week before her diagnosis. Tessa, who was half-Arab and half-Welsh-pony, had been part of Daniel's mother's idea for herself when they had first moved to the plot. She was going to ride Tessa every morning "after dropping the kids at school." It would be her "me time," she liked to tell her friends. Her time away from her husband and children. Well—now she would have all the "me time" a person could ever have asked for.

It was still dark when they left the plot
in his mother's sky-blue bakkie

Tessa was standing tethered by her halter in the rumbling horsebox behind them. In the fiberglass canopy at the back was Daniel's school bag, along with his new cricket bat, his cricket pads and a tin trunk, which was neatly packed with a term's worth of tuck. The tuck was illegal and would have to be buried in the woods above the school—to be visited furtively during break or in the afternoons when no one was looking. The cricket pads had been a Christmas present from his father, who didn't know that Daniel was in fact frightened of cricket and was planning to take tennis instead.

Daniel's mother, who had also been to boarding school in KwaZulu-Natal, had made the journey between Johannesburg and Durban many times before, so Daniel was surprised when she told him an hour and a half later that she was lost. They left the highway and entered a small town in what was probably the Free State. The town was surrounded by crops of dried mealies and fields filled with dusty brown cattle and the main road was lined with tall eucalyptus trees, which leaned in on them, pale and haggard. They were idling along the main road, looking out for any signs to Durban, when Daniel's mother's body locked backward as if she was trying to stand upright inside the car. Her voice started off in a low moan, a rising hum, which escalated rapidly into a scream that a woman might make during childbirth.

The bakkie veered off to the left, toward an oncoming truck, and Daniel grabbed the steering wheel and turned it away so that the truck only clipped the back wheel of the horsebox as it passed. The bakkie then bumped up against the righthand sidewalk and a large-armed man appeared huffing alongside the car. He put his puffy red hand through Daniel's mother's open window and yanked the handbrake and the car jerked to a stop.

The man then opened the door and shouted at his mother to get her attention, but she was oblivious. Her head was lying against the seat and her mouth streaming with pink froth. The man slapped her face hard—and then he slapped it again.

After the third time, Daniel shouted, "Stop! Please, stop! Please stop hitting my mother!"

The man looked at Daniel as if he hadn't even noticed him. But the truth was that the woman in the car was not Daniel's mother. This woman had the face of the Medusa from his book on Greek myths. She had the blank white eyes that turned you to stone.

Daniel climbed out of the car to check on Tessa. The pony was standing there, trembling but unharmed. He talked to her for a while in a low, calm voice, telling the pony all the words of reassurance he wanted to hear. By the time he returned to his mother, there was an assortment of people around her open door. She was sitting there bewildered but awake. It turned out that she knew her name, but she could not provide their address or phone number. Daniel, however, was able to provide these details. His mother then signed a hand-written note—Daniel had no idea where it came from or what it meant—and she announced herself to be perfectly fit to carry on.

There were no police around and there was no sign of an ambulance. Their absence helped Daniel to conclude that nothing out of the ordinary had happened—and that the incident was merely a part of getting lost, of losing their way, and that if they could only get back on track, everything would return to normal. They were told to carry on driving to where the road reached a T-junction and there they were to turn left and continue until they saw the signs for

Durban. The highway they had been using, it turned out, was going in the opposite direction from Durban and it would be quicker to drive across the country on this connecting road than it would be to return to Johannesburg and start again. When they set off, Daniel felt reassured by the idea that he would know how to stop the car if he needed to. All he had to do was keep the steering wheel straight and pull on that handbrake with all his might. What else could there be to stopping a car?

They left the town on a thin, straight road and drove for a long time. But they never came to a T-junction or saw any signs to Durban. They drove through fields of mealies as endless as the sea. Daniel stared down the rows of mealies as row flicked after row, finding comfort in their clean rhythm, their ordered structure. He had the very clear sensation of being in two places at the same time—in the car, with his mother, whose every move he watched like a hawk, and elsewhere, his mind moving from corridor to corridor of corn as if in their dark, green depths he might find a chance of escape.

But the mealie fields offered no escape. He was stuck in the car with this woman he did not know, surrounded by a land that was indistinguishable and without end. At one point, they stopped at an intersection and his mother got out of the car and pissed in the stony sand without even trying to hide herself from the passing traffic. She was like an animal, squatting there pissing, her nose to the wind as large gray ants paused at the edge of her urine to investigate.

They drove on, the car floating just above the road, the horsebox and the horse still there and yet long-forgotten behind them. Daniel stared longingly into the rows of mealies, row after row, row after row, until it happened again—the same jolt—the same rising scream.

This time, he knew what to do. He kept the car straight with his right hand and with his left he pulled on the handbrake with all the weight of his body, his foot against the dashboard. But it made no difference. The engine was screaming alongside his mother's screaming. Her foot was wedged flat against the accelerator.

He wasn't wearing a seatbelt. The car flew off the road and hung in the air and then it was rolling, the horsebox yanking and buckling behind them. Daniel stood inside the car, holding onto the handgrip above his window, his two feet somehow against the dashboard and the seat. Later, he would recall the feeling of cartwheeling slowly through space. He felt like Spiderman. He observed the scene with a strange equanimity, like someone underwater, looking around at a cloud of alien fish.

The car, now on its side, plowed on through the grass and then came to a halt. Daniel found his feet standing on the closed passenger window, the flattened grass visible through the glass. His mother was hanging above him from her seatbelt. She was gagging because the seatbelt was strangling her. As he climbed out of her open window, her seatbelt, which was carrying the whole weight of her body, snapped. She landed with a hard clump on the other side of the car and remained quite still.

Daniel went again to check on the horse. The horsebox was upside down, its wheels streaming with knotted cosmos and khakibos, and Tessa was standing in the horsebox, on the underside of its roof. When Daniel walked across her light, she screeched and jerked her head so hard that the metal clasp of her halter snapped. She backed out of the horsebox and trotted off, vague and dazed, onto the open road.

Already there were other cars there—perhaps three. Daniel managed to catch and calm the horse and bring her back to the car. Tessa had a long cut along her nose, but otherwise she seemed unharmed. There was a crowd of people around the cab of the bakkie where his mother lay. A man told Daniel that his mother had most likely broken her neck and that she was probably dead. He said that they would have to wait for the paramedics before she could be moved. Daniel held onto Tessa in the long line of crushed grass that had been left behind by the sliding car and wept into the silky gray wall of her neck. He was not sobbing for his mother. The woman in the car was not his mother. He was sobbing for himself. He saw the whole of his life ahead of him. He would have to go and live with his father. He would have to live in the eye of that storm. With only him and his father. And his new woman. Mary or Jane. Who held a poisoned apple in her hand.

There are several moments, looking back, when a person might say that their childhood ended. Daniel would later think that he was not sure it had ever been there to start with. Childhood was another fiction we created for ourselves and our children. On that day, however, something died inside him. His relationship with his mother would never be quite the same again. She was two people. The mother he knew and the beast that lay inside her. There was no longer one of anyone. Inside each of us lay a shadow, a madness, a force so huge that in a moment it could obliterate everything you thought you knew about yourself and others. But something else came to life inside him too. That part of him that was there but not there, connected to him but also outside of him. That other part of him was present whenever he walked into a room, but it had already managed to absent itself.

He saw the whole scene that followed from a great height. His mother coming awake inside the car like an animal at the zoo. The car and horsebox being righted. The procession of people walking with them to a nearby farmhouse, with Daniel leading the horse and his mother moving silently next to him, a pale Eurydice, without any sound left inside her. The people who put them up for the night spoke no English and his mother spoke no Afrikaans. Over dinner, seated around a table under a single light, Daniel translated as best as he could. The farmer was a large man with a red, smiling face.

His wife was smaller and thinner and had a pained, slightly aghast expression. They had two sons—fleshy, dark-haired boys who spent much of the meal stifling their laughter. All of their ridicule was directed at the fine-boned city boy—for the mother was only a ghost.

Daniel and his mother slept in the same bed that night. A double bed with a soft mattress that seemed as old as the house. But he didn't sleep. Whenever he closed his eyes, he heard her scream, and the car engine's scream, and the horse's scream. He suspected that he would carry that single scream inside his head forever.

The next day, they were driven down to KwaZulu-Natal by the farmer's younger brother. Daniel said goodbye to his mother at the foot of the hostel's main stairs and then he carried his school bag and his cricket equipment and his trunk full of tuck up to his dormitory. He believed, for some reason, that he would never see his mother again. But he felt safer now. He was already in his imagined land, the landscape in which the storyteller, the weaver of alternative realities, can begin to speak—and begin to make sense of a world from which he has done his best to escape.

He learned later that his mother was epileptic

She had suffered from grand mal seizures as a child following a bad fall from a horse, and these had continued into the early years of her marriage. However, she had never had a fit since her children had been born. Now that Daniel's sister was gone, the fits returned—and, over the years, several other attacks would follow, most of them less dramatic.

Daniel learned to recognize what he would later call her fugue states—a kind of abstraction, a tendency to wander off in thought, word or deed, which would signal the weather-change, the on-coming storm. But the fit itself was always like a lightning bolt from the blue, a crack that would come straight from the hand of God the Father, wielding a metal rake. His mother would be set off immediately—sent howling into the pit of hell. A fit would last for about a minute, sometimes longer, but while it was happening it was without end. His ears would ring with it, his head would ring with it, his whole world would ring with it. Her fits were always followed by a deep sleep, sometimes for as long as an hour. It was such a sleep that had made her seem dead in that second accident on that day—the sleep that had made the bystanders conclude that she had broken her neck.

The worst of the other incidents took place a few years later, in the Eastern Cape, during a summer holiday. On this occasion, Daniel's mother went for a walk along the beach after breakfast. Daniel had been swimming and hadn't noticed this particular fugue state. Sometimes, he missed them—even if, at some level, he was always on the lookout for them. His mother started walking and for the rest of the morning she carried on walking. She went past the row of beach houses that ran along the shore, she passed the old shipwreck rusting in the dark, seaweed-sloppy waves, and she entered an area that was the start of the Addo Elephant National Park—with its network of sand dunes and impenetrable bush. There Daniel's mother finally encountered some hikers in the wasteland of dunes. Although she appeared to be perfectly cheerful, it turned out that she wasn't aware of where she was or how she had got there. When they questioned her further, it emerged that she couldn't remember her name. Or whether or not she had a husband and children. The hikers led her back along the beach, where they found Daniel frantically searching for her—a part of him believing that his mother had simply waded into the sea. Later that evening, she had her first fit, the first of several that would go on through the night.

At the end of that holiday, Daniel refused to drive with his mother back to Johannesburg. She had to take him to the airport in Port

Elizabeth so that he could complete the journey home alone. It was not the first time Daniel had felt bad about abandoning his mother. On the day of the car accident, had he not climbed out of the car window while she was gagging on the seatbelt and left her there to die?

He has asked Natasha Lopez out on a date

Her apartment in Pietermaritzburg is neat and sparsely furnished. The large windows of the living-room look down through some oak trees toward a small, suburban park. Natasha's son is already in his room with the babysitter when Daniel arrives and Natasha does not offer to introduce them. Instead, she slips away to murmur some final instructions to the babysitter, leaving Daniel to contemplate the retro seventies style of the place, and the indoor plants, and the bookshelves filled with books that have been categorized into sections—fiction, poetry, plays, philosophy and literary criticism. There are also some books in French and what seems to be Portuguese. Daniel always studies people's books when entering a room. He believes you can find out almost everything you need to know about a person from their books—which includes those people who don't have any. The only painting in the room is the well-known portrait of a young woman sitting on a bench by the Italian painter Vittorio Matteo Corcos, called "Dreams." The woman is dark blonde and wide-eyed and beautiful, and she stares just below the eye level of the viewer, her mind apparently elsewhere. On the leather couch sleeps a black-and-white cat, which does not stir to look at him.

"I like your apartment," Daniel says when Natasha re-enters with fresh lipstick and a small beaded bag over one shoulder. "Have you lived here long?"

"We moved here when my husband died," Natasha says. "I wanted a place lifted above the earth. The apartment has lovely light in the mornings. Would you like to see the balcony?"

She pulls open the sliding glass doors without waiting for his answer. It is a warm, late summer night, with a freshness in the air that feels like autumn. Here there are two wooden chairs and a wooden table, all painted white. There are more herbs and flowers in pots. Daniel picks a basil leaf and is about to smell it when Natasha steps forward and kisses him.

"I thought we should get that done," she says, "so that we don't spend the whole evening worrying about whether or not it will happen." Her mouth tastes as if she's just come up from the sea. The mouth of a mermaid. "You have lipstick on your mouth," she laughs afterwards.

He booked a table at a restaurant in the hills above the city

Their table overlooks a long lawn that slopes down to a lake. A weeping willow is illuminated on the embankment, looking like a woman in a green dress bent down to find her face in the water. A slender pier disappears into the darkness to the left of the tree and at the other end of the lake there is a road where cars are hurrying home, their headlights scurrying back and forth against a bone-white stand of eucalyptus.

She asks him what his new book is about.

"I thought it would be all about death," he says.

"But?"

"I have started to realize that death isn't something you can write about. At least, not to the exclusion of life. If you aren't working your way toward life, what's the point of doing anything?"

"You could try to beat death," she says, half joking, "like John Donne tries to do in that poem. We do not die, he says. Only death does. When we are born again into the afterlife."

"Do you believe in the afterlife?"

"I suppose I believe in this life," she says. "I suppose I believe—I don't know, that there's some kind of intelligence in everything. Even if we can't access it fully. But this intelligence—it runs through everything as electricity does. It orders the world into birds and bees, snakes and scorpions. And we are part of this intelligence. We're connected to it. Whether we like it or not. You can call it God, if you like. But I apprehend it more as—emotion. More as feeling than thought. I suppose I apprehend it as love. Were it to withdraw from the world, we would simply dissolve back into stardust. There would be nothing left. Not even death."

"So you're a kind of—animist?"

"I'm a humble participant in a miracle that is much greater than me," she laughs.

Daniel is usually self-conscious around schoolteachers, just as he is around priests. There is some part of him that wants to show them that he might be good prefect material. Even though he has never had any desire to be followed by anyone. But with Natasha he feels differently. Natasha could have any job, any function in the world. She comes to him—or so it seems to him—simply as herself.

"Have you had much experience of death?" he asks.

"Some." She sends Daniel an ironic, slightly lopsided smile. "I mentioned that my husband died. It happened when Rafael was still a baby. It was a cycling accident. He swerved to avoid a pothole and was hit by a car. He landed on the sidewalk and broke his neck. He can't have suffered much. It must have been over very quickly. But I often wonder about what he experienced during that moment between being hit by the car and landing on the sidewalk. I wonder what he saw then. Did he have time to think of me? Or to think of his son? Did he look back on his life and repent for his wrongdoings? Did he look back on his life and actually like himself?"

"I'm—sorry."

"I don't mean to suggest he was a bad person," she says with another of her subversive smiles. "The truth is, I'm not sure I ever quite knew him. I'm not sure we ever quite knew each other. We had a baby and decided to get married. Then he was dead."

"But you were happy—up to that point?"

"I remember when Rafael was born, my husband came into the room with his father, holding a bottle of champagne. To celebrate the new birth. There was something about that moment that I knew was wrong. Not once did he look at me properly. I had just been to the edge of the world, to the very limit of what my body could endure, and he looked across at me as if I was still the same woman he had always known. Or thought he'd known. And as for Rafael, he merely looked at him as you might look at something that's just come out of an oven. A loaf of bread. He was looking at Rafael only in order to see himself. To see his own image reflected back at him. It was all a performance, his way of being a father. Perhaps he was trying to convince the rest of us—or himself—that he was actually up to it. But I'm not sure he was ever up to it. Some people don't have much imagination for anything outside of themselves. My husband was such a person."

"You're very honest," Daniel says.

"I try my best to be," she laughs.

Natasha's aquamarine-blue dress brings out the paleness of her skin and the darkness of her hair and eyes. Daniel glances at the slight watermark under her left eye as she speaks, wondering where she might have come from, this woman who is so careful and collected and yet burns with this gem-like ghost of a flame.

"Do you believe you can ever know anyone?" he asks. "I mean—Sartre said that love was impossible, didn't he? We either turn ourselves or we turn the loved one into an object of desire. We can't both be free at the same time. He said that all love is a kind of bad faith. An exercise in objectifying yourself or objectifying the other person. It is a series of lies, of misrepresentations, a hall of mirrors in which you will only ever have access to yourself. Apparently,

Iris Murdoch later responded to this by saying that sometimes the greatest exercise of your freedom is to give up your freedom, to hand yourself over to the life of another person—and I suppose extend your sense of self in the process."

"Maybe they're just looking at love from the wrong direction."

"What do you mean?"

"Who's to say that loving and being loved has to be about freedom? Or the giving up of freedom? Who's to say that loving someone has to be a debate about who has the most or the least power? What if all of that is just—a red herring?"

"A red herring?"

"Do you think the fish inside the wave worries about its freedom? The wave will rise and fall anyway, whether the fish thinks about the wave, or itself in the wave, or itself relative to any other fish in the wave. Maybe what matters more than your sense of self, or of being in control, is being alive. Alive inside the wave. Alive to the wave. At least—that's what I sometimes think."

THE BUTTERFLY COLLECTOR

"Charles, are you awake?"

Charles wakes to find the shape of William at the entrance to his tent. Since their arrival at the mountain called Isandhlwana earlier that evening, Charles has not seen his friend. Their tents have been pitched some rows apart along the left flank of the mountain and Charles decided to miss the usual dinner of fallen ox in preference for a few stale biscuits and what remained of his rum. At the other end of the tent, under a pile of blankets and coats, Tyrell is serenely snoring. He is using a pile of cricket pads to prop up his head.

"What time is it?"

"It has passed one. I couldn't sleep. Would you like to come for a walk?"

"A walk? Are you mad?"

"I told Bayley I would go and check on the Native quarters across the track."

"All right," says Charles, slipping on his boots while Tyrell sleeps on.

Outside, the moonlight illuminates the rows of several hundred tents and the mountain is shaped like a great beast against the densely glittering sky. Charles can see the upside-down crucifix of the Southern Cross and the long stretch of Scorpio. In two days, there is to be a solar eclipse around lunchtime and Charles is interested to observe how the moths might respond. The collective noun for moths is an eclipse, perhaps because most species of moths are of the moon, not the sun. During the eclipse, would the moths ascend into the air, believing it to be night—or would they have been too bedazzled by the light of day to make so rapid a transition? During an eclipse, some bat species have been known to enter the air and some birds have been known to go silent or even to fall to the ground. Some spiders have been observed starting to dismantle their webs, while bees will often return to their hives. Even large mammals appear to be affected by an eclipse. Cows will wander back to their sheds, hippos leave the water to enter their nocturnal feeding grounds—and there are sailors' accounts of dolphins and whales rising in great numbers to the surface of the sea.

As soon as they have left the camp and turned away from the packed Native quarters, where the men have made their shelters out of bits of wood, William places a companionable arm across Charles's shoulders. Ahead of them is a grassy plain where earlier the animals were released to graze—the grass so tall in several places that the beasts had entirely disappeared.

"I have missed you," says William.

"I have missed you too."

"I have something that I should like to say. At least—something I should like to ask."

"What is it?"

"Do you remember our first night together—when we were on board the *Edinburgh Castle*?"

"Of course."

"I was rather drunk, as I recall."

"As I recall, you were."

"Well, I asked you something quite—unusual."

"You did."

"You were terribly kind about it, but you declined."

"I did."

They have arrived at a rocky outcrop that rises up slightly from the plain. Ahead, they can make out the glow of a sentry's pipe—and, in the distance, the creaking of a hundred reed frogs from a distant stream or marsh.

"What if I were to ask the same question of you again? What would you say?"

Charles feels his whole body beginning to shake.

"I—don't know," he says. "I have never done anything like that before."

"It isn't all that different," says William, "once you know how to go about it."

The shivering has grown worse—and Charles walks some distance away and sits on a rock. "Do you mean to say that you have—that you been with other men before?"

"Yes, I have. Only when I'm drunk. But I'm completely sober now."

"With whom? If I may ask?"

Charles is barely listening to the words, but he feels the need to keep talking, if only to avoid what he now knows has always been inevitable.

"A few times in India. Sometimes in London. Usually at a place just off the Tottenham Court Road. Then again here. At Helpmekaar."

"Here? At Helpmekaar?"

"A Private in the 24th. His name is Mowbray. With Mowbray, it has happened twice."

"But Will—that is terrible."

"Not so terrible. Even animals are known to do it. You should know that—being such a naturalist."

"But—what if you were caught?"

"We are most likely going to die here anyway."

William has found a rock across from him. He puts his hand forward to hold Charles's face. The shuddering has not abated. Both men can hear the chattering of his teeth.

"Why are you shaking?" William asks.

"I feel—afraid."

"You love me, Charles. You must admit it."

"I suppose I must."

"I too—have feelings toward you that I have never felt toward any other man."

"Not even to Mowbray?"

"Not any man."

William leans forward and kisses him. This is the first time Charles—a man of twenty-three—has ever been kissed. At the touch of William's mouth against his, his body relaxes and the fever passes out of him. It is replaced by a strange calm. The same exulted calm he felt when lying next to William in Lydia Grace's bed.

"I think your sister knows," he says. "I think she knows what kind of people we are."

"My sister is the very best person I know. One day you must marry her."

During this exchange, the moon has been engulfed in drifting cloud and the land around them has grown quiet. It is odd to imagine that they are in enemy territory, and that all around them they are being watched by spies. But the thought of the enemy presence only amplifies a feeling that Charles has always carried inside him, which is that all of life—except perhaps for all the butterflies in the world—stands opposed to him.

"And what about us?" says Charles. "What about—this?"

"This is something that can only happen once."

There is no point in attempting to go back to sleep

Charles is to be up well before dawn to attend to outpost duty, where the men in his charge are to parade with the remaining men of the 24th before they withdraw for breakfast. The oxen are then to be turned out to graze, after which Charles has been tasked with checking on the new picquet lines beyond the camp. Over the last few days, Sprite has given Charles duties that are sometimes difficult to fathom—not only extra night picquet duties, but the supervision of defaulters in the digging of pit latrines and the carrying of messages to outlying detachments in the most inclement weather conditions. Sometimes, it seems that Sprite simply wants Charles as far away from him as possible—and, at other times, it seems that Sprite wants him where he can observe his every move.

At four o'clock, Sunshine arrives with a bucket of water so Charles can wash and shave. Although many of the other men have been allowed to leave their beards to grow, Sprite has insisted that all the men of his regiment remain clean-shaven except for their moustaches. Sprite himself has a thin, neat moustache that twitches across his lip like a ginger-colored caterpillar.

Charles is walking across to the parade area when he passes Will and Bayley's tent. He is not expecting to find his friend there since he and some other volunteers were to ride out with Major Dartnell's company in the early hours to reconnoitre the ground over some nearby hills—but there he finds Will sitting on a biscuit box with his left foot neatly bandaged and propped up on a recently washed, upturned chamber pot.

"Will—what on earth has happened?"

"I sprained my damned ankle this morning as I was walking out to the horse line. An overgrown porcupine hole right in the middle of the camp, can you believe? I was sure I could ride with it, but Dartnell wanted only the fittest men, and he didn't want me holding them back, so he found a substitute."

"How frustrating," says Charles, nevertheless pleased to see him. "What are you to do today?"

"Rest my damned ankle. I should be able to walk in a day or two—once the swelling's gone down."

"I'll come and find you later this afternoon. Don't go anywhere."

"Believe me, I won't."

Although the mornings in Zululand are cool and the mountains often engulfed in a wet, low-hanging mist, the stone lion is soon shimmering in the heat like a mirage that has wandered down from Egypt. As Charles rides out to inspect the picquet lines, he can see no sign of life amongst the distant blue hills other than another single column of smoke. Earlier that morning, there had been a few scattered shots, but nothing to raise alarm.

He stops at a field officer from the Second Battalion of the 24th, who expresses concern about the defenses at the front of the camp. Except for a few dongas and some raised rocky outcrops—including the place where Hawthorne and Will had lain the previous night—there are few strong fighting positions—and Chelmsford, who had also ridden out that morning to view the country ahead, has done almost nothing to fortify the camp.

"Hopefully, it won't come to that," Charles says. "The land around us appears to be entirely empty. Do they not say the whole Zulu army has withdrawn to Ulundi?"

"They say many things," the field officer retorts.

As Charles continues to ride along the edges of the picquet lines, he sees nothing more than a few women running along with bundles on their heads and an old fellow wearing a loincloth who is wandering about like a man who wakes to find his whole world swept away in a hurricane.

Another butterfly Charles is hoping to catch for the Museum is the spectacular *Precis sesamus*—an azure-and-indigo butterfly with bright-red bands on the uppersides of both wings that is said to roost in considerable numbers in the higher mountains of Natal during the wet season. Charles has seen a few of these agile, fast-flying butterflies already, but these moments have always been under the gaze of Captain Sprite. Now, as soon as he is safely away from the scrutiny of the field officer, he takes out his butterfly net and heads toward a rocky mound—already beginning to make out the iridescent-blue flutterings of the *Precis sesamus* amongst some flowering plants.

When he returns to camp, it is to a scene
that will change his life forever

A young private has been roped to a tripod and is about to be whipped by the drummer boy, McEwan. Charles leaves Clifton Lass with Sunshine and walks across to where a crowd of men from the 24th—as well as some grooms and other Native staff—have started to gather.

"What has he done?" Charles asks one of the privates.

"The official line is that he abandoned his post," the man says darkly. "But you want the unofficial truth? He was caught with an officer."

"Caught?"

"Doing the dirty. You know."

The man performs an obscene and unmistakable gesture.

"What's the fellow's name?"

"Mowbray."

At the sound of this name, Charles understands everything.

"And the officer," he stammers, "what is to happen to him?"

"The officer is too good for a whipping," the private says with readily available contempt, "even if he's the bugger who started it."

Mowbray is pale and grave and doing nothing to defend himself—reduced, as he is, to a state of shamed paralysis. Charles does not remain to witness the scene, but walks directly to Will's tent—where he finds his friend fully dressed and alone, seated on the edge of his mattress with his fine face in his hands.

"Will?"

"Oh, Charles," is all Will says.

"What on earth happened?"

"Bayley walked in on us. Myself and Mowbray. It's all over."

"What is to be done?"

"I have no idea. Bayley went straight to Pope—and now, of course, Mowbray is to be whipped."

"I have just come from there," Charles says. "The poor chap is terrified."

"I said they should take me instead—but Pope said it would be impossible to whip an officer. Not in front of the men I am supposed to command. There is to be an honor committee this evening when they are to decide my fate. Oh Charles, I will have to resign my commission—at the very least. How am I to look the other men in the face?"

"I'm sure they will let the matter pass."

"But with a private? They won't permit that. As long as they thought there was something between you and me, they were prepared to ignore it. But this—this is crossing a line—and it is something they will not be prepared to forgive."

"We don't know that."

"My life is over. Whatever happens to me, my reputation is in ruins. There's nothing I shall be able to do to redeem it."

"Redeem yourself in battle," Charles says. "If we behave honorably in this war, much may be forgiven."

"But I can't even walk!" moans Will.

By the time Charles leaves the tent, the flogging is over and the private has been removed from sight. Charles considers going to look for him, but then he decides that drawing attention to the private would only further implicate Will. Instead, he withdraws to his tent for the rest of the afternoon. Thankfully, Tyrell has volunteered to join one of the scouting parties and has been gone since dawn. With trembling hands, Charles pins the five *Precis sesamus* specimens he caught earlier that day into a larger tin.

"Hawthorne?"

Charles emerges an hour later to find Sprite standing outside with Bayley and some other officers. Sprite is even redder than usual, as if he has been stewing in a cauldron. He looks down at Charles with undisguised contempt.

"Good evening, sir," says Charles.

All around them, the evening sky is an undulating silver-gray and salmon-pink. The mountain stands above them, an enormous megalith with a creaking halo of crows. Charles can see that there are other men watching—men sitting outside their tents playing cards or simply smoking their pre-dinner pipes.

"What can I do for you, sir?" asks Charles as innocently as possible.

"We are going across to Grace's tent to give him a beating," says Sprite. "You are required to participate."

"I beg your pardon, sir?"

"It is a direct order."

"But sir—what about the honor committee that is to be held tonight?"

"In case you've forgotten, Hawthorne, we are in the middle of enemy territory. There will be a formal inquiry at Headquarters when all of this is done."

"I'm sorry, sir, but I can have no part in this. If necessary, I am happy to be answerable to Lieutenant-Colonel Pulleine."

The other men exchange a look that confirms to Charles that they were expecting this response—nay, hoping for it.

"Is that a threat, Hawthorne?" Bayley asks, stepping forward.

"No, sir," says Charles, still addressing himself to Sprite, "but I ask with respect not to be a part of this."

Sprite gives off a laugh. "You are already a part of this, you fool," he says. "In fact, it was probably you who corrupted Grace in the first place. Be assured, Hawthorne—the inquiry in Pietermaritzburg will most certainly be including you."

"Sir, if there is to be an inquiry, and Grace is found guilty, surely he shall receive punishment enough? And if you do anything to him now, sir, in front of the other soldiers—sir, it might be taken amiss. It will not be good for the morale of the men. And the Native soldiers, sir, who serve under Lieutenant Grace, they are extremely loyal to him, sir. You know how fragile and fickle their loyalties are. They may not fight alongside us if we do anything to harm Lieutenant Grace."

All of this is said urgently and quietly to Sprite—so that only the officers closest to him can hear it. As Charles is speaking, however, he knows it to be the truth—and he can see that Sprite knows it too.

"Are you suggesting, Lieutenant Hawthorne, that you are prepared to stand in for him?"

"Stand in for him how, sir?"

"Are you suggesting that you are prepared to take his beating on his behalf?"

"You mean right here, sir?"

"There are other ways to get at a man," says Sprite with quiet intent. "Tomorrow, we are to form a scouting party and ride out before dawn on behalf of Lieutenant-Colonel Pulleine. I want you to ride right next to me. I want you with me tomorrow, and the day after that, and the day after that, and I don't want you even for a minute to be out of my sight. In that time, you will do whatever duty I ask of you, no matter what it might entail. And when the occasion arises, and we are faced with the enemy, if it pleases me, I shall feed you directly into the belly of the beast. Are you prepared to do that—for your Queen, if not for your friend?"

"If those are to be your orders, sir, then I shall be happy to obey."

It is still dark when they leave the camp

Chelmsford and the bulk of the British army have departed some hours before—and Charles and his companions ride out from the northern end of the camp, not far behind Lieutenant Raw and his troops. They follow a narrow animal track and ascend a path that runs along the crest of a spur. The mist gradually thins around them and sinks deeper into the creases of the dark-gray earth—and, as the light grows, they soon make out some Zulus moving amongst the mealie fields far below. These are not soldiers, but appear to be foragers, passing through another rural farmer's land, taking the ripe corn and stuffing it into their hessian sacks. When the men see the line of British soldiers appearing along the spur above them, they run ahead, drawing the mounted troops onward toward a rocky lump of hill that rises in the growing light to meet them.

"You don't think this is a trap?" Bayley asks Sprite.

"We shall soon find out," says Sprite with a casual laugh. "Hawthorne—you ride on ahead."

As they ride onward, soon merging with Raw and his Basotho horsemen, the sun grows hotter and higher in the sky. There is little sound except for the singing of the grasshoppers and cicadas. At one point, Charles sees a large, mottled bird ascend in the blue air and then tumble down to the earth as if it has been shot. This appears to be a mating ritual, however, since the bird soon re-ascends and repeats the display.

He is happier to be out of the hearing of Bayley and Sprite. All morning, the two men have kept up their usual, sly banter—touching on almost every subject other than the one that so recently concerned them. The previous evening, Charles had known better than to go looking for Will, and Will had not come looking for him. Charles hopes that Will has no idea of what had been agreed between himself and Sprite—although, with a man like Sprite, there was no telling what might have been done or said.

When Charles was still at boarding school, he had been a quiet and withdrawn boy, but he had never been so quiet and withdrawn as to draw unnecessary attention to himself. At that school, if a boy did something to offend another boy, the offended boy would say "after supper"—and this meant that they were to meet behind the dining hall after dinner to face one another. By that time, word would have spread and a crowd would be waiting behind the hall in order to watch. As soon as the fight started, the more popular boy's name would be chanted out, and the less popular boy would have to overcome not only his opponent but the growing hostility of the crowd. Back then, it was Charles's worst fear to be in a fight, to have his name chanted or not chanted, to have his face beaten to a bloody mess by some other boy who was larger, faster and less feeling than him. But Charles had always managed to avoid an after-supper fight. He did it by abstracting himself, by absenting himself, by doing everything he could not to cause offense.

Later, when Charles read Aristotle, he decided that the Greek philosopher was wrong when he stated that you could only be called courageous when you acted courageously. You could be a courageous person and choose, for whatever reason, not to act.

Moreover, cowards could disguise their cowardice by not exposing themselves through cowardly actions. Yet cowards would always know that they were cowards, even if no one else did. Watching those fights after supper, Charles was struck by the degree to which they revealed the truth of what the boys were. Savages, down to the last one. To submit to this fight, to this mob chanting for blood, was another kind of cowardice, because in their world it was less dishonorable to be beaten in a fight than it was to decline one. Yet, as Charles had lain awake the previous night, he was curious to find none of that cringing fearfulness inside himself that he had carried with him as a child. As he lay there, waiting for the reveille, he found himself once again feeling strangely elated, if only because, at least for another day, he had managed to preserve the living presence of his friend.

"Hawthorne—ride out further along that ridge!"

Charles does not bother to say anything back to Sprite, but urges Clifton Lass off the animal track and higher up the ridge. Below him, the land has gradually closed in, pushing the Zulu foragers along a gully where a thin thread of water glints in the sun. There Charles can see another group of men herding a clump of cattle forward with broken-off branches, the beasts moaning in protest as they stumble over the stones. When Bayley and a few other horsemen descend to meet them, they turn and flee up the rocky spur at the other end of the gully and soon vanish from sight. Charles continues up the ridge with some Basotho horsemen, Clifton Lass making her way easily amongst the anthills and rocks.

Behind Charles, and not far below him, Sprite takes out his pipe and lights it. They have barely paused since setting off and some of the men have started to grumble about finding water and shade in order to give their horses a rest, but Sprite and the other officers have remained deaf to this. All morning, Charles has also been on the lookout for butterflies, and he has seen several more examples of the *Precis sesamus*—the butterfly that will forever be fixed in his mind with Will's fate.

"I say," says Sprite, exhaling a cloud of smoke, "what on earth is that noise?"

Charles pauses his horse to listen beyond its breathing.

"I do believe it's a swarm of bees," someone further along is saying.

Ahead of them, a few of the Basothos have paused at the crest of the hill. One of their horses makes a reeling, rearing movement, as if it has just encountered a snake. Charles nudges Clifton Lass forward, looking around for whatever it is that could be making the noise, knowing all the while that it could never come from anything in the natural world. This is a sound like the gathering of some horrific force—like God clearing His throat in order to speak.

It is only when Charles reaches the crest of the spur that he discovers the cause of the noise. Around forty thousand Zulus are sitting crouched in the valley beneath him, the men emitting a low hum, the women only now beginning to ululate. On seeing the horsemen appearing on the edge of their horizon, the Zulu army stands with one movement—like a single thought, a single intention, rising up to meet them.

PART SIX

THE WRITER

Water hates a secret

It does everything it can to unearth it. To bring it back to the light of day. Always, it is working its way toward a problem. At every moment, it is busy turning stones this way and that, nudging at earth-cliffs and riverbanks until they subside with a slow sigh back into the water. Children understand this—yet they continue to build their walls of sand against the sea, knowing that such walls are provisional. They build their fortresses not because they want them to last forever, but because they want to see how long they will last, how long they will stave off the inevitable.

Grown men are different. They imagine that they can bury a thing by the side of the river and that it will remain hidden. They come with their shame slung over their shoulder and they dig where the earth is soft. They think that if they bury their secret deep enough, it will remain there, quietly turning into earth. They forget about the river that runs its course at their feet. But the river feels this invasion, this snag of the conscience, this bone of contention. As soon as the man has walked away, apparently unburdened, back to what he trusts will be his original life, the water is already working its way toward his shame. There are some actions that can't be undone. There are some actions that change the world forever.

The dark-blue anorak is found near Fugitives' Drift

It is tangled and torn, but still identifiable. It has a "special offer" tag attached to its collar and a pink ribbon sewn into the front of it. Inside its zipped pockets are a bag of cannabis and a bright-green cigarette lighter. As for the girl who once wore the anorak, she has long ago slipped away, like Cinderella's foot.

The police van appears later that morning

Daniel watches it ascend the muddy track through the lodge, the vehicle dipping into puddles and laboring over rises, the sound of the engine meek and insistent, like an animal in pain. The heads of the detectives are visible inside, faceless and dark, wobbling in unison like two mannequins.

Today, even the living look dead. Daniel remembers what Natasha said. That we are nothing but stardust with the light of God passing through us. That God's intelligence is inseparable from our intelligence. He wonders what kind of god this might be, who allows seventeen-year-old girls to be so casually slaughtered. It is not a human intelligence. It is an intelligence that encompasses female spiders eating their mates after copulation and female fireflies signaling males with the sole intention of eating them. It is an intelligence that encompasses whole galaxies without blinking. This intelligence is merely passing through him, just as it is passing through the two policemen, as casually as a sunbeam enters a room and ignites an ashtray, a sleeping cat, a murder weapon—before moving off again.

"Where the hell do you think they're going?" David asks.

David is sitting across from Daniel, smoking a cigarette and peering. Today, he also looks half dead. A long-faced puppet-man, bright pink and askew, as if some mechanism has given way somewhere at the neck. Instead of following the road up to the parking lot, the van has taken the gravel track toward the Websters' house.

Daniel does not answer David's question since it was more an expression of intrigue than an actual question. They both know the answer.

"Do you think it's got something to do with the anorak?"

It was David who told Daniel about the dark-blue anorak. David sent him a message earlier that morning, asking to meet him for coffee as soon as the kitchen was open. No doubt, David wanted to garner more information from him—not that Daniel has ever told him anything of substance.

"It must have something to do with the anorak—and Sam," David continues, stabbing his cigarette in the direction of the ashtray. Already, he is on his feet, leaving Daniel to sign for their breakfast.

David is the only journalist to have remained at the lodge and no doubt he sees this as his moment to break the news—or whatever the appropriate expression might be. Strangely, Sam does not feel dead to Daniel as he sits on, inhaling the smell of the half-burned cigarette lying on the edge of David's breakfast plate. But perhaps this is because Daniel has lived with the ghost of her so often recently that he does not want to think of her as dead. Not in this world of stardust and ignited light.

At the far end of the deck, on the other side of a new British family fresh off the plane, Tim has been eating his breakfast. He has had his back turned away from them, as if he does not want to be disturbed—and Daniel has had no intention of disturbing him. Soon after David has left, however, he turns to find that Tim has arrived at his side.

"That arsehole a friend of yours?" Tim asks.

"More of an acquaintance."

"What did you tell him?"

"Sorry?"

"Have you been feeding him information?"

"What information could I possibly feed him?"

Tim smells of stale alcohol and hasn't shaved for days. His eyes have a bleary, mad look and are bluer than the cobalt-blue rugby jersey he is wearing along with his signature khaki shorts. Since their conversation about Caroline, about him and Caroline, they have not spoken. Perhaps the knowledge Daniel carries about him makes Tim despise him—or despise himself.

"The police want to talk to me," Tim says.

"The police?"

"I received a message from Bruce. I have to go up to his house."

"The police want to talk to you about the anorak?"

"I have no fucking idea."

Daniel can see the little boy inside Tim now. The little boy who seems to want the whole world to be his mother. Daniel almost feels sorry for him. He is another doll wandering about, being pulled at by strings that stretch all the way back to the ill-lit rooms of his childhood.

"I suppose I'm feeling a bit rattled," he says in tacit apology.

"It's understandable," Daniel says, understanding nothing.

"Would you mind walking with me?" Tim tries to smile, but tears shoot into his eyes instead. "I could do with a wingman, you know?"

The police van has been parked right up
against Bruce's Land Cruiser

The proximity is unnecessarily assertive, as if the police are telling the family that, whatever happens, there is no hope of escape. As they approach the house, Daniel sees long-faced David retreating behind a buffalo-thorn bush. Fortunately, Tim does not see him. Tim is like a man off to meet his executioner—and Daniel is his prison guard, making sure he doesn't attempt a last-minute escape. David waves Daniel on like a villager hoping to witness a death. A death by hanging or bloody beheading.

The kitchen door has been left open and Daniel follows Tim inside. Ndlovu and Dlamini are drinking glasses of mineral water in the dining area and they appear unsurprised to see Daniel with Tim. By now, they probably think of him as part of the family, one of those relatives who is never explained because their presence isn't important enough to require an explanation.

"We were talking to Mr. Webster about the blue jacket," Dlamini tells them by way of greeting.

"Oh yes?" says Tim.

"The dark-blue jacket."

"Right."

Dlamini raises his glass of water as if this is intended to stand for the item. "I have been told that you possess such a jacket."

"A blue jacket? At some point, sure I have."

"And where is this jacket now?"

"I—have no idea."

Dlamini looks across at Ndlovu to share some communication, but the other man is staring nervously at the wolfhound and picking his teeth with a match. Bruce is standing nearer the glass veranda, his shoulder angled away from his wife, who is listening, with her back turned, from the leather couch.

"Did you ever go to Rosie's Place?" Dlamini asks Tim.

"Sure," he says.

"Did you ever go there with Miss Webster?"

"With Sam? Yes, I did."

"You took Sam there?" Bruce asks, furious.

"I did."

"What the fuck did you do that for?"

"We went for a drive. We popped in for a drink. It wasn't a big deal."

"Unbelievable."

Dlamini waits for a father's expected rage to settle before he carries on. "Because Sam was seen there wearing a dark-blue jacket," he says.

"It was more of an anorak—but yes."

"And this was your anorak?"

"It was."

"But now you don't know where it is?"

"We left it there. That night. Afterwards, I don't know what happened to it."

"You mean you did not go back the next day to look for it?"

Tim lets off a nervous laugh. "When I realized I'd left it behind," he says, "I messaged Simon. I asked him to keep it for us, but I can't remember if I got a reply. You can check my messages, if you like. Maybe he forgot. Or I forgot to get it back from him. It's not exactly the kind of jacket you need down here anyway. An anorak like that. I only bought it because it was on sale and I thought it would be useful when I went to college. I was hoping to go to uni at St. Andrew's or Edinburgh—and you may not know this, being from South Africa and everything, but it can get pretty damned cold up there in Scotland."

Tim has started to ramble and everyone is aware of it.

"Who is this Simon?"

"Simon Ngobese," says Bruce. "Moses Ngobese's son. He is studying in Cape Town, but he comes and goes."

"So you were not alone that night? You went with this Simon Ngobese to Rosie's Place?"

"We sort of bumped into him," Tim says. "Sam and I arrived alone."

"You did not arrange to meet Simon Ngobese there?"

"I'd seen him there before. We'd had a few drinks a few times. But really—he has nothing to do with any of this."

"He has nothing to do with any of—what?"

"Like I say," Tim says, readjusting his stance, "he was just there. We had a drink with him and then we left. End of story."

"Until you messaged him to keep the jacket?"

"I must've thought he was still at our table—or that maybe he'd seen the jacket on the chair and kept it for us. But maybe he didn't get the message or see the jacket. And someone else could've taken it. It was a nice jacket."

"You say you bought the jacket on a sale. Where did you buy it?"

"Duty Free. Heathrow Airport."

"It had a pink ribbon sewn on the front?"

"That's right. It was an Eden Park anorak."

"Do you know that there are no shops in KwaZulu-Natal that sell this make of jacket? The only places where you can buy it are in Cape Town and Johannesburg—unless you were to buy one at Heathrow Airport."

"Okay—"

"But it was the same jacket—or must I say anorak?—that we believe was seen on the body of the girl in the river. It was the same make of anorak that has just been found downriver of where the girl was found. Do you not think that this is quite a coincidence?"

"It might be the same anorak," Tim says, "but I lost it weeks before any of this stuff took place."

"So you are stating that you never retrieved the anorak or got it back from Mr. Ngobese?"

"That's what I'm stating—yes."

"And you have not seen the anorak since?"

"Like I said—no."

"Thank you."

Dlamini finishes his water and places the glass carefully on the marble counter.

"Is that it?" Bruce asks, moving into the overhead light.

"We would like Mr. Greene to come with us," says Dlamini. "To make a formal statement." He turns to Ndlovu, who now has his full attention. "And we will need to speak with Simon Ngobese—this so-called friend of his."

Daniel finds Matthew alone at the stables, killing flies

The boy is still wearing his tennis clothes from school. The shorts, T-shirt, socks and shoes. Each item perfectly white. But instead of a tennis racquet, he is holding a bright-red plastic fly swat. He swings it with his bony wrist like a professional. He is so intent on his game that he does not notice Daniel's approach.

Daniel has never had much to do with Matthew before. He is the kind of boy who sends a quick smile in the direction of unknown adults and then looks for the closest means of escape. Daniel has found him to be polite, quiet and entirely unavailable. Yet Daniel has always felt a kinship with him. Perhaps because he has found himself projecting some version of his younger self onto the boy. But even if Matthew is nothing like Daniel imagines him to be, he feels for him anyway. Even when Sam was around, Matthew conducted himself like an only child who had been left too much to his own devices. Not exactly neglected, but never sufficiently considered. While Caroline clearly loved him very much, Caroline did not strike Daniel as a person who was able to love someone without complicating that love with the complication of herself.

"What are you up to?" Daniel asks—more to alert the boy of his presence.

"Killing flies. So far, I've killed one hundred and sixty-two."

"Is that your record?"

"My record is one thousand three hundred and sixty-seven."

"All in one day?"

"All in one afternoon." He sends Daniel a breathy laugh without quite looking at him. "There are always more flies at the stables than anyone can kill."

All around the rough, whitewashed walls of the stables, Daniel can make out the blood smears and bundled corpses of dozens of dead flies. Meanwhile, Matthew has moved onto the wall outside Spare Pony's stable. He has barely paused in his game. He has the same mesmerized, crazed expression Daniel associates with addicts—and artists.

"How have you been doing?" Daniel asks him more generally.

"One hundred and sixty-three," Matthew says, having just smacked another fly on a wooden pole polished from years of sweaty saddles. "One hundred and sixty-four."

"I hear you're in your second year at your dad's old school?"

"Yeah."

"What's that like?"

"It's school, you know?"

"Yes. I know."

Daniel sees that the spell Matthew was in has been broken—and that he is now only using the fly killing to mask his awkwardness. Daniel remembers that Matthew and he have spoken at some length before, when Sam was still alive. They had gone for a walk so that Matthew could show him a malachite sunbird's nest. The nest had been constructed above a small waterfall and you had to climb up the rock in order to peer inside. There they found two greenish, blotched eggs, waiting to hatch.

"Did those sunbird eggs ever hatch?" Daniel asks.

Matthew looks at him for the first time. His face is glowing from his exertions. He has the kind of skin women dream about. Without a blemish. Except for the single smear of fly blood on his left cheekbone, close to a concerned blue eye.

"I think a snake or another bird got to them," he says.

He sounds pleased that Daniel remembers the nest and their desire to see the eggs hatched. The event took place in an altogether different world. For both of them.

"I'm sorry about Sam," Daniel says.

Matthew holds his gaze as an animal might, his nostrils flared for danger. "Thanks."

"Do you believe she's still alive?"

Matthew stares down at the fly swat in his hand. They both do. Matthew is left-handed, like Daniel. He holds the swat more like a squash player than a tennis player. Perhaps his favored game is actually squash. "I think she's probably dead."

"Did you know they just took Tim to the police station?"

Daniel knows that Matthew can't possibly know this. Although he will soon know it because the whole world will know it—thanks to David. David tried to speak with Daniel straight after the interview, when Daniel was walking back toward his room, but Daniel said that he knew nothing. He had been making coffee in the kitchen when the police and Tim Greene were talking. The glass doors to the veranda had been sealed shut. David knew that he wasn't telling the truth, and he probably knew that Daniel wanted him to know that—and leave him alone as a consequence.

"What for?" Matthew asks.

"To make a statement. They also want to question Simon."

"Simon? What's Simon got to do with any of this?"

"I don't know. I think it's got something to do with the anorak they saw on the dead girl."

"Oh."

"Do you think Simon could ever do anything bad—to someone. To a girl, perhaps?"

"I don't know," says Matthew.

Already, he is looking around for more flies, but there is an edge to his voice that feels less directed at Simon than at the whole story, the whole disappearance of Sam. He kills another fly. Then another. He seems to have no desire to kill. Only a need to mark the time and fill it with something tangible. If only to prove to himself that he is still there.

THE GHOST OF SAM WEBSTER

Sam

Tom is waiting under the bloodwood tree by the old school bell

Sam knows why he has chosen this place. One Sunday morning after chapel, he rode his bicycle across to her school and waited for her here, exactly as he is waiting now—and that was the first time he officially asked her out. They went for a pizza at a nearby restaurant that overlooked a parking lot. There they saw Dr. Lopez with her son, who looked like a dark-eyed elf, twirling a long silver spoon in what was left of his lime milkshake.

Tom has never seemed impatient to Sam. He's one of those people who leaves those around him to work at their own pace—and he extends this allowance to himself, which sometimes frustrates Sam, since she likes to move quickly and efficiently through the world, seldom stopping, seldom retracing her steps. This means that she often leaves Tom behind, sometimes miles behind—as has happened with the whole shameful business of Tim Greene.

She's been planning to break it off with Tom for weeks now, but she didn't want to upset him during their final exams. Tom is like one of those elegant, steady yachts in which every rope is tight and secure, and the sail and the wood and the golden hinges gleam with perfection. Yet it sometimes feels to Sam that there's little actually directing him. Over the last months, he's settled into her current as you might into a bright summer's day—and, because he suspects only the best from everyone, he has had no idea that she abandoned ship weeks ago.

He smiles and stands the moment he sees her.

"Hey. How was it?"

Her last exam was Further Studies English. There were three questions in the exam and it was three hours long. The first question was about two films and two novels she had studied, the second was about four poets and an unseen poem, and the third was about three novels from her own reading—the so-called philosophical question, for which, unusually, she ran out of time. Sam generally finished an exam with time to spare, but these days there's a dead weight inside her that she's had to lug about. She has never thought of herself as a coward. In everything, she has always been without fear. But this new, dead feeling feels like fear. It's the terror she felt as a child when the dead left their graves in the side of the mountain and assembled around her bed, peering down at her with their blank moth-faces, sucking all the air out of her.

"It was great, thanks."

She said the same to Dr. Lopez after the exam. She tried to use a voice Dr. Lopez might recognize, but she only managed to sound fake—and a bit like Jessica.

"Ben and them are meeting at the Italian place for a beer," Tom says. "I said we might drop by."

"I'd prefer be alone with you," she says, "if that's all right?"

"Of course."

Tom brightens at the sound of this and Sam remembers their agreement. That they would only make actual love when they were done with school. Little does he know that Sam has already given herself away. First in the light of that fire, with her brother listening from the shadows of the cave, and then again the previous weekend, in Tim's drummer-boy room, the rising moon huge in the window and a thousand frogs creaking from the reeds along the river.

"I borrowed my mom's car," Tom says with a note of irony.

Tom is six months older than Sam and he has already passed his driver's license. His mother's car is a mustard-yellow Nissan bakkie that is being held together with rust and spiderweb. Sam hasn't yet bothered to take her learner's license, even though she and Matty have been driving around the lodge since they could first see over a steering wheel. When Sam climbs into the bakkie, she finds everything covered in a fine layer of dust. There are bits of plumbing clanking underfoot amongst mysterious papers, and there is an empty tin of cherry-flavored travel sweets, a comb, a vintage Nokia phone and a pair of sunglasses with only one lens—all crammed into the cubbyhole, which is without a door.

In Sam's house, everything is beautiful and functional and dead. In Tom's house, objects could be removed or multiplied and no one would notice the difference. This was how Sam has just distinguished between realism and symbolism in her Further Studies English essay. In the symbolic realm, every teaspoon had a totemic significance and if you removed it the meaning of the space would be changed. In a realist setting, Sam argued, you could introduce as many teaspoons as you liked and the meaning of the space would remain pretty much the same.

"I've missed you," she says.

"Yeah—me too," says Tom, oblivious to the shadow in her voice.

Tom has no doubt ascribed her recent cooling to the pressure of the exams. Although they both have only one more week left of school, Sam knows that Tom has been directing each of his days toward this moment, to Sam's last exam, when they can start to relinquish the indignities of school and enter the world as young adults, free to do whatever they liked. They have both applied to go to the same university in Cape Town next year and they have already been accepted into neighboring residences—two towers that were built decades ago and are ugly and cylindrical and whipped around by the same, incessant wind. Sam hasn't told Tom that she no longer intends to go. Soon it won't matter anyway, since today is the day she has chosen to break up with him.

They pass through the village and enter the hills. The Midmar Dam is the same color as Tim Greene's eyes, sunk deeper into the earth than usual, so that the red earth rims the blue-gray water, separating it from the dull green that is carried into the furthest hills. The rains have only just started and the whole summer lies ahead of them. It is gentler here, where Tom lives. There is a softness and an abundance in these hills. They have been farmed for generations and each part of the land has been assigned a function. Everyone has agreed that here they will establish a dairy herd, there they will grow some wine, this will be a pine plantation—and that will be a gated community with a tennis court, a golf course and a dam stocked with rainbow trout.

Where Sam lives, it feels as if death threads itself through everything. Where she lives, everything already has its own ghost standing inside it. This is how she is accustomed to thinking about the world. Everything under threat, everything provisional. For Tom, there has always been time. Time to be yourself. Time to enjoy a full, rich life. Even now, he is driving as if he has all the time in the world. He might not know where he is going, but it does not matter because he already knows where he is meant to be. For Sam, life has always been about clinging to a rock while all around you the world is howling.

No one knows this about Sam except for Tim. Everyone else has only ever seen her shining surface. Only Tim knows what it is like to look beautiful but never feel beautiful. Tom, on the other hand, is so at home inside himself that he has never been ruptured out of his goodness, which is also a form of ignorance. His goodness, she now sees, has been inherited, not earned. It is easy to be good when you've never been tested. But for Sam there has never been any goodness, any security. And her parents have never been of any help in this. Perhaps because they have always been so endangered themselves. When the dead came to stand around her bed at night, it almost felt as if her father and mother had ushered them into the room.

"Where should we go?" Tom asks as they drive further into the hills.

"It doesn't matter. Wherever you like."

Something died inside her at the death of her cat. How was she ever to feel at home in a land where the people around her wanted her and her family dead? Sam knew that whatever the Websters thought about themselves, they were already ghosts in that place. When that wall of thorns had been built across the entrance to their road, cutting them off, barring their escape, she had been reminded of the walls of thorns the European pioneers used to construct in the bush to protect their livestock. They did this to keep the lions at bay—but they also did it so that when they wanted to slaughter an animal they knew exactly where it stood.

"We could go to my place. My parents are out."

"Let's just—drive around."

A mountain shaped like a woman's breast lies milk-blue and recumbent against the pale horizon. Sam once climbed to the summit of that mountain on a school outing and she thought at the time that it was the very opposite of her mountain. Everywhere she looked, all she saw was evidence of life.

That first time between herself and Tim—it was so shocking, so violent, somehow. Yet it was the most natural thing in the world. They fitted together so neatly. Their bodies felt as if they had been designed for each other. Which, she supposes, they had. But the first time was over too quickly and it happened in the shadow of Matty's presence, his disapproval. The second time—that was the time that changed everything between herself and Tim. He hovered above her like a dancer. Without weight, floating. Although he was on top of her, it was as if she was the one carrying him. He was so soft and open and absolutely hers. It was probably the least lonely moment of her life.

"Are you happy?"

Afterwards, he'd slipped some of his colorful beaded bracelets off his wrist and onto hers. They were a bit large for her arm, but she wore them anyway—and she hasn't taken them off since.

"What?"

"Are you happy?" Tom asks her again.

"I just—I thought I'd feel different, somehow, you know?"

A long, brown train carrying timber runs alongside them for a while until the road rises and dips, rises and dips—and rises again to a landscape where the train no longer exists.

Tom turns up a dirt road lined with eucalyptus

The road is badly corrugated from milk trucks and everything inside the bakkie stutters and jumps as if subject to a sustained electric shock. They pass a long, meandering fence of white wooden posts where a silvery stallion tosses his head and trots away through the grass, his tail lifted, his nostrils flared as he nickers toward a group of interested mares in a neighboring field. Tom slows at a dairy where

Friesland cows are emerging dutifully from a tin-roofed shed, the smell of muck reaching them through the dusty air conditioner.

"Where are we going?" Sam asks.

"I don't know," says Tom. "I've never been here before."

There is another, rougher track leading up to a row of pines. The trees stand there, dark as midnight and hissing like an instrument made to measure the breath of God. Sam watches Tom as he climbs out of the car and opens the old metal farm gate. Dead fronds from the trees are stuck to the wire and there is an old sign saying "Shut this Gate."

They continue up the track, which winds through taller, older grass toward the mound of a bright-green hill. Here they climb out of the bakkie and walk toward the summit. The grass is cool and soft and rubbery. Along the far horizon ahead of them, the uneven wall of the Drakensberg is clearly visible, from Giant's Castle to Champagne Castle—and, beyond it, the distant line of The Bell and Cathedral Peak. There is no longer a cloud in the sky and the air around them is a crazy blue. This is the new world, Sam thinks. The clean world. The world that has always been entirely available and waiting for her to step inside it.

There are few houses ahead of them—only the unfolding hills, the creases in some of the valleys brimming with shining water. A few Friesland dairy cows are visible at the far end of the field, where it slopes down toward a row of workers' cottages, which are masked off by a stand of black wattle. From a nearby rock, a long-claw shrieks in their direction—and above them in the blank sky some grassbird twitters and dives.

"It's lovely here," Tom says.

"It looks as if it's only just been made," Sam says. "Like a new sky and a new hill, covered in new grass."

Tom lays his black school blazer on the grass at the summit of the hill and she sits on it. In the inside pocket of the blazer is a neat row of pens. She smiles as this. Tom is one of those people who always has a pen handy whenever you need one.

"We should've brought a picnic," he says.

"I don't think we'd be able to eat anything," she says. "Are you feeling nervous?"

"A bit."

He kneels in front of her and kisses her mouth. Everything about Tom is so warm and calm. He's as clean as this mountain, as this air. He is entirely a part of them, as if he has also been made new by this place. Their teeth click together and they laugh.

"Are you sure you want to do this?" he asks.

"Totally. Are you?"

"Totally."

She pulls off his tie and unbuttons his shirt. He is still kneeling in front of her, his smooth tanned arms rested reassuringly on each of her shoulders. They have done this before, undressed like this before, but this time they are undressing for a different and more serious reason.

"I read somewhere," Sam says, "that you only really know a person once you've made love to them. Do you think that's true?"

"I feel that I do know you," says Tom.

"I wish that were true."

He leans back to get a better look at her. He has finally registered the snag in her voice.

"If I don't know you," he says, "then I don't know anyone."

She kisses him again to silence him and she pulls him down on top of her. His elbows are on either side of her head, and she runs her hands along the silky length of his back, along the neat contours of his muscles, down the deep groove of his spine. She can feel him through his trousers and she unbuckles his belt and unbuttons his trousers and pulls his clothes away from him so that he is lying entirely naked on top of her.

"You're so beautiful," she says.

She knows there is something bad about what she is doing to him. She should be telling him about Tim. She should be admitting that she is a liar. That she is not the person he thinks she is. She should be telling him that he's about to make love to a stranger. To someone wholly unworthy of him. Yet she wants this. And she wants to be worthy of him. And she wants to be known by him in the best way that a person can be known by anyone.

Caroline

His bedroom is full of dead flies

There are smears of fly blood on the walls, the windows, the door. There are iridescent-green fly corpses everywhere, lying on their backs on bedside tables and windowsills, like broken toys that have folded in on themselves. The silver bomber revolves above the bed slowly, tracking the carnage. A plastic alarm clock that Caroline does not remember ever buying ticks thickly, unstoppably.

It has always been easier to know what Sam is thinking than it has ever been with Matthew. Sam has always had some diary somewhere, conveniently filled with all her worst thoughts about herself—and, especially, others. There Caroline read how she stank of drink in the mornings and how she became all slushy whenever she tried to express her affection. There she read how Sam wished her father was some other father. A man who knew how to behave in public and didn't forever show off at the top of his voice. There she learned when Sam first kissed a boy and when Sam first tried to smoke. It was also in these pages that Sam described how the dead used to come and stand around her bed—but that these days she is only ever haunted by a single figure, elegant and patient as a bullfighter, intent on cutting her throat.

But Matthew has never left any such diary. He is a scrupulous and increasingly private boy. Every morning, he makes his own bed, as he has learned to do at school, and he even empties his bedroom dustbin into the kitchen bin. If he has anything to say about anything, he is keeping it firmly concealed inside his little flaxen head. Matthew has always been the kind of boy who takes the nearest exit during a scene of conflict, returning only later, like a cat reentering a room in which all the furniture has been rearranged.

Matthew's housemaster recently said that what has happened to Matthew happens to most boys his age. They disappear for a few years. But the love that is laid into the foundations of the boy when he was a child, the housemaster continued—that would emerge to determine the man he would become. This idea was supposed to be of comfort to Caroline, but she hated the thought that her son's fate was already set in stone. How could the kind of man Matthew would become have been established when he was still merely the outline of a boy, a dance of light with only the slightest whiff of his adult persona quivering through him? How was such a thing possible? How was it even fair? At the very moment that Caroline was preoccupied with some other thing—irritation with her husband, the search for a cigarette lighter—Matthew had been needing her in some fundamental way to help draw some line inside him, some curve of pathway, that would later provide the space to hold a particular door or window, or that would be able to hold in place some crucial foundation stone. Why had no one told her about this? Why did all the important information always come to her one heartbeat—or ten years—too late?

"What are you doing?"

She turns to find Bruce in the doorway behind her, taking up every available bit of it.

"Nothing," she says.

Which is true.

For a man with such a large, bear-like presence, Bruce has always moved around on padded, sound-proofed paws. She knows that he can see that she has been snooping. Coming into Matthew's private place the moment he has gone back to school after the weekend. Sniffing out all the evidence while it still had something pungent about it.

"You need to leave him alone to work things out for himself," Bruce says.

"But what if he doesn't? What if he doesn't know how to work things out for himself?"

"You need to have a bit of faith."

"In what? In him? In us? The boy has had no decent role models to draw from. For years, he's been walking around in the dark."

Bruce stiffens, noting this for the insult that it is.

"Don't you know that this is the exact age at which many boys kill themselves?"

"Oh for God's sake," says Bruce. "Do you really have to be that melodramatic?"

"Just look at this place," Caroline says. "Who makes his bed so neatly and then leaves his room full of disgusting dead flies? He's trying to tell us something—but I have no idea what."

"He's just a boy. What could he possibly have to say?"

"I don't know. That he's unhappy?"

"Then he can join the boat. If there's enough space left in it."

"Or maybe he knows something that we don't."

"You sound drunk," Bruce concludes.

Caroline wonders whether this is true. These days, it is difficult to know. No matter how much she drinks, she never gets drunk. Which might mean that she's permanently drunk.

"Anyway," says Bruce, "it's Sam and not Matthew we should be worrying about."

"What has Sam done now?"

It has always been Caroline's job to worry about Matthew and Bruce's to worry about Sam. These are their long-established allegiances—and their battle lines.

"There's this whole business with Greene, for a start."

"What business?"

"It's completely obvious that something is going on between them."

"But they both said very clearly that there wasn't."

"Right."

"So—you think there is?"

"Anyone with eyes in his head can see that there is," says Bruce. "She barely seemed to study for her Finals—and I kept seeing them together down at the stables, and in the restaurant. Anyway—I spoke to Greene again and he assured me that nothing has happened between them. But that's not to say that nothing will."

"What are you going to do about it?"

"I haven't decided. But I'll definitely have to ask him to go."

"You can't do that."

"Why not? She's still a schoolgirl. If anything happens—legally, it's rape."

"I can't believe the slut."

"I'm sorry?"

"You heard me."

Bruce looks at her long and hard—as you might into the face of a mad person. "I don't understand how a mother could hate her own child," he says slowly, his voice full of contempt. "I just don't know how to begin to digest that thought."

"Of course I don't hate her," says Caroline without conviction. "But you must admit—there has always been this thing running through her. This insatiable, self-serving vanity. This thing that makes her take whatever she wants—regardless of the consequences."

"Don't you think you're talking about yourself?"

"What is that supposed to mean?"

"Do you really want me to spell it out?"

When Caroline stares back at him, he continues:

"He doesn't belong to you either, Caroline."

"Who?"

"Greene—obviously."

"I don't know what you're talking about."

"You know exactly what I'm talking about. And the worst thing is—everyone else can see it. Sam, Matthew. Even Moses."

"Moses?"

"He tried to warn me some weeks ago. For obvious reasons, I wasn't prepared to listen. But it's clear that you've developed this strange infatuation with the boy and can't help yourself. And you've become the laughing stock of all the staff at the lodge. The drinking, I could stomach. After all, I'm hardly one to get onto that particular high horse. But to slaver over a boy only a few years older than your own son—it's hopeless and disgusting. And it's embarrassing to everyone else who has to witness it."

"I have no idea what you're talking about," Caroline says again.

Bruce turns away, as if, having delivered his speech, he has lost interest in the argument. "Just leave Matthew alone," he says. "That's all I ask."

She circumvents the circle of stones and starts to run

Every part of the house is hostile to her because every part of it belongs to Bruce. Every window and door out of it encloses a view he has chosen, over a landscape for which he has spoken. The only place Caroline has been able to find in recent months that does not contain Bruce, and Bruce's gaze, is Tim. Their secret felt like a victory, like something active and alive at last. But under Bruce's gaze it has become something coarse and defiled, and she is a shameful animal, a disgrace, an object of ridicule. And what is Tim Greene? Some predator moving between a mother and a daughter, using them for whatever he wants? What person could do a thing like that? To look so perfect, to behave so sweetly and tenderly, and be all lie? She had thought of him as someone in need of her care, in some way. As a mother, yes. But more than a mother. Also as a lover. As someone who could meet him in the most fundamental way and arrive at some kind of good, some kind of truth. And it hadn't only been about the sex. She had seen through sex many decades ago. It had been about something more urgent and important. As vital to her continued survival as her own beating heart. But it turns out that what she thought of as good and true was neither. It was some other thing her imagination is too meek and ignorant of evil to grasp.

Only when her ankle twists in a runnel in the road does she realize that she's still wearing her sheepskin slippers. But it's too late to go back and change. She has left Bruce alone in the house. A house she will never be able to re-enter again. Her only hope is Tim. Perhaps he'll be able to persuade her that all is well between them and that this spectre Bruce has raised is nothing more than one of his macabre inventions.

She finds his drummer-boy room unlocked, as usual

He is lying on his bed, on his back, his left arm over his face so that his torso and a ripple of ribs are exposed. The mosquito net has been knotted above him and hangs there like a large jellyfish. Two flies are resting on the place where his belly breathes. He often sleeps like this, with his body laid out like some sacrifice, one long limb raised to counterbalance the raised arm. The room smells of beer and cigarettes and his clothes are on the rug where he stepped out of them—the boots, the jeans with the boxer shorts still inside them, and a single yellow sock protruding from a leg. They might be the clothes someone left at the edge of the shore before going swimming, or the clothes of someone who suddenly found themselves capable of flight.

Caroline has brought a shaft of afternoon light into the room by opening the door, but still Tim does not stir. He is breathing slowly and luxuriously—and, as she watches him, his mouth moves with what might be a smile, or a particular phrase that is running through his head that pleases him. She has kissed that mouth. She knows now, on seeing him, that Sam has too. It's clear that the large doll lying there belongs to no one. Least of all to Caroline.

"You animal," she says, trying out her voice in the room.

She pulls away the sheet, exposing the length of his nakedness. There at the heart of him, as expected, is the dark bone, mid-dream, flailing and full of yearning. Some blind, burrowing creature that has finally been brought out to the light. Tim smiles again in his sleep and his hand feels for the sheet and finds nothing.

"You fucking animal!"

Only now does he open his eyes. He looks at her from an ironic distance—as if he always knew, in some part of him, that she would come in here like this, looking like a mad old woman in a dressing gown shouting at her own demons, her own ghosts, which have nothing to do with him.

"What's going on?" he asks, trying to sound an optimistic note.

"You tell me," she says.

"I have no idea of what you're shouting about."

He has made no attempt to cover his body. Now he looks down at himself as if it is his body, and not himself personally, that Caroline is fighting over.

"What have you done with Sam?"

"Sam?"

"I'm asking you a question."

"I'm aware of that, Caroline. But I don't know why you would think I have done anything with Sam. As far as I'm aware, she's safely back at school."

"Oh don't play games with me," says Caroline. "You have been fucking her, haven't you?"

The word sounds terrible, stated like this—but then it is terrible.

"Really, Caroline."

A normal person would have covered himself up by now, but still Tim has made no attempt to do this—even as that thing has withdrawn back into something revolting and risible, looking around for its shell.

"How could you betray my trust like this?"

"Your trust?"

He sounds thrown by such an idea.

"She's still a child."

"Believe me, she's not a child."

"She's still at school!"

"Wasn't it today that she had her last exam? FS English, I believe it was."

"I should be calling the police!"

Now he laughs. "What the hell for?"

"It's rape!"

"Believe me," says Tim, "Sam is not about to go to the police and accuse me of that. Whatever happened between us, she was the one who asked for it."

He sits up now—the sheet back over his hips as if by magic. Caroline holds onto the door frame. She is finding it difficult to breathe. She is having to hold hard onto the edge of the spinning world.

"Don't you get it?" he asks after a sufficient pause.

She looks at him, waiting for him to say it, waiting for him to say that they love each other, that they're going away together. Instead, he says something far worse.

"She hates you. And she hates this place. Me? Even if she doesn't know it, I'm just another means of escape. She wants to get as far away from you people as possible. As soon as she can, she's going to run and run, and she won't stop running until she's as good as dead."

"And—what if I told her? What if I told her—about us?"

"She would only run further. And hate you more."

Caroline sees that he is angry, finally. At the very least, she has accomplished that.

Not knowing what else to do, she walks away from him, not bothering to slam the door. She finds that she is only wearing one slipper—and she kicks it away from her like a dead rat.

PART SEVEN

THE WRITER

The school's psychologist had glasses the color of dirty water

He had a soft voice and skin that glistened like a snail. He showed Daniel pictures of squashed butterflies and asked him to make sense of them. He gave him sets of multiple-choice questions that were clearly intended to assess the extent to which Daniel had a borderline personality disorder—or was a psychopath. He even handed Daniel a play in which a boy gouged out the eyes of a stable-full of horses because he had a complicated relationship with his god. Yet Daniel left school with the idea of becoming a psychologist. Perhaps he simply wanted to make sense of his own phantasms, which screamed back at him in his dreams the way a Medusa does when you mistake it for your own mother.

Daniel left school with no clear idea of what he was, of what his woodgrain was, in spite of his teachers, the housemaster and the priest all urging him to "know thyself" and making him recite such poems as "Invictus" and "If"—which were less poetry than thinly veiled masculine propaganda. But on the day Daniel stood in the queue to register for his university subjects, he found that Psychology clashed with History of Art and he chose the comparatively useless subject of History of Art instead.

Daniel had also more or less stopped writing by then. The bright stories, poems and drawings he had made at his junior school had given way to rather wild and speculative essays that a few weeks later even he could barely decipher. His senior school English teacher—a failed writer himself—had also discouraged Daniel from writing, stating that his style was turgid and pretentious. Daniel was simply trying too hard. The poems he tried to write were bristling with such complicated metrical and rhyme schemes that they soon exhausted themselves—and, by the time they had reached the final full stop, there was little of their original life left inside them.

A boy called Adam with whom Daniel had never been close at school came to live with them. Adam's mother had been at school with Daniel's mother and Adam and Daniel were supposed to be friends. Adam's parents lived on a small and unprofitable farm somewhere in the KwaZulu-Natal Midlands. He was to stay at Daniel's house for almost no rent. Every morning, Daniel and Adam would drive into the university together with Daniel's mother—she was the Secretary of the Fine Art Department—and every afternoon they would all drive home. Adam was doing a Drama degree and Daniel was doing a straight Bachelor of Arts, studying History of Art, English, Linguistics and Philosophy.

In the evenings, Daniel and Adam would climb onto the roof of the house and smoke Adam's homegrown cannabis. Sometimes, Adam would strum songs from Supertramp and Led Zeppelin on his acoustic guitar. Adam had a mop of blond hair and a jolly, high-colored face—and Daniel, who was good at finding ways to like people, soon learned how to like him. Daniel spent much of his time when he was not studying working his way through the Penguin Classics catalog, although he shied away from any book that smacked of a happy ending.

One day, Adam came home with a girl called Jade. She was already in her final year of a Drama degree. Jade had a reputation on campus for having had several boyfriends, sometimes simultaneously, and for taking dangerous drugs. She was also reputed to be a very talented singer. Jade always wore black and bright-red lipstick and she had a Jacobean air about her. She was funny and ironic and for some reason she found Daniel hilarious. They soon became a threesome and Jade more or less moved in—especially over the weekends. The roof of the house had a good view of the Nazi-designed Voortrekker Monument—and from this vantage point they would talk for half the night. They were directly above the room in which Lucy had died. Although Daniel never mentioned it, he sometimes felt the presence of his little sister, sitting there beside them in the dark.

It soon emerged that Jade was a bit of a witch. She knew all about Glassy Glassy and tarot cards and star signs and she claimed to have telepathic powers. She called Daniel Monkey Man—actually, Affemann, because she had a German father and she spoke the language fluently. Daniel would sometimes ask her to read the "Duino Elegies" in the original German—and although Daniel didn't understand the words themselves, the night air would become thick with angels freshly unearthed from the Underworld.

> Wer, wenn ich schriee, hörte mich den aus der Engel
> Ordnungen? und gesetzt selbst, es nähme
> einer mich plötzlich ans Herz: ich verging von seinem
> stärkeren Dasein. Denn das Schöne ist nichts
> als des Schrecklichen Anfang, den wir noch grade ertragen,
> und wir bewundern es so, weil es gelassen verschmäht,
> uns zu zerstören. Ein jeder Engel ist schrecklich.

One weekend, when Adam went home to visit his parents, Jade asked Daniel around to her flat for dinner. It was near the university in Auckland Park. Her room was in the basement of an old miner's cottage. It consisted of a large double mattress on the floor, a jungle of indoor plants, candles, incense holders and dreamcatchers. There they drank red wine and listened to Sigur Rós and smoked a few joints and ended up having sex. Daniel had never had sex before. The sex happened without Daniel considering whether or not he even found Jade attractive. Jade introduced the idea as a joke, a game, and this helped Daniel into the experience with some dignity. But for Daniel it was deadly serious. It was not only a betrayal of Adam, whom neither of them had ever quite taken seriously, but it would mark the beginning of Daniel's new life.

As soon as Adam returned from his parents' house, he was told about this new development. Within a week, he had moved out, taking with him his collection of guitars, cannabis plants and home-made pipes. For some reason, Daniel's mother hated Jade from that moment onwards—and so Daniel moved in with Jade in her basement room, only sometimes crossing paths with his mother at the university. Perhaps Daniel was exacting revenge on his mother for their history of dislocated attachments, but at the time it did not feel like revenge. Daniel believed himself to be happy. Properly happy. For the first time in his life. Finally, he could locate inside himself someone who was worthy of being loved. Whether this was an illusion conjured up by a combination of the novelty of sex and Jade's witchcraft, or whether it was something real and enduring, Daniel did not care to contemplate. Jade's plan was to move to Bremen, where her parents lived, at the end of the year. There she would record her first album and become famous. All Daniel had to do was finish his degree and learn German before joining her. With his marks, a post-graduate scholarship to a good European university would be almost inevitable.

Although Daniel did visit Jade in Germany a few times, their relationship soon ended. Jade found a spotty journalist who sported a Stetson and modeled himself on Humphrey Bogart and she wrote Daniel a long letter in which she severed herself from him forever. A year later, when they met up in London for a drink, she told Daniel that even during their first blissful months of being together she had started to feel unsatisfied. Although Daniel had seemed wholly available and present at first, he had soon moved off to some other place that she could never access. Even when he emerged from this private place, he continued to carry it with him, as a man might carry a secret lover. She told him that his declarations of love were always more about his own feelings than they ever were about her. She could have been anyone.

These words were difficult for Daniel to hear. Little did he know that they would be repeated, with variations, by practically every girlfriend afterwards. But he remained deeply indebted to Jade. In those first months, she had wanted to reach into every part of him and bring each part into the light. There she had found a young boy driving with his mother through a field of mealies. There she had found the same boy watching his father beating a goose to death. She had taken this boy and led him elsewhere, back to the scenes of happiness that he had experienced with his mother, father and sister before sickness and death moved in on them. She had also taken him to new places. The first of these was her own body, which fitted together with his in a way that was miraculous. Another was a new kind of laughter. An embodied, forgiving laughter. This inspired Daniel's long essay on James Joyce's novel *Ulysses*, in which Daniel found a new way of being-in-the-world, a Rabelaisian embodied laughter that was a laughter of the body, of forgiveness and democracy—instead of the intellectual, censorious laughter he associated with Nietzsche, which placed itself on the highest mountains and laughed at all tragedies, real or imaginary.

Within days of first making love with Jade, Daniel also regained the ability to write—the clarity and conviction and intensity of thought and feeling required to delve into language and bring something new to life. Almost overnight, he found he could write poetry in whatever meter he chose for himself—iambic, dactylic, anapestic—and any rhyme scheme, however baroque. These devices—and all the other poetic devices at his disposal—simply appeared in his poems already up and running, the content finding its form as organically, spontaneously and miraculously as if Daniel was writing out something that someone more resolved and resolute had already felt and written.

His first poem returned to the boy trapped inside the car. He started with the rows of mealies, with row flicking thickly after row, and the mother transcending the car with a scream—and the car flying off the side of the road and hanging there like a toy car before dropping and rolling and sliding. The poem ended with the boy climbing out of the car and leaving his mother lying there—knowing that she was dead.

Daniel would later reflect on this poem, this starting point, and he would wonder whether or not there was something Oedipal about every act of creation. The killing off of the parent, the failed figure of authority, in order to make a new homeland, a new motherland or fatherland, that had a better chance of sustaining him. It was no wonder that Daniel's mother had hated Jade. Jade was complicit in this final act of abandonment, this final killing off of Daniel's mother. She was the one who had handed Daniel the knife—not knowing that he would not only use it to kill off his mother, but to sever himself from her forever.

Natasha has invited him for dinner at her apartment

He arrives with a large bunch of lemon-yellow roses and a bottle of pinot noir. He has not seen her since their first date, their first kiss, although they have spoken a few times on the phone. In each of his exchanges with Natasha, she has stuck him as a new kind of person. There is something about the way she lives in the world that wakes him up to the world. Seen through Natasha's eyes, everyday reality reveals surprising new vistas. It is like opening your bedroom window to find a day rinsed clean after a long night of rain and flooded with golden light and birdsong. Natasha's world—or so it seems to Daniel—is a world in which everything is permitted to live fully. Where everything that lives is holy.

This may well all be an illusion, of course. A mirage after a thunderstorm. Another bout of wishful thinking on Daniel's part. He has had his fair share of such misconceptions over the years—and they have never ended happily. But where before his days have felt like the same day repeated over and over again, there is something about Natasha's arrival in his life that feels like a fresh beginning, a day one.

She opens the door as if she has been waiting right there, at the threshold, all day, for him. This is another thing about Natasha. She never hesitates. She comes at whatever it is she wants clear and straight—and Daniel finds it impossible to resist.

"There you are," she says. "Come inside."

She moves quickly into the room before they have a moment to regard each other properly. He realizes that she might be as nervous as he is. This thing between them has been building up like a great, green wave—and neither of them has found the words to comprehend or contain it.

Her apartment smells of frying onions, garlic and freshly chopped parsley.

"Where's Rafael?" Daniel asks.

"Away at camp. It's the first time he's been away from me for the night. And it's two nights. And I must say—it's terrible. Why do you think camp has to be a rehearsal for Vietnam?" she asks with a laugh. "Why does it have to be all about war? Why can't it be all about love? Singing around the campfire? Learning the names of the different stars? Making a play about the birth of the world?"

"Does he at least have a group of friends?"

"Rafael can only take in one person at a time. He's only ever had one friend, which means that when that friend is being nice to him, he is happy—and when that friend goes away or has a fight with him, his life is hell."

"That sounds familiar."

"He's the same when he eats," Natasha continues. "He likes his ingredients to be separated out on his plate. He'll eat all of the tomatoes and then all of the carrots. I'm not sure what he'll do at camp—with their unfamiliar food and with so many other boys surrounding him. Usually, it's only him and me. Which I suppose is exactly why he needs to go on this damn camp."

"I'm sure he'll be absolutely fine," Daniel says, doing his best to sound hopeful. "These flowers are for you."

She turns and looks at him and steps forward to take the flowers—and she kisses him instead.

"I really do need to stop doing that," she says, laughing. "I'm sorry—I just feel this overwhelming impulse. You must think me very forward."

"Honestly—you can do it as often as you like."

They laugh again, sounding more relieved, as she turns away to find a vase large enough for the flowers.

"Would you mind opening the wine?" she asks, gesturing toward a chilled bottle of green wine.

Grateful for the activity, he looks for a bottle-opener in the drawers and finds one in the most logical place. This apartment is the very opposite of his mother's house. In the house in which he grew up, nothing was where you expected it—and, as soon as you had learned to expect it in the unexpected place, its position had once again shifted.

"I'm making my grandmother's Caldeirada," she says. "I hope you like fish."

"I love fish."

"I don't usually make it when Rafael's at home. Too many ingredients."

By now she has arranged the flowers and she places them on the dinner table, which, like the rest of the apartment, is all neatly laid out, with everything in its allotted place. Only now does Daniel pay attention to the music in the background—a woman singing to the accompaniment of a guitar, her voice full of melancholy and loss.

"What's this music?" Daniel asks.

"Fado," Natasha says. "Don't tell me you've never heard fado before? It's full of what we call saudade. The longing for something or someone that you know, deep down, will never be encountered again. My grandmother used to sing these songs while cooking. I like to have it playing whenever I'm making one of her meals. I'm sorry if it sounds a bit mournful, but it has the odd effect of raising my spirits. It's such a celebration of life, of living—even if to be alive is sometimes to be in pain."

"I like it," Daniel says.

He watches Natasha as she pours half a cup of white wine and one cup of chicken stock into a mixture of onions, tomatoes and garlic. Then she adds a squeeze of fish paste, a pinch of saffron and some crushed cloves, followed by a handful of olives and a teaspoon heaped with burned paprika, which immediately gives the room the smoky aroma of chorizo sausage.

"You're supposed to add potatoes," Natasha says, "but my grandmother always baked sliced sweet potatoes separately, in olive oil, and then fried them up with garlic and rosemary to make them golden and crispy. We would eat that instead of bread. She also used shellfish, usually—but today we're having some of the trout that Rafael caught on a farm near Nottingham Road."

"It sounds lovely."

"Do you like fishing?"

"I used to fish for trout and bass as a kid. But I haven't done any fishing since."

"Rafael likes it very much. I find it so awful—the way you have to club such a beautiful creature over the head with a wooden stick. A priest, I think you call it. Although heaven knows why they would want to call it that. But I am grateful for the fish. It goes very well with my grandmother's Caldeirada."

Daniel hands her a glass of wine and they clink glasses, smiling into each other's eyes. Looking into Natasha's face is like looking at a constellation of stars. He wants to kiss the watermark under her left eye, but instead he tastes the wine, which is dry and fruity and reminds him of holidays by the sea.

"To us," Natasha says.

"To us."

Natasha has baked the trout separately. She takes it out of the oven and places a small trout in each of their wide bowls. Over this, she pours the broth, sprinkling the dish with black pepper, chopped parsley and chilli flakes. Then she arranges the sweet potato slices around the bowl on a large plate.

"You'll have to eat it with a spoon," she says.

The dish is layered and fragrant and it sends a warm glow through him.

"This is delicious. Thank you."

"You can thank my grandmother."

"You mean—she's still alive?"

"Alive and well in Mozambique."

"And your parents?"

"My parents are both dead. They were killed not long after I was born. During the civil war in Mozambique. It was my grandmother who brought me up."

"I'm sorry."

"Yes—we have always been surrounded by such violence. It's why evenings like this are precious. And important. I'm very happy that you're here, Daniel."

"I am too."

They eat silently—the food and the drink and the music carrying them to some other place and some other time, which is also this place and this time, and like no other place or time Daniel has ever experienced.

"We have both been surrounded by a great deal of death," he says.

Natasha looks at him, saying nothing.

"And yet, it seems to me, you have carried on living. You haven't been brought down by it. Or drawn away from wanting to live because of it."

"Where I come from," Natasha says, "death is not such an important thing. It is very soon absorbed back into life. My grandmother said you must always have a packed suitcase at the foot of your bed—so you are always ready to catch the next train. Her favorite thing was to travel on a train. Whenever I couldn't sleep at night, she would lie next to me and we would imagine we were lying on our bunks inside a train. We would travel all the way across Africa and across Europe. We would visit all the cities along the way—always with a suitcase ready and packed for the next train, the next city."

"You must miss her, living all the way down here."

"Raffy and I see her a couple of times every year. We always spend Christmas with her in Mozambique. She has a very busy life, with lots of friends. She is happy to think of me and Raffy out in the world, going to new places, meeting new people. She would be happy to see the two of us sitting here, like this."

By now, Daniel has finished his plate. He pours more wine.

"I also traveled after university," he says. "I lived in London for a while, working in the theatre. And I lived in Paris, where I taught English. What I realized, though, was that it doesn't matter where you go. It doesn't matter where you live. When I was living in Paris, for instance, I would occasionally look around and realize that I was living in Paris—but most of the time it was myself I was living in. I was either asleep or eating or cooking or reading or working—and I could have been doing these things anywhere. The pastries were better and there was a wider choice of cheese. The people around me were also generally speaking French. But otherwise Paris could have been anywhere."

"That sounds quite sad."

"I think it was, in a way. I was always most concerned with writing my next book. Where I lived was not so important. Which meant I never really lived. I never lived in London or in Paris. I was too lost inside myself. I was too sad, somewhere. Or not sad, exactly. I lacked the will, you know? I lacked the appetite to go out and meet the place, the people. I think I was trying to fix something inside myself. I had to try to fix this thing, resolve this thing, before I could be available for the world, for living inside the world. I suppose I thought I'd be able to resolve this thing through writing."

"And did you find this thing, resolve this thing?"

"I never did," Daniel laughs.

"Oh well—you have at least written some interesting books along the way."

"It was coming back to this country that made me resolve one important thing, at least."

"What was that?"

"The idea that this is where it matters. For me. This place, the people inside it. They are what matter. I could have lived in London or Paris for the rest of my life, but the place and the people would never have meant very much to me—and I would never have had anything of any interest to say about them. Here, in spite of everything—this is where I belong."

"So where you live does matter. It isn't only about what's going on inside yourself?"

"I'm finally beginning to understand that—yes."

Daniel doesn't know what the woman in the background is singing about. She sounds very sad about something. Maybe some man she has lost. He looks at Natasha and finds himself smiling. She is wearing red lipstick and a white cotton dress with mother-of-pearl buttons down the front of it. Her hair is the color of a crow's wing. She is the most beautiful woman he has ever seen, and she is smiling right back at him.

He carries their plates to the sink and when he turns he finds her already fitted neatly inside his arms. Soon they are swaying to the music. They are inside the same sea. She smells of lemons, of honeysuckle and sunlight. His mouth is one movement away from her neck. Now and again, his lips brush past her skin. He smells the summer of her hair. He isn't thinking about anything. He is mute and numb with wonder.

They move across the room, beginning to unbutton each other's clothes. Their clothes float to the floor, but their beating hearts remain. Daniel is shuddering. It is a sensation close to weeping. Their hands move over each other's bodies, but their hands belong to both of them—they are two parts of the same desire, the same mystery that is very carefully being opened out, like a strange flower, into the waiting world.

Afterwards, they lie in each other's arms

They are two bodies afloat, adrift in two bodies made of light. Around them, there is only the night, and the golden circles coming in from the streetlamp, yawning and straying with the movement of the autumn wind.

"Are you still here?" Natasha asks, wiping a tear from her cheek.

"I am."

"I had forgotten how—frightening it was."

"What?"

"This."

He knows what she means—and he knows that she means nothing bad.

"Really living can be more frightening than anything," he says.

"That is why people find it so hard to sustain."

"So how do you sustain it?"

"I have no idea," she laughs. "Perhaps you let it sustain you. You relinquish the idea of control. Perhaps that's why it's so frightening. And liberating. I think you have to be completely open to the world if you want the truth to happen."

The next morning, he drives back to the lodge like a man emerging from a dream

The world filters back to him like an idea that had been forgotten about—yet he finds himself coming toward it from a wholly new direction, as if he is returning from a long holiday in some distant land. He drives through an old avenue of oak trees, crosses a bridge over a shimmering stretch of water, pauses to allow some goats to skitter across the road—and all of it comes to him like a story he has heard before, a story about some other man in some other time who once passed through this place.

Only now does Daniel realize that he never spoke to Natasha about Sam's disappearance and the latest speculations about the young woman's death. There exists between them an instinct for tact, for some unspoken level of decency, that he is happy to find intact inside both of them.

Reality returns, however, in the form of David

Daniel finds him sitting on the wooden deck in the shade of the fever tree, drinking a slim pint of German beer. Daniel realizes that he has been avoiding David ever since he saw him hiding behind the bush. But in his new state he is happy to see him. He is happy to see anyone.

"You're looking very pleased with yourself," David says. "A good morning of writing?"

"A good morning of—not writing," Daniel laughs.

He orders a beer, even though it's not yet time for lunch.

"So how are your orcs getting along?" Daniel asks.

"Never better, thanks."

"And your investigations?"

"All very interesting."

David clearly wants him to ask more about this, but Daniel finds he has no interest in the latest facts. Sam is gone. That other woman is dead. The details of how it happened are no longer important. Whatever happened to Sam, he only hopes that she didn't suffer. That whatever came to end her life did so quickly.

Moses emerges from the building, carrying Daniel's beer on a plastic tray, staring at it owlishly. Daniel can see at once that he's drunk—and he realizes that he's never seen Moses drunk before. He has always been the very embodiment of sobriety.

"Nawu ubhiya wakho," Moses says.

"Thanks."

"Ngingakunika ingilazi?"

"Sorry?"

"Do you want a glass for it?"

"The beer? No thanks. The bottle is fine."

Moses gives out a humph and turns and walks inside.

"They have arrested his son," David says conspiratorially.

"Sorry?"

"The police have Simon Ngobese in custody. Ngobese was seen at the lodge with the hooker before she disappeared. They were seen at the bar and later they were heard arguing. They think that Ngobese is the one who killed her—and threw her body in the river."

"And Tim Greene? Have you spoken to him recently?"

"I saw him around here two days ago, but the bugger refused to talk to me. Threatened me with violence, in fact."

"But—does any of this have anything to do with the disappearance of Sam?"

"Who knows?" David says, clinking the top of Daniel's bottle with the side of his glass. "But it feels like we're getting closer to the truth, old chap, don't you think?"

"You know what?" Daniel says, suddenly standing. "I think I've changed my mind about the drink."

"But I wanted to tell you more about my orcs!"

"I'm sorry, David, but I couldn't give a fuck about your orcs."

THE BUTTERFLY COLLECTOR

There are times in human history when people rise up
to meet each other in a force
that can no longer be called human

Years later, Bruce Webster would assure his listeners that the Zulu soldiers understood this. When you were a soldier, you were no longer a man. You were no longer a father, a husband, a son, a brother. You were an instrument of death. You had been handed over to some other heightened thing that was outside of everyday life. What you did in those twilight hours was what you might have done in a dream. You were not yourself, but a shadow-self. The darkness you dragged behind you during your hours under the sun, shaped like a shadow, slipped back inside of you—and you became that other phantom thing, that clear killing thing, that had no known name and was free to do whatever was required of it in order to endure.

This did not mean that you were not responsible for your actions. What you did during those hours defined you forever. The stories that were told about you afterwards were the stories through which much of your worth would be measured. You would be remembered for your acts of courage and your acts of cowardice. Those who survived would tell those stories about you whether you lived or died—or liked it or not.

Before going into battle—at least as Bruce liked to narrate it—the Zulu soldiers assembled at the king's homestead and underwent ceremonies in order to gain the blessing and support of their ancestors, who later came into the field of battle with them, as alive and present as any living man, to influence events. The healers gave each man an emetic that caused him to vomit and purge himself and cast out the presence of those spirits—known and unknown—that stood in his way. The younger men were each tasked with killing a black bull with their bare hands. Once the bull was dead, the hide was stripped and the beast was cut into strips, roasted over open fires and eaten so that its strength passed into those who consumed it. The meat was treated with medicines that offered strength and protection. When the ceremonies were finished, those who had participated were no longer themselves. They were bound together into a single entity and prepared for the shedding of blood. This state of openness made each man vulnerable to spiritual corruption, so he had to abstain from any activity associated with his former life.

Before leaving for battle, the weapons of each soldier were treated with medicines that gave them extra power. The soldiers assembled at the banks of the White Umfolozi where the bodies of celebrated warriors from before King Shaka's time had been laid to rest. The men sang songs and praises that lifted the spirits of the dead from their slumber so that these men could rise again and walk with them into battle.

Shortly before the army was to attack, the healers splashed the soldiers with protective medicines that contained the body parts of enemies who had been killed in previous battles. Each soldier also had his own privately procured medicines that were carried in pouches around their necks or in containers inside their earlobes. These were inhaled through the nose in the form of snuff. Many contained stimulants and hallucinogens including aloe juice and cannabis. In the heat of battle, the soldiers were often in such a heightened state that they killed everything they saw, including horses, oxen, mules, sacks of wheat—and, in some cases, the figures of those who may not have been there in physical form. It was essential to disembowel the enemy after you had killed him so that his spirit did not remain to haunt you and could be released into the afterlife. Zulu soldiers wore the clothes of those they had killed for a period after the fighting was over, and they often removed body parts of the dead that were associated with fecundity—like a man's beard or genitals—so that they could be used for medicine.

Those who returned after battle were considered still "wet with yesterday's blood." They were to remain away from their homesteads until they had cleansed themselves of the blackness of spirit that had been produced by those they had slaughtered. Those who had killed were believed to be spiritually contaminated and they ran the risk of bringing this corruption into their communities. Special isolated homesteads were made available to these men and for several days they were cleansed by the healers. Each man would be wearing the clothes of those he had killed and he would have with him the bloodied weapons they had used during battle. The soldiers were taken to a nearby stream, where they removed all their clothing and washed themselves and were treated with purging medicines. Only then were they allowed to return to their communities with the stories of their deeds in battle firmly established inside them, and all around them, for all their remaining days on earth, and forever afterwards.

There is a particular cricket—the short-tailed cricket—that eats its own wings

It may be that the cricket does this because it no longer needs to fly. It may be that it has arrived at the place for which it was intended. A new territory, a place for breeding—or a place for dying. But to eat your own wings? That is worse than Icarus. There are also rat snakes and cobras that are said to consume themselves, either drawn to the movement of their own tails, or attracted to the scent of their prey on their own bodies, and so they begin to swallow themselves until they are stuck there, somewhere between the predator and the prey, until starvation overtakes them.

In the natural world, the act of self-cannibalism usually has a biological function. The human body, for example, naturally digests its own tongue cells or cheek cells. There are accounts of people in some cultures wanting to gain nutrients by eating their own skin or drinking their own blood, and some women have consumed their placenta after birth to ward off post-partum depression. But self-cannibalism has also been practiced as a punishment. As recently as the 1990s, young refugees in Sudan had their left ears cut off because it was claimed they were not listening to the Koran—and before they were released they had their ears returned to them and were forced to eat them.

There is also the mythic Greek serpent or dragon, the ouroboros, which is famous for consuming itself. The ouroboros entered Western iconography through Egypt and Greece and became a potent symbol in alchemy, where it represents the merging of the phallic tail and the yonic mouth—and is seen as a representation of the eternal cycle of life and death.

On the day of the dead moon, however, the only thing that Lieutenant Charles Hawthorne would experience was the cycle of death, of men killing men in a cycle that had no way out, no alternative course, until there was no longer a living enemy to stand on the earth and fight.

We find him in the middle of a strange dance

When at first the Zulu army rises to meet them, Charles's first impulse is to watch it as you might a huge wave coming toward you. In that first moment, it is difficult to believe that what he is seeing exists, and is not some mad dream, of earth becoming blood, of a whole land ascending into a sea of moving human forms, each one filled with one purpose—the single intention to kill. Yet at the same time he understands with every part of his body the meaning of this moment. He understands that he, and the other men around him, have entered a place where they do not belong, and where they have no rights—and he understands that this incursion into an alien land has unleashed a force so ageless and inevitable that there will be no stopping it until the last of them is gone.

Clifton Lass moves first. She swerves around and starts to gallop away down the crest of the spur. It's as if the whole of the land is alive beneath them. Charles quickly passes Sprite, the blank face of Sprite, his pipe sitting forgotten in his mouth like the key to a wind-up toy. Further along the spur, he is joined by the galloping spectre of Bayley, who for once in his life has nothing left to say. Although several men have already arranged themselves into little units, and are firing into the great tide that is moving toward them, it is as effective as throwing pebbles into the sea—and soon they are lost in the oncoming wave of the Zulu army.

Charles rides for a while alongside a riderless roan-gray horse, given over to the wild blood of his horse. The horses are galloping in one direction and it takes a while for Charles to realize that they are returning instinctively to the safety of the camp. They do not know that there is not much left there to defend. No trenches, no laagered wagons, no coherent lines of defense. Chelmsford and most of the army are already many miles away. He has left the remainder of the camp under the command of Pulleine, along with some men from the 24th and the Native Contingent—and Durnford's column, which left that morning on an excursion of their own.

Only when Charles realizes that he is riding alone does he rein in his horse. The Zulu army is now well behind and many of the British have dismounted along a more secure rocky crest to fire back at them. Charles rides up to where some men from his contingent are lined along the ridge, firing volleys toward the opposite hill—and he fits himself between them and starts firing. The Zulus are no longer rushing toward them, but have dropped into the grass and are advancing man by man, rock by rock.

On a flanking crest, Charles sees Tyrell running toward his horse and being shot in the back. Tyrell's arms are thrown out for a moment in a gesture like an attempted embrace, before he is shot again and does an absurd pirouette and disappears into the grass. Charles feels nothing. He observes the scene from far away. He is watching an inevitable natural event taking place. As though each of them in those hills is already dead and is playing out some re-enactment from the forgotten past.

"Hold the line!" Sprite is shouting—as some men from the Native Contingent dissolve around him and retreat back down the hill. Sprite continues to fire into the opposite slope, and then he too turns and runs down to his horse and mounts and gallops off—deeper into the valley. When the men around Charles see this, they too clamber onto their horses and leave. Charles continues to shoot, even managing to injure one man, before he sees that the wind-rippled grass not twenty yards ahead is alive with creeping human forms—and he too mounts his horse and flees.

It takes them an hour to return to the camp

The men are withdrawing toward the shadow of the mountain shaped like a lion, which is faced away from them, as if it has not noticed this latest activity—staring, as it is, toward all the stars in heaven. From a spur to the side of Charles, there is the sound of bugles as a stronger line of defense is established by what look to be Durnford's men and the able-bodied who had been left in the camp. The column of what is most likely the 24th can be identified from a hanging white column of smoke from the powder of their rifles and artillery—and, from the left, what sounds like rounds from a mountain gun screams across the sky.

It would appear that much of the threat is coming from the north. Ahead of them are a series of dongas that provide relative shelter for the advancing enemy—and, as the shooting continues, some of their soldiers try to maneuver themselves so as to be able to shoot into the dead ground ahead of them. From where Charles is positioned, this appears to have almost no effect—and it does not take much longer for the Zulus' rifles to come within range of the camp. Charles hears the drum-roll of the infantry volleys and the popping of the British carbines—and all the time the humming and buzz of the Zulu soldiers, punctuated now and again by their unintelligible war cries.

By now the sun is at its height. The smoke of the guns and rifles is hanging thickly in the windless air. An opened ammunition box is delivered to Charles's men, but moments later they have to withdraw from their position and are forced to abandon it. As the Zulus advance, it is impossible for Charles to see what is happening. Everything around him is slowed and slurred and deliberate. His tongue is an alien thing inside his mouth. His hands are burned and bleeding. His jacket has come undone and one of his boots is torn—by a bullet or a rock. He hears a man moaning—half sobbing, half speaking to himself—and then he realizes it is he who is jabbering thus, in a language never heard by human ears before. He knows that Will is somewhere in all the chaos not far behind him.

Barely able to walk. Barely able to defend himself. Each of Charles's decisions since the Zulu army was first mobilized—he only now realizes—has been, in some way, connected to Will, connected to the only thing in all of this madness that he understands and that means anything.

Some yards to his left, he sees a man being cut to pieces by five other men—a straw man dressed in a red coat, his arms flailing as if pulled by strings. Then a horse comes galloping straight toward him and he steps out of its way and watches it continue toward the Zulu line, dragging the dead sack of its rider, who still has his boot caught in a stirrup and appears to be dead. An artillery shell explodes a few yards away from them—and both horse and rider hang suspended in the air before they disappear in a cloud of earth and smoke.

As they continue to withdraw toward the lines of tents, several yellow butterflies that Charles recognizes as *Terias brigitta* ascend through the air ahead of him—and he wonders whether he might be dreaming them. The ground beneath him—the earth and the grass and the stones—feel curiously numb. Everything is heavier, as if the magnetic pull of the earth has increased tenfold, infecting every animate and inanimate thing. It's as if there is no feeling left in the world. Only this dumbness. This fumbling about in the gathering dark. With Will lost and alone somewhere at the other end of it.

The bugles soon sound again and the men mount and ride back to the camp on their horses. As soon as the Zulus see this, they let out a triumphant cry and come charging toward them—many of the men discarding their shields so they can run faster. Although some of the British stop to fire dislocated volleys as they retreat, they do nothing to stem the advance of the Zulu soldiers.

Orders are being shouted to defend the camp, but from where Charles is riding it is difficult to see where the line of defense begins and where it ends. In several places, the grass is so high that the enemy can hardly be seen. In one area that appears entirely still, dozens of Zulus stand and overwhelm a position and more men are killed. One of these, he notes, is Sprite. Sprite stands to find a spear already running through his heart. He drops to his knees as the shadow-form of the enemy flows past him—his body kneeling as if in supplication—but already he is irrelevant—and again Charles finds that he feels nothing. He knows that Sprite no longer exists. That the man kneeling there is merely the afterthought of Sprite. Nothing that is known is known. Everything Charles knew was a lie. This scene—this is the truth. This is merely God communing with two aspects of Himself. Using whatever forms are available to Him.

As the Zulus close in, the only coherent thought that remains with Charles is the idea of reaching Will. The closer he gets to the shadow of the stone lion, the less he cares about the necessity of keeping the advancing Zulu army at bay. His fellow soldiers are all dead anyway, even if some of them are still running around inside living bodies. They are each ghosts, the ghosts of men—floating around in bodies, in lives, that in reality never belonged to them.

All around him, the few remaining men from the camp who can carry arms are advancing toward their death. Other men are retreating through the dongas and the grass, no longer bothering to bring their horses, some of them calling out for more ammunition boxes to be brought to them. The cloud of smoke hangs thickly above all of them, the air punctuated by the dying splutter of musketry and the occasional thud of artillery. Some men who were from the band in another life pass Charles, carrying stretchers. Cooks and grooms and other bandsmen are running back and forth, in random directions, trying to locate more rifles or ammunition. It is like a whole village looking around for anything of value that they might be able to offer up to the unknown gods as a sacrifice. Charles stumbles across a Scotch cart marked with its little red flag to find that there is only one opened ammunition box left—and he fills his belt and jacket with more useless bullets.

He recognizes the rocky outcrop where two days previously he made love with Will, and something very still and simple resolves inside him—and he climbs onto his panting horse and abandons what is left of his men—some sergeant major he does not recognize all the time yelling at him to keep to his position.

By the time the moon comes to cover the sun, the world
has grown dark

Charles has lost track of his horse. He is running through a mass of moving forms and tangled tents and guy ropes. He passes Sprite's pet monkey, hopping off, trailing a broken leg. He encounters a man he immediately knows from the shape of him is the Welshman, McEwan. He has been hung from a meat hook on the side of a wagon and disembowelled. One of the grooms McEwan whipped is feeding McEwan's genitals into his mouth as you might a reluctant baby—the wounds McEwan inflicted still raw and swollen across his back.

Many of the tents have been flattened by the fleeing animals. One of the horses that passes Charles pulls a tent behind it. The camp is littered with cooking pots, tobacco pouches, unravelled bandages, helmets, saddles, blankets, tin mugs, playing cards, letters. When Charles arrives at the place where he expects Will's tent to be, he finds a bull lying on its side in the grass, spraying scarlet blood from a long gash in its neck. Only then does he see that he has been following the wrong line of tents. Will's tent is higher up. Further back toward the ridge. He passes a man fighting off three Zulu soldiers and does nothing to help him. One Zulu soldier is running straight for Charles when another Zulu soldier collides into him. Men and animals are appearing from every direction, not knowing where to run, where to defend or where to attack. Another man does not even have the time to fix his bayonet before a flying spear is lodged into his flesh.

As the darkness thickens, a man with a bandaged foot and a face blackened by blood—his own blood or someone else's, it is impossible to know—arrives shouting Charles's name.

"Will? Will? Is that you?"

Charles's voice sounds strange in his ears—the voice of some other man, crazed and existing in some other realm. He sees very clearly that Will has a cut across one thigh and what might be a wound somewhere under his tattered blue jacket. He is holding his pistol in his left hand, by the barrel, as you might a small club. His eyes have never looked so wild or so blue.

"We're completely surrounded," Will says. "There's no way out."

"We must make for the nek," Charles says.

"The what?"

"The nek. Have you seen a horse?"

"There's one over there," says Will, indicating a place through the smoke somewhere behind him.

"We will ride out together."

"The colors have been taken," Will says—as if this means that all is lost.

"We have to abandon camp." Charles pulls Will's familiar arm across his shoulder. "Come. We must move. We don't have a moment to waste."

He holds tightly onto Will's wrist and leads him in the direction he indicated. One man passes them, muttering a prayer. Charles sees Sprite's monkey again, sitting upright in the grass, nursing its shattered leg. Three chickens rather absurdly run ahead of them, as if expecting Charles to throw them some grain.

The horse is standing tethered to a wagon wheel, mad-eyed and huffing, its mottled gray flanks streaked with sweat—but it is apparently uninjured. Lying under its legs next to more unopened ammunition boxes is a man with an assegai in his chest and his intestines unravelled like a pile of sausages. Charles recognizes him as young Mowbray, Will's ill-fated friend.

"I'll help you up," he says to Will.

He helps Will to step over Mowbray's twisted leg. Will does not think to look at the dead man's face. Charles lifts Will onto the horse's withers and Will wraps his arms around its neck. All around them are the cries of men, the staccato of rifle fire, the chants of the Zulu soldiers growing louder and more triumphant. Hundreds of animals and men are bellowing and moaning and running back and forth in a cloud of smoke.

"We'll follow those mules," says Charles, gesturing with his head toward two brown mules that are galloping away from the last row of tents. Will is sitting forward, holding onto the horse's mane, and Charles can see that his jacket is ripped at the back where an assegai or a bullet has passed through. Not far below them, at a thicker scattering of rock, they pass a group of soldiers from the 24th, fighting at close quarters with some Zulu soldiers. Once again, Charles calmly circumvents them.

"Charles," says Will, "am I dying?"

"No, Will. You are not dying."

"But everything has gone dark."

"Don't worry," Charles says, realigning Will's body with the horse's neck. "It is only the moon passing across the sun."

PART EIGHT

THE WRITER

Daniel has been invited to the Websters for Sunday lunch

He finds Bruce sitting alone in his wicker chair, staring toward the view. Today he has a doomed and impatient expression. A man scheduled for execution who would prefer to get it over and done with. He has a tumbler half filled with neat whisky, which is excessive even for Bruce. He seems surprised to see Daniel, standing there with his usual offering of pinot noir—as if Bruce is wholly unaware of the invitation to lunch.

"Where have you been?" Bruce asks.

"What do you mean?"

"You look as if a light has been switched on inside you."

Not knowing what to say to this, Daniel laughs and glances across at the table. It has been laid, presumably by Caroline, very elegantly. Everything is silver and pale-blue, except for the peach-colored roses that come from the garden. Caroline might have been far happier living in the suburbs, working as an interior designer, instead of being stuck out here as Bruce's wife.

"Who else are you expecting?"

"I don't exactly know," says Bruce. "It's all Caroline's idea. I must say—I have no idea what the hell is happening with my wife. She's turned into Lady Macbeth."

"Oh yes?"

"I mean—what can she be thinking, having people over to lunch at a time like this?"

"Maybe she wants to feel normal again."

Bruce laughs. "We haven't felt normal for a very long time, my friend."

Daniel sits in his usual chair. He hasn't been offered a drink and he doesn't want one. There is something about the moment that requires a ruthless sobriety. The stillness that might be required of a soldier before going into battle.

"Is Simon still in custody?" Daniel asks.

It has been two days since Daniel heard the news of Simon's arrest from David. Since then, nothing appears to have happened, and there has been no further sign of Tim Greene at the lodge.

"He is," Bruce says. "Fucking ridiculous, if you ask me. The kid's got himself into trouble before. And yes—it seems he was with that young woman before she died. And that they may or may not have been arguing. Simon is always arguing. With himself and everyone around him. That's the whole point of Simon. But I know that he's also a good boy at heart. He'd never be able to do a thing like that."

"Unless it was all a mistake?"

"Well, perhaps. But even so—"

Bruce gulps down his drink as if it is apple juice. They stare at the recumbent stone lion. It has been days since Daniel last looked at the mountain—but there it is as usual, outstaring the final endeavors of the world.

"And Tim?"

"What about him?"

"I gather he's been released?"

"Some days ago. But he hasn't had the courage to show his face. No doubt Caroline knows where he is, but I haven't bothered to ask. They're probably still fucking each other, for all I know."

Daniel keeps his gaze fixed ahead as Bruce drinks.

Caroline and Matthew enter a moment afterwards with platters of bread, olive tapenade and mashed-up artichoke—and more silver buckets for the wine. Caroline has an ardent, faintly terrified expression. She only looks at Daniel when he greets her by name.

"Daniel? Oh hello, darling—I didn't hear you coming in. How are you keeping?"

"I'm fine, thanks," says Daniel. He doesn't ask how Caroline is. The question is too large and difficult.

"Hello, Matty," Daniel says instead.

The boy glances at him. He also looks strangely afraid, as if the enemy hordes are finally advancing—and there's not enough ammunition to defend themselves. Daniel remembers only when it's too late that it was Sam alone who called him Matty.

"Hey," Matthew says.

He comes across and sits next to Daniel. He has a piece of buttered ciabatta in his hand and he chews on it abstractedly. There is something so odd about the Webster family today. They're all sleepwalking, or acting out some scene not of their choosing, as if there are hidden cameras amongst the bowls of roses and African masks. A setting to pin down the murderer at last. Although, in this case, there is no detective in charge of the proceedings, sifting the evidence—and there is no apparent desire from anyone to get to the truth.

"How's school?" Daniel asks.

"Sorry?"

"School. How is it?"

"I don't know," Matthew says. "I think it's fine, thanks."

He has a flushed look in his high, velvety cheeks—as if he ran to get here. Yet there is also something fated and calm about the boy that makes Daniel feel foolish.

"At least it'll be half-term soon," Daniel says.

"Yes."

"Do you have any plans to go away?"

Matthew looks across at him, something in his expression wavering with a distant humor. "I won't be going anywhere," he says flatly.

Daniel notices that Bruce has finished his drink. The tumbler sits at an angle in his large hand, the rim where Bruce's mouth touched it gleaming in the silver light. Matthew hasn't once looked at his father, but he can feel the boy absorbing everything. The empty glass, the weight of his father's breathing, the horror of his tunnel-vision gaze across the hills. Daniel also grew up with parents who were never able to anticipate pain in any form and shield him from it. Daniel and his parents always encountered suffering like three separate boats fighting against the same sea.

"When's Tom coming?" Matthew asks his father.

"Tom? Is he coming?"

"He's coming with Jessica."

"I have no idea," says Bruce.

As if on cue, they see a golf cart threading up the hill. The two faces in the windshield are too obscured to identify, but it is clear to everyone that the two people in the golf cart are Tom and Jess. Two surviving aspects of Sam, driving back into the scene of the crime.

Matthew stands and runs out and Daniel follows him through. Tom and Jess soon appear, Tom wearing jeans and a white T-shirt and Jess a leaf-patterned dress. They enter the room as tentatively as meercats, peering and pausing and smiling.

"Hello, Tom," says Matthew with a kind of rapture.

For a moment, they all look at one another—Tom radiating the stillness that a tree might, standing alone in the middle of a neatly plowed field. Matthew steps forward and takes his hand—and Jess starts to move around the room, a bit too fluttery and gay. Perhaps she is trying to demonstrate her closeness with the family, her enduring love for Sam. She greets Daniel and Matthew and then she rushes through to the brooding place of Bruce.

"Can I get you something to drink?" Matthew asks Tom.

"Some water, maybe?" Tom asks.

"Right away," says Matthew, moving off.

For a moment, Daniel and Tom are left alone. They have met only once before, when Tom was still fresh on the scene, appearing as Sam's shiny new boyfriend. But he has less shine on him now. He is closed off somewhere inside himself, carrying a weightedness that could mean just about anything.

"I'm sorry about everything," Daniel says. "How have you been—through all of this?"

Tom looks properly at Daniel. Like Sam and Jess, he would also have studied Daniel's book. He would also have had to work his way through the pages, puzzling out its opaque areas, forming his own connections. Yet Tom looks at him with a polite neutrality. Perhaps he knows, as Daniel knows, that the book no longer has very much to do with Daniel.

"I've been okay, thanks," Tom says.

"It's awful—this thing about the woman they found. But maybe it's a good thing it wasn't Sam. For Sam's sake, I mean."

"Yeah, I'm glad it wasn't Sam," says Tom.

Caroline enters and pauses at the edge of the room like a woman peering into a shop window. An art gallery, perhaps, where a life that is more accomplished carries on.

When Tom sees her, he steps forward.

"Mrs. Webster. It's good to see you."

"I'm so sorry," Caroline says, gripping his hand in a way that is almost fraternal. "I was still putting on my face. Is Jessica here?"

"She's there with Mr. Webster."

All of this is unnecessary—since Jess's voice is clearly audible from where they are standing—and, were they to look beyond the fronds of a potted palm, they would see the two figures sitting companionably together.

"It's so good of you to come," Caroline says. "I have been thinking so much about you, Tom. I have been missing having you here. I have been—longing to see you again."

"It's very good to see you too, Mrs. Webster," says Tom.

"I just—I thought that if Sam were here we'd all be together like this. I thought—if Sam's friends were here, then maybe she would appear too—maybe we could conjure her up."

"She is here," Tom says. "I'm sure of it."

Matthew brings Tom's water and Tom takes it with a smile. Matthew has added ice and a wedge of lemon and he watches Tom take the water and drink.

"Thanks," Tom says.

"Can I get you something to drink?" Daniel asks Caroline.

"Let's stay realistic," Caroline says, laughing with a ragged bitterness. "I'll have a large gin and tonic."

Bruce presides over the table like a forgotten god

Jess is performing the role of the loyal friend, as if taking up a place where Sam left off. The young girl who outshines everyone around her simply because of her beauty and youth. But Caroline appears to be grateful for the distraction. Perhaps because Jess takes up so much space that any other vacant spaces around them—and between them—can be forgotten for the moment. Tom sits there, patient as a horse, and Matthew leans toward him. Only sometimes does anyone remember Bruce, who sits before two fragrant roast chickens that have already been carved in the kitchen by Tom. Whenever they do defer to Bruce, it's with a rush of apology and guilt, like old believers who have forgotten about their god—and replaced him with something less tedious.

Real grief is, of course, very tedious. It goes on and on—a flat, dry landscape where nothing moves. Few can linger there for long. If they do, they are soon left alone. They are left there with a huff of impatience, as if grief is a place of their choosing. But this grief is not of Bruce's choosing. These days, it is all he knows, all he believes in. Living is for others. It's a delusion. A place you go to in order to distract yourself.

Daniel is sitting to Bruce's left, across the table from Tom. He is the only person who seems close to Bruce. Maybe he is the only person who is comfortable to sit alongside Bruce's grief—as you might sit alongside an old mountain, resting in its cool shadow.

"Do you remember that time Sam cut all the dormitory curtains?" Jess is saying. "She got into so much trouble from Matron. She didn't see how she had done anything wrong. The curtains were too long and they needed adjusting. She said they looked much better and didn't understand what all the fuss was about."

"Dad had to buy new ones, didn't he?" Matthew asks with a wan smile toward the blank wall of Bruce.

"That was just like Sam," Caroline says. "It never crossed her mind that whatever she wanted might not be the right thing to do."

"She used to say that she was always in the right," Jess says, "and that if she was ever in the wrong, it was always for the right reasons."

They ponder this for a moment. The mood is almost humorous, almost affectionate. But there is a note of unease running through everything. Daniel thinks again of that image he had of Caroline when she appeared alongside Bruce on television several weeks ago. That sense of a neatly folded napkin inside which a piece of meat was quietly festering.

"So where do you think she is?" Caroline asks suddenly.

She looks around the table at everyone except Daniel. No one looks back at her properly. Perhaps each of them is carrying their own burden of complicity.

"I thought at first that she had run away, to be honest," Caroline continues. "She seemed to hate us so much, in those last weeks. But then after a week I knew something unspeakable had happened. I understood that this wasn't just one of our fights. She was gone and she wasn't coming back. And then that girl was seen—and then her body was found—and she wasn't Sam, as it turned out. But we knew that already, didn't we?"

Matthew looks at his mother—but no one else does. Daniel can see a kind of trembling running through the body of the boy, like someone who has just been missed, by a few inches, by a lightning stroke.

"How does a girl simply disappear like that? Tom—did she say anything to you? Jessica—how about you?"

"She didn't, Mrs. Webster," says Tom.

"In those last weeks, she didn't say much to anyone," Jess says. "Except for Tim. He's the one who knows anything—if anyone knows anything."

"Believe me—Tim doesn't know anything," Caroline says.

"How about we eat?" says Bruce.

"And I have no idea what Simon has said to them," Caroline continues. "But the police say they're getting close to the truth of what happened to that girl—and then, they believe, the mystery of Sam will be the next thing to be resolved. They believe the two things are connected. No matter how many times we tell them they're not."

"How do we know they're not?" Daniel asks. "It's a reasonable assumption. Two young women going missing in the same place within a few hours of one another."

"In this country, people go missing a dozen times a day," Caroline snaps—glaring across at Daniel. "That woman was a hooker. Sam was still a schoolgirl. They traveled completely different paths."

"Until they perhaps converged," Daniel says.

Bruce bangs his fist on the table.

"I said we should eat," he says. He looks around the table and his eyes land on Jess—who is sitting in the chair where Sam always sat. "Jessica, which part of the chicken do you prefer?"

Halfway through the meal, Caroline wanders toward her room

Matthew excuses himself soon afterwards and moves to the kitchen door. After a moment, Bruce mutters something and stumbles off after him, no doubt sensing some issue with the boy, who has retained a shocked, bleached look throughout the meal.

As soon as the Websters are gone, Jess and Tom visibly deflate—the strain they have been under only now becoming apparent.

"Bloody hell," Jess says. "It was even worse than I thought."

"Was it? It was pretty much what I expected," says Tom.

Daniel takes the plates through to the kitchen and rinses them at the sink. Through the large sash window, he can see Bruce and Matthew sitting in the circle of stones where the kitten was killed all those weeks ago. Matthew is talking quietly, rapidly, while Bruce sits one rock away, holding his head. There is something tragic about the scene, although Daniel has no idea why—or what they might be talking about. After a moment of standing there, rinsing the plates, it feels indecent to remain, so he returns to Tom and Jess.

"Do you think we should go?" Tom is saying.

"I have no idea," says Jess. "All I can say is thank God you and I are escaping to varsity." She glances across at Daniel, "I'm telling you—these people have always been completely barking. Sam was the only sensible one. But even Sam couldn't escape their madness in the end."

"What do you mean by that?" Daniel asks.

"I don't mean anything. I only mean that Sam disappeared long before she disappeared."

Daniel looks at her carefully. "That's exactly what Natasha Lopez said."

"I'm quoting her," says Jess. "Because it's the truth. Sam really did become someone else toward the end. And if I blame anyone, I blame the Websters. And yes—obviously, I blame Tim."

"But I thought you and Tim—got along?" Daniel says.

"Tim always gets what he wants. If he wants to get along with you, you will get along with him. That's the way he works." She shoots a look at Tom. "I mean—he stole her from Tom, didn't he? There was nothing Sam could do to protect herself."

"Is Tim a very bad person? Is that what you're saying?"

"Who the hell knows? I have no idea who he is. I'm not even sure that Tim does."

Daniel looks at Tom. "Do you think Sam is dead?"

Tom looks back at him, as solemn as a totem. "Yes."

"Why do you think that?"

"Because it's the only explanation. It's like Mrs. Webster said. Sam loved me. I know she did. She even showed me that she did. After our last exam, when we had only one week left at school, we went for this drive, and we went to this hill, and—something happened, something that changed things between us forever. And afterwards, when I drove her back to school, she started crying. At first, she wouldn't tell me what was wrong. She kept saying how sorry she was. How shameful she was. Eventually, she told me about Tim Greene. She said she'd been with him before. She said she was all confused and didn't know what to do anymore. I said I knew her. I knew her better than anyone. And I knew we belonged together. I said if she took some time to think things over, and let everything settle, she'd know this too. She told me she loved me. And I believed her. I said we should talk in a few days. We'd sort everything out. But we never saw each other or spoke to each other again. It's like she was halfway through a sentence and then something really bad came and silenced her. I know she'd never have been able to walk away from this thing between us without another word. That's how I know something really extreme happened. And I also know that someone in this family knows more about what happened to her than they're letting on. I can feel it. They're hiding some really horrible thing. I don't know what it is. But it's sitting there. Right in front of us."

THE GHOST OF SAM WEBSTER

Bruce

"I have come to hand in my resignation"

Tim Greene is standing at the door to Bruce's office in the reception building. He is dressed in the pale-blue linen shirt, khaki shorts and leather boots that have become his uniform when giving tours of the battlefield. Bruce has reflected before that Tim is the kind of person who spends a lifetime in one uniform or another. The school blazer, the rugby jersey, the chinos and jacket. Everything outwardly standard, like a disguise, while inwardly the man was altogether elsewhere, out in the wilderness, playing by his own rules entirely.

"Well, where is it?" Bruce asks.

"Where is what?"

"Your resignation."

Tim seems thrown for a moment. This is clearly not the response he was anticipating. "I'm doing it—verbally."

Bruce twists his mouth so as not to laugh. "Okay."

They both wait.

"Where are you going next? Back home, perhaps?"

Tim seems to think about this. "I thought I'd travel around."

"I see."

"Maybe go east."

"Right."

Bruce can see that there is more. The resignation was only a part of it.

"I'd like Sam to come with me."

"Sam?"

"What I mean is—she wants to come with me."

"She does?"

"Yes."

"She would like to "go east"?"

"Yes."

Bruce feels a stirring of rage, but he swallows it. "Why on earth would she want to 'go east' with you?"

Tim hardens his gaze. Bruce can see that he's quite prepared to fight, if that's what it takes. He can see that the boy, if necessary, is ready to use violence.

"I suppose you'd better ask her that yourself."

Bruce stares at Tim without blinking, as if he is only a recent intrusion at the edge of his horizon. "Have you spoken to Caroline about this?"

This question appears to surprise Tim. "I thought I'd—talk to you first."

"Take the old bull by the horns?"

"I suppose you could think about it like that."

"Tell me something, Tim. Have you also been fucking my wife?"

Tim does well to hide his shock—and chooses to smile instead. "What gave you that idea?"

"She did, as it happens."

"She said that?"

"Of course not."

Tim smiles again. "Crazy idea, right?"

"But you have been fucking my daughter?"

"I have—we are—"

"Yes?"

"We have become—very close."

Tim is acting offended by all this swearing and Bruce realizes that for a while now he has hated this little bastard. There is something properly wrong with him. Some internal mechanism that has been set in the wrong direction—and has inverted everything. Tim sees again that the other man is capable of the most extreme violence—and that he would be capable of anything in order to protect his hallowed patch of ground.

"Well you're fired anyway," Bruce says, "whether you resign or not. By the time Sam comes home on Saturday, I want you gone from here. Is that understood?"

Tim is looking pale and angry. "Fine."

"Fine."

Tim stands there as if looking around for one more reason to stay in the room.

"Now fuck off."

Caroline's car is parked behind his car, so he takes
the silver Audi instead

He drives quickly and recklessly down the track and out of the lodge and along the rutted road. He doesn't care about punctures.

He doesn't care if he wrecks this car. He's never understood why Caroline has always held onto it. He's offered her a new car often enough. It turns out she's surprisingly vain in some areas and entirely without vanity in others. In the side door is a packet of frequently re-melted chocolate biscuits and some headache pills. Signs of his wife's various addictions. He wonders what will happen to Caroline after he's gone. He knows that her addictions, like his, are stand-ins for living. They're fake leaps of the heartbeat, artificially generated endorphin and dopamine rushes, each one a rehearsal for the real thing—the thing that goes by the name of happiness.

Only when he reaches the highway does he realize that he's driving toward his children. He's feeling an urgent need to see them, to gather them toward him as some primate might at the approach of a predator. They're all under attack from previously inconceivable angles. As a father, he has to anticipate and protect their weakest points.

There is a restlessness in the trees around him. A large weather front is on its way. It is anticipated to last for at least a week. But there's not much evidence of it now—only this sense of something out of sight coming toward them, announcing itself through a configuration of contradictory murmurings.

He finds Matthew first

The boy is standing alone at the tennis court, hitting a ball against the wall, practising his forehand. Bruce can see that Matthew has already registered his presence and is waiting for him to approach. He probably saw Caroline's car being parked nearby and waited to watch his mother emerge—only to find the surprise of his father. Only when Matthew's ball hits an uneven place in the wall and shoots off to one side does Bruce step out of the shadows of a bloodwood tree and approach quietly.

"Hello, Matthew."

"Hey, Dad."

"You're getting a lot of spin on the ball."

"Thanks."

Matthew comes toward him, his smooth face almost feverish, his blue eyes shining. "Is everything all right?" he asks awkwardly.

"Sure. I just—wanted to talk."

"About what?"

"I don't know. This and that. How about we take a walk to the tuck shop? I could do with something cold to drink."

"All right."

Matthew knows that his father knows where the tuckshop is. It has been in the same place since Bruce was here as a boy—under the old pin oak, next to the second-hand shop. He trots to catch up with Bruce, who is already walking fast up the lawn toward the turreted castle-walls of the school, which stands against the blueness of the sky like a great fortress made from rock. Bruce has always hated the sight of the school from this self-important angle and he wonders why he sent his son here. Of course the boy is unhappy. What chance did a thin suggestion of a boy like Matthew have against the force of a place like this? The best Matthew can do is to slip into its shadows, or bounce a ball against its worn-down surfaces, waiting for the minutes and the years to pass.

"The first thing I wanted to say," says Bruce as soon as Matthew has caught up with him, "is that you don't have to stay here. We can find another school for you, if you like."

"Thanks, Dad, but it's okay—really. I'm actually getting used to it."

"Getting used to being unhappy? That can't be a good thing."

"I'm not unhappy, really. I mean—starting at any school would be just as hard. And you went here. So I'd like to make it work, if I can. It isn't so bad after a while. It's actually quite nice. I'm beginning to make friends. And some of the teachers are—quite kind."

"Let's see how we go, okay? At any moment if it gets too much for you, I'd like you to tell me. If you're unhappy, we can fix it. Okay?"

Matthew nods briefly, not believing him—knowing that all of the evidence from Bruce's life and Caroline's life contradicts this.

"To be honest," Bruce continues, "I couldn't stand this place either. But then I don't think I'd have been able to stand any school."

Matthew sends him one of his breathy smiles—half politeness, half gratitude. "I know what you mean," he says.

"And I know that things at home have been strange, lately."

Matthew looks at him again but says nothing.

"I mean—me and your mother have been pretty strange. We've been having a harder time, these last few years. I sometimes think that everyone would be happier if we lived apart for a while, just to see how it would work for everyone. What would you think about that?"

Matthew gives off a non-committal shrug.

"My main concern in all of this is you and Sam. I want to do what's best for you two, you know? I want to make sure that you both know that you are loved. By both of us. Your mom and me. I want you to know that we will always do everything we can to look after you. And to keep you safe."

"Are you saying you've decided to get a divorce?"

"No, my boy. I'm not saying that. It hasn't come to that. It's just that—well, as your parents, we have a job to be happy. We should be showing our children what a happy family looks like. And if we find after we've both tried really hard that we can't do that, well then maybe it's time to do something different. Because people can be happy. In your life, you should expect nothing less than happiness. I want you to know that."

"Thanks, Dad. I do know that."

"Sometimes, it can even be quite interesting if your parents get divorced. People live in new houses. They have new chances for something else to happen. Something unexpected. Also, whenever it's their birthday or Christmas, they get double presents. And there's nothing worse in life than this feeling that you're stuck. That you're doomed to living the same day over and over again. Because life is a miracle. Every day, we have to stay alive to the miracle."

Usually, Bruce's verbal escapades leave Matthew restless and resentful, but today he absorbs it with some earnestness.

"Would I live with you or would I live with Mom?"

"It's a bit early for that kind of talk, but you could live wherever you wanted to live. You could come and go as you liked. I'd imagine your mother would want to live closer to town. Have a chance to work, maybe. I know that sometimes she finds it very isolating out at the lodge. But if she lived in Maritzburg, for example, you could go to one of those day schools. You wouldn't have to be a weekly boarder. You could maybe come to the lodge for the weekends—or for the holidays. But that's only a suggestion. You'd be able to do exactly as you liked."

All of this has taken Bruce by surprise, but he sees now that he has been coming to this point for months—for years, even—and that he can only see it now. He and Caroline have to separate. Before his death, which is now imminent and inevitable. Caroline must set herself up elsewhere, away from the lodge, so that when he dies the property can be sold and the family can finally move on. He knows that the rest of his family have always hated it there. They have been prisoners. Forced to live in a graveyard of Bruce's devising.

"Okay, Dad. Thanks. I'll think about it."

"As I say—none of this may happen. But if it does, I'd like you to know that you will be okay. Your mother and I will make sure of it."

By now they have reached the tuckshop and Matthew moves ahead. "What would you like, Dad?"

"I think I'll have a Coke."

"Two Cokes," Matthew says to the small Zulu woman behind the counter.

"And some wine gums—for your sister."

Sam is waiting for him in the carpark

Bruce has phoned ahead, knowing she would mind being ambushed—and for reasons that would never have occurred to his son. She is wearing her bottle-green tracksuit and she has her hair tied back in a high ponytail—an arrangement she only ever uses when she is about to play sport. It gives her a different, elastic air, like a hare preparing to leap over moonlit fences. By now, the first evidence of the oncoming storm is beginning to gather against the horizon—an immense, dazzling stand of cumulonimbus.

"I brought you wine gums," Bruce says, offering the sweets like a peace offering.

"Thanks, Dad. Is everything all right?"

"Sure it is. I felt the need to see you. I hope that's okay."

"Has something happened to Mom?"

Bruce hesitates before answering. A great deal has happened to her mom. "No, your mother is fine. As far as I'm aware."

"Okay—"

"But I have fired Tim Greene."

Bruce watches her for a response. All she does is go still, holding her breath.

"Why did you do that?"

"Because I don't trust him."

"You don't trust him?"

"I don't think he's a good person."

"A good person?" Sam gives off one of her humorless laughs. It is the only thing, as far as Bruce knows, that Sam gets from Caroline. "Is there such a thing as a good person?"

"I don't know. But there is such a thing as a bad person. A person who is somehow—sick. A person who is sick and doesn't mind that they are sick. A person who gets a certain secret gratification out of feeding off the lives of others—and feeding their sickness into the lives of others."

"And you think Tim is like that?"

"I think if Tim had been a German soldier during the Second World War, he would not have batted an eyelid at the gates of Auschwitz."

Sam rolls her eyes with an attempt at scorn. "Gee, Dad, aren't you being a bit over-dramatic? What has he actually done?"

"I'm not sure. I was hoping you could tell me more about that."

"You don't know what he's done," says Sam, evading the question, "but you fired him anyway? Why? In case he tries to get a job at Auschwitz—and asks you for a reference?"

"He was going to resign anyway."

Sam is slightly quelled by this—and Bruce can see that it does not come as a surprise.

"He says you two are going away together. Apparently, you plan to 'go east.'" Is there any truth in that?"

"We've talked," says Sam carefully. "I said I'd maybe like to take a year out. Travel around for a while."

"With him?"

"With him. Without him. It's not really about him, Dad. I just feel the need to get away. To get some perspective on things, you know?"

"But you're going to Cape Town. We have already paid all the deposits."

"I was hoping to delay. Only for a year. So I can find my feet."

"Okay," says Bruce, trying to re-establish a place from which to think. "But I thought you had a boyfriend. Have you broken up with him?"

"Tom? No—me and Tom are still together."

"But—you're also with Tim?"

"It's confusing, Dad."

Sam says this with a sudden rush of honesty. She has never been able to sustain a lie with him for long. When she was a girl, he knew she was carrying a lie as soon as she entered a room. She held the lie inside herself in a way that was distressing—mainly to her.

"You probably don't want my advice," he says, "but I don't think Tim is the right person to be spending your time with. He doesn't have your best interests at heart. He strikes me as the kind of person who is only ever able to look after himself."

"What are you saying, Dad?"

His children keep asking him this—and he has no idea.

"I suppose what I'm asking you to do is to wait. Let Tim go. By the time you come home for the weekend, he'll be gone anyway."

"But Dad—I think I might be in love with him."

"Really? And what about Tom?"

"Well, I'm in love with him too. But in a completely different way. Maybe a better way. I don't even know. But it's like I'm two people at the same time—like two snakes trying to kill each other off—and I don't know which one of them I should be rooting for."

"There is never one of anyone, Sam. Aren't you always telling me that?"

"That's the sort of thing I write about in FS English. But it's not the same in real life. In real life, we have to choose who we want to be."

"No, we don't. And it doesn't matter who we think we are anyway. All that matters is what we do. Where we choose to care. Only our care matters. Nothing else exists."

Sam has opened her wine gums and already eaten the three green ones. She hands Bruce the three black ones—as is their custom.

"I wish you hadn't fired him," she says. "I wish you'd spoken to me first."

Sam wipes a tear from a green eye. Her eyes are the most beautiful thing Bruce has ever seen. Soon he will be gone, he thinks. He will never be able to experience the green of his daughter's eyes again.

"I'm sorry," he says. "But you were in danger, Sam. I had to get rid of him."

He drives, without stopping, toward the sea

The road is the only place left to him. For a while, it's enough simply to be driving, to be moving. It gives the illusion that the tormenting circumstances of his life are shifting, and that the dark configurations arranged around him will move off, like a moon moving away from the sun and bringing back the half-forgotten light. He has decided to keep driving until he reaches the edge of the land, the edge of the continent that he has, for a lifetime, tried to call his home. He will find the place where his world comes to an end—and the world that is not his can finally begin.

He threads his way through the sugarcane fields north of uMhlanga, taking a series of tracks that he has known since he was a boy. The wind has gathered in strength and the bush lining either side of the red dirt track is being tossed about with a casual violence, as if by a force intent only on uprooting it. Bruce can hear the weeds running thickly along the bottom of the car, and the occasional clunk as he connects with a rock, but he makes no attempt to slow down. Even if Caroline's car gets stuck in the mud or damaged beyond repair, he is close enough to the beach by now to be able to walk the rest of the way to the sea.

He can hardly blame Sam for wanting to leave. He remembers when she was younger—how she would sometimes cry out at night, and he would come into her room to find her sitting up in bed, looking around a room crowded with ghosts. But to escape with Tim right now would be like asking some fallen angel to lead you out of Hell. All he would do is draw you into a deeper darkness.

Bruce had thought he had understood all there was to understand about Tim Greene. But since Moses's allusions, Bruce has been doing some observing of his own and it has become clear to him that Tim and Caroline are in some sort of unholy alliance. Whenever the two of them are together, Caroline lights up like a Christmas tree and speaks in a false, high voice that sounds exactly like the voice of her long-dead mother. But even when the two are apart and in Bruce's company, he feels their alliance staining the air. Tim thinks that their liberties give him the right to treat Bruce with a casual complacency, an amused disregard—and Caroline thinks that they give her a new independence, as if she has individuated at last. Bruce knows it is also a horrible game—a game that is also a kind of revenge on Bruce. Neither of them understands the extent of Bruce's indifference. But this thing with Sam is real, real in a way that the relationship with Caroline is not—and that was exactly why he'd had to fire the bastard.

It is also why he needs to get treatment. Before this morning, he believed he had nothing to live for. He believed his children no longer needed him—and that his presence was quite possibly doing more harm than good. But now he sees that his role isn't necessarily to be a source of meaning for his children. His role is to be their protector. His role is to keep the beasts at bay wherever he finds them, and to remain as strong as he can in order to do so. As soon as he stops the car, he will phone his doctor to make another appointment and he will drive to Johannesburg to see him. The thought of returning to the lodge with Tim leaving and Caroline grieving is too much for him anyway. He will wait until Tim has gone and the children return for the weekend. Perhaps then the family can find a way of regrouping—or separating out into safer units, units that will endure with and then without him.

He parks under a large leopard three, takes off his shoes and walks across the yellow sand to meet the ocean. He is the only person there. The only person crazy enough to be walking directly into such a storm.

The first rain arrives as his toes are touched by the surf. The storm comes in a thick wall, drenching him and everything around him. The waves ahead of him are roving and gray and enormous. They are run through with red mud from all the rivers of Zululand. Only a few white gulls are there to see him, moving in overhead, thrown off by a new, wet blast of wind—but coming back again, and back again, perhaps mistaking him for a fisherman with a bucket full of bait.

Sam

It's her last day, but already she has left the school

The girls around her feel like the memories of girls she once knew. All she wants is to get away from them, to hide in the corner like some wounded animal. She does not know why she feels this woundedness. For far too long, she has been a member of this tribe and not a member of this tribe. For far too long, she has had to disguise herself by performing their version of her back at them. But now all the right words have dried up. Like little dead fish inside her mouth.

It has been raining hard for three full days. As if this perpetual wetness is not enough, Jess and some of the other girls have brought water guns to school. They are running through the corridors and bursting into the puddles in the quads with peals of laughter, sounding like a bunch of unruly bells. Some of them are wearing the uniform of Matty's school—and it's as if a whole lot of wet, androgynous boys have been released into the school.

Sam finds them dumb and frightening and she has no idea of what they think they're celebrating. She has seen through the series of hoops through which a girl is supposed to jump—under the watchful eye of some circus-trainer God waiting to see if you will turn out good enough to be picked for his team. The last thing she wants is a husband and children. She has seen what that did to her mother. The photographs of her mother around the time she was leaving this school are unrecongnizable. A pleasant-faced girl smiling coyly with her head rolled to one side, her hair fluffy and sunlit, like a baby chicken. Her teeth, which are now horsy and brown, were as bright and even as unchipped china. Then she married the man she thought she loved—and that man and his children have taken twenty years to kill her.

Sam isn't exactly sure why she and Jess stopped talking. It had something to do with the confusion around Tom and Tim. Of course, Jess had liked Tom before Sam. She was the one who had drawn Tom to her attention. Jess later accepted her defeat as one who is used to coming second—with a good-humored forbearance, as if coming first wasn't really worth all the sacrifice. In a weak moment, in the wake of Matty's disapproval, Sam had a few weeks ago confessed the whole Tom-Tim situation to Jess—and Jess hadn't responded in the way she had hoped. She simply gave off a hard bleat of laughter:

"Sometimes in life we have to choose," she'd said. "Who's the lesser of the two evils?"

"Tom, obviously."

"Then choose Tim. At least then your life will be more interesting."

This had been a joke—but the subtext was not only that Sam's life was not particularly interesting, but that Jess thought it was high time Sam suffered—and that she wanted Sam to suffer. Since then, Sam had tried to re-establish contact with Jess—and, at moments, it seemed that Jess was trying to do the same. But in the end they found that their ways of thinking about each other had become nothing more than places of hurt.

Sam withdraws from the weather to the safety of Dr. Lopez's

classroom, where the rain keeps up its steady percussion on the tin roof. She has decided to bunk the final chapel service, the final prayer. She knows that her mother will be sitting somewhere at the back, wiping her tired eyes at familiar hymns, her voice quavering like a deranged hen. And she knows that her mother will not think to look for her—or that, if she does, she will give up easily and assume that one of those brown heads ahead is Sam's.

Perhaps it's not the idea of leaving school that has so unravelled her. Perhaps it's the thought of returning home and never being able to get away. There could be Cape Town, as planned, in a couple of months. She knows that Tom is still waiting for her, still waiting for her to call. Since they made love a few days ago, they have not communicated—as they agreed in the car. Every minute, she has wanted to call him, to hear his voice, his breath in her ear—but then the idea of Tim drags at some other part of her, like something coming up from some dark place inside her, a beast without a face, or with a face so beautiful that she immediately disappears right into it. This is why she needs time to separate. To try to get her feelings straight. At the moment, she's all knotted and tangled up—with each thought that tries to reach outward just turning back in on itself again.

The whole idea of escaping to England with Tim also feels impossible. She would need a visa, for a start, and she recently spent most of her savings on a new phone. But she can't believe that Tim is as bad as her father says. Maybe she doesn't want to believe it. But the image of him standing at the gates of Auschwitz will not leave her. She knows this is wrong of her. It's like the way Sylvia Plath appropriated the suffering of the Jews for her own self-dramatization. Sam has recently written about this form of appropriation in one of her FS English essays. Yet she suspects Tim's brokenness. She doesn't know what caused it—or what it might lead to. She suspects her own brokenness too. Is she simply handing herself over to Tim as a sacrifice? If Tom represented health and life, does Tim represent sickness and death? There is something so comforting about the circle at the center of Tom's name. Round and ripe as a tomato. A thing complete and enclosing. Whereas at the heart of Tim's name is that little insistent "i," with its dislodged head floating above its station.

"Sam?"

Dr. Lopez is standing at the door, holding a broken school umbrella. She's perhaps the only clear figure in Sam's life, standing there so slim and decided, straight and clean as a blade of grass.

"Hello, Dr. Lopez."

"What are you doing in here? Is everything all right?"

"Everything's fine, thanks."

"Aren't you going to chapel?"

"To be honest, I thought I'd give it a miss."

"You did?"

Dr. Lopez is always like this. She lets you sit with your decisions and leaves you to work out their consequences on your own. She thinks that a girl, when given the space to do so, will almost always come to the right conclusions. Even a girl like Sam. Dr. Lopez is one of those teachers who comes at you from underground. She never comes into class with a whole lot of notes and she never speaks much, or even seems to teach much. She asks lots of questions, allows for silences—and just when you think nothing is actually happening, you look around to find that the room has become alive and electric. Sometimes, in her classes, it feels as if you aren't at school anymore, but in some dreamland. You're all out at sea somewhere—and everyone around you is plunging right down deep inside themselves and bringing to light the brightest fish.

"Well it's only a ceremony anyway," Dr. Lopez says. "A final farewell."

"I feel like we've been saying goodbye for months. It's like—enough already."

"I know what you mean. But you are precious to us. You do know that, don't you? And I have always felt it is important to be able to say goodbye properly. We don't always get to do that. Sometimes, a person can suddenly be gone and they've never had the chance to say anything meaningful—and those left behind aren't able to say anything meaningful back to them."

Sam wonders whether Dr. Lopez is talking about her dead husband. Her dead husband gives her an added meaning, an added definition. Dr. Lopez is what people call a strong woman. But Sam doesn't believe in that idea. Strong women. Strong men. She's sure there'd be a whole lot of mess even inside Dr. Lopez if you were able to dig around for long enough. In her classes, it's always as if Dr. Lopez is inside each one of them, but she herself is never quite visible.

"Are you happy to be leaving?" Dr. Lopez asks.

"I'm not sure what I feel about it. I feel scared—but I don't know of what."

"It's a moment of transition. Those are always unsettling. But they are also necessary. We realize that we have to move on—even if it feels impossible."

"But what happens if you have nowhere to go?"

"Take it a step at a time—that's my advice. One step leads to the next. It's the only way to move beyond a place of difficulty."

"I feel all tangled up," Sam says. "I have no idea how to take one step forward—let alone two."

"What do you think is causing this?"

"I don't know. I'm supposed to be breaking up with my boyfriend."

"You are?"

"I lied to him. I was unfaithful."

"Have you told him the truth?"

"I have. Or what parts of the truth I have the words for. As you have taught us, the truth is seldom pure and it's never simple. So now we're giving each other some space. But the thing is, even if he manages to forgive me in the end, will I be able to forgive myself? We had something so good. So—healthy. And there's a part of me that is intent on destroying that. As if I mistrust it. I'm not even sure that I won't do it to him again. Be unfaithful again, lie again. And he's too important. He's too—fine. I can't do that to him. I don't want to hurt him anymore. The better thing would be to leave him—to leave him alone. If I was to go back to him, I'd only ruin his life."

"Are we talking about Tim?"

"Tom. His name is Tom."

"I see."

"He was the one good thing in my life—and I've been doing everything I can to kill it."

"Remember the Oscar Wilde poem we did," Dr. Lopez says. "Every man kills the thing he loves. Every woman does that too. Maybe it's because love is a burden, a kind of responsibility. I mean—it's also a great miracle, a great source of bliss. But to really carry it, and keep carrying it—that can prove to be too hard for many people."

"So there's no point? All love fails anyway?"

"No—but it has to keep adapting, like any living thing. You can't idealize it. And you can't idealize yourself or the person you love. Because no one can live up to that—not even Tom."

"What are you saying?"

"I'm saying that maybe you need to be gentler with yourself. You've made a mistake. You can learn from it. And even if you don't make the same mistake again, you'll make other mistakes. You're a person. All you can do is try to turn up—with your best self—and see what happens next."

Sam nods and smiles, all the while knowing that these words are intended for some other type of girl, a girl with a healthier appetite for living—and for the idea of happiness. "I'll go to the service," she says, as if some positive step has been taken. "Thanks, Dr. Lopez. For everything."

"Goodbye, Sam."

"Goodbye."

She doesn't stop to look for the last time at Dr. Lopez's face—or to see whether the teacher has been persuaded by her words. It doesn't matter anyway, since pleasing Dr. Lopez was yesterday's concern.

PART NINE

THE BUTTERFLY COLLECTOR

They leave the camp with a herd of screaming animals

All around them are oxen, cattle, horses, dogs, chickens and goats—and several hundred men. With the smoke from all the powder and the effects of the eclipse, they are wading through a twilight fog. Men are climbing onto anything that moves. Charles sees three soldiers trying to mount the same horse. Another soldier, an officer in red, attempts to mount the back of an ox that is still wearing the remains of its harness—until he is pulled away by three Zulu soldiers and stabbed to death from every angle, repeatedly, interminably. Charles urges his horse forward and pulls the slumped body of Will closer toward him, holding tightly onto his ammunition belt. Although Will appears to be breathing, there is no way of knowing the extent or seriousness of his wounds.

They crest the nek of the mountain only to find another horn of the Zulu army coming around from the back of the mountain to meet them. Surrounding them are the slaughtered remains of non-combatants who tried to abandon the camp earlier, as well as soldiers, both Native and British, who tried to leave on foot. Ahead of them is a covered wagon drawn by a dozen mules, a large red cross painted across the canvas, trying to evacuate some of the wounded. Charles watches as several Zulu soldiers emerge from the cover of the grass and advance on them. The mules are immediately slaughtered by the first two men to reach them while the rest of the Zulu soldiers climb into the wagon and silently and systematically kill each of its inhabitants.

Charles turns the horse away from the scene of carnage and toward the open country to the left, where two other horsemen are riding free from the bulk of the Zulu attack. They enter a steeper valley cluttered with larger rocks and thicker grass—where a Zulu soldier, no more than a boy, appears from nowhere and Charles shoots at him with Will's pistol—only to find that the pistol is unloaded or jammed. All Charles has left is his sword—which he is yet to use. He unsheathes it and is about to swing it at the Zulu soldier when the boy is shot by someone riding closely behind them and drops to the ground.

"Hawthorne?"

Charles turns to find Bayley riding close to his horse's haunches.

"Make for the river," Bayley yells—not even glancing at the body of Will. "Only a few miles away from here!"

"Which direction?"

With the tall grass and the crops of aloes around them, they can no longer see the position of the mountain and they can no longer work out the direction of the river. Ahead is a deep donga into which a soldier and his horse have already fallen. From Charles's vantage point, he can see the horse struggling to stand, its hind leg at an unnatural angle. Its rider is lying against some rocks, broken and still.

"I have no idea," Bayley says.

It is then that Charles sees a shimmering blue dragonfly, the *Anax imperator*, a species he first caught as a boy on the Norfolk Broads. At the time, he was mesmerized by the apple-green thorax, the metallic cobalt-blue abdomen and the silvery, gossamer wings. He knows they are found near water and he turns his horse to follow it. The dragonfly zips along an animal track and descends another gulley that is so narrow Charles and Bayley's horses can barely scrape through it.

The dragonfly dips around some thorn bushes and disappears, but they have reached another eroded gorge, this one running with floodwater, and they follow a path down which their horse and Bayley's horse easily descend. They canter across an old riverbed, weaving between large boulders and stunted trees, where the path is again strewn with the remains of others who have come before—assegais, hats, rifles, saddles, more bandages and ammunition belts—and more dead animals and men.

When Charles and Will are faced with three Zulu soldiers, the soldiers run straight past their horse and instead make for Bayley—who is wearing a red serge coat. Charles has noticed that the Zulu soldiers are tending to attack the men in red, perhaps believing that the men in blue patrol jackets have less status. But he does not stop to help Bayley. From the sound of Bayley's high cry, he knows that the other man is as good as dead.

After several hundred yards of broken ground, their horse ascends another, steeper hill—the lion-shaped mountain rising up again behind them. Here they pass an open cave and they turn off to the right and gallop along the top of a ridge. They can see the sweep of the Buffalo River not too far below them to the left. Charles is about to turn toward it when he encounters a marsh. Here there are two more soldiers, trapped in the mud and under Zulu attack, so Charles steers their horse off to the right, circumventing the greener area and making toward a crop of bush.

As they begin their descent on the other side of the ridge, down toward the river, they encounter more Zulu soldiers with rifles, shooting across at them from amongst some rocks to the left. A man and his horse come tumbling down through the vegetation to Charles's right, only to be shot. Charles passes another standing horse, large and black, with its saddle still attached under its belly, screeching with a sound Charles has never heard from any animal before.

The path steepens again as two more *imperators* criss-cross their path—and Charles follows them down another, steeper donga off to the right. Will has made no movement for a long time now, and Charles has to nudge his friend to ensure that he is not dead. Already they can hear the roar of the Buffalo River ahead of them. The long length of the river soon becomes visible, blood-brown and roiling with floodwater. It looks completely impassable. Yet, if they are to leave Zululand, Charles knows they must cross it.

"Almost there, Will. Are you a good swimmer?"

"A very bad swimmer."

"You'll have to hold onto the horse's mane. If you lose your grip, grab onto its tail—or one of the stirrups."

The river ahead of them is about seventy-five yards wide and flowing fast. The crossing is a mass of men, horses and cattle—some dead, some living, all of them being swept as if toward some great abyss. Those gathered on this side of the riverbank are looking for a way to cross—and they are being shot at from several directions by Zulu snipers. A few men and animals are visible on the far bank. Some too wounded or exhausted to move away from the enemy fire. As Charles watches, a barely clothed man is climbing out of the water only to be shot in the shoulder. The man slips back into the torrent and is swept away into a whirlpool and lost.

The approach to the river is strewn with hidden rocks, but Charles urges their horse forward, steadying Will by holding onto his ammunition belt. The horse slithers and grunts as they descend through some reeds toward the water's edge—and before they have made the decision to enter the river, the water is all around them and the horse is sucked into the current. It groans with the effort to remain upright, its legs scrabbling to find a hold where there is none.

Almost immediately, Charles is dragged off in a different direction, finding himself alone and floundering in the rolling water. But he is a strong swimmer and he manages to gasp in air and keep himself more or less afloat as he is carried downstream. Ahead of him, he can soon see their horse's head straining above the water—and the dark-blue body of Will still somehow attached to it. The horse does not seem to understand where it is to go at first, but another horse meets it from the left and their horse veers off toward the opposite bank.

Charles passes a coffin-shaped rock where three men are holding onto a long pole that Charles realizes are the regimental colors—and then he too is pulled into a whirlpool. He can no longer see any sign of their horse or Will. He can no longer see anything. But he ducks under the water and swims hard toward what he hopes is the opposite bank—and when his boot strikes a rock, and then another rock, he starts to lodge himself against the current and climb his way across the slimy boulders toward the shore.

He reaches the earth and pulls himself onto the gravel and lies there for a long time, too tired to move. He has lost his ammunition belt and his pistol and his damaged boot. His breeches are ripped and he has a large cut on one of his calves. He can't recall when this happened—whether it was a wound from an assegai or a cut from a rock or a broken branch in the river—but he can feel no pain. His body still belongs to some other man. In his ammunition pocket, he can feel the shape of one of his collection tins. The water in his mouth tastes of salt and when he touches his lip and looks at his hand he sees it is brown with watery blood.

All around him, men and animals are climbing out of the water, or lying there wounded or dead. Charles tries to lift himself up to locate Will—or their horse—and he sees the mottled gray form of their horse floating on its side further downriver—drowned or shot. Of Will, there is no sign.

"Will?"

"Hawthorne, is that you?"

Charles sits up to see Bayley sitting behind a rock, removing the Wellington boots from a dead Native.

"Left me for dead, did you?"

Charles does not answer. He gets to his feet and wanders away from the shore and toward some bushes, where more men are huddled behind rocks to avoid the rifle fire. But Will is not amongst these men either.

"We need to get out of here," a man who has caught hold of a dark-bay horse is saying. "Further upriver I saw some Zulus trying to cross. Here," he says, looking at a Native man, "you help me up and the two of us can ride out together."

The other man—whom Charles now recognizes as an associate of Sunshine's, his groom from another life—helps the soldier up. As soon as the soldier is mounted, however, he is shot. He slips off the saddle and lands with a heavy flop on the ground, and he doesn't move.

"Excuse me," Charles says to the groom, "have you seen my friend, Lieutenant Grace?"

Sunshine's friend stares hard at him. It is the first time a Native soldier has ever looked at Charles without a preformulated smile across his face. He looks at Charles as you might at a madman. Without a word, the groom gestures downriver and then walks away, up the bank, like a man merely walking home.

Charles secures the dark-bay horse and finds a boot in the rubble—a boot several sizes too large for him and molded for the wrong foot—and he pulls it on. Then he mounts the horse, which he realizes is badly lame, and makes his way downriver, trying to keep the rocks between himself and the rifle fire where possible, but no longer caring very much if he is hit. Behind him, he hears Bayley shouting out to him—saying something about taking the horse—but he ignores Bayley and carries on.

He passes the body of their previous horse and then he passes a crocodile on a sandbank—an eight-foot beast that keeps its primeval yellow eyes fixed only on the limping horse. Still there are men trying to cross from the other bank and they are drawing most of the Zulus' attention. Charles follows a slight bend in the river and finds his friend sitting in the sunlight on a rock, wearing only his torn cord breeches.

"Charles? Is that you?"

"It is," says Charles.

"I'm afraid I can't use this leg."

From where Will is sitting, the opposite bank is too steep and rocky for any Zulu soldiers to reach and they are in an area of apparent calm. Charles dismounts and lifts Will's arm over his shoulder and helps him over the last of the rocks and up a steep animal track through the bush. The track is too sheer and narrow and rocky for the injured horse, so Charles leaves it standing there, cropping some bright-green grass.

The path continues to ascend steeply away from the river and Charles has to stop every few minutes to catch his breath. He can see that Will's wound is not too severe—more of a glancing blow from an assegai or a bullet than something that has penetrated the flesh. The wound on his thigh is worse, but fortunately it's on the leg with the twisted ankle, so Will's other leg is able and strong.

"Do you think the Zulus will cross and continue their attack?"

"I have no idea," says Charles. "But it's possible they might."

"I saw some of them linking arms in order to cross, but the current was too strong and they turned back."

"We need to keep moving, if we can. We need to find another horse."

They encounter a stream and drink deeply and carry on. All around them, Charles can see good examples of the bright-yellow *Eronia varia* butterfly. He realizes that his collection and most of his equipment are still back at the camp in Isandhlwana—except for the butterfly books and reserve equipment he left behind at Helpmekaar. Well, it was unlikely that he should ever return to the area. Those butterflies would have to be caught and collected by other men—if those other men ever entered Zululand.

"Why don't we leave?" he says to Will.

"What do you mean?"

"Who says we have to face the hearing in Pietermaritzburg? Who says we have to face anyone? We could return to Durban and catch a ship back to your sister."

"Still hankering after my sister? Remember—she's marrying the ostrich farmer chap."

"Not if I can reach her first."

This is intended as a joke, and Charles is pleased that Will can find the resources to laugh.

"But I am being serious," Charles continues. "If we don't turn up, it will be assumed that we're dead. Then there won't be any hearing—and the whole story—the whole business with Mowbray—will be lost."

"Did you see Sprite falling?"

"I saw Sprite being killed—yes."

"And Pope?"

"I'm not sure about Pope."

"And Bayley?"

"Bayley saw me here at the river—not long ago."

"There we go, then. You know Bayley. He won't let the matter go."

“So would it not be better to run away?”

“I’m tired of running, Charles. Come—let’s rest. This leg is beginning to hurt.”

They find a place away from the animal track and under the shade of some soft-leafed shrub. Charles removes his jacket, which has almost dried out in the heat, and puts it over the pale shoulders of his friend. Then they lie down together in the grass, Will’s head rested on his shoulder. There is still the sound of distant rifle fire and the occasional human cry, but this is all taking place somewhere else. Instead, the sounds of the natural world move back in around them—the cicadas and the crickets in the grass and the rich and various birdsong, coming from birds whose name Charles has never had the opportunity to learn. At one point, some Natives pass them on their way back toward the river—and a few minutes later a British soldier runs back up the path and disappears over the ridge above them. But Charles and Will are not seen by anyone, hidden as they are amongst the bushes—and, following some animal instinct for secrecy, Charles does not call out for help. Already, Will is asleep in his arms and Charles holds him and leaves him to sleep.

He is woken by the sensation of a beast breathing in his face

He opens his eyes to find a horse standing over them. Will is still lying heavily in his arms. Charles nudges at him with his shoulder to ensure his friend is alive—and he is pleased to hear the other man’s breathing. He loosens his hold on Will and rests his head back in the grass—and then he catches hold of the reins of the horse. It is a large bay without a saddle, but its bridle is perfectly intact.

“Will, I believe we have a horse.”

“Oh Charles,” Will murmurs, “I’m tired. Can we not remain here—for a short while longer?”

“We should keep moving,” Charles says, placing his hand on the clammy forehead of his friend. "We don't know where the Zulu army is located at present."

"Well they aren't here, so surely this is as good a place to hide as any?"

"It will soon be dark. We need to have your wounds attended to. We can ride across to the field hospital at Jim Rorke's place."

"I don't think I have the strength to move."

"Come—I'll help you up."

Charles lifts Will and manages to hoist him onto the horse's back. The horse is a few hands higher than their previous horse and more skittish. Will makes an involuntary moan as he adjusts his weight on the horse, but he says nothing about the obvious pain of his wounds. Charles ties the reins into a knot above the horse's withers and climbs on behind him. He notices that Will is shivering—even though it is a warm midsummer's evening.

He regains the animal path they were using earlier and soon encounters a wagon track. Above them, the sky is the slate-gray of dusk. There is no moon and the heavens are, as yet, without any stars. But there is enough light to see the river below, which veers off to the right, the overgrown track shadowing it.

They ride in this way for about an hour as the night closes in, perhaps for longer—now and again coming across remnants of other soldiers along the way. At one point, they encounter a pack of wild yellow dogs feeding off a dead man. The dogs don't look up from their meal as Charles approaches. One is missing an ear. The evidence of some other battle, some other war. The dogs snarl and jostle for a better angle, a better piece of flesh—and Charles does nothing to stop them.

Ahead of him, the sound of continuous rifle fire gradually emerges beyond the sound of the river. Charles suspects it may be Chelmsford's forces closing in on the Zulu army from the interior. Surely they must have come upon the camp later that day—and swept the Zulu army back? It is doubtful that the Zulu army would have remained in the area when the bulk of the British army were advancing back toward them—trapped, as they would have been, between Isandhlwana and the Buffalo River.

The track on which he is riding reaches the crest of a hill and what Charles sees in the darkness of the valley makes him stop abruptly. Below him, a few miles distant, the buildings of the field hospital at Jim Rorke's place are alight. Charles can clearly see an open flame on one of the roofs of the buildings. He realizes that the rifle fire has been coming from there—and that the field hospital is under attack.

"Will?"

Will is lying clutched to the horse's neck—and he makes no sound.

"Will—the hospital is under attack. I don't know where we are to go."

Still—Will says nothing.

Charles moves his horse off the road and up to some higher ground to the left. Here the grass feels taller and thicker and they soon lose sight of the pale strip of road and the valley below them. Charles has no idea whether he should cut across and ride around in the general direction of Helpmekaar. For all he knows, that camp may also be under attack. This is unlikely, given the distance the Zulu army would have to travel across enemy territory to reach the camp—and yet they risked crossing the river to attack the field hospital, so there was no telling what they might have done. There was also no telling how many Zulus there were around them or from which direction they might advance. In an area that the British had believed to be entirely unoccupied, they had come across over twenty thousand fighting men.

Not for the first time, Charles wonders what they are doing here. What possessed people to leave their island on the other side of the world to come to a land about which they knew nothing and attack people about whom they knew nothing? A soldier must do his duty. That is what Charles's father had always said. But his duty toward what? His duty in the service of what? What Charles has experienced over the last twenty-four hours had nothing noble or honorable about it. It was merely butchery. Men killing other men in a manner that was bestial and base. It did not take much for the uniform and the flag to disappear. It did not take long for the animal that is inside each of them to slip out and take over—and do whatever it needed to do in order to survive. And now the madness was happening all over again, right in front of him, at the field hospital.

"Who goes there?"

Charles halts his horse. "Lieutenant Hawthorne and Lieutenant Grace. Who is that?"

"Private Brown, sir."

"Good evening, Brown. Are you alone?"

"Yes, sir. My horse died right under me, sir."

"I'm sorry to hear that."

"I was riding toward the field hospital when my horse just died right under me, sir. So I was continuing on foot when I saw thousands of Zulus crossing the river and advancing toward it, sir. So I came up here to wait—and to see what might happen next. I have no weapon, sir."

"Don't worry, Brown. I'm sure you did the right thing. Could you help me with my friend?"

Brown comes forward in the dark and helps to catch Will as he slides off the horse's neck. They drag him across to where Brown has been sitting on a coat.

"Do you have water?" Charles asks.

"Yes, sir. And I have a biscuit, sir."

"Would you be able to give some water to the lieutenant?"

"Absolutely, sir."

Charles lifts Will's head so he can drink. Will's head is hotter and he is still trembling.

"Has the field hospital fallen yet?"

"I believe it must have, sir. It was on fire when I last looked and I am sure that the men there would have been overwhelmed."

"Do you think the Zulus have continued on to Helpmekaar?"

"I couldn't see, sir. All I saw was the flames."

"Well there's nothing we can do now except wait for dawn. What regiment are you from, Brown?"

"I was under Lieutenant-Colonel Pulleine, sir. I was also working as his groom. I was the last of our post to be standing, sir, so I took a horse and fled with the others. Sir, it seems that everyone else is dead."

"We're still here, aren't we?"

"Yes, sir."

"So there is still some hope."

"Yes, sir. Thank you, sir."

All night, he listens to the crackle of rifle fire

Will feels clammy whenever Charles touches his face—and, no matter how hard he holds onto his friend, Will's body continues to shudder, punctuated now and again with an abrupt jolt, like a body drifting off to sleep and then waking again with a start. Private Brown finally dozes off—and then later Charles feels him watching them with a level and interested gaze. It must be clear to Brown that there is something more than friendship between the two officers—but, whatever their relationship, the younger man does not appear to be perturbed by it.

Only when the sky is growing paler toward the east does Will begin to speak.

"I have been bad, but I'll be better now, you'll see. We shall spend much more time together."

"William?"

"You wouldn't come down. No matter how much everyone pleaded, you refused to come down. You didn't eat any dinner that night, and I went to bed, knowing that you were still up there, in the old yellowwood, outside my window. I knew it was all my fault. That one kind word from me would bring you down. But I never said it. I wanted to hurt you. For you to wait for me and to learn I'd forgotten you. That I was happy and asleep. Oh, Lydia. Are you still there?"

"I am here," Charles says.

"The next morning you were in your bed and we never talked about it again. I think you forgave me. You always forgave me. But I'm a very bad person. I never deserved your forgiveness. Oh God, oh God. You should have hated me. I think I wanted you to hate me. Something would have been settled. I could have carried on. But you never did. You carried on loving me, didn't you?"

"I did," Charles says.

"Even after everything. After you saw me and learned what I was. You never stopped loving me. You never turned away. You always looked at me with love. But I am bad. I am a very bad person, Lydia."

"You are not a bad person," Charles says, stroking his friend's knotted head.

Charles drifts off an hour later and wakes to find the morning sun all around them—once again arrived to light the world. But it is no longer the world as Charles knows it. The previous day—which started with an unsuspecting ride out of the camp and into the hills with Clifton Lass—feels like something that happened to a man from long ago, from another time. That man died somewhere between that moment and this. That man had only been dreaming about the world. He hadn't been awake to its true nature.

Charles relinquishes Will's body without waking him. Then he slips on his mismatched boots and walks across to an outcrop of rocks to get a better view of the valley. There is a thin haze of smoke drifting up from the ruined buildings of the field hospital, but otherwise there is no sound except for that made by the birds and the wind through the grass. To his right, the line of the Buffalo River is marked by a long trail of mist. There is a darkness moving slowly into it, like a shadow cast by cloud, and Charles realizes with horror that it is a shadow made of men. The Zulu army retreating, perhaps. Or maybe it is merely the shadows of the dead moving back to their ancestral lands, looking for a way home.

Closer to where Charles is standing, the river is more visible, carrying on as it did before, still blood-brown and swollen with floodwater. Soon, it will seem that none of them was ever here. There will be some bones left to whiten in the grass and a few regimental badges to rust into the earth. There will be some stories, too. Of the red soldiers from a distant land who came here to die like beasts. But otherwise their passing will be like that shadow of men moving into the mist, disappearing forever.

"Good morning, sir."

Charles turns to find Brown standing at his shoulder.

"Morning, Brown."

"Lieutenant Grace just ate the biscuit, sir."

"I'm pleased to hear it."

"Do you think it's safe to go down, sir?"

"I think the Zulus may be retreating. We should at least try to get a better view."

"Absolutely, sir."

They approach the field hospital from the direction of the river

They are near the place where Jim Rorke is buried—far away from the house and the former chapel because the poor man was said to have killed himself—when they see another shadow advancing toward them through the mist. Charles thinks at first that it is the Zulu army returning, but then he sees that it is what appears to be the whole of the British army, walking as if entirely intact—and as if the events of the previous day never took place. "That must be Chelmsford and his men," Charles says down to Brown.

Brown is walking alongside the horse. Will is in his usual position on its withers, doing his best to sit up.

"Should we wait for them, sir?"

"Let's ride ahead. There may be a wounded survivor at the hospital in need of help."

Charles remembers the ambulance wagon and its chain of mules from the previous day—and how every living thing and wounded thing was killed by the Zulu army, without discrimination—and he doubts that there will be any survivors in this field hospital.

The few buildings of the hospital are still smoking and surrounded by what look like piles of burned branches—until Charles sees that they are the bodies of men.

The dead Zulu soldiers are piled up all around the settlement, too many to count. In some places, the individual bodies are no longer even distinguishable. Most of the men are wearing nothing but beads and leather bracelets and the usual loincloth. Their bodies are a golden brown, entirely new and untested.

Some of the dead, Charles notes again, are little more than children. Amongst them, a few are slowly moving and groaning, but there are too many to attend to and Charles would not know where to start.

He continues toward the burned-out buildings and only stops his horse when he sees a man arriving on the roof of the one building that appears to be still intact. The man is waving something red back and forth. It looks like a flag—or perhaps it is merely a coat.

THE GHOST OF SAM WEBSTER

Sam

She finds her mother in her father's car

Her mother usually does everything she can to avoid driving the Land Cruiser. She hates the scale and self-importance of it. But Sam knows that her father intends the opposite by driving this car: from the outside, it is old and shabby, and it is only when you're inside that you experience the new engine, the new interior. Around them, it is still raining thinly—and the other cars in the parking area are filing along the entrance with predatory intent, their wipers slick and silent, their headlights glowing like the eyes of wolves.

Sam saw her mother standing at the back during the chapel service. She was wearing her only raincoat for the occasion, her lipstick applied like a temporary measure to overwrite the weakness of her mouth. As far as Sam could see, her mother wasn't trying to find her daughter's face in the confusion of faces. She seemed more intent on her own internal landscape—perhaps on tracing the paths back into her own childhood, which she always talked about as if it were some sacred garden denied to everyone else.

"Hey, Mom. Where's Dad?"

"He's up in Joburg. He said he'd be back today—but I've seen no sign of him."

"You mean he took your car?"

"Don't ask me to explain your father's actions. These days, I have no idea what's going on with him myself."

Sam gets in next to her mother. They do not touch. Sam can't remember when they last touched—or felt the need to touch. She fastens the seatbelt and pulls her blazer sleeve down to cover the beads around her wrist—Tim's rainbow-colored charity beads, which he'd bought from a shop to help raise funds to save the rhinos—or was it the whales?

It was like hell, coming back into her mother's orbit. It was not her mother herself, but the forcefield that sat between her and her mother, like a long argument that could be taken up at any point, no matter how much time had elapsed since they last spoke.

"I hear Dad fired Tim," she says.

"Oh yes? How did you hear that?"

"Dad told me."

"Yes—I'm afraid Tim has gone," Caroline says, a pigeon-quaver running through her voice. "He left yesterday for Durban. Simon drove him down to the airport."

Sam knows this isn't true. Since Tim has been messaging her throughout all of this. The truth is that he's still waiting for her, hiding out in the tin shack that Simon sleeps in whenever he comes back from university to see his father. It is some distance from the rest of the staff houses, higher up on the ridge, and it recently provided refuge for another twelve-foot python—which was found lying there with one of Moses's chickens half-digested inside it.

"Oh well," says Sam, affecting disinterest. "It was probably time he went anyway."

Caroline shoots her a scandalized glance. "You mean you don't care?"

"Why would I care?"

"You two seemed—close."

"Ag, he hated this place," says Sam, moving away from the subject. "He couldn't wait to get away."

Caroline takes this as a slight on her—as Sam half-consciously intended. Sam immediately feels bad, however. Her mother has always been such an easy target. An already plucked chicken walking around, waiting to be roasted. But soon she won't be seeing her mother anymore. She wonders whether she'll ever see her again—and what the two of them might feel about this. They must love each other somewhere. It's just that they've become too blurred against each other's faces to see it.

Another weather front is moving in

But she takes Meg out anyway. She has been thinking about this outride all week, looking toward it as a moment when everything might become clearer. She has always been happiest on the back of a horse. She likes the sensation of being lifted above gravity, her body handed over to some higher intelligence. Meg is her one remaining friend—the only presence that can still locate a continuity inside her, so that Sam can find, after all, that she is still the same girl.

As she leaves the stables and takes the familiar track toward the high plateau, she talks to her horse, gently and continuously, as you might talk to a very old woman or a child. She knows that Meg can hear her and understand her. The words themselves are not important. She has left her phone behind with its line of messages from Tim and its absence of messages from Tom—switched off and slipped into her bedside drawer. She wishes briefly that Matty could have come with her. But Matty is playing squash and will be fetched only later in the day. And these days Matty isn't prepared to indulge her latest boy dilemmas anyway.

When she arrived in her bedroom earlier that morning, she nearly succumbed to phoning Tom. This has been her habit—to phone him the moment she entered her room and lay down on her bed. It was often the first moment during the week in which she could be alone in a room, and alone with her body—and she usually found that she wanted to share that body with Tom. She would talk to him as she touched herself, as he touched himself. She knew that this was somehow an outrageous thing to do with a boy like Tom. It was like taking someone who didn't know how to swim on a little boat far out to sea. She always had this feeling with Tom—of him being one horse-step, one oar-stroke, behind.

Even when they went to that green field after her last exam, it was she who had found the right way to fit them together. It was not that Tom was unwilling—it was simply that, out of some learned politeness, he seemed slightly outside of himself. It was a thing she found in many boys. They had been told that they were trash and toxic enough times to believe it. Even when Tom was safely inside her, he was somehow one movement behind his own body, as if his body was the body of someone else, or was being drawn into a room that he himself was too afraid to enter. The feeling of him inside her was right and good, and Tom was more careful and tender than Tim had ever been—but it felt that Tom wasn't quite there to experience their togetherness together. Perhaps he was trying to concentrate all his energies on not coming. Perhaps he was hoping to give her pleasure before he could satisfy himself. But the consequence was that it felt like a missed opportunity. They had made love, but she had been left feeling unfinished, alone and misrepresented. She had cried in the car going home as much for this reason as because she had betrayed him. Although she hadn't realized all of this until days later. At the time, it had all been too painful to admit.

Maybe if she gave him another chance he would be able to be there, more fully, at their moment of coming together. It had felt like a missed opportunity the first time with Tim too. It was only the second time, in his drummer-boy room, that she had experienced the real life of him. That second time with Tim had been almost like a meditation. There was a place that he reached inside his body, which was also inside her body, that felt like a landing place. More than anything else, sex with Tim had felt like healing. Something in him was being healed. Or something in her. It was difficult to tell. But he became so alive when he was inside her. He became full of some current that flowed right through him, and right through both of them, like something lit up and deeply personal—and wholly impersonal too. When their bodies were together, some other thing moved through them, spoke through them, knitting every nerve together in perfect symmetry.

Right now, this is the only source of life and of truth on which Sam feels she can rely. For it, she is almost prepared to sacrifice everything. The boy she loves, her education, her parents, her home, her friends—and everything else she has ever held close to her. Yet it has no name, and she has never even talked about it with Tim. From his point of view, this source of certainty might not even exist. Yet she doubts it. Wasn't it also in him too? Wasn't it the meaning of "Tim Greene" in the best possible sense?

She knows the black mamba is there before she sees it. It is half-hanging over the water of the kidney-shaped pool. She knows without knowing it that this is one of the snakes she and Simon saw before. At first, the snake laps at the water with its black tongue and then it dips its mouth into the slick plane of the pool, very delicately, barely causing a ripple. Then it starts to gulp, the sides of its face flaring with each swallow. She wonders what happened to the other snake—the other side of this same snake. Did it move away to another territory, or did this snake finally manage to kill it off?

Meg has also seen the snake, with both sides of her brain. She stands and snorts while Sam makes no move to get away. Sam watches the drinking snake and then it pauses to watch her. They stare at each other for one long heartbeat—and nothing else moves.

The rain reaches her on the journey home

Instead of going up to the house to change, she walks across to the tin shack where she knows she will find Tim. She has only ever been inside this shack when she was a child. As far as she can remember, Simon has always lived there. At first, he lived there without thinking much about it. Then he learned to be ashamed of it. In more recent years, he has almost become proud of it. It stands there as proof of the injustice of the world. As long as he is sleeping there, he can justify his hate.

The rain is falling in thick, pulsing waves as if some machine is behind it. There is something determined and insistent about the rain. It leaves nothing in the landscape untouched. Every bit of the earth is soaked with it. Sam does nothing to cover herself. The rain has already won before she has even registered it—a wall of water so enormous that one life is immediately lost inside it.

She opens the door to the shack without knocking and finds Tim sitting on the makeshift bed, smoking the stub of a joint. He is wearing his khaki shorts and old rugby jersey from school—striped red and white.

Sam can see that he hasn't shaved for a week and he is looking tired, like someone who has been up all night, having an argument.

"Hey," he says. "I thought you'd never come."

"Sorry. I went out with Meg. I needed some time to think."

"Is your father back?"

"Not as far as I know."

"And your mother?"

"I think she's gone to fetch Matty from school."

"We need to get out of here," says Tim. "With weather like this, we could get trapped. They say it's going to rain for at least another week."

Because the lodge is surrounded by two mountain streams, in bad weather the cement bridges would often become submerged, and the lodge's inhabitants would be stranded. Even if you could get beyond these streams during a flood, the nearest bridges across the Buffalo River would also be underwater.

"Typical," says Sam, sitting down next to him.

He takes her hand and presses it to his mouth. "Are you sure you want to do this?"

"I am," she says, almost believing it.

"Maybe you should go home and pack. Simon says he can give us a lift to the airport. I've booked us two tickets to Johannesburg."

She leans forward and plants a kiss on his mouth.

"I love you," she says.

It's the first time she has said this to him—and once again she almost believes it.

"I love you too," he says, as if this were the most natural thing in the world.

She finds Matty alone inside the house

He is sitting at the kitchen table, eating a cheese sandwich, a tall glass of milk standing in front of him. Jane is watching from her folded rug alongside the leather couch. Even though Matty's school has officially broken up for the year, he is still wearing his clothes from squash. When he sees Sam, who could not be wetter, he looks unsurprised. Neither of them has ever given the rain much importance.

"Where is everyone?" Matty asks.

"I don't know," says Sam, shaking out her jacket and leaving her riding boots at the door. "Didn't Mum pick you up?"

"She sent Moses instead."

"Are you—okay?"

There's a bereft and hopeless look on Matty's face. His eyes seem smaller and closer together, as if his whole vision of the world has shrunk downwards, inwards, to one nugget of pain.

"I'm fine," he says.

Sam is about to carry on through to her bedroom when she realizes that this is the last time she'll be seeing her brother—for a long time, at least. She realizes he's the one person she'll miss, the one person she doesn't want to abandon. He's always been a constant, moon-like presence in her life. Once a chattering companion—more recently, a source of obscure unease that she hasn't had the headspace to worry about.

"I'm going away for a while," she says.

"Oh? Where?"

"I'm going east."

"You mean—to the sea?"

"I'm going very far away."

"By yourself?"

"With Tim."

"I don't understand," says Matty, something visibly shutting down inside him. "What are you doing that for?"

"To get away."

"From what?"

"Everything."

Matty looks at her with undisguised disappointment—an expression that has only recently found its way into his face. He had never looked at her like this before.

"What about Tom? Does he know?"

"No."

"Have you even bothered to break up with him?"

"Of course I have," she lies.

"I don't understand it," Matty says, turning away from her and back to his glass of milk.

"What don't you understand?"

"When you have everything."

"I don't have anything."

"What more can a person want?" Matty asks, standing up quickly and knocking the table so that the glass of milk trembles. "And you choose to run away with Greene?"

"I'm not running away."

"What about next year? What about varsity?"

"I'm taking a year off to think about it. Maybe I won't go to varsity."

She sees that Matty is crying. "You're destroying your life," he says.

He moves away from the table so violently now that the glass of milk wobbles and falls off the edge of the table. Sam catches it—so that only a splash of milk hits her hand.

"Matty? Where are you going?"

But he has already run out into the rain.

Not knowing what else to do, Sam lifts the glass of milk and drinks it. It enters her body the way milk entered her body when she was a child, cooling everything but leaving her unsatisfied.

PART TEN

THE WRITER

Daniel is sitting on the balcony of the library, looking down at the Buffalo River

The water catches the morning light and steams slightly. From here, he can hear the rush of the current over the sleek, black rocks. Rising up from either side of the river is the dense and singing bush, where a leopard moves like a ripple under the surface of reality, and a python lies twisted against a rock, patterned with all the patience of the evolutionary world. There are purple-crested turacos calling in the bush not far below from where he sits—and in the blank sky vultures are carving wide circles through the air, hungry for any available evidence of death.

On Daniel's computer is a job offer. The role of Script Editor on a new television show. This one is set in a busy governmental hospital in Johannesburg. Daniel knows little about the life in a busy governmental hospital in Johannesburg, but then he knew little about the taxi industry, illegal goldminers and the life in a traditional Zulu homestead—the story worlds of his previous shows. The idea of starting on a new television project sends a dull, bleak sensation through his blood, but he is about to run out of money, and he not only has the lodge's bill to pay, but all the expenses that come with his mother's house.

He knows that it is also time he left the lodge. Watching the suffering of the Websters has been like witnessing the final disintegration of a volcanic mountain from some distant land. There is nothing Daniel or anyone else can do to stop it and its collapse seems inevitable. He would have left two weeks ago had he not met Natasha—and started this strange, new relationship, which is like experiencing something intricate and miraculous taking shape very rapidly, like the pattern across the surface of a leopard—or a python—being established right in front of your eyes.

He came here to find Sam Webster, or what remained of her, but all he has done is find echoes of her, traces that lead to more echoes, more ghosts. He wishes he could save her from her fate, and write a different story for her, with some other ending, but everything that he has imagined taking place around her in the months before her disappearance keeps conspiring against her, forcing her final moments into a singular runnel—reminding Daniel of those few surviving British soldiers fleeing iSandlwana and working their way toward this very river, which lies there smoking and whispering, the color of molten lead.

"Daniel?"

He turns to find Bruce at the darkness of the door, the cool interior of the library behind him. Bruce is looking more like his old self today. Recently showered, his hair combed, with a white, collared shirt and a pair of khaki-colored slacks that have been ironed crisply.

"Hello, Bruce."

"Moses said I'd find you here. Are you working on your book?"

"Trying to."

"Where are you at?"

"About to arrive at Helpmekaar."

"You're nearing the end."

"I am."

"Good. That's very good."

"I'll send you the final pages as soon as I'm done with them, if you like?"

Daniel can see, however, that Bruce's mind is elsewhere. He is merely acting out the exchange, like a man providing himself with an alibi. Bruce goes to the edge of the wooden balcony where Daniel is sitting and he stares across at the sliver of river, which shines on under its drifting cloud of mist. The bush on either side of the river feels alive with the density found at the very core of a bee swarm—or a termite nest.

"Listen," Bruce says, "I'd like you to do something very important for me."

"Of course. Anything."

"This evening, at six o'clock, I'd like you to come up to the house. I'd like you to come alone and I'd like you to tell no one else about it."

"Okay."

"Daniel, it's important that you arrive at exactly six o'clock."

"I'll be there," Daniel says.

Bruce gives him a nod and a smile—and then, as he is about to withdraw back to the library, he stops himself. "By the way," he says, "I want to thank you."

"Thank me for what?"

"For what you're about to do for me."

"That sounds—very mysterious."

"Just be there at six."

Some people are built like churches

They walk through the world like moving churches, where people can come to dwell. They provide cool, quiet places away from the noise, the hurry, the stress. You can dwell with them and absorb the silence. They provide a space in which you can gather yourself, recollect your thoughts in tranquillity, find within yourself structures and resources with which to once again face the world.

Daniel has never experienced this with a person before. He might have in his early years, with his mother, but his mother's gaze was always turned away from him. Her windows faced in some other direction, away from a landscape in which he might have been found. Jade provided this feeling briefly, but that turned out to be an illusion, since she was in urgent need of a sanctuary of her own. Was it possible for two people to provide a sanctuary for one other? Was it possible for two people to occupy the same church?

Daniel is thinking about this as he drives through the hills toward Natasha. The cloud has moved in and a new coldness has entered the air. He leaves the dirt road and passes the ruined house repaired with rubbish and pauses while a herd of cattle crosses the road between two farm gates.

Autumn will be coming soon. Winter will be coming soon. Daniel has always liked the winter. It is a time when it is permitted to withdraw, to be alone. He has always done his best work during winter, when the outside world offers fewer distractions. But this coming winter feels endangered. He is not sure what the world might look like without Natasha in it. If he is to return to his new job in Johannesburg, will that mean that he will lose sight of her? Will she cook alone in her kitchen, listening to her grandmother's music, feeling saudade for the man she found and then lost—and knows, deep down, she will never see again?

He has to walk through a sea of schoolgirls to reach her

They are chattering happily, oblivious to the dark-haired, blue-eyed poet moving through them like a creature from another land. He is neither parent nor teacher. He is barely a man. He has always had this gift for invisibility. He has always relied upon it. What he hasn't yet understood is what Bruce saw so clearly inside him before that Sunday lunch. A light has been switched on inside him. He is as radiant as an angel, as illuminated as a figure made from stained glass. If the girls do not look at him, it is not because they don't notice him—it is because they do.

"Hello," he says, entering the cool interior of Natasha's classroom. As he steps into the room, a sensor ignites the lights. Natasha has been sitting so still that the sensor was no longer aware that she was there. She looks across at him and smiles, her whole frame softening.

"What is so urgent?" she asks.

On the phone, he said he had some news and he needed to speak with her as soon as possible. This moment—ten o'clock in the morning, at first break—is the earliest she is available.

"Has something happened?"

"Nothing bad. It's just that I've had a job offer. A new TV job. I wanted to talk to you about it."

She manages to retain her smile through this—her thoughts, her feelings, remaining still inside her, like birds on a branch, shifting silently against one another in the dark.

"What do you want to talk about?"

"What I should do. Whether I should accept it or not."

She gives a frown of what might be impatience. "I'm not sure I'm the person to advise you on that."

"I know. And I'm sorry—I'm not trying to put you on the spot, or anything. It's just that—I thought I'd take it. At least until I could find another kind of job. I thought I might go into teaching. Teaching English—or maybe Drama. But I thought I'd make one condition."

"Oh yes? To whom, exactly?"

Now she seems faintly amused.

"To my employers. The producers. I thought I'd say that I wanted to work from here, from down here. I could drive up for story meetings once a week, if necessary, but for the rest of the time I could be living down here. Of course—I'd need to sell my mother's house. But I could do all of that while living here."

"While living where, exactly?"

She is looking even more amused.

"Well, I didn't want to seem too presumptuous," he says. "But I thought I'd try and find a place near you. Rent an apartment or a cottage. So we could spend more time together. If you'd like that."

She is watching him now with open warmth and humor.

"Daniel," she says, "I would like that very much."

The mountain casts a shadow across the battlefield

He leaves his room five minutes before the appointed hour. The sky is low and gray and moving quickly. All around him, the birds are still. There is something strange in the air, some air of expectation. There has been an idea inside Daniel that he has been pushing back all day—as something he can return to later, when he has a moment to think. There has been much else to think about. The new job, the consequences with Natasha, the idea of moving down to KwaZulu-Natal and looking for work as a teacher, the decision to sell his mother's house. There would be Victoria and Legion to consider. He would have to pay their pensions and help them to buy off Victoria's mother's house in Zimbabwe. There would be other consequences of each of these decisions, going in different directions, that he hasn't even started to consider. But this other idea, this suppressed idea, comes pushing up again inside him, making him pick up his pace as he takes the track across the top of the stables and toward the Websters' house. What on earth had Bruce been talking about? This morning he looked so much better than usual. His hair was brushed, he had on a new shirt. He was like a man on his way to an important meeting or an interview. But what was he planning to meet? Whom was he hoping to interview?

Only now does Daniel remember the dream he had the previous night. In the dream, Sam was alive and well. She was a much older woman, her features tired but happy, a streak or two of gray running through her still-dark hair. She was walking across the battlefield, between the whitewashed cairns, with her two grown children, a boy and a girl of around nineteen or twenty. When Daniel turned to greet the children, he found only a blank space where their faces were meant to be. When he looked back at Sam, he saw she was not a living woman, but the ghost of a woman, her children still sitting somewhere inside her, waiting to be born. They had no father. Sam had died before she had met their father. So they were merely the ideas of children, the potential for children. But they had no fingerprints on their fingers and they had no names.

He is awakened from this memory by the sound of a dog howling. Or a wolf howling. It is coming from the shining shape of the Websters' glass house, which is just discernable above the thorn trees. The path re-joins the gravel driveway and Daniel continues toward the kitchen door. Bruce's fawn-colored Land Cruiser soon becomes visible—and then Daniel sees that Jane is sitting outside the driver's door, her head raised as she emits that wolf-howl, long and desolate.

Daniel starts to run—but he already knows that he has arrived too late. He has been punctual, as Bruce insisted. Without needing to look at his watch, he knows that it is exactly six o'clock.

THE BUTTERFLY COLLECTOR

Charles is pleased to be reunited with his butterfly books at Helpmekaar

Even though his net and much of his equipment are still somewhere in the rubble at the base of Isandhlwana, he has enough here to start his work again. Until he can acquire a decent net, he will do some "treacling" and concentrate on moths. Amongst his belongings are the butterflies he collected in Durban—the beautiful *Papilio demoleus* that he killed under the gaze of Will's dark-haired cousin, Isabella, and the *Papilio nireuslyaeus* that he caught the next morning at the stables shortly before they took the omnibus up to Pietermaritzburg. The gaze of Isabella, he realizes, has stayed with him ever since, each time he has killed a moth or a butterfly—or indeed a living man.

Nonetheless, the evening is warm and misty and favorable for moth-catching—so, while Will lies dreaming in their tent, Charles takes some molasses from the feed storeroom and buys some wild honey from a kindly cook and boils down a concoction, which he spices at the end with rum. This he paints on a fencepost behind the stables to attract whatever moths might be in the area. He catches two *Sphinx atropos* specimens, which are large moths with a distinctive skull-shape on the back of the thorax. Charles would occasionally find *atropos* moths in the potato fields behind his family home in Somerset—and previously, when he was still posted in Sandspruit, he saw one of the Zulu grooms killing an excellent specimen—believing, it turned out, that it was a bad omen and possessed a deadly sting. Charles's *atropos* specimens are large and docile from his concoction and soon extinguished with a drop of cyanide.

Gradually, the picture of the last two days is beginning to emerge. The bulk of the British army leaving the camp at Isandhlwana more or less undefended, the unexpected discovery of the Zulu army a few miles from the camp, the massacre that followed and the escape of a few hundred men over Fugitives' Drift—and then the attack late that afternoon at the field hospital at Jim Rorke's place, where around a hundred and fifty men, many of them wounded, held back a force of thousands of Zulu soldiers through the night.

It was clear when Charles had first reached the burned-out field hospital that the survivors were in no position to help Will. Private Brown and several other men were soon ordered to kill any surviving Zulu soldiers, whose bodies lay intertwined amongst their dead. Powerless to intervene, Charles rode on to Helpmekaar with Will. There Will's wounds were immediately dressed, he was given a strong sedative and Charles took him back to his tent to care for him. Their tent was situated at the edge of a precipitous krantz that overlooked the old road to Jim Rorke's settlement and the undulating green hills beyond it. A herd of wild hartebeest was roaming freely there, unconcerned by the proximity of the tented camp, and the rocks around them were alive with rock rabbits. Charles was too tired to hunt anything, however—and, for the rest of that day, the two men slept soundly, only occasionally waking to eat a biscuit or to drink some water laced—like Charles's concoction—with rum.

Charles and Will have made no mention of the hearing that is planned for them. By now, they have heard of the death of Lieutenant Pope at the base of Isandhlwana, and their hope is that the matter—somewhere under all the mountains of the dead—will be laid to rest. On their third evening at Helpmekaar, however, they receive a note asking them each to appear the following morning at the quarters of Major Upcher. Grace at eight and Hawthorne at eight-thirty. The private who delivers the note knows nothing about the reason for this summons, but Charles suggests afterwards that many men are being asked to consult with the Major—so perhaps this is merely a part of the fact-finding session that has been continuing regarding the events of the last few days.

"Charles, I think we both know that is a lie," Will says.

They are sitting on the edge of a krantz off to the side and well away from the camp, overlooking a long stretch of land that becomes Zululand. A floating of pied crows is circling not far below them and the slow curve of the Buffalo River catches the declining light, making it look for a few moments like a river of gold—until it sinks back into the failure of lead.

In the middle distance, at Jim Rorke's, they can make out the trenches where the Zulu dead are being buried. Thousands of men thrown into a few long ditches, their spirits condemned forever to be away from home. In the far distance, to the left, they can also see the smoking lion of Isandhlwana, where the thousands of British dead are still lying unburied at its feet like some pagan sacrifice.

"It's a matter of honor with men like Bayley," Will continues. "It does not help that we left him there to die on the battlefield."

"It was every man for himself."

"There is no such thing as that. Not amongst real soldiers."

"Are you and I not real soldiers?"

"I managed to be in the middle of the battle at Isandhlwana and I did not kill a single man. Is that the work of a real soldier?"

"You should count yourself fortunate. It's not pleasant to kill a man. The odd thing is—whenever I did so, I had that feeling of shame I first experienced when I was with your cousin."

"My cousin?"

"Isabella—in Durban."

"Ah—young Isabella. How long ago that seems. We were great fools, Charles."

"We were?"

"We wasted all that time we had together."

"We still have time ahead of us," says Charles. "We have survived the worst of it."

"If only that were true."

Charles takes his friend's hand and is surprised at how hot it is.

"How are you feeling?" he asks.

"Much better, thanks."

"Did you see Mowbray?"

"Mowbray?"

"Lying killed at the camp. He was lying there at the feet of our horse."

"Oh God. Poor Mowbray."

"It feels odd," says Charles, "to know more men who have perished than those who have survived. We have a duty to such men as Mowbray, Will. We have a duty to live long and to live well. This matter tomorrow—it will be something we will have to endure, something we must overcome. There will be more life after it, if we are patient, I promise you."

"What kind of a life—when you are living in such shame?"

"The world is large. And there are many ways of looking at a man. We do not need to be defined by this one—interlude."

"We shall be defined by it, Charles. Whatever we try to do."

The next morning, Charles finds Major Upcher sitting outside his official quarters

There is no sign of Will—but Bayley is there, standing one step behind the major's chair. Charles has not seen Bayley since their last encounter on the banks of the Buffalo River, although Charles has heard that Bayley has been one of those responsible for burying the dead and cleaning up the field hospital. He must have come up to Helpmekaar specifically for this hearing. Major Upcher is a large-framed, imposing figure who is also known to be a good friend of Bayley's—the two men having schooled together at Harrow.

Charles has shaved for the occasion and cobbled together what uniform he could from the supplies, but his regimental numbers and badges are naturally missing.

"I'm pleased to see that you are not continuing to disgrace your regiment," is Upcher's opening remark.

"I beg your pardon, sir?"

"I have been speaking with Lieutenant Bayley about you," Upcher continues. "It is evident that you have disgraced your regiment both on and off the field of battle."

Charles knows better than to respond to this, and he does not look across at Bayley, although he can feel the smirk coming off his old antagonist like an unsavory smell.

"There is going to have to be a formal hearing at Headquarters," Upcher says. "But I need you to know that, as of this moment, you are unofficially suspended from your commission. You will be expected to appear before General Clifford on Friday morning at ten o'clock. Is that understood?"

"Yes, sir."

"Lieutenant Bayley has also claimed, Lieutenant Hawthorne, that on three occasions you prematurely abandoned your men and your position. Once on the way back to the camp, once after leaving the camp, and once after you had crossed the Buffalo River. Is this correct?"

"I am not sure that I understand any of these claims, sir."

"Well are they true or not, man?"

"Sir, I did everything I could to keep the enemy back—but, as with everyone else, I retreated whenever my situation became untenable."

"Well that is all very interesting. Lieutenant Bayley, however, has suggested that you may have been far more interested in serving the interests of your friend—or should I say servicing the interests of your friend?—than you ever were in serving your regiment."

"I made a promise to his sister, sir, that I would do what I could to protect him. But I believe that I fought as long and hard as any other man, sir."

"We shall never know that, shall we? Almost all the men who fought alongside you are dead."

"That is correct, sir. With the exception of Lieutenant Bayley, sir."

At this, Bayley glowers, but he says nothing and Upcher allows the insinuation to pass.

"Lieutenant Hawthorne, you are no doubt familiar with the story of Captain Rowlston."

"I am, sir."

"It is interesting that you two shared the same regiment in Templemore."

"Why is that interesting, if I may be permitted to ask, sir?"

"Because the two of you appear to have been cut from the same cloth."

When Charles does not reply to this, Upcher continues:

"Rowlston knew what had to be done. Now that we have had our little chat, I believe that Lieutenant Grace does too."

"I beg your pardon, sir?"

"My suggestion to you, Lieutenant Hawthorne, is that you go for a good, long walk. To reflect on your conduct. Perhaps you could catch some of your famous butterflies along the way."

"What are you suggesting, sir?"

"That is all for the present, Hawthorne. I am sorry that it had to come to this. I expect you to have left the camp before first light tomorrow morning. Your presence has corrupted the atmosphere of your regiment for long enough."

Charles runs as fast as he can back to his tent

He finds Will sitting neatly on his bed, fully clothed in the uniform of his regiment. The small, uncorked bottle marked with the skull and crossbones is in his left hand.

"How long will it take?" Will asks his friend.

"Will, what are you talking about?"

"How long will it take to die? Will it take longer than a butterfly?"

"Please, Will. Pass me that bottle."

"I don't think I can do that, Charles."

"William—please. Do not let them win."

Will laughs at this—and then he empties the little bottle into his mouth.

THE GHOST OF SAM WEBSTER

Caroline

The road is a dark river rolling toward her

Rocks are piled up where the entrance to the driveway is meant to be, a wall of thorns backed up behind it. All around, the rain roars. The dim world is on the move. The surface of everything is melting and shifting. The windscreen wipers are busy, but useless. The headlights light up only more darkness. She waits, waiting for nothing. There is nowhere left to go. She has come as far as she can. Bruce's car is the one thing that is still. It sticks to the side of the mountain like a sucking tick. It is only a matter of time before the mountain takes it, with her inside. The lights are angled upwards, into the empty air. The whole car already feels lopsided. Dislodged. Disengaged from any known road. Caroline has never felt herself, or known herself, to be so alone.

She could try to back the car up and turn around and return to where she came from, but she isn't sure where that is anymore. Even if she regained her original road and followed it back down the hill, where would she go? What home would welcome her? What person out there would open their door?

To the one side of the car, she can feel the mountain rising up in the night. A huge presence brooding with ancient knowledge. She remembers the talk about this being a burial mound. Of those who lived here long before. The bones of the dead. An old grudge, directed against her and her kind. On the other side of the car is empty space—the sheer drop down to the stables. With one quick move, she could steer the car downwards, plunge into the abyss, roll all the way down to the bottom of the hill. The idea thrills her. To blast this bit of metal to pieces. To see Bruce's face afterwards. The wreck of their lives reflected back at them. Or even better—to die with it now. To steer herself toward her own death. To own her own death—since she has never owned her own life. It's not that she wants to die, exactly. But she likes the idea of the experiment. How would it feel? Would her last moment be one of clear euphoria, of blissful release—or would it be full of aguish, of terrible regret? She moves the steering one inch toward it—then two. She can feel the tires sliding through the gravel, the whole car adjusting its weight.

All around, the storm carries on, indifferent to her fate. The safest place is to remain as still as she can inside this car. If she waits for long enough, the storm will have to pass—like all storms. She sits and waits, listening for some change in the weather, some evidence of a slackening off. But there is only an answering rumble from the heavens. And more rain. And more thunder. This storm feels intended specifically for her. Some higher judgment. It might rain for forty days and forty nights. It might rain like this forever.

She is also very drunk. She doesn't know how this happened. She can barely remember the drinking. She wasn't even aware of it. She needed to be drunk so badly, so instinctively, that the drinking itself passed unnoticed. "She hates you." She remembers the words. The way he said it. "She hates you and she wants to get as far away from you as possible." But how was that possible? What had Caroline done, exactly, to make her child hate her that much? Was it merely the drink? The smell of the drink that came off her every morning? The stale sweet smell of her own failure, her own desolation? A child would, in time, take such a thing personally. The abandonment. The knowledge that, for your own mother, you are not enough. Your mother has to keep looking elsewhere for something her life appears to lack. Or even worse—she had to look elsewhere to numb the disappointment, the pain of your existence. But no—it can't have been only that. The drink was a later development, a later source of conflict. One that was useful because finally there was visible and tangible evidence. Sam knew that Caroline had been absent from the start. From the start, she had left Sam to fend for herself. And now that's what Sam was doing. Fending for herself. Herself and no one else. As Caroline had. She was isolating herself, cutting herself off. As Caroline had. Such a thing—it only led to this. This storm, this car, this tempting drop toward your death.

Caroline sees that she has to stop her. She has to salvage something between them before it's too late. Without thinking, she opens the door and steps into the storm. The river is there to meet her. It reaches around her knees, drags at her skirt. With her first step, she loses a shoe. With her second, she loses the other. But she knows where to go. The rain is stinging her face. The wind is tossing her about like some pale and naked plant. With only two branches and a wailing head. But she knows what to do. She wades on uphill through the water. A thorn goes into her heel, but she can't stop for it, she can't stop for anything. It feels as if the whole of life is coming together to meet her. Everything life can throw at a person is being thrown at her now, slapping her in the face, pounding her with its fists. But she has to stop her daughter before it's too late. She has to save her daughter from the devil that bewitched Caroline, bewitched each of them.

She wonders why she delayed. Why wait for the storm before acting? There were whole days, whole years, when she could have saved her child. Saved herself. But instead she drank. She shaped every day around the next drink. Just to get through the day. Just to make it endurable. But while she did that, the rest of life was going on, and the lives around her were hardening against her, all around her. Was there anything left to salvage?

But the hill is just a hill, after all. The storm is only a storm. Soon she can sense the shape of the glass house in the darkness. She can feel its magnetic pull. Of course, there is always something left to hope for if you look hard enough. There is always a second chance. To be human is to fall. To fail. Everyone should be allowed to get up again. And what has she done? Her sin has been to do too little. Her sin has been to give up. Surely that was worse than doing active, conscious harm? She has been ill. Does she deserve to remain unloved for that?

Her obstacle was Sam. Always Sam. Sam's judgment. She has always been the judge of all of them. None of them has ever been good enough for Sam. Perhaps Caroline took to drink because she was afraid of her own daughter. She could never say this out loud. The thought was unforgivable. Ridiculous. But with Sam's gaze on her, it often felt as if there was no air left in the world. No air for Caroline in which to be happy. Sam was a monster. Yes. And if there was a reason Caroline went off with Tim it was not because she wanted to defy her husband, it was because she wanted to defy her daughter.

Caroline sees the house and slows. She stands in the middle of the circle of stones and understands that the ghost she was walking toward through the rain was some other daughter, the mere ghost of her daughter. The real Sam would never forgive her. The real Sam might still be there, standing in the house, but in truth she went away a long time ago. Even if Caroline wasn't too late, she would be too late.

She enters through the kitchen. A woman made of mud and twigs, leaves and misery. Jane is watching her arrival from the rug, but Caroline ignores the dog and moves through to Sam's bedroom. There she finds Sam packing the small, red suitcase she used to take with her on tennis tours and hockey tours and weekends at the sea. Caroline bought the suitcase for herself, she remembers. But Sam, liking the look of it, had acquired it.

"Sam?"

Sam turns and stares at her. "What happened to you?"

"I left the car down the road. The road is closed. Blocked off."

"You look like a scarecrow."

Sam turns away and folds a blue linen shirt into the neatly piled suitcase. Sam has always been fastidious. Since she was a girl of seven, and stopped allowing Caroline to brush the knots from her hair, every single hair has always been perfectly aligned on her head.

"Where are you going?"

"I'm going away for a while."

"Where to?"

"I haven't exactly decided yet."

"You're going alone?"

"I'm going with Tim."

Sam hasn't looked at her during this last exchange, but she looks at her now.

"But he left yesterday. He's already gone."

"He's still here. He waited for me."

Sam picks up a white silk scarf patterned with blue swallows. Another gift from Caroline. This one intended. "I'm sorry, Mom," she says. "But I have to go. Please don't argue about it. I'll keep in touch, I promise."

"Listen, Sam. I don't want you to go."

"You don't want me to go, or you don't want me to go with Tim?"

"I don't want you to go."

Sam places the scarf across the shirt. The suitcase is almost full. On Sam's bed, Caroline can see her passport slipped under her phone.

"Tim isn't who you think he is," Caroline says.

"How would you know?"

"Because he's a liar. He's been lying to all of us."

"Oh please."

"He doesn't love you. He doesn't love anyone."

"Mom, you're drunk."

"Listen to me, Sam. He's a very bad person."

"Rubbish."

"If you go away with him, you're going to come to harm."

"You're just jealous that I have a life. I love Tim and he loves me. I think he's the only person who's ever seen me. I mean properly. He's the only person I've ever felt safe with."

"That's what I thought too."

"What's that supposed to mean?"

"I also thought he was somewhere to—escape to. But he isn't. He's a monster."

"I have no idea what you're talking about—and I don't think you do either."

"I know exactly what I'm talking about. Since the very first night he arrived here, Tim and I have been lovers. He walked in here for dinner and by the end of it we'd had sex on the couch. I have no idea how it happened. Or why. I know it's grotesque. Unforgivable. But sometimes people do—very self-destructive things."

"Wow." Sam looks at her. "And that was the only time?"

Caroline feels the temptation to lie, but she knows that the truth is her only hope—and Sam's only hope. "We've been lovers all this time. Even while he's been with you."

Sam looks at her with something like admiration. "I can't believe you'd stoop to this."

"I'm telling you the truth."

"If anyone is a monster, it's you!"

Sam is looking at her with such rage that Caroline can see that some part of Sam, some part that she isn't yet ready to admit, must believe her.

"I can tell you everything there is to know about his body, if you like. He has some fluff in the small of his back. Just above his buttocks. He has a scar on his chest where a mole was removed. He has a rugby wound on his left hand. On the ring finger. Where his nail doesn't grow properly. He has vitiligo. But you have to look very carefully to find it. It's high up on the inside of his left thigh. He says it's shaped like the Welsh dragon."

She can see that Sam knows none of this. She can see that she, Caroline, knows more about the man's body than she does. She carries on.

"When he's done with you, he usually has a lukewarm shower and a large mug of coffee. Sometimes, when he has an orgasm, he gets a migraine. Like his brain is trying to split in half. He thinks it's got something to do with narrow blood vessels at the base of his skull. But I believe it's guilt. I believe he isn't one person, but two. I believe he's constantly at war with himself. And that the worst in him always wins through. I think he's the Devil. And I think he seduced you just as he seduced me. But I'm older and I've experienced more of the world. I know what men are. I know they're weak, shadowy, self-serving, duplicitous. And Tim is the very worst of them. He will take what he wants from you and then he will dump you. Like he's dumped the rest of us. So please, Sam. Don't go. Don't go anywhere near that evil man again."

Sam has continued packing during the course of this speech as if Caroline is not speaking at all. When the red suitcase is full, she zips it and picks it up, slipping her phone and passport into her pocket. Without even looking at her mother, she walks out. By the time Caroline has thought to call her back, Sam has already disappeared into the night.

Sam

The storm hits her like a great wave

It's like being at sea. Surrounded by an endless darkness. Immediately, she is sucked into it, taken over by it. The hill on which she stands is a huge swell, pulling her deeper into the storm's current. Behind her, the house disappears. An abandoned ship. Its lights extinguished. She has no idea where she is going. She is going wherever the wind and the rain will carry her. She left the house with such wind in her sails, but already she is tattered and torn, drenched by the storm, sloppy and adrift—with only the little red suitcase to connect her to the familiar world.

The only thing left to move toward is Tom. She betrayed him, and she had almost dismissed him, but now she realizes that he is the thing she has been using all along to arrange her inner map—a star, a sun, a bit of light that for a while Tim almost managed to extinguish. She knows that he will take her back. She knows that he will allow her to make this mistake and come back from it. She only has to find a way to reach him. Which is when she remembers the estate bakkie down at the compound. Moses usually leaves the key in the ignition, which was why Simon can use the vehicle at night and come and go unnoticed.

She had to get away from Tim and her mother. She would never see them again. She would never come back to this godforsaken place again. She would find Tom and she would ask him to take her away. They would find a place at the far end of the world, on the other side of this death valley, on the other side of this storm, where they could have another chance at life. In the morning, she would write a message to her father telling him that she was going away. But for now she had to get away. She had to get as far away as possible. She especially had to get as far away as possible from Tim. He frightened her. Far more than this storm, which was nothing. She was used to the weather in this place. The lightning was bad, but it was worse on the top of the mountain where the wildebeest were. If she stuck to this river—which was once a road—she would be able to find her way out of here and get away forever.

She is just beginning to feel better when she finds herself in the middle of a bush of thorns. The thorns have surrounded her, like some trap closing in. She only knew which direction she needed to move in because of the flow of water, but now her path is blocked. She stands there, unable to move. A fly waiting for some giant spider to climb up out of the night to come and take her.

That is when the light floods in.

She has no idea what it is at first. It's as if the sun is coming out, or the gate of heaven is miraculously opening. She almost expects an angel to climb out of the light and fly down to find her, and raise her up, and carry her off like those souls she saw being flown into heaven in that painting by Hieronymus Bosch. Then she hears the engine and realizes the light is coming from a car. It sounds like her father's car.

She looks up to the light as it closes in on her and says:

"Daddy, is that you?"

Caroline

She pours herself another drink

She is alone again inside the house. Standing in the glass veranda in the dark. The dog asleep at her feet. The storm rattling all around her. It is difficult to know who she is or where she is. This is a living nightmare. Yet she feels a new clarity. A new finality. She has arrived at the place of desolation that she has spent her whole life warding off. But here it is. She recognizes it at last. This is what it feels like. To be completely alone. It's easier than she thought. There's no pressure to be anything. To do anything. She can drink this whole bottle of gin and then another and there will be no one left to care. No one left to notice. Finally, she can do no more harm. She has already done all the harm one person can be expected to do.

"Mummy, is that you?"

She turns to feel the presence of her boy. Matthew. She had forgotten about him. Even when things are at their very worst, she never forgets about him. Of course. There is Matthew. The only thing that makes her necessary. Bruce, Tim, they were only markers of death, of dying. As for Sam—first she was taken by Bruce, then she was taken by Tim. But Matthew has always been there. Waiting for her. Believing in her. Believing that she will one day take the chance to come back to him.

"Where have you been?"

"I found Dad's car."

"I left it there at the bottom of the driveway. The road was blocked."

"I thought I'd be able to drive it back to the house."

"In this weather?"

"Yes."

Matthew waits for her. He has the air of one who hasn't spoken yet. Even though he has been speaking.

"What is it?" She can feel the fear in her voice. The fear she picked up from him. "What happened?"

"I'm afraid there's been—an accident."

"What?"

"It was an accident."

"What was an accident?"

"I hit her. I think I hit Sam. I think I drove right into her."

"You what?"

"She's there, lying in the road. I'm afraid, I—"

He doesn't say anything more. He doesn't need to.

Caroline takes out her phone and dials Tim's number as she starts to move toward her coat, her boots. He answers at once—as if waiting for her call.

"Tim. It's me. Is Sam with you?"

"No."

"Please—don't lie to me."

"I promise you. She left a few hours ago. To pack. I haven't seen her since."

"Can you come here?"

"Haven't you noticed that it's raining rather badly?"

"I need you to come now. Meet me at the bottom of the driveway—"

"Caroline—"

"There's been an accident."

"Caroline—"

"Come to the wall of thorns. Bring a torch."

She doesn't say more.

She is already moving outside when she hangs up.

She tells Matthew to stay in the house.

Then she is moving back into the dream-dark. But she is no longer alone. She is a mother now. You can never be alone when you have a child in the world. But it's all nonsense anyway. It's some mistake. Matthew must've been mistaken. A wild boy, given to occasional fantasies. Sometimes, he saw things that he later found had never been there. Like the snake he saw under his bed when he was a boy. And everyone rushed there to find nothing. No snake anywhere inside the whole house. So maybe he'd hit a rock with the car and thought it was a life, a living thing. Maybe he'd hit a duiker or a bushbuck. Wasn't there always a little duiker lingering around in the bushes down there? Recently, it had become almost tame. Perhaps it had been drawn to the light.

The rain is falling thick and incessant, moving this way and that, swaying in time to some ancient earth-song, some terrible drum. Caroline stumbles and realizes she has been running all along, falling and running and getting up again, and never quite falling or running or getting up again, and never quite knowing what is happening.

But what is happening is definitely happening.

She sees a light in the dark. She sees Tim already somehow standing there as if he's been standing there all along. She thinks for a moment that maybe it was Tim that Matthew hit, not Sam. But then she remembers that she has just spoken to Tim on the phone. She was the one who summoned him.

She can't be relied on to think too clearly.

Tim says something as she approaches. The words are lost in the storm. At his feet is some pale thing. A rock, a fallen tree.

She sees now that it is a girl.

Tim is standing over a girl's body. The torchlight on her heart.

"Did you do this?" Tim asks her.

The lie emerges already formed. As she says it, she knows she was always going to say it.

"Yes."

"What the hell happened?"

"I—drove into her."

"She's—"

"I was drunk. I am drunk."

"You will go to prison for this."

"It doesn't matter."

"It does matter. Matthew needs his mother. So does Sam."

"Sam?"

"We'll have to get the body away from here," says Tim.

"What body?"

"Don't worry. I'll take care of it. I'll take it far away from here. You go back to the house."

"What?"

"I'll bring the car back later."

Bruce's fawn-colored Land Cruiser is parked there unevenly. Reared up against the earth-bank where Matthew left it. The two headlights pointed into the vacant heavens as if expecting an attack. An image of war, of enemy invasion.

"I'll clean up everything."

Tim is taking off his dark-blue anorak, placing it over the body.

"But Sam—"

"What about Sam?"

"Is she—is she dead?"

"Sam?" says Tim, standing up.

He shines his light on the girl's face.

It's not Sam's face. It's the face of someone else. A young woman. Someone else entirely.

Caroline looks around in the dark.

"But then—where is Sam?"

EPILOGUE

THE BUTTERFLY COLLECTOR

The white butterflies came late that year

There had been a dry spell in the Kalahari and the Karoo, followed by unseasonal rains. Every year in southern Africa, millions of brown-veined whites—which Trimen called *Pieris mesentina*—hatch in the desert and lay their eggs as they emigrate in an easterly direction, toward their deaths, some say as far as the Indian Ocean, north of Mozambique. Trimen and his contemporaries knew little about the concept of butterfly migration, and even today it is not known why these butterflies continue to fly such a distance to die. There is no self-interested reason for this behavior. Having relinquished their duty to the next generation, perhaps they simply take pleasure in the sensation of inconsequential flight.

As Charles traveled toward Lydia Grace, he was surrounded by the same crop of white butterflies as she was, although they were moving in the opposite direction, toward the land of his disgrace.

There was also a bewildering array of small electric copper, blue and green butterflies wherever he looked. Where before he might have tried to catch and name a few of these specimens, on that day he let them pass. He had already telegramed Lydia ahead of his arrival to inform her of her brother's death.

According to family legend, Lydia was surrounded by a thousand white butterflies when she received the news. She collapsed in the dusty yard outside the corrugated-tin farmhouse of her fiancé, Tertius Grobbelaar. When Grobbelaar returned from a feather auction in Mossel Bay, she told him that she would not be able to marry him. She would remain on the farm until her brother's friend, Lieutenant Hawthorne, could take her back to Cape Town. There was to be no funeral for Will, whose body, she would later learn, was buried in an unmarked grave at Helpmekaar. The cause of his death was not mentioned in the telegram and she had assumed that he had died in battle.

Later, Lydia would tell her children—of which there were to be seven—that she was already in love with Charles when he came to find her in Oudtshoorn, which wasn't much more than a settlement arranged around a church on a dusty plain, surrounded by a distant wall of wrinkled rock. Charles arrived in a Cape cart and stayed the night and the next day they left Grobbelaar's farm, the dog Pip happily restored to his position under Charles's left arm.

Charles and Lydia were married within a month in the stone church at Kalk Bay. Several months later, they had their first child. A healthy boy they named William. For the rest of his days, Charles never killed another butterfly. The last living creature ever to die from one of his cyanide bottles was to be William Grace. But he continued to work closely with Trimen at the museum, researching his butterflies and his moths in the mountains around the Cape of Good Hope. He also taught at the local school in Kalk Bay with Lydia, teaching Natural Sciences while Lydia taught Latin and

English. It was a happy marriage, by all accounts. When Charles died, he carried two great loves and seven children inside his heart.

It would take several generations of historians to establish that other version of Charles Hawthorne—the famous coward who had three times abandoned his fellow soldiers at the height of battle. The man who had driven across the desert through a sea of white butterflies to claim the hand of the woman he loved—or hoped to love—that man soon became nothing more than a family anecdote.

THE WRITER

Dear Daniel

By the time you read this letter—if all goes as planned—I shall be passed.

This is the only meaningful act I have left. Soon my body will close down and the landscape of my life will be in ruins. In that other letter you found with me—the letter addressed to the police—is my confession to the murder of the young woman from Durban.

I did not mean to kill her. She appeared like an apparition out of the rain. My car hit her before I even knew what had happened. I went to look at her but she was already dead. I had been drinking. I knew a scandal like this could ruin my name, my family and my business—and so I took the body far away and threw her into the river. I wasn't thinking straight. I just wanted to get the hideous fact of her death as far away from me as possible. This is also what I have told the police.

I don't know what you will think of me. It doesn't matter now. The wonderful thing about death is how it changes the scale of everything. Very little matters from this strange promontory. Already the events of my life are barely visible. I would need some kind of powerful and falsifying lens to bring them back to life. I know that when I am gone I will be labeled a coward. I can live with that. Or should I say that I can die with that? I have nothing left to defend and nothing left to lose. With the one exception of my son.

This is why I am writing to you. I need you to stay close to Matthew. As a stand-in godfather. Or simply as a friend. I need you to talk to him and to listen to him and to help him in every way that you can. I don't mean financially or practically. I mean in the way that really matters. I need you to help him to straighten out his idea of himself. I need you to help him to find the right perspectives. He will need a tree to stand under. I am asking you to be that tree.

Many things will be said about him and our family after I am gone. Many things will be said about me. I am not asking you to represent me or even to defend me. I need no representation and no defense. I am asking you to help Matthew to find a way of thinking about himself that will enable him to live a good life. A life without shame. A life with enough air around it to enable him to be many things, for himself and others. I am worried that if he is left too much alone he will live forever inside a self-constructed prison.

I am going to swallow this handful of blue pills now. I have been storing them up like a squirrel for the winter. Autumn has always brought out the best in me.

Finish your book.

And tell Natascha (sic) Lopez what you feel about her.

Thank you for everything—

Bruce

On the day of Bruce's funeral, Daniel straightens his tie in the mirror

He looks at the laughter lines around his eyes and wonders where such lines might have come from. A lifetime of laughter? It seems unlikely. But not impossible. Perhaps he has laughed more than he has realized. Perhaps he has also been happier than he has realized—having never had his eye much on happiness.

Looking more closely at his face, he can see the face he will have as a middle-aged man. His ears have already softened and grown slightly creased. He realizes that he has inherited the ears of his mother. That pair of rather large, indecisive, defeated ears he always pitied her for having. But his face is still essentially the face of his father. Very much a Hawthorne face. It is unmistakable and has been carried down over the generations—from the watercolor of Charles Hawthorne's father, Brigadier General Arthur Hawthorne, which now sits under cracked glass in a cupboard somewhere in his mother's house—and all the way to Daniel, the first man in his family line to be without a child, without an heir. It is a conventionally handsome face at first glance. Classical and English, like the face of Rupert Brooke—but also dark-shadowed and haunted, as if the Hawthornes are doomed forever to too little sleep, or a sleep that is too superficial ever to relieve the alarm bells running along inside each of them—like those service bells in old country houses that were once intended to summon the servants.

Daniel sees now that they have all been running away from something. Losing themselves in the name of action. But what were they fighting against? Was the antagonist something external or something internal—like most enduring antagonists?

He puts on his jacket. He is dressed in black. He is dressed for death. He knows—and has known from the moment he read Bruce's letter—that Bruce can't possibly have been responsible for the young woman's murder—or accidental death. He was never guilty enough. Around the subject, Bruce always showed the disinterest of an innocent man. And in the police interviews Daniel witnessed, there was never a single question or statement from Bruce that suggested he had anything to hide.

There was also this idea that after Bruce had hit the woman with his car he had somehow loaded her into the back, driven her miles upriver and then carried her body through the mud and thrown her body into the flooded water. Was Daniel expected to believe that Bruce—an old and cumbersome man who was not only drunk but dying of cancer—had transported the woman such a distance under such conditions? Even if he had managed to do all of that, why had he dressed her in nothing but an anorak, another man's anorak that had somehow appeared out of the ether?

It was clear that Bruce was protecting someone, someone close to him. His letter—which was characteristically lacking in commas—stated very clearly that the only thing he had left to protect was his son. Was this his way of telling Daniel that Matthew was responsible? Was this as close as Bruce had dared to go to telling Daniel the truth? He knew that Daniel was a writer, "a man of letters," as the epithet went. Was Bruce relying on Daniel to be the one person who would truly be able to understand his letter?

It is Matthew who has been behaving like a guilty person, not Bruce. Had Matthew been the one driving the car? There was something about Bruce's description of the event that sounded authentic. She had appeared like an apparition out of the rain. But if Matthew had really been responsible for the woman's death, when had Bruce found out about it? That night? A week later? Over the past weeks, Bruce had appeared to be wholly unaware of such a possibility. So more recently, then. Recently enough to trigger this event—and this line of defense.

If all of this were true, it meant that Matthew had been carrying his secret alone for weeks, for months. Yet the idea of the boy dressing the dead woman up in someone else's anorak and taking her miles upriver was just as improbable as it was with Bruce. No—if Matthew had done this thing, he would most likely have run straight back to the house and told his mother. His mother would have turned for help to the one person close to her, the one person able to take the body miles away and be dumb enough to wrap it up in his own anorak. That was why Tim had been arrested. He had been the one to dump the body, even if he had not been the one to kill the girl. Had he killed the girl, Bruce would never have protected him. So it must have been Matthew. The only thing left for Bruce to defend. And now the police were moving in on them—they were moving in on Simon, on Tim and on Caroline—and soon, following Daniel's reasoning, they would be moving in on Matthew. Bruce had stepped in at the very last moment—not only to save his son, but to save them all.

There seemed to be no other plausible explanation. Yet Daniel knew enough to know that he would never be able to test his theory on anyone. The killing of the young woman would be something they would each have to carry with them forever. Hadn't Bruce already understood this? This was what his letter had been about. Matthew would have to find a way to live with himself that would not be solely defined by this event. It was Daniel's job—the writer's job—to help Matthew find some other narrative with which to live. A narrative with what Bruce had called "some air around it."

In all of this, Sam is the one thing that keeps eluding Daniel. She is the reason he came to the lodge and started writing again. She is the reason he met up with Natasha and had another chance at life. Daniel owed her—or the ghost of her—no less than everything. Yet even as she had drawn him back toward the living again, and helped him to redeem some of his best ideas about himself, she had continued to evade him—as she had evaded each of them.

Daniel liked to think that at the last minute she managed to escape her fate. Perhaps, as she was running toward the light of what she thought was her father's car, the other woman ran across her path and saved her. Daniel liked to think that Sam stopped in her tracks and turned away and ran toward some other world—a world with no more ghosts, no more hauntings—or that she simply turned away and slipped off into the realm of myths, the realm of archetypes.

An hour later, he enters the school chapel

The wooden cross and the emaciated Christ are still hanging there. The two policemen, Dlamini and Ndlovu, are flanking the heavy wooden doors like security guards. Moses is sitting one pew from the back with Brian and some of the other staff from the lodge. Off to the side, under a stained-glass window of pinks and reds and blues, is Simon, who was released a few days previously following Bruce's signed confession.

The Websters—or what is left of them—are already sitting in the front row and Daniel finds a seat in the row behind them. The coffin is almost within reach of Matthew's arm. Matthew is wearing his school "number ones," his feathery golden hair still wet from the shower, the teeth of the comb still marked through his fine hair. Perhaps feeling Daniel's gaze on him, Matthew turns and looks at him and sends him the whiff of a weighty smile.

Caroline is sitting pressed against her son, wearing something straight and black. Her hair has simply been washed and left to dry, as if she feels she has a duty to her body to keep it clean, but nothing else. Daniel wonders what she might be feeling. She must know what Bruce has done for Matthew, what Bruce has done for all of them. Was this enough to retrieve some old idea of Bruce, some version of the man she had loved? This final act of Bruce's would leave her a wealthy woman, free from her current life. Or would she decide to take up where Bruce had left off, and keep her claim to the land of ghosts and shadows, the giant graveyard over which she and her husband had for so long presided?

Tim Greene is sitting next to her, dressed in a dark-blue suit. A suit the same color as his anorak. He appears to be entirely unchanged by recent events and looks as perfect as he would have when he first arrived at the lodge. Tim is the one person out of whom Daniel might have been able to get some of the truth—over a drink, perhaps, or over several drinks—but Daniel has had no desire for this. He knows enough of the truth to know what to do with it.

Next to Tim are Jess and Tom. From where Daniel is sitting, he can smell Tom's cheap deodorant. The smell of school dormitories and locker rooms. The smell of dead sisters and adrift mothers and quiet misery. In a week, Tom and Jess will be moving down to Cape Town to start the life that had also been mapped out for Sam. Daniel knows that Tim—who has also finally been cleared by the police—has already booked his plane ticket home. Within a matter of days, he and the others will be gone from this place forever. Even if they returned a month later, or a decade later, the world as they had left it would no longer exist. That world was dying today with Sam and with Bruce.

"Is this place reserved for anyone?"

Natasha is wearing a black dress that gives off the same electric-blue sheen as her hair. Daniel looks up at her as you might toward a friend in a crowd of strangers—an ally in the very place where you least expect it. She is smiling at him as if she knows all of this already and is somewhere pleased and amused by the idea of it.

"Yes—it's reserved for you," he says.

She sits next to him and takes his hand. Her hand is cool and soft and determined. A source of coherence and strength, of enduring decency.

The simian school chaplain whom Daniel recognizes from before steps onto the lectern and raises his arms. He introduces the first hymn, "Amazing Grace."

This is a song Daniel has sung a hundred times before, but he has never experienced it as he does today. Never before has he felt more lost, more blind. Never before has he felt such an absence of meaning, such a knowledge of the futility running through everything.

Afterwards, the chaplain steps up to the lectern and looks around at the congregation with an expression of long-suffering hope.

"Bruce Webster was a good man," he says.

This opening statement comes as a surprise. According to almost everyone sitting in the chapel, Bruce is the man who killed a young prostitute and then killed himself, being too cowardly to face justice. Exactly what happened between Bruce and the prostitute before her death is a vacant, windy area of speculation upon which few are brazen enough to dwell.

"He was also a dying man," the chaplain continues.

Daniel can feel the people around him exchanging glances of surprise. These are not Bruce's friends, he realizes. They knew next to nothing about him. They are here for some other reason. Obligation toward Caroline. Or the family. Or simply because they want to be a part of the closing chapters of this story.

"Bruce knew he had a few weeks to live. He had cancer that had metastasized and entered into every vital part of his body. He had been prescribed powerful pain medication that, for reasons he is no longer here to explain, he declined to take. It was with these opioids that he terminated his life.

"Bruce could have gone to his death having never confessed to this appalling thing that happened to him, this appalling mistake. But he wanted to settle his accounts with the world. He wanted the world to see him as he really was. He wanted the world to know what he had done. It was a thing that could have happened to anyone. Bruce's crime was to hide away what had happened and then to hide this poor, dead woman away—a woman who deserved our full attention and care.

"The next day, by some cruel justice, Bruce woke to the world to discover—as he believed at the time—that his own daughter had run away from home. As the days followed, however, he came to believe that something far graver had occurred to his child—and he phoned the police, expecting the worst.

"Since then, Bruce has had to carry the knowledge of his mistake, the knowledge of his illness and the loss of his own daughter all at once—a burden few of us would be able to bear for a single day, let alone for these last months. But, at the final hour, Bruce Webster stood up and he told the world what he had done, and he made peace with himself and the world, and he made peace with his god."

As the chaplain continues, addressing himself mostly to Caroline and Matthew, Daniel looks across at Natasha. She is still holding his hand, as steady as before. Ahead of them, Matthew is sitting forward and sobbing silently into his fists. His mother has her hand on the back of his blazer, while Tim and the others stare straight ahead.

It is odd that Daniel's life has arrived here, in this place, surrounded by so much suffering and stoicism. He thinks of his sister, Lucy. He remembers her milky smile, her tentative grasp on the world, her defiant note of bravery toward the end. He remembers his mother hanging from the seatbelt, gasping like a dying fish, and her mutedness as she walked along the road afterwards toward the farmhouse, the horse and the farm workers walking like some unfamiliar collective noun along with them. He remembers his father—now living with his new family at the other end of the world – beating the goose to death with a rake, and the way his mother pushed the creature into a dustbin bag afterwards, hiding away their family's suffering and shame. He remembers Jade and Adam sitting on the roof of his mother's house, the squat fortress of the Voortrekker Monument in the distance, the words of Rilke sounding like a prayer, like medicine, through the highveld winter air. He remembers the almost merry smile of recognition from Sam when they first met and the leap of remembrance in his heart that he experienced. The kind of leap you feel at the sight of something that is very precious and still at the start of its radiant life. He remembers Bruce's abrupt and abundant laughter, and the way he listened deeply, like the widest of lands welcoming the rain. He remembers all of those he has loved and lost. As Tom and Tim and Jess would soon be gone. As he himself would soon be gone.

We are all passing through this place, he thinks. No one belongs to anyone or to anything. No one owns anyone or anything. We don't even own our own lives. They happen as the sunrise and the sunset happen. We are born into a body that is not of our choosing, into a world that is not of our choosing—and we have little control over what happens once we are here. Illness takes away a child, or it takes away a mother. A young woman is removed from the world at the very moment that she is entering it. An old man thinks he can end his own life, but the truth is that it had already been ended for him.

As the organ blasts around them, they stand for the next hymn. None of them is choosing to stand. They are simply standing because this is the next thing that is expected of them. Daniel can feel the wetness leaking from his face—his laughter-lined face—and he does nothing to stop it. He can do nothing to stop anything. He is weeping for the loss of everyone, for the loss of everything. He is weeping for Lucy and his mother, and he is weeping for Bruce and for Sam, and he is weeping for the young prostitute whose name he never even bothered to learn. He is also weeping for Charles and Will, and for all those who have come before and who have died in this place.

When he looks up into the rafters of the room, he understands that the world, the whole meaning of the world, has been changed for him forever. He doesn't know at first what to name this new sensation, or how to comprehend it, but the phrase that comes to him, the words that announce themselves inside him, are: I can finally feel God.

He understands that God is not somewhere else, in some better or more heightened place, as he has always imagined. God is not some other, separate presence that you have to be good enough or spiritual enough to access. God is everywhere. God is what is here when you are no longer here—and, when you were here, you are God.

And you don't have to believe in it or have faith in it, as the priests have always said. This thing called God isn't elsewhere. It doesn't need capital letters in its name in order for you to be able to summon it up or access it. It isn't in a word and it isn't the Word. It is inside language and outside of language—and it is in the gap between. God is everything that is. And there is nothing else.

It trembles through the room, this knowledge of God. It moves through everything. It is entirely present, here in the present. God is in the exactitude of Matthew's tied shoelaces. In the sleek lines left by the comb through the boy's hair. In the velvety light catching the contour of his left ear. In the way he still stands so upright after a life that has been intent on bringing him down. God is also in the resignation in Caroline's shoulders. The creases around her mouth. The softening of the flesh under her throat. The line of gray growing from the base of her skull. Daniel once read that to make a single pot of honey, six hundred bees have to visit two and a quarter million flowers. Well, God is in every bee and every flower and every grain of pollen.

And what makes God worth acknowledging, and even worshipping, is that this force feels like love. There is only love. Even the spider and the fly. Even the two armies engaged in mutual slaughter. Even the dead woman being washed away by the bloated river. Even they are love. They are love sent off in the wrong direction, perhaps. Ignited by the wrong ideas. Triggered by some horrible, ungoverned or ungovernable wound. But everything—everything is love.

Daniel remembers something Aristotle once wrote that he was never able to understand or accept. We only do wrong when we are ignorant of the good. When we become aware of the good, we want to become a part of it. And we are happier that way. We feel at home in the realm of the good. Well, Daniel now sees that God is the good—and the good is everywhere.

THE GHOST OF SAM WEBSTER

Matthew

Matthew is at the stables, killing flies

His mother is alone in the glass house. Today, they are going to spread his father's ashes at the foot of iSandlwana because there is to be an eclipse. His mother has waited especially for this day to come so she can set his father free, as she calls it. When there's an eclipse, it's as if a door has opened to the spirit world. People can move into the spirit world and the spirits can come down and move amongst them. When there's an eclipse, you can speak to your chosen god. It's a day when such a god is listening. A day when something might get shifted. This is why it's important what you do on a day like this. What you ask for. If you do the wrong thing, or ask for the wrong thing, you might have to live with the consequences of it forever.

Matthew doesn't know what to ask for. Daniel says it's enough to be there. He says it's important to be there for his dad. His dad will want to see him standing there, upright, when he passes into the next world. He will want to see that Matthew is all right.

Matthew has killed five hundred and sixty-four flies now and he'll only stop when it's time to go. He likes killing flies. He knows he shouldn't. They are living creatures. They have the same right to be here that he has. He also knows there will always be too many to kill and that they will always outlive him. But it's comforting to kill them anyway.

"Five hundred and sixty-five."

They are also at war with him. They are little machines from a science fiction movie that are forever trying to eat him. They circle him all day, smelling his skin, tasting his sweat, looking for a place to lay their eggs. Like his mom once said—all the flies want is to turn them all into food for maggots. Not because the flies hate them. They don't even think about them. They only see them as walking food for their eggs.

"Five hundred and sixty-six."

Matthew knows that Daniel knows something. He doesn't know what Daniel knows, but he looks at Matthew with knowing eyes. Perhaps Daniel merely feels sorry for him. It's like he's trying to be nice, but not because he wants to be, but because he has decided to be. He keeps trying to find a way to get closer to Matthew. As if he wants Matthew to share some part of himself that so far he has never been able to share with anyone. But Matthew is wary of such an idea in the same way that he is wary of the housemaster or the school priest. These men pretend to be nice to you. They trick you into saying things. But in the end they take away what you say, what you reveal, and they find a way to use it against you.

The truth is that no one will ever be able to know Matthew. They will never be able to look into the heart of him. The truth is—and he never even told his dad this when he told him the truth—the truth is that, for a moment, he actually decided to kill his sister. He saw her running in front of the car, and there was nothing he could do to stop what was happening—the car was moving, and she was moving, and all of a sudden there was a brief thump. The sound made when a car hits a rabbit at night. Then it was over. But there was that moment when Matthew decided to hit her. He saw he was going to hit her and he saw there was nothing he could do to stop it—and then he had to accept that he was going to hit her, and then he had to decide to do it—and then he did it.

The other part of the truth is that a part of him wanted to do it. A part of him really wanted to hit her. He wanted to hit her because he hated her. He hated her for being loved by Tom. He hated her for not loving Tom back. He hated her for always getting what she wanted. He thought it was maybe time she didn't get what she wanted for a change. So yes. He thought the woman was Sam and a part of him wanted to hurt her. He doesn't know about kill her. But hurt her—definitely.

Because the next part of the truth is that he loves Tom. He has never been able to admit this to anyone, but every part of him is in love with Tom—and he loves every single thing about him. The way he walks with his feet always clipped and shining. The way he moves his hands when he speaks, as if each of his words has a shape to them. The way his eyes soften when he smiles, as if smiling is a thing close to tears. Most of all, he loves the silence of Tom. The stillness with which he lives in the world. There is something about Tom's silence that is entirely physical. Tom is so completely alive inside his body. Every part of him hums with light. And to be near Tom is to be near an angel, near a god. He gives the world meaning. Value. Everything about him is beautiful—and all Matthew wants is to disappear into him. He knows that this may be terrible and wrong. Yet it is the only right thing in the world. The only thing that has ever made any sense to him.

This is why Matthew is miserable at school. This is why he is so alone. He doesn't have any friends only because he isn't interested in friends. He is only interested in Tom. The whole of the school arranges itself around Tom. Matthew has even memorized his timetable. He knows exactly where Tom will be at every single minute of the morning and the afternoon. He does whatever he can to cross paths with him. Or simply to experience him from a distance. He is neglecting his studies at school because all he wants to study is Tom. He wants to learn everything about him—like a soldier studying the map of the most dangerous and unknown of all territories.

And the fact is that Sam could have had him. She could have had all of him. She could have lain in a bed with him and pressed her skin again his skin. She could have touched his lips with her lips and placed her head against his chest to listen to his heart. She could have smelled every part of him, tasted every part of him, touched every part of him. But instead she had chosen someone else. Some other body. Some other beating heart. She could have been completely at peace in Tom's silence, his stillness, his light—and instead she had chosen Tim Greene—she had chosen the dark.

So when his mom said it wasn't Sam that he'd hit with the car, he'd felt a strange fear and disappointment. He had tried to kill Sam—or that's what it felt like—and she had escaped. In that moment, he was doing it for Tom as much as for himself. He was doing what Tom was too good and too pure ever to contemplate. But he had killed someone else instead. That quick rabbit-thump. The sound would stay with him forever.

He started to cry when his mom told him what had actually happened. His mom thought they were tears of relief, but in reality he was feeling sorry for himself. He was imagining the years he would spend in prison. The years he would spend away from Tom. He had wanted a bad thing and that bad thing had happened. And when Tom heard about it, he would make a new decision about Matthew that would close Matthew off from Tom forever. Matthew would become no more than a spectacle. A sick and unsettling story. An alien to Tom's world that would have to be shunned and shamed and condemned forever.

His mom explained that Tim had taken the woman far away and that he would hide her body. She said he knew nothing about Matthew's part in it—and that the whole problem would soon be forgotten. But not a single detail of that night was ever forgotten.

The next day, Sam was gone. It felt all over again that he'd killed her. And these days he thinks that he actually did kill her. In that moment, he had wanted to hurt her with his father's car—and, in that moment, he had killed her. She went away and she would never come back. He had done that. He had done that more than his mom had or his dad had or Tim had. He was the one who had hated her so much that he wanted her gone. And then she was gone. And if Tom ever got wind of what he'd done, he'd hate him even more. He had wanted to hurt Sam, but he'd only ended up hurting Tom. And his mom and his dad. And everyone else he had ever loved.

"Five hundred and sixty-seven. Five hundred and sixty-eight."

Now his dad is the third person he's killed. He's the third person he's killed in the last few months. Matthew should never have told his dad the story. But he was tired. He was tired of carrying it around with him all day. Day after day. They sat in the circle of stones behind the kitchen. For some reason, it was easier to confess from there. He sat on the smallest rock and his dad sat on the largest rock and Matthew told him the whole thing. From the beginning to the end. Leaving nothing out. Or almost nothing out.

"I don't understand," his dad said. "You were driving my car?"

"I was trying to get back to the house."

"And this girl came out of nowhere?"

"Like a ghost in the rain, coming out of nowhere."

"And Mom covered up for you?"

"Her and Tim."

"And she told Tim it was her driving the car?"

"Only Mom knows I was driving the car."

"Are you sure about that?"

"Only Mom—and now you."

His dad shook his head. He shook his head so violently—and, just like that, the idea popped into his head. Matthew saw it arrive in him. A large bird landing in a tree. A vulture, perhaps. A bird with death inside it.

"Listen, my boy," his dad said. "This is not going to go away. The police are moving in on us. They have spoken to Simon and they have spoken to Tim. They are following the dark-blue anorak."

"And they won't stop until they find me?"

"I'm not sure your mom will be very good at hiding the truth."

"What must I do, Dad?"

"Nothing. I will arrange everything. But you must promise me one thing, my boy."

"What?"

"That woman you hit. Apparently she was with Simon. They'd been drinking and God alone knows what else, and they'd had a fight. She was running away from him. She wasn't even dressed. And she was running for her life. You—you were just a boy trying to drive his mother's car home."

"You mean his father's car."

"His father's car. And he collided with that woman through no fault of his own. His mother should have called the police right there and then. But she lied for him, don't you see? That was her mistake, not the boy's."

"Can't we tell the police now? Can't we tell them the truth?"

"No, my boy. Too much has happened. There's Sam's disappearance. They will try to connect the two—and you'll get dragged into that. No. Let me handle this in my way. I will put an end to it—once and for all. So you must promise me this one thing. That you won't tell anyone else about this. Not even a single person. Not ever. Can you promise me that?"

"Yes, Dad."

"You do trust me, don't you?"

Matthew didn't trust anyone.

"Of course."

"Good. Then you have nothing more to worry about."

That was the last time Matthew had a proper talk with his dad. But his dad carried on the lies. He carried on the idea of rescuing Matthew from the thing they said he hadn't done—or meant to do. None of them knew that he did mean it. He did intend it. None of them knew that he was a killer at heart.

"Five hundred and sixty-nine. Five hundred and seventy. Five hundred and seventy-one."

Caroline

They are standing at the foot of the lion-mountain

They are a small family of pilgrims, dressed in black. Above them, the sky is rippled a pale iron-gray. Around them, the whitewashed cairns spilling their bones of the dead are a pale blue-gray. They are standing in the last light left in the world. Not far from them, a troupe of goats is nibbling a thornbush, oblivious to the occasion. Daniel is there with Dr. Lopez and her son. He looks older, standing next to them. And taller. Moses and Brian and some of the other staff from the lodge are also there—wearing suitably uniform expressions.

Otherwise, there are no other witnesses to the scene. All of Sam's friends have already left to study overseas or in Cape Town. Tim has returned to England, where he has accepted a rugby scholarship at a university whose name escapes Caroline. It might be Durham, it might be York. There is only Caroline left. Caroline and Matthew.

It's a strange thing, but Matthew didn't want her to sell the lodge, after all. He didn't want to move away from this place and escape to the city. He said he liked it here. He didn't mind the ghosts of this place. So for now Caroline has agreed to remain. She has given a great deal of the land away to old Mpanza. The whole section of grassland at the top of the mountain where the wildebeest dwell. The old man claimed not to mind that the animals there were periodically struck by lightning. He said that his cattle would be protected. Caroline knows that this is only a small victory for Mpanza and his followers. A brief battle in a much longer war. She knows that Mpanza will never rest until Caroline and her people are dead or gone. And Matthew knows this too. He said as much. Yet still he says he wants to remain. He says that this is the only place that makes sense to him. It's the only place where he can keep his new ideas about himself intact—whatever the cost might be of staying.

Since that decision, Matthew has seemed happier and more settled. He has started to ride Sam's horse, Meg, up into the mountains every day when he is home from school. He and Daniel have also become firm friends. Matthew is even starting to pay more attention to his schoolwork. His housemaster says that in the last few months he has become an altogether different boy and that he has "finally managed to find his feet."

To be honest, Caroline has nowhere better to go anyway. She has made her bed here and she may as well die in it. And yes—it will be good to have the freedom to do what she wants with the place. She has already raised the rates. She is only interested in foreign visitors with proper money to throw about. She will make the lodge profitable in a way Bruce never managed. As for his famous stories, she still has the recordings of his accounts of the battles, and she has the rights to his books. She will train the Zulu staff where Bruce left off and they will keep telling the tale of iSandlwana and Rorke's Drift from what Bruce so confidently called "the Zulu perspective."

"Don't look at the sun when the eclipse happens," Caroline tells her son.

"I know that, Mom."

Daniel looks across at them and smiles some encouragement.

"Isicabu," Moses says, "today we honor you. Hamba kahle, mfowethu. Siyohlangana kwelabangasekho, lapho kukhona khona injabulo kuphela. Mvelinqanga, sinxusa ukuba wamukele umphefumulo womfowethu ngoba esendlule kwelabaphilayo, ebheke kwelabangasekho."

As the moon comes to cover the sun, and all the cicadas and the grasshoppers and the birds go silent, Caroline unscrews the lid of the biscuit tin that contains Bruce's ashes, and she releases the gritty thread into the wind. There are some bits of what must be bone at the bottom of the tin at the end—and she has to give it a final shake, as if not wanting any of the ash to go to waste.

THE RIVER

In the week Sam disappeared, the earth was moved
by forces it never knew existed

Mountain streams bounced beyond their bounds to join rivers that had never been there before. Where there had once been an elegant waterfall hemmed in by bracken and ferns, there was now a mound of rubble. Where the river circumvented a pasture filled with grazing, honey-colored ponies, there was now an abandoned lake. Where the river curved left, it now veered right.

All the roads around the Websters' lodge were deep underwater—and the bridge that the locals called Ghost Bridge vanished completely. Most of the houses that had been built on the floodplains were reduced to a handful of sticks, and an old stone church that had been standing at the river's edge for over a hundred years melted back into the mud. Some of the dead who had been concealed in the ditches along the edge of the graveyard were revealed in their resting places, their bones shining like polished ivory in the black earth, their dislodged skulls left to roll through the water amongst the stones.

Further downriver, a petrol tanker outside the Durban Country Club was washed into the sea. Fourteen crocodiles from a crocodile farm between Tongaat and Ballito reappeared later in the surf of the Indian Ocean—creatures from another era, clawing their way through the blood-colored amber. The young woman's body that Zwelibanzi Zimba saw on the rocks while tending his grandmother's goats was only one amongst five hundred drowned bodies that would be found in KwaZulu-Natal that week.

When it stopped raining, the people didn't notice it at first

As the sun ascended, the roads and the rivers lay tangled and smoking. A golden haze sifted across the land. The first bird called and then the second bird answered it. In a field stood a small yellow car without a driver, far away from any road. All around iSandlwana, the world lay brim-full of muddy water, of washed-up rubbish, of broken-down houses, of drowned rats and cattle, dead dogs and children.

Everything lay there for a long time, quietly floating

Everything was waiting for the first seepage, the first outlet—and then, at last, the water started to nose its way forward, runnel by runnel, toward the sea. A single chicken murmured and hopped down from an uprooted aloe, leaving crooked crosses in the shining mud, sharp and inquisitive. Zwelibanzi's father emerged from the mud, and then his mother emerged from the mud, and they held each other's faces and looked for the person they had lost there—and, after a moment of looking, they found each other's faces again. Zwelibanzi's grandmother, who lived in the neighboring valley, looked around for her homestead and found nothing there. She looked around for her goats, and she found nothing there. But under a pile of roofing thatch, she found someone else's children—somehow alive, somehow asleep, somehow dreaming.

Slowly, the land around the lion-mountain started to repair itself—as a butterfly, fresh from the chrysalis, knows how to assemble its own mouth. The grandmother cleared the rubble from the yard and made a shelter out of the thatch for the children. The goats were gathered in from the drowned fields. Then the family lit a fire and threw wet wood into the flames. They heated some water and cooked their first meal of crushed corn. Already they knew everything they needed to know about how to repair the world.

Over time, the activities of the people in that half-forgotten place started to feel like a dance, a tentative song. The little yellow car became a den for a pack of wild dogs. The broken-off pillars of Ghost Bridge became a roosting place for the vultures. Although the bridge would never be replaced, the people realized that the new bridge further down the valley served them just as well.

Sometimes, there were sightings of a pale, wild-looking girl holding a small, red suitcase. She was seen at the edge of the road, flagging down cars, asking for a lift to the next town. There were some who claimed to have spoken to this girl. There were some who claimed to have seen her face. One man said that he had asked the girl if she knew what happened to people when they were dead. She looked at him with incomprehension, as if to suggest that death was only a dream of the living, and that life was only a dream of the dead.

ACKNOWLEDGMENTS

This novel was written to honor the several hundred children who go missing every year in South Africa. Most of their stories are never heard—and their spirits, like that of Sam's, are quietly absorbed back into the land from which they emerged.

I would not have been able to write this novel without the help of South Africa's premier butterfly expert, Steve Woodhall, who answered my many emails about butterflies and gave of his time and energy at all times of the day. His *Field Guide to Butterflies of South Africa* was my happy companion through the writing process. I am grateful to the historian Ian Knight for his feedback during the construction of the war narrative as well as for his account of the ceremonies the Zulu soldiers went through before and after battle (see *Companion to the Anglo-Zulu War*). *The Zulu War Journal* by amateur entomologist Colonel Henry Harford was also formative reading.

I would like to thank Terry Morris and everyone at Picador

Africa for their continued support. I am especially grateful to Andrea Nattrass for her comments on earlier drafts, and I would like to thank my editor Michael Titlestad and my copy-editor Sally Hines for their rigor and care. I would also like to thank Aoife Lennon-Ritchie for facilitating the sale of this novel to Catalyst Press in the United States. Finally, a huge thank you to the brilliant Jessica Powers and her wonderful team at Catalyst Press, including Fourie Botha, Matt Powers, and Jessica Parker.

My wife Leila and daughter Phoebe continue to be my still point in the turning world.

This novel is dedicated to my sister
Martinique Higginson
25 March 1979—30 July 1982

ALSO BY CRAIG HIGGINSON

The Book of Gifts (2020)

"As readers, we turn to specific authors when we don't want to be disappointed. The internationally acclaimed writer Craig Higginson has become one of these for me. His novel, *The Book of Gifts*, is another gem in his impressive oeuvre ... This finely layered, mesmerising novel will cement Higginson's position as one of the most gifted ... writers in South Africa and beyond. His ability to shine a light into the darkest places of the human heart and confront them with empathy is remarkable."

– Karina M. Szczurek

The White Room (2018)

"In prose pared to the bone Higginson explores the complex nature of love. Most importantly, we realize love can become what you will it to be—and that once you've grasped it, you should guard it with all your life."

– Fred Khumalo

The Dream House (2015)

Winner of the 2015 University of Johannesburg Prize for South African Writing in English

Shortlisted for the 2015 *Sunday Times* Barry Ronge Fiction Prize and the Jenny Crwys-Williams Fiction Book of the Year 2015

"It's here at last—the South African novel that throws off all the literary baggage of political cliché and posturing, and gives us an honest exploration of not only what it is to be human, but what it is to be South African."
– *City Press*

The Landscape Painter (2011)
Winner of the 2011 University of Johannesburg Prize for South African Writing in English
Shortlisted for the 2012 English M-Net Literary Award

"It is in *The Landscape Painter* that Higginson unfolds the mastery of his craft on all fronts … Haunting long after the last page is turned, *The Landscape Painter* is one of those rare gems which allows readers to rediscover themselves. Higginson is already one of the finest South African writers around, but his star is surely and steadily on the rise."
– Karina M. Szczurek, *Sunday Independent*

Last Summer (2010)
Shortlisted for the 2011 English M-Net Literary Award

"This is a tale of understated elegance and empathy, piercing in its honesty, and utterly beguiling from the very first sentence."
– John van de Ruit

www.ingramcontent.com/pod-product-compliance
Lightning Source LLC
LaVergne TN
LVHW041057080826
845145LV00007B/1611

* 9 7 8 1 9 6 0 8 0 3 4 3 6 *